dancing

in the

dark

T.L. MARTIN

Published by Koru House Press.

For information address Koru House Press, Koru House, Remuera, Auckland, New Zealand, 1050 www.koruhousepress.com

Dancing in the Dark
Copyright 2018 T.L. Martin

All rights reserved. No part of this book may be reproduced or transmitted in any form without written consent of the author, except by a reviewer who may quote brief passages for review purposes only.

This is a work of fiction. Names, characters, places, and incidents are used fictitiously and are a product of the author's imagination.

Cover Designer: Qdesign, www.qcoverdesign.com

Interior Formatting: Champagne Book Design, www.champagnebookdesign.com

Editor: Sarah Collingwood, www.sarahac36.wordpress.com

"I love your rough edges
and soft parts
that bleed.
The ruins of your soul are poetry
to me."

—Anita Krizzan

playlist

Billie Eilish—*Lovely (with Khalid)*

Ciara—*Paint it, Black*

Son Lux—*Easy*

Melanie Martinez—*Dollhouse*

Two Feet—*Her Life*

Sabrina Claudio—*Orion's Belt*

Karliene—*Become the Beast*

Portugal. The Man—*Modern Jesus*

Billie Eilish—*Six Feet Under*

Sabrina Claudio—*Belong to You*

Konoba—*On Our Knees*

Ruelle—*Deep End*

Noah Cyrus—*Again*

Aurora—*Murder Song (5, 4, 3, 2, 1)*

Portugal. The Man—*Evil Friends*

Melanie Martinez—*Cry Baby*

Erutan—*Come Little Children*

prologue

"The devil asked me how I knew my way around the walls of hell. I told him I did not need a map for the darkness I know so well."
—T.M.T.

Adam

THERE'S NOTHING LIKE IT.

Nothing comes close to the soothing, hypnotic wails of a grown man who knows these will be the last sounds he ever makes. His cries are a soft symphony set on repeat in the back of my mind, even as he stands in front of me, mouth agape, eyes squeezed shut, head thrown back. With each new scream, the tendons in his neck bulge beneath a mesmerizing cascade of red. With each new scream, the outside world quiets a little more, my grip around the knife loosens, and my shallow breaths ease into an even rhythm.

Soon, his cries morph into choked whimpers. I'm so relaxed my eyes grow heavy, but I refuse to let them close and miss even a second of the scene playing out before me. The scene I orchestrated with little more than my bare hands.

They said go to therapy. No one ever specified what kind.

My lips quirk. The knife's handle is thick and damp in my

hands. The scent of blood and pain fills my nostrils, along with a high I know will fade all too soon, as it always does.

It's not until the silence—the only sound comparable to the heavenly screams I just savored like a fine wine—returns to my ears that I remember my audience. I let the weapon slip from my fingertips. It hits the ground with a clatter as I lean against the concrete wall behind me. Kicking a leg out, I cross it over my other ankle and suck in one final, intoxicating breath.

I can't take my eyes off the sight. Or maybe I can, but I don't want to. It's too perfect—the way his head's angled a little too far to the right. The slight, red stump on the left side of his face—all that remains of his ear. The streams of crimson intertwining as they leak down his body, tiny drops staining the ceramic tiles with my mark.

Fuck, that's good. Some might even call it artistic. I tilt my head, absorbing the terror still etched into the tight lines of his face. His hair is a little grayer than I'd hoped it'd be by the time I got to him, but it only adds a certain charm I have to admire.

Huh . . . She always thought she made epic pieces of art. If this isn't epic, I don't know what the hell is.

"Wanna take a picture?" Griff's gruff voice snaps my head to the right. His bulky shoulders are broad enough to fill the entire doorway he stands in.

He's being snide, of course, but I almost smile while I consider it. It is a shame to see years of meticulous preparation disappear as quickly as they do. But, no. I don't need a trophy. What I need is my goddamn sanity—something I'm not quite sure I've ever had, and I certainly will never gain as long as this lifeless piece of shit is clouding my view.

And just like that, the familiar, dark claws of bitterness tear their way into my chest and eat away the high.

Frederick Ferguson. Fifty-six years old. Elementary school

bus driver. Two ex-wives, one grown child he hasn't seen or spoken to in eleven years.

I make a mental slash across his name on my list. Took longer than usual to get this one, but that's only because my hands were otherwise occupied with numbers five and thirteen.

Staring at the body sagging against the column it's tied to, I kick off the wall. "Burn him."

I don't exit the room until smoke blankets the air. Ash and dust, death and murder. Some drink it down like a poison until it kills them, leaving nothing more than a shell without a soul. Others, like me, are the poison. When you have no soul, there's no threat of losing it. With no threat, there's nothing to fear.

And without fear . . . you're limitless.

chapter one

"Do not judge my story by the chapter you walked in on."
—Unknown

Emmy

ONE BRONZE, OVAL BUTTON. ONE PUSH. ONE *DING*, ONE *DONG*.

And it will all be real.

I suck in a breath, my chest straining against the skin-tight uniform. A cold rush of unease flits down my spine as I tug at the mid-thigh hem of the little black dress. A dress I received on my doorstep. A dress that's worth more than Mama's entire trailer home. A dress that had a one-way plane ticket to New York and five crisp hundred-dollar bills stuffed inside its inseam pocket when it arrived.

Before yesterday, I'd only ever heard of designer *Oscar de la Renta* on reality television. Today, I'm not only wearing his clothes but also matching four-inch pumps.

Shifting my weight from one foot to the other, I adjust the black, rectangular-rimmed glasses sitting on the bridge of my nose and shake my head at myself. *Stop being a coward and get it over with already.*

If Frankie were here, she'd smirk and shove my shoulder to

edge me toward the door. But she isn't here, is she?

Before I can talk myself out of it, I press one chewed fingernail to the doorbell and wait for the ring.

Anticipation builds with each second, gnawing at me until my palms are sweaty. *Ugh.* As though I don't already have enough personal issues to deal with without adding this whole scenario to the mix.

I can hardly believe I'm really here. Not that I know where in the hell *here* is, exactly.

Angling my head, I try to inconspicuously scope out my surroundings. The black limo that dropped me off a few minutes ago is now a distant speck, disappearing down the endless driveway. Each side of the smooth, narrow path is lined with perfectly trimmed hedges tall enough to resemble a maze. A maze that threatens to swallow me whole if I dare venture back the way we came.

It's impossible to see far enough, but I know the limo had to pass through a gate to get here.

Blacked-out windows blocked any clues as to where I was headed from the second I was picked up at the airport and escorted into the shady vehicle. Tinted glass hid even the driver's seat from view, but they couldn't mute the occasional sounds. After what felt like hours of driving with only tire noise, my ears had perked at the subtle rumble of a gate opening.

My heart thumps a little harder against my ribcage as I gaze into the clear blue sky above my head. As far as I can tell, there's nothing to reveal my location. The plane may have delivered me to New York, but for all I know, we've veered all the way into Jersey or Massachusetts.

I turn back to the door, taking in the actual property, and shit . . . the place is massive. I'm a tiny speck of dirt standing before the house. No—mansion. The building is all high arches, intricate engravings, fancy terraces, and polish and shine, stretched out enough it could consume our entire trailer park.

Deep breaths.

After a soft click, the mahogany door swings open and a stunning woman stands before me. She probably has fifteen years on my twenty and looks like she just stepped off a runway. Sleek blond hair is pulled into a complex twist at the top of her head. Her high cheekbones are rosy. Her tanned skin is smooth and flawless.

"Emmy Highland?" she purrs, glossy red lips curving as she extends her hand. "Stella Larsson. So pleased to finally meet you."

I shake her hand and try to force my shoulders to relax as I latch onto the familiar name. "Nice to meet you, too. In person, I mean."

Her smile widens, and it only emphasizes her beauty. Stepping gracefully to the side, she releases my hand. "Please, come in."

It's not until she turns and I follow her into a long corridor that I notice her outfit: a little black dress ending mid-thigh, with matching four-inch pumps. Almost identical to mine, except when she shifts I see that hers has a steep V-neckline while the one I was provided has a modest sweetheart cut. She also wears a thin gold scarf curled around her neck like a choker, but the way it's tied neatly on one side somehow makes the entire look radiate class.

My footsteps halt on their own when the corridor ends, which leads to an enormous living room. A breathtaking sea of gardens lay outside the grand windows that eat up the entire far wall. Rays of sunlight pour over the seating area, creating a glow that casts a shimmer against my skin. When I look up, I notice most of the light's coming from a glass ceiling.

The dazzling warmth feels deceiving when I know what really goes on here. What role I'm expected to play. I take a few steps to the right until the shimmer vanishes and I'm standing in a shadowed corner.

My arm brushes a canvas on the wall. It's a stiff, traditional landscape of a century-old mansion. Bronze and regal looking, the piece is all kinds of wrong. Definitely not how I would have done it. The building's paint should be chipping, the garden full of weeds, reminiscent of the days come and gone. Long shadows would stretch across the cracked steps, teasing the house with ghosts of its past. A thick streak of red would mar the windowsill, an abandoned bucket of paint knocked sideways and spilling its heart.

Even states away from the sketchpad tucked so carefully in my corner of the trailer, where Mama won't find it, my fingers itch to get lost in the brushstrokes they always crave. Each stuffy painting calls me closer with its pleas for sharp strokes of red and black, making me wish I hadn't been instructed to leave all my belongings behind.

Of course, I never had proper materials to work with, but Frankie did what she could to get me supplies, even when I was little. Paints and sketch pads from second hand stores were easier to come by than new items. Otherwise, pencils and scraps of paper would do. No matter what, she made sure I was stocked with something, and whenever Mama caught me and threw it all away, Frankie would go out and find more.

Frankie used to say when you feel the urge to do something, it's your soul's way of leading you to where you're supposed to be. *Never ignore your impulses, Emmy. We'd all be lost without them.*

I swallow, shoving the thoughts down and flicking my gaze from one painting to the next.

"Would you like some tea before we begin?" Stella's smile

wavers as she gazes into the dark corner I've chosen.

I glance down, tugging at the hem of my dress again. The thing crawls closer to my panties with each step I take. "No. Thank you."

"Of course. Just this way."

We cross the room, our heels clicking with each step, and reach a wide, winding stairwell. She leads the way, her hand brushing over the railing. We don't stop until we're standing inside a small office with a single desk at one corner and a lounging area with a glass coffee table in the center. She gestures toward the cream-colored sofa.

"Have a seat, Emmy."

She waits until I'm sitting before taking a seat beside me and retrieving a glossy briefcase from beneath the table.

"So," she says without looking up, her slender fingers skimming over the files, "the contract I have here almost replicates the one we reviewed last week via our long-distance correspondences. There is one minor difference you'll notice. Where we had blacked out any suggestions as to who your new employers are for confidentiality purposes, this contract will reveal their company's identity. All right?"

My fingers grip the hem of my dress tighter, but I quickly release the fabric and nod. If I'm going to be convincing enough to pull this off, I can't let my unease show.

"Very well. Now, assuming you've had enough time to consider all aspects of what this position entails and that you're ready to begin—seeing as you boarded the plane—we'll move forward with the signatures, with me as your witness."

The pounding against my ribcage evolves into a flutter, light and fast. My dress is suddenly too tight and itchy against my skin. Yes, I did consider all the aspects, but not in the ways she's suggesting; more along the lines of what will happen if my new employers figure out what I'm really doing here. *When* they figure it out.

Because, eventually, they will.

Honestly, I can't believe I've made it this far. Even though Frankie and I are only half-sisters and don't resemble each other at all, there are obvious things that would reveal our ties if they ever find a reason to dig for them.

"Ah, here it is." Stella withdraws a stapled packet and a pen, then sets the briefcase aside. Finally, she meets my gaze with a reassuring smile. "I realize how uptight and formal this all seems now, but I promise you'll feel more comfortable once the basics are out of the way. Just a few more t's to cross and i's to dot, and you'll officially be on our payroll."

Payroll.

Money.

Ridiculous sums of money. Figures too large for me to admit, even to myself, without feeling like a criminal. There's no way a secretary would ever be paid this much, and it's the very reason I assume Frankie signed up. One flickering thought of all the things money like this could mean for her, and I get it. I really do. We always talked of big dreams and getting ourselves away from Mama. Away from Mississippi altogether.

"Yeah..." I let out a breath, hoping Stella can't see the questions and nerves in my eyes. "Of course."

"Excellent." Her grin broadens, and she extends the thin packet and pen toward me. "Just your initials here"—she points to the small line beside each paragraph, flipping through the pages as she does—"here, and here, and then your primary information at the bottom there. Leave the witness section for me to fill out. Then we'll be all set."

A thin layer of sweat makes my grip on the pen slippery, but I do as instructed, initialing as I go. Though my eyes skim through each familiar paragraph, I try not to pay too much attention to their words for fear I'll back out. I'm not usually a nervous person, but then again, I don't usually find myself in a position like this one.

Some paragraphs stand out more than others, specifically the ones revealing my new employer's identity:

Section 13, Clause 4:
"I understand that my duty as a Matthews Secretary is to serve in any and all ways asked of me. I am here as a servant and as a servant only. Signature of this contract indicates that I, Emmy May Highland, agree to my role as a servant and will strive to ensure everything asked of me is seen through to completion and full satisfaction."

I've read my variation of this document so many times I no longer bat an eye at *full satisfaction,* but *Matthews*? Still vague as hell.

I look up and raise an eyebrow. Stella just smiles and nods for me to continue.

Section 13, Clause 5:
"I understand that certain tasks may be highly demanding and cause physical and/or mental duress, and I do not hold Matthews House, Inc. or any of its staff or affiliates responsible for any such occurrences or damages in any shape or form."

Section 23, Clause 1:
"I understand that being selected by one of the Matthews as his loyal servant will bind me to him in more ways than one. I will become and remain his willing and loyal servant

throughout the duration of my year-long contract, and he will become my master. As such, I will only address him as Master."

Section 24, Clause 1:
"I have had a full physical as required, including a health check for any sexually transmitted diseases. These records have been provided to Matthews House, Inc. and reviewed prior to arrival. In addition, I agree to adhere to the mandated regulation of birth control during my entire term of employment."

Section 29, Clause 2:
"I understand if I do anything to displease my master, he reserves the right to disclaim me as his servant at any time throughout my year-long contract."

Section 29, Clause 3:
"I understand if none of the Matthews claim me as their servant, I will make it my primary duty to serve all four of them at their individual requests. I also understand it is my sole responsibility to present myself to the Matthews in such a way that will appeal to them, and if none see me fit to claim, either my end-of-year bonus will be cut in half or my time at Matthews House will be terminated."

My eyes have almost glazed over by the time I reach the final clause.

Section 42, Clause 4:
"I understand anything done, seen, or heard within the walls of Matthews House during my contract is bound by

complete confidentiality laws, and my full discretion is required. If I, Emmy May Highland, do anything to hint at the activities I may observe or partake in at Matthews House, this will result in my end-of-year bonus being rescinded, and matters will be further taken at the will and discretion of Matthews House, Inc. however they deem fit."

The Matthews.
I swallow the knot in my throat. The more times I read the name, the more it feels like invisible handcuffs cutting into my wrists. Handcuffs. Restrictions. I've never been able to stomach the idea of being confined.

Despite the name not ringing with any familiarity, something about it twists in the pit of my stomach. It had been difficult enough convincing myself to commit to something like this back at home, when I didn't have a name to pair with the creepy title 'master' and I wasn't sitting on their expensive leather. But now . . .

The lines of my printed name and signature at the bottom of the form are squiggly enough to look like a five-year-old's. I can't stop my hands from shaking at the finality of it all.

This is it. There's no halfway, no probationary period. Once I hand this contract over, I'm all in.

Which, if I do this right, also means answers. It means finding Frankie, being able to see with my own two eyes that she's okay. And maybe in the process some of the guilt will lift enough so I can breathe again.

The reminder helps calm my pulse. *Frankie*. She's what matters. She's *all* that matters.

I shut my brain off and give the papers to the woman beside me. Stella fills in the bottom section, then stores them in the briefcase and stands. She extends her hand. "Shall we venture onto phase two?"

I take her hand and rise. "Phase two?"

She smiles. The too-perfect curve of her red lips sends goose bumps up my arms. "I'll escort you to the ladies' quarters where you'll be groomed and prepped for an introduction with the Matthews. This is your chance, Emmy. Your chance to be claimed." She closes her eyes and inhales deeply, then opens them again as she releases the breath. "I'll always remember my first time being claimed."

A dreamlike spark flits through her doe eyes as if she's lost in another moment, and it makes me take a step back.

Oh, Frankie. What the hell did you get yourself into?

chapter two

> "You think I'm just a doll. A doll that's pink and light.
> A doll you can arrange any way you like."
> —Harley Quinn

Emmy

MAMA DIDN'T BELIEVE IN TELEVISION, SO FRANKIE AND I USED TO SLIP into a neighboring trailer where an elderly woman, known endearingly as 'Batshit Crazy Betsy,' let us borrow her cable to indulge in our addiction of reality television and the Home Network channel. I've seen my fair share of fancy properties from that little box TV sitting on her kitchen counter.

This place pales them all in comparison.

When Stella first led me outside through the back door, the quaint garden I'd glimpsed from within the living room greeted me. The same massive hedges lining the front driveway circled the garden's border like a fence. Which is why I was so surprised when she revealed a thin opening hidden behind a cherry tree. We passed through it and continued beyond the wall of shrubbery.

I never expected to see the quarter-mile field of grass leading to another, *larger* mansion.

It's a secret guesthouse—if a mansion this big could be called *secret*—with intricate moldings decorating its exterior and the kind of terraces that keep guests like me in awe. This building is narrow enough to hide behind its counterpart, yet twice the size of the front house in length.

We cross over a slim driveway, and Stella stops as we approach the mahogany front door. It automatically unlocks with a distinct click. My brows furrow, and I shift my head upward. Sure enough, there's a small, black bowl protruding from the door's archway, the kind that hides a camera so you can't tell which way it's pointing.

I'm not yet sure whether the knowledge that we're being monitored so closely should make me feel safer or more uneasy. How closely were they watching Frankie?

I follow Stella into the foyer, and my movements slow as I look around with wide eyes. This building might match the front house on the exterior—all soft earth tones and elegant designs—but the interior is something else entirely. Our dresses blend right into the jet-black walls. Polished, white marble stretches beneath our heels, enhancing every click with an echo that bounces off the corners.

The constant *click-clack* grates on my ears, but the dark settles around me like a soft blanket. Shadows soothe the goose bumps on my bare arms. The pumping in my veins calms. At least, in this place, the deceptions are gone. No frills or frosting to dress up and distract from the truth.

Each massive room we pass looks identical to the next in style. The furniture is minimal, modern, and in only the purest shades of black or white. The few windows hide behind velvety black curtains, rendering the entire place dim and shadowed in a way that should probably send a shiver down my spine.

It doesn't.

Three women casually stroll from one room to the next. Each of them is blond, stunning enough to make me do a double take, and wearing high-end dresses and heels similar to mine and Stella's. They also wear thin scarves around their necks like Stella's, except only one matches hers—gold. The others are blue and red.

The scarves seem to be the only splashes of color in the entire building, other than the occasional piece of abstract art hanging from the walls.

Something icy uncurls in my stomach as I watch the women come and go. The sensation hits me with a sting, deep in my gut, because at first glance any one of these young women could be mistaken for Frankie. Tall, blonde, tan, curves in all the right places. Beautiful enough to appear photoshopped.

I'm attractive, but it's the kind of beautiful men only appreciate until a girl like them—like Frankie—enters a room and wipes any trace of me away.

Ordinarily that wouldn't bother me, but with my thick, black hair falling straight down my back, ivory skin, and a petite frame that barely reaches 5' 6" in these four-inch heels, I'm chillingly aware of how much I stand out next to the others. How much attention my mere presence here might draw. How long do I have before one of the girls—or worse, the Matthews—gets suspicious?

I nod toward a girl nearest us, who's setting a fresh bouquet of roses on a glass table. "Will I be getting a scarf?"

Stella follows my gaze. "If all goes according to plan."

We reach a pair of tinted glass doors. Once they open automatically for us, Stella leads me through a short hallway, and soon we're in a sterile room with a wide desk before us. She steps forward and rings a silver call bell.

I can hear that *click-clack* of heels well before another

stunning woman appears. With vibrant red locks spilling over one shoulder, she's the first non-blonde I've seen. The left half of her head is closely shaven, accentuating her heart-shaped face and adding a distinct edge to features that would otherwise be considered soft and dainty.

When her gaze meets mine, she doesn't smile. Doesn't nod. Doesn't greet me in the least. I watch in admiration at the way she moves with such natural, confident ease behind her desk to slide a sheet of paper into a drawer. Then she leans her hip against the oak wood and eyes Stella expectantly.

"She's ready to begin phase two," Stella says, gesturing to me. She peeks at her black wristwatch and adds, "Be sure to have her prepped by dinner. They'll be expecting her."

"What exactly will they—" I start, but Stella takes my hand in hers and squeezes.

"Relax, Emmy. Aubrey here is the best of the best. She'll get you in tip-top shape for presentation and have the Matthews fighting over who gets to claim you." Her proud smile makes me doubt whether she realizes how strange her words are.

Presentation. Claim. Am I really the only one here who thinks these are not normal terms to drop into casual conversation?

My gaze shifts to the redhead, Aubrey, whose lips quirk when she takes in my expression. Then her green eyes scan me up and down in a brisk assessment. "Consider it done."

"Very well. I'll leave you to it, then." Stella nods and exits the room.

Aubrey reaches down, retrieving a wicker basket with a folded white towel and washcloth draped over other items I can't make out. She holds it out to me. "For you."

"Thanks." I grab it and peek inside.

"Private baths are down the hall and to your left. You'll use our provided hygiene products for now, but tonight you can make a list of any specific items you want, and I'll pick them up for you tomorrow." She flicks her gaze up and down the length of me once more and shakes her head. Something about the look prompts me to tuck my chewed fingernails into the wicker until they're hidden from view. "Not sure how you wound up here, Emma—"

"Emmy."

"—but I'll have you shinier than Stella's lip gloss by the time I'm done with you."

The private baths look nothing like any I'd seen back home. Large and round, the whirlpool tub makes me feel pampered. *Too* pampered, like it's trying to convince me I'm something special, and I find myself hurrying through the motions to get the whole thing over with.

After slipping out of the tub, I pat myself dry and spot a white, silk robe hanging on a wall hook. I slip it on just as a knock strikes the door.

Aubrey's standing there when I open it. She turns and gestures for me to follow. "Spa time."

Turns out 'spa time' is code for excruciating pain. She soon has me stretched out on a massage table, my legs spread as she yanks the final strip of muslin from the area between my thighs. I don't make a sound, but my fingers dig into the vinyl leather. I've never waxed anything but my eyebrows until now.

"I know. Hurts like a bitch the first time," Aubrey says.

I suppress a grimace. "Just the first time?"

"And the second. And third. And—you know what, I should've left it at 'hurts like a bitch.'"

I snort out a bitter laugh, the sting finally cooling as she spreads a thin layer of cream over the area. When she straightens my legs and applies the soothing balm to my freshly waxed calves, I open my eyes. She stands to the left of the table, the shaved side of her head facing me, and, for the first time, I notice her bare neckline.

"You don't wear a scarf?"

She smirks but doesn't look up from my legs. "Nope."

"Are you not one of the secretaries then? I figured it was, like, a part of the uniform or something."

"Oh no—I am. I just haven't been claimed."

I swallow, one of the contract clauses floating into mind: *I understand if none of the Matthews claim me as their loyal servant, I will make it my primary duty to serve all four of them at their individual requests.*

My throat is dry when I respond, "Oh."

Aubrey lets out a chuckle as she gently helps me into a sitting position and closes the robe around my front. "I like it this way, if that's what you're wondering."

"You *like* it?"

We stand, and she leads me to another room then guides me into a chair surrounded by mirrors. I'm hardly paying attention. How could she *like* serving four men to 'full satisfaction'?

I'm no saint when it comes to sex. I lost my virginity at fifteen and never looked back. I like sex, or, more accurately, I *need* it, despite knowing I don't enjoy it the way most women do. For me, the act serves a specific purpose.

I don't have a place at home, a mama who wants me, or a clue who my daddy is. I definitely don't have any control over the secret, forbidden places my mind sometimes goes. But art and sex? Those are the two things I can count on. My sole releases in this world. The only things within my control powerful enough to drown out the rest of the world.

This place—signing a contract, acting as a servant, accepting payment for my body—this is entirely new territory. Territory that threatens to rip away any sense of control.

Aubrey tilts my chin up. She inspects my face, then skims the display of makeup topping the vanity. I've never seen so many beauty products in one spot.

"Yeah," she eventually murmurs, "I do. That's not to say none of them *want* to claim me . . ." Her lips lift, and she uses a brush to blend concealer over my skin. "But I made a choice. And it's liberating. Isn't that why you're here? Searching for something? The kind of freedom you can't find anywhere else?"

Freedom? I don't know what I'd call identical dolls sharing a mansion to do the bidding of men, but *freedom* isn't exactly the first word that comes to mind.

My thoughts must be written in my expression because Aubrey pulls back, her eyes narrowing. "Or maybe what you're looking for is different. Maybe the *reason* you're here is different."

My stomach clenches as her words hit too close to home. I keep my expression blank, but my voice falters. "Wh-what do you mean? They found me, contacted me. Just like everyone else here."

It's a truth blended with a lie. The faded phone number I found scrawled on the bottom of Frankie's nightstand might not have been left there for me, but, as I learned, this place is invite-only in the most exclusive sense. You don't seek out the Matthews House; they seek out you.

When I picked up the phone with trembling fingers the day I realized Frankie wasn't just gone—she was missing—the woman who answered my call had assumed I'd been selected like everyone else.

Aubrey shrugs, then leans forward again and starts working

on my eye makeup. "What I mean is that sometimes the things we're drawn to tell us more about ourselves than we realize. There's a reason you decided to get on the plane, Emma—"

"Emmy."

"—and it's not just the money. It's never just the money for something like this."

Her words sink into my brain, clear and heavy. Could that be true? Was Frankie here for something else? But what could she have been searching for? She's never the one looking for answers; she's the one people get answers from. Never a follower, always the leader.

"Then what?" I ask, my voice small, fearful of the response I might get. "What for, if not the money?"

Another shrug as she glances around, eyes flicking from one black wall to the next. "There's something raw about the darkness here, don't you think? Something honest. Real. In a place like this, you can't help but let yourself go to your deepest secrets and desires. Your darkest corners." Her fingers wrap around my chin as she tilts my head once more, this time so I'm staring straight into her sharp, green eyes. "And everyone has dark corners, Emma. Even the angel who never sins just wants to be set free."

chapter three

*"The sun watches what I do,
but the moon knows all my secrets."*
—J.M. Wonderland

Emmy

I HAD A DOLLHOUSE WHEN I WAS SEVEN. WE GOT TO KEEP IT FOR THREE whole months before Mama found it. She labeled it a game of the devil and banished it from our trailer.

It was a hand-me-down from Batshit Crazy Betsy's granddaughter, and its walls were bent and caving in. The tiny furniture pieces were so faded we couldn't distinguish their color. Even the finger-sized dolls were chipped, their clothes torn.

Frankie had eyed the pieces when we first got them, picking them up one by one and inspecting their damage closely. Within seconds, she found a way to fix them. That's one of the traits I've always admired about my big sister, how she takes things into her own hands.

She'd borrowed—and I use that term loosely—another neighbor's makeup and fabrics then gave the dolls full makeovers, complete with posh dresses and eyelash extensions. She used the extra scraps of fabric to add rugs and curtains to the house's interior.

"You see, Emmy," Frankie said, modeling one of the dolls and having it do a full body spin. "Now no one has to know."

"Know what?"

"About the damage, of course. You show people what they want to see, and they'll never suspect what's underneath." She stroked the toy's hair, which was now combed and tied back with a ribbon. Then she leaned forward, toward its ear. "You'll be the perfect little doll now, won't you?"

If dolls could feel, I imagine that one would have felt exactly as I do now. The black-walled corridor I follow Aubrey down is lined with small mirrors. Each one only serves to cement the odd, hollow sensation in my chest. If I took a moment to stare at my reflection, I might find myself on the surface eventually, but our brisk pace means that each step only teases me with fleeting glimpses of a stranger.

My hair is still straight, hanging to my waist, but the black strands are sleek and glossy, shining in a way I've never seen before. The extensions sealed to my already thick lashes feel heavy on my eyelids. Shimmery specks from the golden shadow create an unnatural sparkle in my sky-blue eyes. The concealer hides any trace of the light freckles sprinkled along my nose and cheekbones, making my fair skin look porcelain against the black of my hair and dress.

And all I see is another doll.

Aubrey stops so abruptly I almost crash into her. I glance around, seeing that we've reached a small sitting room with a single bench.

"Sit here," she instructs. "I'm going to check if they're ready for you."

She disappears through an open doorway that leads into the dining room. I shift on the bench, craning my neck to try to catch a peek of the men who are to seal my fate in this house. The men who've likely already sealed Frankie's.

A stab of unease pricks my spine, forcing me to sit straighter. The Matthews. Brothers, maybe? Family of some sort? Whoever these men are, they're the only lead I have to Frankie's disappearance. The last place I know she was headed before her letters stopped coming.

Mama could assume she's still out chasing paper all she wants, but I know better. Since I've never had my own phone, and Mama didn't make it easy for me to sneak over to Betsy's trailer and use her computer, Frankie made sure to write me through snail mail at least once every month. Always. I knew something was wrong the instant that second month arrived with no mail. By month three, I called the police station and tried to file a missing person's report. None of the officials took the claim seriously. When half the town, law enforcement included, has paid the woman in question for an 'adult evening,' it's almost impressive how quickly she loses credibility.

The truth is I can't say I blame them. Frankie left Mississippi the second she turned eighteen, off to pursue modeling in New York. It wasn't unusual for long stretches of time to pass without anyone in our neighborhood seeing her. She liked to pop up without notice and surprise me, then disappear without a word until a letter would arrive in my mailbox the following month explaining whatever new dreams she was chasing at the time.

You and me, she'd always say. *One day we're gonna forget all this and be sipping rum off the coast of Hawaii.*

At twenty-five now, her lifestyle choices—flirting with both the law and the boundaries of common sense—have always come with repercussions. She knows this as well as I do. Like me, her choices have left permanent marks imprinted on her life. But then, she's always been larger than life.

Which is why when she showed up out of the blue eight months ago, shoving the few belongings she still had in our trailer home into a duffle bag, I didn't blink. Her movements were wild, frantic, as she stuffed the bag till it overflowed, a nervous excitement radiating off her.

"This is it, Emmy," she'd said as she pulled open the drawer of her nightstand and ruffled through some old photographs. "The real deal."

I propped a hip on the side of our dresser and folded my arms over my chest. "You say that every time, Frankie."

"No." She paused, her hand frozen mid-search as she looked up at me. Her deep brown eyes went a shade darker, her expression shifting to something serious, thoughtful. "I mean it this time. If you had the chance to get away, and I mean *really* get away—forget Mama, forget it all. Would you take it?"

I frowned, parted my lips, but I didn't know what to say. What I really wanted was to ask her not to leave me again, to beg my only friend in this world to stay just a little while, but I knew I could never voice those thoughts aloud.

I'm a bird trapped in a self-made cage. Frankie is as free as they come.

"If your honest to God answer is no, then I'll call the whole thing off," Frankie said, taking a slow step toward me. "I'll stay home for a month. Maybe two."

"Really?" Skepticism trickled into my voice.

She nodded once. "Really. But no bullshit, Emmy. Just truth. What if . . . what if there was a place you could finally just," she shrugged a shoulder, glanced sideways toward the box that hid my artwork, "be you. *All* of you. Without consequence. Without judgment." When she looked back at me, her eyes were wide, lips tilted downward. She wore all the innocence of a little girl depending on the honesty of my answer. "Would you do it, Emmy?"

A knot formed in my throat. I wanted to lie, to beg, to insist. But we both knew my answer. I couldn't even imagine that kind of freedom. "Yes." My voice cracked. "I would."

Looking back now, the words we shared that day take on a whole new meaning.

"Emma?" Aubrey's voice pulls me back to the small sitting room, and my eyes find her standing in the open doorway. "I said they're ready for you."

"Oh." My response comes out shaky as I stand, my new contacts making me blink rapidly. *This is what I wanted*, I remind myself. *Don't fuck it up.* Spine straight, chin up. I clear my throat. "Thanks."

Aubrey nods toward the dining room behind her. "You'll do fine," she whispers as she starts to steer me past the doorway. "Just remember the contract. Unless you're like me, do what you can to get claimed."

The contract. Get claimed.

Deep breaths.

The second my foot crosses the threshold, four male pairs of eyes hit me. My chest rises and falls. My skin feels clammy against the tight dress.

The dining room is dim, enclosed by the black walls I'm becoming accustomed to. It's lit only by a modest chandelier above the small, rectangular table where the Matthews are seated. I don't know if it's the shoddy lighting or the adrenaline suddenly pumping through my veins, but I can't seem to focus on any one man long enough to make out his appearance.

All I see are frames of *big*, *dark*, and *suits*.

"Matthews," Aubrey greets them with a nod, "meet Emmy Highland. Your newest secretary."

For a moment, the room is so still I'm afraid to breathe. My chest is too tight. Their silent, concentrated stares are tiny needles prickling beneath my dress. When another long minute passes and still no one speaks, I flick my gaze to Aubrey, hoping I'm the only one feeling the awkwardness.

Except she isn't there.

My fingers start to fidget, but I catch myself and clasp my hands together. *You show people what they want to see, and they'll never suspect what's underneath. Right, Frankie?*

A throat clears. The sound is rough and whips my attention to one of the two men seated directly across from me. The other two sit at each head of the table, one to my left and the other to my right.

"Emmy." The throat-clearer speaks with a strange sort of authority. It's the kind of voice that trails off, like it has a secret. Like he knows my name better than I do. "Well, aren't you going to join us?"

It's not until then that I see the empty chair positioned across from the speaker and the silent man beside him. I force my legs to bring me forward, hoping my movements are fluid despite the unease rolling through me as I slip into my place at the intimate table.

"Ah, much better," the man drawls. "No use having a beauty like this one under our roof if we can't even see her." He winks, nodding toward one of the other men who chuckles.

With the lighting directly above our heads and my pulse settling, I can finally see them clearly.

Since only one man has spoken directly to me, I focus on him first. His face is all sharp angles with a long nose and pronounced cheekbones. His dirty-blond hair, parted mostly on one side, is smooth and long enough to stroke his collar—a very expensive looking collar. I don't know suits, but his reminds me of wedding attire.

Looks too high maintenance to be my type, but he's the

kind of handsome Frankie would fall right into.

"Excuse my rudeness," the man says, amusement dripping through his tone. "Allow me to introduce myself." He stands, and I would have cocked an eyebrow if I wasn't so on edge. Does he think standing for introductions makes him more of a gentleman? He extends a hand. "Raife Matthews."

I force a smile I hope is charming as I rise to slide my hand into his. "Nice to meet you, Raife."

"Aha," he says, something dark dancing behind his golden-brown eyes, "so she does speak. I was beginning to worry this one was defective."

Bitterness bites at my tongue, begging to be unleashed. But then, what kind of men did I expect to find in a place like this? Remembering the reason I'm here, I swallow my distaste to humor him. I need to play the part if I'm going to get close enough to these men to figure out their role in Frankie's disappearance.

My lips curve just a hint, my index finger playfully stroking his palm when he releases my grip. "I do more than just speak."

A low chuckle slides past his lips as he tilts his head. His eyes narrow. "We'll see about that." Before I can respond, he's gesturing toward the man at the left end of the table, and I lower into my seat. "This is Felix, the brains of us Matthews brothers."

Brothers.

Raife smirks again, and I swear it's like he can read my mind. A shiver crawls up my spine at the thought, reminding me to watch every tick of my expression.

Felix holds out a hand, but he doesn't stand, and I'm glad. At least that's one less pretense. "Don't mind Raife here," he mutters, giving me a lopsided grin while we shake. "Not all of us are creeps."

Raife rolls his eyes. "Don't let him confuse you, sugar. He's just as fucked up as the rest of us. Some of us just wear our creep on our sleeves."

I glance back at Felix. He's probably a good five years older than me, but he's got a younger face than the others; soft edges and wide eyes beneath a mop of light brown hair. My gaze lowers to his bright suit—such a contrast to the darkness of the room. His white button-down shirt is layered under the thin straps of suspenders and a crisp, grey vest, but it's his bowtie that steals the show. The thing is large enough to look like a caricature, and it's a vibrant shade of blue I'd love to paint with.

I expect Felix to argue or deny Raife's statement, but instead he shrugs, something dangerous flickering in his eyes. "Touché, brother."

The tiniest spark of hope that I may have found a decent brother quickly deflates.

"Although," Felix adds, nodding toward the opposite end of the table. "If any of us have mastered our creepy sides, it's that one." I glance to my right, then fight the urge to shrink into my seat at the sight of the third brother. "Emmy, meet Griff."

Griff doesn't say a word. Even seated, it's obvious they're all tall, well-built men, yet Griff is far bulkier than the others. His massive frame crushes the chair beneath him.

He wears a black and white tux like Raife's, but his arms are wide enough they threaten to split the material. His brown hair is shaved in a military cut, his lips are turned down in a scowl. His eyes, however, are enjoying a slow perusal of me, starting from my waistline and inching their way up until they land on my chest.

When he runs his tongue over his teeth, I suppress a shudder. The darkness I'd glimpsed in his brothers' eyes is nothing compared to the black holes staring at me now.

"And then there was one," Raife murmurs, turning to the man sitting beside him. A hint of amusement is back in his voice as he looks to the remaining brother, almost deviously.

For the first time, I shift my eyes to the silent man sitting across from me. He's staring straight at me, still partially shadowed as the weak rays of light above the table struggle to reach him. His head is angled a fraction, his thumb stroking a lightly stubbled jaw. Like he's assessing me. Judging me.

My skin flushes, heat rushing to my cheeks, and I hate it. Has he been watching me so closely the entire time?

Broad shoulders dipped, his posture's more relaxed than the others. The top of his black button-up is undone, hinting at a sculpted chest. No jacket, no tie. The glass table reveals that his long legs are spread. Comfortable. And yet a wave of tension courses through him, beneath it all. He's rolled up the sleeves of his crisp shirt, allowing me to see the tendons of muscle straining in his forearms as he clenches a fist, then releases.

His hair—shaved on the sides, longer on top—is as black as my own, blending into the walls that encase us. But where my skin is porcelain, his is olive-toned.

I dart a glance to the other brothers. He doesn't resemble them. Come to think of it, none of them look alike.

"Well, don't be shy, Adam." Raife nudges his brother's shoulder. "Introduce yourself to the beauty."

The man, Adam, doesn't take his gaze off me, but one corner of his lips twitches up. His eyes, though, flash dangerously. Deadly. They're such a dark blue they almost look black in this lighting. I can't tell who they mean to threaten more: me or Raife.

His eyelids lower, his gaze burning me from within as it drags down to my lips. Then stays there.

Somehow the subtle movement feels more obtrusive than Griff staring blatantly at my chest. My throat goes dry. I try to swallow but can't. Suddenly being claimed by any of the others doesn't seem so bad.

"Of course. Brother." The words are bitter. The deep baritone of his softly spoken voice prickles my skin as his eyes break away from my lips.

He aims them at Raife, whose own lips curve as though the pair of them are sharing some sort of private joke. A joke only Raife seems to find amusing. A silent dare colors each of their expressions, tainting the air with something dark, heavy.

Felix shakes his head at them as though in warning, but Griff remains far more interested in me. Neither of the men is as sucked into the interaction unfolding before us as I am. Something flips inside my stomach as their stare-down begs me to look away. But I'm stuck, held hostage by the strange and twisted energy filling the room.

What is the joke, exactly? And why does it feel like it's at my expense?

"I hope you're enjoying your first day." Adam's chair scrapes along the white marble as he pushes back and stands, the motion shattering the intensity and flooding my lungs with relief. The relief quickly turns to ice, though, because then he's walking around the table, right toward me, and I can't suck in a breath.

He stops directly beside my chair, then lowers himself just enough to put his lips by my ear. Warm breath strokes my cheek, my neck. When his thumb comes up and brushes my hair from my eyes, a fiery tremor runs down my spine.

"It's going to be interesting," he whispers, his voice so soft, so smooth, it would almost sound soothing if I weren't listening to the words, "watching you break. *Emmy.*"

chapter four

> "You get lost out of a desire to be lost.
> But in the place called lost
> strange things are found."
> —Rebecca Solnit

Emmy

"That went well." Aubrey slinks into a chair beside me as I stare at my plate of food. Food I haven't touched. My stomach is still on fire from the hot breath on my cheek and the dark words in my ear just twenty minutes ago.

I blink, easing out of my trance and angling my head toward the beautiful redhead. "Well?" I repeat. We must have different definitions of the word.

She reaches for a bread roll in the center of the otherwise empty dining table. Not *the* dining table; the one in the ladies' quarters is for secretaries only. Thankfully. "You gained the attention of Adam Matthews. Not that he's going to claim you, but still, impressive."

"He's not—I thought—"

"What?" The roll halts just before reaching her lips. "You thought that was him claiming you?"

My eyes dart to my untouched plate of pasta as I only internally admit that, yes, that's exactly what I thought. I grab the fork and twirl the linguine around it, stuffing the food in my mouth if only for a distraction.

"Adam is . . ." Aubrey takes a small bite of the roll, chewing as she contemplates. "Selective, you could say. I've been here four years and have only seen him claim one girl."

One girl.

"Who was she?" The question is out of my mouth before I can stop it. I didn't intend on asking questions about Frankie right away, but I have to jump at the window of opportunity. If there was any doubt these men could have harmed my sister before, it's completely vanished now.

Aubrey snorts but doesn't answer. When I continue to stare at her, she tilts her head. "You're serious? It's forbidden to name or discuss girls who have been here previously. Confidentiality and all that."

I let out a breath and dig into the dish once more. *Of course it wouldn't be so easy.* Throwing a sideways glance her way as I chew, I try a less direct approach. "Was it recent?"

"No. Not even close."

My muscles relax for a split second. It couldn't have been Frankie then. But that still leaves the other three brothers. "Do they all like the same type of women?"

She pulls a loose red tendril behind her ear. "Not always," she says with a wink. "They usually share a specific physical type, yeah, but I assume you've already figured that out." I nod and take another bite, trying to appear less interested than I am. "Griff can be kinda picky. He's rough, you know, so he usually likes girls who can take it. Felix is more laid-back, and Raife, he claims almost everyone at some point. Even if it's just for their first month, before one of the other brothers takes over."

I stop mid-chew. "Everyone?"

"Pretty much. There are some exceptions, but it's rare. He likes to get to know each of the girls personally, and claiming someone is really as personal as you can get here."

I lift the glass of water to my lips and inhale a few large gulps. Setting the drink down, I turn to her. "And Adam?"

She squints and taps her lip. "I haven't gotten him figured out. I doubt anyone has." When I don't respond, she adds, "Listen. Don't worry about Adam Matthews. Even without him, it's clear that you're wanted. You'll have your master by eight o'clock tomorrow morning."

Though a tinge of alarm runs through me at knowing the exact time I'm to be claimed, I can't fully process it while that particular brother's name still lingers in the air. Just like that, his soft lips are back on my ear. *It's going to be interesting watching you break, Emmy.*

I try to keep my expression neutral when I meet Aubrey's cool, green gaze. "Adam, he said something to me before he left the room."

She waits patiently for me to continue.

"Something about watching me break." When I realize I'm twirling the pasta again, I set down my fork. "What did he mean by that?"

She cocks an eyebrow and pulls back. "He wants to watch?"

"Watch what? What does that mean?"

"He's talking about phase three, Emma." I open my mouth to correct her again but then bite my tongue. She knows my name. "But you know, he normally sits those out. Not like the others." Her lips twitch, and her eyes sparkle. "They always watch—"

"Phase three?"

Aubrey turns to me with a frown. "Did Stella tell you

nothing? Yes, you have exactly"—she eyes a clock hanging on the wall across from us—"six minutes to finish eating, and I have orders to make sure you finish all of it. Then it's on to the final phase before claiming."

When I say nothing, her frown deepens.

"You didn't really expect men like the Matthews brothers to make a year-long commitment after ten minutes of formal introductions, did you?" I stare at her blankly. Guess I hadn't really considered that. "Look, you'll be taken through a series of tests, that's it. Everyone's tests are different, so I can't tell you what to expect, but they want to see what you can handle, what you can't. If you pass, you'll go to your room and get your beauty sleep for tomorrow."

"And if I fail?"

She shrugs. "It happens. Not everyone's cut out for this, and there's no shame in that. You'll be sent home on a first-class flight to return to your life as normal."

I close my eyes and take a breath. *I can't go home.* Not when I'm so close. Not when Frankie might be out there somewhere, hurt or in danger. Or worse. No thanks to me. My exhale comes out shaky as I open my eyes again.

"Everything will work itself out." Aubrey leans closer, lowering her voice even though we're completely alone. "Trust me, phase three is all the Matthews will need to make their decision on whom you will serve."

I've never been afraid of the dark.

When we were little, Frankie would sneak into my corner of the trailer so we could fall asleep together. Later, when

Mama took away my designated spot completely, Frankie let me share hers. She would leave a lamp on all night long. It was the only way she could sleep. For me, though, something about the brightness irked me. As though blinding me wasn't enough, it got greedy and snuck under my skin, gnawing at me like an itch I could never scratch.

The dark, however, has always been there to comfort me. I love that fleeting moment of pure power that pumps through my veins right before I cloak myself in its shadow. The world is quickly shut out with a simple flick of a switch. Just like that. It's the only shield no one questions or expects you to justify.

But tonight—with the cold, steel chair sending goose bumps down the backs of my bare thighs, my wrists tied behind me—it's quickly lost its appeal.

I can handle a small, windowless room cloaked in darkness. Confinement is another thing entirely.

Tingles spread through my legs when I shift in the chair, my muscles begging to be stretched. I don't know how long I've been sitting here, but the skin around my wrists is sore, and strange shapes are beginning to blend in the dark.

After a while, my shoulders slump.

My head whips to my right at the grating sound of a steel door opening, and a woozy sensation rushes from my chest to my scalp at the movement.

Jesus.

How long have I been in here?

Shaking the feeling away, I squint at the door. Any hope of glimpsing more than a shadowed figure entering the room vanishes as the door closes. Footfalls glide toward me until clothing crinkles right in front of me and a light stroke of air flutters across my skin as the figure kneels.

I narrow my eyes but can't make out anything more than a

broad, masculine outline.

"Welcome to the Dark Room, Emmy." I recognize the amused, almost taunting tone immediately. Raife. I'm not surprised he finds entertainment in my obvious discomfort. "How are you feeling?"

"I've been better," I manage smoothly.

He lets out a chuckle. It's low, throaty, and sexy even to my ears, despite my lack of attraction. There's no question all four of the Matthews brothers are genetically gifted. The fact only makes me wonder why they'd need to hire anyone for sexual favors. "Tell me, lovely. Is it the darkness that bothers you so, or is it the wrist ties?"

I open my mouth to answer honestly but lick my lips instead as I recall Aubrey's words. *They want to see what you can handle . . . He wants to watch? . . . The others, they always watch.*

Are they watching me this very second? Even Adam? Can he see me clearly even while I'm practically blind? His dark eyes flash in my mind, secretive and scrutinizing as he looks down on me.

Heat warms my flesh.

It's going to be interesting watching you break.

Not tonight, Adam Matthews.

I force my wrists to relax against the binding, then bat my lashes in case Raife, too, can somehow see me clearly. "Maybe I'm just not used to being alone when I'm tied down."

That earns me a groan as he leans closer, the deep shadow of his face hovering in front of mine. "I knew you had some bite under those soft lips," he whispers, just as I feel his thumb brush over my bottom lip. "Shame they're not for me."

I frown, then mumble through the next wave of dizziness that rolls through me, "What do you—"

"No questions." He snaps upright, voice sharp as a whip. I

shrink back into the chair at the sudden shift, then inwardly scold myself for the reaction. "Tonight we're going to get to know each other intimately. If at any point you find yourself too uncomfortable to proceed, you'll let me know, and I'll release you."

A thick swallow passes through my throat. "Meaning . . ."

"Meaning you'll be sent home." He lowers and leans closer, his arms dark shadows that cage me in as he grips the chair's armrests. "Because if you can't stomach tonight, you won't last a week. Fun fact: my brothers don't seem to think you'll last ten minutes. However"—he bends his head until his nose is on my neck, and I shiver when he inhales deeply against my skin—"something tells me you'll surprise them. Something tells me you'll surprise us all."

When he kneels before me and slides his large hands up my bare thighs, my knees snap together automatically. He lets out a dark chuckle. "Relax. All you need to do is relax. Can you do that for me?"

Relax?

His grip tightens, and my back stiffens. I don't want to relax. Not while my wrists are bound, my surroundings are blind, and I have no idea what the Matthews have in store for me.

And yet, I do feel oddly . . . warm? My eyes close as the new feeling sinks in. His cold palms are a strange contrast to the warm caress soothing my limbs.

Alarm bells ring in the back of my mind.

Taking a deep breath, I open my eyes again and target the figure before me. *Focus, Emmy*. The only thing I need to be thinking about is getting some semblance of control while in this toxic room. Except something tells me Raife won't have that at all.

A man like him needs to be the one in control at all times. Or maybe . . . maybe he just needs to feel like he is.

I slowly let out the breath I was holding, then soften my

voice for him. "I can do that for you."

"Excellent." His thumbs brush small, circular strokes along the insides of my thighs, as though rewarding me for my response.

The subtle movement is so skillful I'm sure it's had other women sighing, but I have to make a conscious effort to keep my body from tensing up.

The door opens again with a loud groan, and we both look to see Stella entering the room. Light seeps in from the hallway, illuminating her like a beautiful, blonde angel. She's quiet, even demure, as she lowers a tray carrying two lit candles to the ground, just beside the wall.

When she stands, she sneaks a glance at Raife and holds it for a moment. I turn back to him, thankful I can finally see his sharp features even if we're still shadowed, and I'm surprised to find him watching her just as closely. I don't think I've seen this look in his eyes when they're aimed at me. Twisted amusement, yes. A challenge, curiosity, and even raw hunger, yes. But never the pure possessiveness darkening his brown eyes now.

"Will this be all, Master?"

Master? A glint pulls my eyes to his right wrist, to a shiny watch I hadn't noticed before. It's gold, just like Stella's scarf.

"For now," he murmurs, his tone full of suggestion.

Ruby-red rises up her cheeks, and she flashes me a small but friendly smile before turning and closing the door behind her.

His thumbs continue their caress as he pulls his gaze back to mine. Just like that, the heated expression's wiped away, replaced with the strange, devious curiosity I recognize. I'm not sure if I should be grateful or regretful for the candles' subtle lighting.

I lift my chin, and he cocks an eyebrow. "Tell me something, lovely." His tone is still. Deadly serious. "Have you ever wondered what it feels like to burn?"

Goose bumps race along the skin he continues to caress.

"No. I can't say I have." I clear my throat at the odd sound of my voice bouncing back in my eardrums. It's muffled, like I'm speaking from under a blanket.

Raife removes both hands from my legs to loosen his tie. His movements are quick, almost rushed, yanking the material down and popping open the top buttons of his shirt.

I open my mouth to ask what he's doing when he turns away. He takes a few steps toward the candles and raises the tray.

An orange glow dances along the sharp lines of his face as he returns to stand in front of me. The trick of the light makes his pale skin look almost olive, and it makes me think of Adam.

After pushing the uninvited image away, my eyes dart down to the flames. A spike of fear uncurls in my stomach. Raife wouldn't really burn me, would he? When I slide my gaze back to his face, the fear tightens into knots. A crazed spark that feels somehow personal blooms in his eyes, and it's fixed right on me. The look cuts straight past my skin, ripe with a desire I can't comprehend, and it's eerily similar to the way Griff stared me down earlier.

I suppress a flinch. It's impossible, but it feels as though I've wronged him, and he's out to get revenge. The thick material keeping my wrists captive feels tighter than ever, curling around me like a snake determined to suffocate.

"Shh," he coos, lowering until he's kneeling again. Setting the tray to rest on his knee, he keeps it steady with one hand and, with the other, runs a finger along the corner of my jaw. His touch is cold, and I shiver. "Don't look so afraid, lovely. It's just a little fire."

His cool finger slips from my face as he lowers his lips toward the candles. With a single puff, darkness drenches us once again. Thin tendrils of smoke hit my nostrils, sweet currents of vanilla laced with a bitter spice.

Heat prickles along my skin, from the apex of my thighs to my toes, and the feeling makes my legs press together. There's no way a candle could cause such a physical reaction.

A low, knowing chuckle vibrates right in front of me, and it pounds in my ears before trailing off with an echo. I squeeze my eyes shut, noticing that the rhythm matches the sensation suddenly brewing in my chest. What the hell's happening to me?

Get a grip, Emmy.

When something hot and thick oozes over the top of my thigh, a yelp spills from my lips and into the darkness. The syrupy liquid slides down the inside of my leg, hot enough to make me squirm. It takes a second to place the sensation—candle wax.

My breathing turns shallow, my pulse racing. The tingles only intensify; the softest needle points running from my fingertips to my toes, and my skin is flushed with an awareness I don't understand.

I want to give in to the feeling. Everything in me screams to submit to it entirely. Like I've been drugged, it's a thick, black tar wrapping around my skin, hot and heavy beneath the surface.

A rush of sensitivity flows over me like an electric current, making each rub of the ties around my wrists burn enough to sting. Black and grey shadows meet my eyes no matter where I look, flashing *danger* in my mind like a glowing sign.

I twist and writhe against the binding, but it just digs and digs. I swear the walls are caving in on me, crushing my chest until I have to open my mouth to suck in a lungful of air.

What has he done to me? *Could* he have drugged me without my knowledge? Oh god, was it in my freaking food? With nothing to compare the feeling to, I have no idea.

I need to get these things off me.

I need to gain *control* before my chest collapses in on itself.

Squinting, palms sweating, I angle my head toward the outline that is Raife. I can't make out his expression as he saunters behind me. Cool fingers brush my neck as he gathers my hair and wrenches it over my left shoulder.

"Just let go," he continues, his voice ringing in my ears even when the words stop. "Show me who you are, Emmy Highland."

Show him who I am? I don't know about all that. I don't know if even I've seen who I really am.

But maybe I can show him who he wants to see.

chapter five

"Even a white rose has a dark shadow."
—Unknown

Adam

I'VE NEVER STARED DIRECTLY INTO THE EYES OF A GHOST.

Not until today, anyway.

The wall is cold on my shoulder as I lean against it, arms crossed. My eyes narrowed, I gaze straight into the screen with a camera view of the room she's in. A few footsteps and a closed door are the only things separating her from me, but she doesn't need to know that.

She's certainly a petite little thing. A mouse trying hard to come off as a lion. The camera's night vision allows me to see everything, and it's the details that give her away—the slight shake in her voice. The way her knees are clenched tight, as though she expects forceful hands to pry them open at any moment. The slow lick across her plump lips before she speaks, a sign of hesitation. And Raife's enjoying every second of it.

Fucking Raife.

My fists tighten, but I release the frustration through a long exhale. I knew the bastard was sick, but this is impressive even for him. The girl shouldn't be here, and Raife's little charade won't seem so amusing when one of us loses our shit from having to stare at her every goddamn day.

I admit, seeing her in the dining room for the first time, not ten feet away from me . . . it was certainly unexpected. Her soft, porcelain skin identical to the image still burned into my brain, even years after the fact. The same thick, black hair. Those eyes—the exact shade of sky blue.

Yeah, she got under my fucking skin. The searing heat vibrating through me this very moment tells me she still is. Raife succeeded in that much. I wouldn't be surprised if the crazy son of a bitch gave her contact lenses to perfectly replicate that eye color. For all I know he had her dye her hair, too; such fair skin against the blackest hair isn't common.

What I intend to find out is *why*. There's a reason we only hire blondes, with Aubrey being the exception. And Raife is many things, impulsive and manipulative being at the top, but he's not usually such a fool.

I rip my gaze from the girl to steal a glance at my brothers, who stand at the opposite end of the small viewing room. Felix's focused stare is sharp, assessing, like my own, except he's not looking at the girl. He's watching Raife. Breaking him down into tiny, manageable pieces that can be inspected and evaluated, like the complicated techy shit Felix spends his days knee deep in. Probably trying to figure out what the hell Raife thinks he's pulling.

Felix is the least of my concerns. He may be a lost cause like the rest of us, but there's not an aggressive bone in his body—outside of our agenda, that is. If he snaps, the worst he'd do is cave in on himself, and I'd be right there to bring him out of it.

Griff, on the other hand—with his nose almost pressed against the duplicate screen, his unblinking gaze centered on the girl, and his grip squeezing the edge of the frame so tight his knuckles are white—all he knows is aggression.

Ever since that day fifteen years ago, when the four of us were forced to sacrifice our souls to change our fates, Griff has had tunnel vision when he sets his sights on something. It's one of his strengths, being able to black out everything but his target, and it serves our agenda well. This thing with the girl, though . . . I push off the wall and take a slow step closer to the monitor, trying to ignore the way her body trembles when the wax hits her thigh for the first time. Gritting my jaw is the only reaction I allow myself.

Griff, he takes her presence here personally. But no one knows just how personal this is to me. No one knows the full extent of my past, my secrets, where *she* is concerned. Dressing up some look-alike to screw with my head isn't only going to cost Raife; it'll cost the girl just as much.

Emmy Highland. A picture-perfect match to what *she* would look like today, if she had survived that night. *Ah, fuck.* I squeeze my eyes shut at the mere thought of *her*. She's attached to memories I've successfully kept locked up tight for the sake of my own survival.

Emmy Highland is not *her*. What she is, is a pawn in Raife's twisted game. But if my past has taught me anything, it's that even innocence is not always as it seems. And her little tells confirm as much; especially now, with the wax sliding down her bare leg.

Whether she's seductively stroking my brother's palm at the dinner table or helplessly tied to a steel chair, there is something undeniably fragile about the girl with raven hair. Something that threatens to crack with a single touch. In fact, I get the feeling I wouldn't need to touch her at all to make her bleed.

My eyes fall shut, the thought of blood against her little

body taking over until it's all I see. So familiar, yet not at all.

Crimson rivulets slowly dancing down her fair skin . . . A deep shiver running through her spine at the thick, warm sensation . . . I wonder how those plump, pink lips would look with her tongue flicking out to catch the drops of red. The blue of her eyes would reflect so clearly in the silver edges of my knife, her pale palm such a stark contrast against the blade's black handle, and I have to know . . . if I slipped the weapon into her delicate hand, would she startle and drop it? Or would she wrap her grip around it and squeeze?

Fuck. Heat cuts down my chest and straight to my cock, burning through my skin until I'm swallowing down a groan.

Goddamn Raife and his mindfuckery. He knew exactly how this girl's presence would screw with me.

I need to get the hell out of this room. I need to get the hell away from her.

Just as I take a step toward the exit, a soft whimper from the other side of the glass has my head tilting. Raife's got the girl's head pulled back by her hair, blue eyes wide at the ceiling, hands still tied behind her back. He's looming over her, a smirk on his face as he holds the candle over her shoulder, just close enough to make her quiver. Likely trying to work out if his next touch will leave far more than a sting.

He's toying with her, seeing what she unwittingly reveals in moments of fear, intimidation, pleasure. Or pain. He tends to get more of a rush from screams than whimpers, but then, so do the types of women that sign up for his ridiculous charades.

Raife's methods today are nothing new, if slightly more . . . strategic than usual. But what is new is her reaction. I hardly notice I'm taking another step forward until I'm almost as close to the screen as Griff. I dip one hand in my pocket, the other stroking the side of my jaw.

Emmy has angled her head back enough to see him, her slender neck fully exposed. One corner of her lips curves, but just slightly. Seductively. When she whispers something too low for me to hear, Raife lowers his head enough his dirty-blond hair brushes her forehead. His grip loosens, and soon his fingers are teasing the material around her hands.

He tugs at the coarse material. Her body stills, her eager anticipation visible from all the way over here. I almost think he's going to untie it completely, but then he slowly backs away with that obnoxious smirk etched across his face.

When the girl grits her teeth and something vicious flashes in her angelic eyes, my gaze narrows, and that fucking heat runs straight to my groin again.

So she failed at her weak attempt to get free. Unsurprising. But she did attempt—and in wolf's clothing no less. Some of the girls may get a little excited in the Dark Room, may even nip when Raife goes too far, but they never fight it. They always want it.

Hmm. No, this won't do. This won't do at all.

It's one thing to walk away from a girl who's fragile, quiet, easily frightened. Submissive, sure, but someone who *wants* it all the same. How easy it would be to break her with a single squeeze. But this—there's something too familiar about the maddening gleam sparking within her eyes now.

Something no mouse would be capable of replicating.

Unless, of course . . . the mouse really is a lion after all.

The girl is hiding something. And the sick part of me is suddenly determined to be the one to discover all her secrets.

Calmly rolling up my sleeves, I turn on my heel and walk leisurely toward the door connecting the Dark Room to ours.

There's only one way to really see who someone is, past

all the bullshit. Let them have their moment of control, then pull their legs out from under them and watch them reach for you before they shatter. It's fascinating how fast the truth spills when they're on their knees, without them ever needing to utter a single word.

chapter six

*"If you are afraid of darkness,
you are afraid of your own soul."*
—Unknown

Emmy

As Raife's shadow looms over me, the fire in my stomach only burns hotter.

I knew it was a weak effort, whispering promises in his ear. *Untie me, and I'll show you everything you want to see.* But the tingles dancing along my body just a minute ago have transformed into a fiery, slippery blanket, and I feel like I've been left in a sauna too long.

My skin is damp everywhere, flushed. My thighs rub together, seeking something. *Anything.* Friction, wax—I'll take any of it. The knowledge makes my insides burn twice as hot.

The only thing keeping my butt on this chair and my mouth clamped shut is that I need these men to want me here. At least enough to keep me under contract until I figure out what happened to my sister.

Even through the haze, the more I watch Raife and see his fixation on pushing limits, the more my curiosity grows in thinking he could have claimed Frankie. Aubrey did say he claims almost all the girls at some point, even if it's just temporary. Based on looks, he's definitely her type. But more than that, Frankie believed, or maybe insisted, she didn't have any limits. She loved nothing more than a man who wasn't afraid to test them. To test her.

A sharp sting jerks my shoulder forward, and I bite back a hiss through the pain. There's no warning, no hot trickle of wax this time. All I'm left with is a throbbing sensation, a tender spot above my right shoulder blade. He must have lit the candle again while standing behind me. I was so lost in my head I didn't notice the light come to life.

"You know, the red flames really are exquisite against your fair skin." Discomfort bristles across my shoulder when something thick and cool is gently rubbed over the fresh wound. The more he rubs, the more the sharpness soothes into a dull ache, and the more I want to turn my head and sink my teeth into the asshole's fingers until I see red.

So many sensations are tumbling through me that I can't tell if I'm turned on, scared, or pissed off. But knowing Raife did this to me makes me focus on the latter.

His touch retreats when a door I hadn't noticed on the wall opposite us opens. Light seeps into the room, and I squint at the bright intrusion. A tall, broad figure strolls toward me, not bothering to close the door behind him. Even before I'm able to make out the smooth lines of his face, I know who it is.

Adam Matthews.

My heart swoops before fluttering against my chest. My already flushed skin heats up at the strange look in his dark, chilling blue eyes as he inches closer. One step, two steps . . . each soft footfall feels like a threat. His posture appears so at ease. I'd never guess the tension coiled inside him if it weren't for the shadowed way the lighting hits each hard angle of his build. The golden streams highlight every flex of muscle beneath his fitted button-down.

I don't know if it's from fear or whatever Raife did to mess with my head, but I can't stop myself from squirming under his icy gaze.

He halts right in front of me, his shoes almost brushing the toes of my designer heels. He dips his head, eyes narrowing to slits as he leisurely rakes them over me. "You drugged her."

His voice is more distant than it should be, yet the low sound vibrates down my spine as he confirms what I already suspected.

"Just a little concoction I'm experimenting with." Raife's hand lands on the curve of my neck, then he strokes me like one would a cat. The crisp material of his suit tickles my back, and I cringe. It's sandpaper to my hypersensitive skin. "If I didn't know better, brother, I'd think you almost sound disappointed."

"Disappointed? No. I'd have to have expectations for that."

Adam's face materializes directly in front of me when he kneels. His hand comes up, then strong, warm fingers grip either side of my jaw. His hold is tight, almost uncomfortably so, but when he slowly angles my head to inspect me closer, the movement is surprisingly gentle.

My eyelids droop, and my limbs become too heavy as a dreamlike haze clouds the corners of my vision, the drugs making a home in my bloodstream. I'm pretty sure the only thing keeping my head up right now is the strength of his grip, because the rest of me has melted against the hard chair.

It's surprising, all the details you notice in a person's features when there's nothing but a few inches of empty space separating you. Like the thick, masculine stubble around his square jaw. I'd noticed it earlier, but being this close makes me wonder if it's the kind that's shaved smooth every morning and grows back by evening. The dark blue of his eyes doesn't look so black now, even while shadowed beneath a row of dark lashes. His olive skin appears exotic so close up, and I find myself wanting to know where he's from. Why he and his brothers all look so different.

A strange shiver flits down my spine when he uses his other hand to sweep my hair over one shoulder. He leans in, inspecting the fresh wound that still throbs faintly. The cool material of his pants brushes the insides of my bare thighs, and awareness rushes through me as I realize he's right between my legs.

A breath pours from my lips.

He pulls his head back, then looks straight at me. His gaze darts down to my throat when I swallow.

Something lethal flashes through his eyes. The tips of his fingers dig into my cheeks a split second before he releases me completely, forcefully enough my head falls back.

Raife's chuckle is the only thing that reminds me of his presence. He walks to the tray along the right wall and sets the candle down. "I knew you wouldn't be able to resist watching this one, but I've got to say, I didn't expect you to join in quite so quickly." He gestures to the candles near his feet, both now unlit, then raises a brow as he removes a square lighter from his pocket. "Care to do the honors? Personally, I enjoy the romantic look of a candle's flame, but I'm thinking straight from the lighter is more your style."

Adam doesn't move from between my legs. He doesn't take his eyes off mine either. "Since when do you get off on burning our hires in the Dark Room?" he asks so casually you'd think he were asking about the weather.

Raife's footfalls head toward me, the sound reverberating in my eardrums as I think about the lighter still tucked in his palm, but I refuse to be the first to look away from the man right in front of me. The one who looks at me like he sees something the others don't. Like I'm a puzzle to be worked out and he's got all damn day.

Whatever drugs I've been subjected to have already screwed me to the point I can hardly hold myself up, hardly trust myself to speak if I tried. But a staring contest? This I can win, even with heavy eyelids.

Fingers stroke my hair as Raife settles behind me again. "Since Emmy Highland, of course. Just look at that face." I wince when he jerks my head back, and I'm almost forced to break my gaze from Adam. I manage to hold it, barely. "So familiar, don't you think? It's uncanny, really." The dark humor laced through Raife's tone is unnerving enough I almost miss the words. *Familiar?* "Come on, brother. You know I've fantasized about fire on that woman's skin for years."

That woman? What woman?

When a tongue slides over the back of my neck, it's so unexpected and teasing to my hyperaware skin that a strangled sound escapes—something between a moan and a growl. For one intoxicating moment, I can't bring myself to care that the man with a fixation on burning me is the one touching me. Not when his brother's deep blue eyes are boring into me, body heat radiating mere inches from the emptiness between my thighs, and—*shit. What the hell did Raife give me?* This time the noise that rumbles through my throat is an unmistakable growl.

Raife tsks and leans closer until his breath is on my ear. "You should know, I like it when you struggle."

"Enough." The quiet word slices through the air as Adam stands.

His fist clenches at his side before he dips the hand into his pocket and looks at Raife.

I win.

I smile. It feels awkward and detached, thanks to the drugs, like my body is not my own, but still. Maybe a staring contest isn't the greatest accomplishment right now, but it's all I have.

Adam only cocks his head to one side, then slowly runs his tongue over his full bottom lip.

My smile falters.

"Emmy, Emmy, Emmy," he murmurs. Thoughtful. His deep, smooth voice commands my attention so effortlessly it makes my thighs rub together. His eyes are bolted to mine when he says, "Untie her."

"But she's a gift to you," Raife scoffs, throwing his hands up. "Gifts are meant to be wrapped. Honestly, it's basic etiquette—"

"A gift," Adam repeats. One corner of his lips lifts as he watches me, but it disappears just as fast. He flicks his gaze to Raife, his expression hardening to stone. "Un. Tie. Her."

Raife lets out an agitated sigh. When he tugs at the rope around my wrists until my arms fall to my sides, my eyes widen. I glance down at my hands, at the line of raw skin circling the area below them like bracelets, and then I slowly stretch out my fingers.

I'm still staring downward, in awe of the way a spark zips through my fingertips as they graze the soft fabric of my dress, when Adam's deep voice pulls at something low in my stomach. "Get up."

I glance up. Both brothers stand right in front of me. They eye me like I'm a circus clown who's just been presented on stage, and they're my audience of two, waiting to be entertained. Waiting to get what they paid for.

"I said, get up," Adam repeats.

I continue to stare dumbly at him.

"You've been set free."

Free?

Two figures form near the open doorway as Griff and Felix step into the room. They keep their distance as they, too, wait for my move. Felix's bright blue bowtie catches the light as he leans against the wall, arms folded over his suspenders, while Griff's massive frame remains motionless in the doorway, darkening the already bleak room.

I don't understand. What do they expect me to do when my body weight feels too heavy to lift on my own? My tongue is thick in my mouth, my throat dry, and I fear that only garbled sounds will come out if I try to speak. That I'll try to stand and fall straight to the ground in front of them. That I'll be made to look even more weak and breakable than I already do.

Adam takes a step forward. I try to lift my head to see him better, but it's like an anchor on my neck. As if he knows this, he slides his warm fingers beneath my chin and tilts it for me, until I'm forced to look straight into his eyes.

His voice drops to a murmur. "Isn't this what you want, Emmy? To be free. To call the shots."

I swallow. The man doesn't even know me. So why does it feel like he sees right through me? Am I really so transparent?

He lowers his head until his stubble gently scrapes my cheek, and it sends a tremor down my body. "Or have I overestimated you?" His large hand slips from my chin to my throat, his fingers squeezing lightly. "Maybe you're truly as weak as you look."

Before I can respond, he pushes away from my throat. The heat of his touch still burns my neck. We're not alone, yet he may as well be the only man in the room. His face hardens as he watches me. After a long, uncomfortable moment of me staying rooted to my seat, he grinds his jaw.

Still, I don't move.

He finally shakes his head, his lips thinning into a firm line, and blows out a breath.

Without another glance my way, he turns and walks toward the exit.

"Not weak," I croak, slurring. The words are out of my mouth before I realize I'm speaking. Adam stops but keeps his back to me. "Just trying to get a feel for the brothers I'll be spending so much time with."

He turns his head just enough for me to see the sharp angle of his jaw, the way the longer strands of his hair have fallen over part of his forehead, the way his eyes narrow.

He's daring me to make a move.

I push off the chair and wince when nausea tears through me. My legs wobble, skin breaking into a fresh sweat. I don't know how long I have until my knees are bound to give out. Allowing myself to drop, I catch my weight on my hands and knees, then cringe. I clear my expression before looking up at Adam through heavy lids as I kick off my heels and crawl toward him.

I'm making this up as I go, but they don't need to know that. *He* doesn't need to know that.

"Do you want to know what I've learned so far?" I ask, keeping my pace slow so my shaky arms don't collapse.

Finally, Adam faces me. He tucks his hands into his pockets, angles his head, but doesn't respond.

"For starters . . ." I let my voice hang, then shift sharply to the right so I'm crawling toward Raife instead.

Raife's eyebrows shoot up.

I fight the irritating urge to look over my shoulder and see Adam's expression. A chill runs through me as the skirt of my dress rides up above my thighs. Once I reach Raife, I stop and sit back on my feet. My breath is heavy and my bones are quivering, but I try to play it off like I'm just turned on.

I lock my eyes on Raife's brown ones.

"I've learned"—my focus blurs, Raife's face doubling, tripling. I shake my head, try again—"I've learned that some of you really know how to tease a poor girl." Bile rises in my throat, but even being drugged doesn't subdue the voice deep in my gut tying Raife to Frankie. Raife, the one apparently running this operation. Right now, in a mansion filled with black walls and the unknown, the only thing I'm certain of is that I'm not leaving this room until I've sold myself to the devil. "And no one likes to be left hanging . . ."

I frown, unsure if I finished my sentence or if that last word was only spoken in my head.

Raife squints down at me, adjusts his tie. "Felix? Griff?" Holding up a hand for show, he snaps twice, as though summoning trained dogs. "I believe the girl is asking for some relief." He pats my head. "I'm nothing if not selfless."

My insides churn as heavy footfalls approach from behind me. Griff's wide, towering build appears beside Raife, and my throat constricts. He cracks his knuckles, rolls his neck, then takes one long stride toward me and halts.

"Felix?" Raife looks over my shoulder, and I imitate the movement. Anything to avoid Griff. Adam still stands behind me with his hands in his pockets, obnoxiously looking as calm and at ease as ever, but I make a point not to look at him. "You surprise me," Raife continues. "Don't you want a taste?"

Felix, still leaning against the wall, only shrugs. "Nah, not tonight. Whatever this"—he gestures toward me, making a circular motion with his hand—"is, I'm pretty sure I want no part of it." He meets my gaze and winks. "Family drama. Nothing personal."

His words swim in my ears like a school of fish racing in endless circles.

Raife huffs. "Suit yourself."

A huge hand grips my neck, and I'm yanked to a standing position. I gasp, pain shooting through me, but the sound catches in my throat. My knees buckle from holding my weight, and Griff steps closer, then flips my body so he's right behind me. Something long and thick rubs against my back, and I squeeze my eyes shut. The fucker's hard over this.

When I open my eyes, Raife's settling into the single steel chair in the middle of the room. He kicks his legs out, then leans back and clasps his hands behind his head.

He grins at me. "Front row seats and everything."

Heat rises in my chest, my neck, my cheeks. I can't bring myself to look at Adam. I don't know why—I'm sure he's enjoying this as much as the others, if not more. He's one of them, after all. But for some ridiculous reason, I'm embarrassed knowing he's watching. The man who wants so badly to see me break.

Griff squeezes tighter, then tighter, until I'm straining to suck in a breath as he hunches forward and grinds against me once more.

I clench my teeth but don't fight it. Not that I'd stand a chance in this state anyway. I signed up for this for a reason, and I'm not going anywhere until I find my sister—even if it means allowing them to think they've shamed and broken me in the process.

Enjoy the show, Adam Matthews.

Finally, I slide my gaze to the man in question. Lie or not, there's something empowering in telling myself I'm *allowing* this to happen.

Adam gives nothing away, his expression a hard wall, but I take some satisfaction in knowing he sees the challenge in my eyes.

Griff releases my throat to grip my waist, and I gasp as cool air fills my lungs. Before I can catch my breath, he lifts my dress and squeezes my bare ass hard enough to leave a bruise. I choke out a pained sound but quickly turn it into a moan.

"You like that, do you? Some pain to go with your pleasure." It's the first words Griff has ever spoken in front of me, and the rough sound makes my skin crawl.

I suppress a cringe, sloppily grinding my ass against him. "I like whatever you'll give me," I garble.

Griff groans then crushes my ribcage between his hands. I can't hold back my wince this time, but it only takes a second to recover my expression. He presses his nose against the crook of my neck, then bites. Hard. I bite down on my tongue before a yelp escapes.

Motherfucker.

"And this?" Griff mutters, his breaths growing heavy as he licks the fresh ache with his slimy tongue. "I fucking know you like this."

"Mmhmm."

I think I start to sway, but then his fingers appear as he roughly rubs my shoulders, holding me up in the process. I tilt my head to eye his hand better, wishing I could sink my teeth into his skin and see how he likes it. Wishing I could see him curl up in pain. Writhe on the floor. Beg me to stop.

He slides my thong to the side and strokes his fingers over my bare slit, then stops between my ass cheeks. "Fuck, I'm gonna enjoy this." He angles two thick fingertips into the one spot I've never let a man touch.

Just as I take a lungful of air to prepare myself for the pain, Adam strolls toward me. Griff freezes but doesn't release me.

Each slow, measured step is intentional—whether to torture my nerves or anger Griff, I can't be sure. Probably both. Adam stops when he's close enough my chest grazes the warmth of his shirt. I lift my chin, set my jaw, and he dips his head as his gaze wanders down to my lips.

"So this is what you like?" Adam asks softly, his voice too calm, too soothing.

Griff's grip around my waist tightens, staking his claim, but Adam lifts a hand and slowly brushes the hair from my eyes, as though he and I are completely alone. His dark eyes flit back and forth between mine, searching them. Waiting for my answer.

"Yes," I lie, my voice a weak whisper.

He nods, then leans closer. Tilts his head. Presses his lips to my neck so softly I wouldn't be sure he's even touching me if it wasn't for his hot breath on my skin.

Awareness kicks through me, and a shudder wracks my body.

"And you're sure?" he murmurs. The hand in my hair travels past the curve of my jaw and lands gently on the other side of my neck.

My stomach dips, his touch pulsating every vein inside me.

"Mmm." I hardly register what I'm saying, only that his caresses are hypnotic. My head falls back against Griff's chest. Revulsion sobers me slightly when Griff slaps my ass. My head pops back up, and I find Adam looking straight at me. A barely perceptible smile tugs one side of his lips, amusement flickering in his blue eyes.

He glides a thumb across my bottom lip, then pulls it down. "Just . . ." Releasing my lip, he bends enough to wrap both warm hands around my naked thighs, wandering higher, higher. "Like." *Higher.* "This?" When his fingers tease the hem of my panties, Griff grunts and grinds into my back again. I try to hide the disgust from my face, but Adam's crooked smile twitches, and I know I've failed.

I narrow my eyes and stare him down. "Yes," I finally

manage, then add a sultry edge to my voice when I repeat, "Just like that."

Adam's eyes fall shut, and he lets out a husky groan, the sexy sound sending goose bumps down my arms. His fingers squeeze my upper thighs as he leans into me again, then nips my earlobe. I gasp, and he grabs my hair, tugs my head back with one rough move. My head spins as tingles flutter across my scalp.

"Bullshit."

It's one word, two syllables, and spoken in such a soft whisper only I can hear it. But it may as well be a slap to my face with the truth it reveals. My eyes widen, but I don't say a word.

I'm too afraid my shaky voice will be my confession.

chapter seven

*"The woods are lovely, dark and deep.
But I have promises to keep, and miles to go before I sleep."*
—Robert Frost

Emmy

I'VE NEVER ACTUALLY HEARD A SWITCHBLADE WHIPPED OPEN, BUT IT turns out the sharp whisper of the movement pierces through a silent room with the magnitude of a gun being cocked. My breathing hitches as I glance toward the sound. Toward Adam.

He's distanced himself from me, one hand in his pocket, the other lazily flicking the weapon open and closed. His movements are so fluid, so casual, it's like the knife is more than a tool. It's part of him, an extension of his limbs. My spine tingles as I watch him. His expression is thoughtful, broad shoulders relaxed.

The silver blade draws my focus. It's longer than I expected. Sharpened to perfection. Deadly.

My stomach knots as my eyes—still drooping as though my lashes are made of bricks—flick to him. I swallow through my dry throat. "What's that for?"

One eyebrow quirks, then his gaze falls to the knife as

though noticing it for the first time. Ignoring me, he drops his arm and nods toward Griff, whose hands unfreeze before he proceeds to grope me. He cups one breast with his left hand and chokes me with his right. I sputter, my mouth gaping as I struggle to swallow air.

Jesus. There's nothing sensual about Griff's movements. He's a freaking machine, inhuman and mechanical.

The hand on my breast slips downward until he's cupping me between my thighs instead. He lifts me off the ground and grinds his erection against my ass.

My face reddens as I grasp onto the slivers of air I manage to gulp down between squeezes. I stare at Adam in bewilderment, though I only have myself to blame. I don't know what I expected from him.

Adam examines every inch of me. He folds his arms over his chest, rubs the side of his jaw with his thumb, tilts his head. "Who are you, Emmy Highland?"

Griff's hold on my neck loosens just enough for me to answer. Once the thumping in my chest evens out, I bring my wide eyes to Adam. "Wh-what do you mean? You know who I am." I blink to clear my doubling vision. "You just said it—Emmy Highland."

Griff's fingers wander from between my thighs to my ass. He pulls my panties to the side once more, his breathing turning into loud, heavy pants against my shoulder.

I close my eyes for only a second, swallowing thickly.

Adam shakes his head. "Who are you?"

When Griff jabs the tip of one dry finger between my cheeks, I bite my tongue hard enough to taste metal. Pain slices through me as he shoves in a little farther, and my eyes water.

A deep craving to hurt the son of a bitch climbs up my throat. Even in this drugged state I want to whirl around and dig my sharp fingernails into his balls.

Instead, I remind myself why I'm here and grit out my answer. "Twenty years old. Just a girl." I pause, concentrating on stringing my words together so I'll stop slurring. "A waitress. A nobody—"

"You're wasting your breath." Adam's dark eyes sharpen on me as he works his jaw. "There's nothing more dishonest than words."

With a heavy grunt, Griff licks the back of my ear as he wiggles his finger in deeper. My legs snap shut, and a sweat breaks out on my forehead. The only thing getting me through the burning pain is envisioning all the ways I want to hurt him, scratch him, claw him, until red clouds my vision. And Adam's pointless, insistent question as he watches it all happen only makes my anger blaze hotter.

"Wh-what do you want from m-me?" I barely manage, keeping my eyes locked on his.

He takes a step forward. Then another. His hair skims my forehead when he leans in and gently says, "What do I want?" His fingers slowly brush the curve of my neck. "I want you to *show* me. Show me who you are, little mouse."

Without warning, Griff plunges his finger farther into me, then pulls out in one movement. Suppressing a shudder, I don't look back when the asshole grips either side of my shoulders, his blunt nails pressing into my collarbones.

His possessive hold sinks into my pores, and something small inside me withers away.

In this moment, he owns me.

They all do.

The *crack* of my last thread of control snapping in half is a thousand times worse than any physical damage Griff can do to me in this room. Butterflies take flight in my stomach, swirling so fast I'm spinning with them, and I may as well be hanging off the roof of one of New York's finest skyscrapers by my pinky.

My sister's wide, brown eyes float into my mind. Her contagious smile. Loud laughter that turns heads. Floral shampoo reminiscent of wild gardens in the spring. A dull ache burrows its way into my racing chest.

As I watch Adam, I know what I have to do. There's one way to *show* him and his brothers I want this. It's either him or Griff, and there's no way I'm about to do this with the latter.

Shrugging out of Griff's hold, I keep my eyes on Adam's and drop to my knees. I sway for a second, placing one hand on the floor before finding my balance. Once I'm steady, I straighten and deliberately lick my lips, hoping my seductive side will appeal to him. His brows furrow, but he says nothing. I raise my heavy arms to his belt, undoing it with quivering hands. I've done this enough times before, but never in a room full of observing men.

Never to a man like this one.

I fumble with unclasping his belt, then lower his zipper. I hear a low whistle from the middle of the room, where Raife sits. My breathing quickens, nerves tightening my stomach until I feel sick. Just as I start to slip my fingers into Adam's pants, his strong hand curls around my wrist, stopping me.

I glance up at him, my lips parted in a silent question.

This is what he wants, isn't it?

When I try again, his grip tightens painfully. He grinds his teeth, gives a slight, barely noticeable shake of his head that feels a lot like a warning. "Who. Are. You."

It's then that I notice the tip of a black handle protruding from his pants pocket, mere inches from my fingers. My gaze darts back to his, the pounding in my chest quickening. His grip stays firm, but his eyes dance with a challenge.

He knows exactly what I saw. What's within my reach.

My throat constricts when Griff kneels behind me, sidling his stomach against my back. "You wanna watch Adam while I'm inside you? Is that it?" He presses his chin into my scalp and slides his sweaty hands to my outer thighs, rubbing up and down. "Mmm. You're gonna beg for it when I fuck you, aren't you?" His voice is low, thick, and crazed, like a man possessed, and I'm relieved I can't see the look in his eyes right now. "Down on your knees just like this, your mouth wide open for me."

Blood boils beneath my skin. Images of what I'd *really* like to do to his dick resurface and make my lip curl. If he ever laid a hand on Frankie . . . A ringing stirs in my ears, and I wonder if it's from the drugs or the rage building inside me.

Adam cocks a brow, dark amusement flitting through his eyes as he takes in my expression. My gaze drifts back to his pocket, my fingers burning with an itch I can't explain. Would Adam really let me grab the weapon? Or is this part of the test? I angle my wrist toward the knife to test him, and his hold loosens, barely.

A rush of air escapes my lips.

Griff slides his slippery tongue from my shoulder to my ear. "I wonder how fast I can get you to scream." His words are muddled between heavy breaths. "Minutes? Seconds?"

He frees one leg from his grasp. The sharp buzz of a zipper hits my ears. His thumb slips beneath my panties, yanks until the material digs into my skin, and rips them off me. I suck in a sharp breath, unable to tear my eyes from the black handle that teases me.

I've never held a knife as a weapon before. With the intention to do harm. To see actual blood spill. But when Griff's hands grab my hips, knocking me backward and positioning me over his lap like the doll I'm meant to be, the urge seeps steadily into my veins.

I can't go through with it, can't risk losing the only lead to my sister. But I can certainly imagine it, as vividly as the ink splattered across my paintings.

My veins turn to ice when I feel it—Griff's erection stroking my sore ass, then dipping between my cheeks. He adjusts me so my legs are spread over his wide lap, my weight resting on my wobbling knees instead of on him, and shoves my back so I lurch forward. I barely catch myself by my hands around Adam's ankles before my face hits the ground.

Black dots cloud my focus, blurring together then scattering apart, and my noodle-like elbows almost buckle.

Raife's snicker echoes in the otherwise silent room. When I glance around, Felix has already left. Too boring an evening for him, I suppose.

I struggle to lift my head, finding Adam in time to see him casually tuck his hands into his pockets, then he's inching the knife higher little by little. I drag my narrowed eyes to his face, and the handsome bastard's lips twitch. He truly believes I'll go for the knife before going through with this.

As Griff realigns my hips, I give Adam one final, half-assed glare then inhale deeply and brace myself.

Griff leans over me, his giant shoulders warming my back, his teeth finding my ear as he sniffs me. "You know," he groans through a broken grunt, sliding in just enough to make my eyes squeeze shut at the threat of tearing. "I fucking hate the way you smell. What is it with our recent hires smelling like this?" He pauses to wrap a hand around my throat, and I open my eyes.

Waiting for the rest of the pain to hit me.

Ready as I'll ever be.

I lift my chin, ensuring Adam sees all of me. My unflinching expression. Just how *breakable* I really am.

Adam's jaw ticks, any amusement wiped clean from his face. His nostrils flare as he looks from Griff to me and back again, as though only now realizing I'm not going to stop his brother. That I really am about to be, literally and figuratively, fucked.

"Hate your black hair, your starry eyes, and now that fucking smell," Griff repeats, choking me just enough to make my lungs tighten at the threat of losing air. "Like some kinda hippy, flowery shit—"

The heavy thumping in my ears drowns out his voice, waves of manic energy vibrating from my fingertips to my toes.

Flowery.

He mutters something else as he digs into my throat until any trace of feeling drains from my face, but that particular scent being uttered by his spine-tingling voice is all I can hear on repeat.

Frankie's scent.

I hardly notice the rush of fresh air pouring into my lungs, the sweaty grip suddenly gone from my neck, before I'm rising up and my hand is curling around the warm handle in Adam's pocket. Shit, my muscles are mush under my weight, and my vision blurs through the rage and drugs. But I flip the knife so its sharp point is aimed behind me and slice blindly where Griff's body heat touches my back.

A garbled noise sounds from over my shoulder. I take a few deep breaths but give up when they fail to calm my frantic heart rate.

Finally, I look back.

Adam towers over me, his blue eyes dark and cold in a way I've never seen. He's got Griff locked in a chokehold, less than a foot from me. I was right—even red-faced and drained of air, Griff's eyes are wild, rabid. And fixated on me. My hairs stand up, bumps rising on my arms and legs.

Though his face gives nothing away, the muscles in Adam's forearms strain as he intensifies his grip, until suddenly, Griff snaps out of it. His eyes glaze over, then die down to the black holes I'm familiar with. Adam relaxes his hold some, and Griff fights for what little air he can get. Despite the veins bulging in his neck as he loses more oxygen than he gains, his expression shifts to irritation, even impatience. Not a shred of fear. Almost like he's used to these types of warnings.

His eyes turn to slits as he flicks them to me, his hands wrapping around Adam's wrist, and a splash of red pulls my eyes down to just above his elbow. It's not much of a tear, but a light layer of blood drips from the jagged cut, and it stirs a surprising flutter of satisfaction within me.

Eventually, Adam releases his brother and steps back so I'm sandwiched between them again. As Griff grapples for air, the ice in Adam's expression thaws. He leisurely smooths out his shirt, readjusts his rolled-up sleeves.

Tension rolls off Griff in waves as he straightens and stares me down. His breaths are steadying, but an angry red tinges his coloring. His shoulders stiffen, and for a second I'm sure he's going to lunge for me, but Adam stops him with a single look.

"You'll calm the fuck down before you move." Adam's voice is low, controlled.

Griff withdraws a dark red handkerchief from his breast pocket and presses it to the wound. He aims his laser stare above my head, at Adam. His face morphs into a scowl, but he tucks himself back into his pants and zips up. He glances at me, rakes his tongue over his top teeth. "You like blood, do you?" He steps closer until his shoe hits my knee. "I'll remember that when this one lets you off his leash." He nods toward Adam, then shakes his head and backs away. He whirls around when he reaches the door and exits without another word.

My ears are still pounding when Adam slides his gaze down to me. He lowers until he's kneeling, then shifts his eyes between mine. In heavy silence, I wait—for what, I don't know. For his approval? For him to throw me out?

His mouth curves, just barely. "Not bad, for a mouse."

My brows knit at the second use of that reference, but my heart rate only picks up as he continues to stare at me. Analyze me.

His gaze drifts down, landing on my thigh. His Adam's apple bobs and a muscle in his jaw tightens once, twice. My lips part, but then I look down to see for myself. It takes a second for my vision to focus. A smooth line of crimson decorates the outside of my upper leg. It's a bold shade of red, like something I'd paint with. Thick on the white canvas of my skin, curving down at the corners in a dramatic frown. I hadn't even realized I cut myself.

I flinch at the sting when Adam slowly drags a finger across the open cut, but he doesn't pull away, and neither do I. His eyes are locked on the wound, and mine on the mesmerized look set across his face. He closes his eyes, his hand curling around my leg and warming my skin. His expression is pained, his grip clenching, as though forcing himself to stop.

He doesn't look at me when he abruptly stands. A shaky breath escapes me, my skin cooling in the absence of his touch. Like Griff, he turns for the exit. "Clean yourself up," he mutters, irritation clipping his voice.

Then he's gone.

A slow, dramatic clap fills the room, making me start. I groggily shift my head to find Raife rising from the chair. At some point, I'd forgotten all about him. He walks toward me, still clapping with each step until he stops in front of me.

"Well I certainly didn't see *that* coming, though I think I should praise you." He beams as he looks me up and down. "Worth every penny." He extends a hand. After a moment, I take it, allowing him to carefully pull me to my feet.

My legs wobble, a rush of awareness still pulsing beneath my skin, and this time, I don't have an excuse. As much as I'd like to pretend otherwise, I wouldn't be fooling anyone if I tried. I think we all know that, in the end, the drug's influence over me had little to do with losing my sanity.

chapter eight

*"So collapse. Crumble.
This is not your destruction. This is your birth."*
—N.T.

Emmy

I wrap my wet hair in a towel, slip into a robe, and exit my private bathroom. The bedroom Raife had Aubrey lead me to is nestled deep in the ladies' quarters and matches the rest of the mansion in its obsession of all things ebony. Unsurprisingly, an enormous bed serves as the centerpiece, although I wasn't expecting to see the sheer canopy pulled back by lace ribbons on either side.

Fit for a princess. Or a devil's harem.

My limbs are still shaking from the events in the Dark Room earlier this evening. I glance down and angle my leg. The wound is fresh, raw enough to make me wince every time the silky robe brushes it, but something looks off without the red. The torn skin is a pale, drained shade of pink, like a coat of lipstick that's reached its end or a faded painting.

Heat floods my stomach as I relive Adam's large hand curled around my thigh. The way the muscles in his arm strained when he squeezed. His deep blue eyes going dark while he stroked the wound. A shudder runs through me, and I tell myself it's only out of fear.

What kind of man is so captivated by the sight of blood? What does that say about the kind of person he is? More importantly, what he's capable of?

I let out a breath and pull my gaze toward the ceiling, forcing the wound from sight. Guilt churns in my gut as Mama's narrowed eyes flash in my mind, her chapped lips curled in pure revulsion as she hovers over me. I try to swallow the unwanted shame back down. Except it's stuck, a solid lump in my throat, because part of me knows she's right about me. A part of me has always known. I may not have any say over the disturbing images that crawl into my brain and demand to be let out, but as Mama used to remind me, I do have a say over giving in to their temptation.

I'm the one who picks up the paintbrush. Dips it into the crimson, ruby, and candy apple reds. Shuts out the voice of reason until all I know is the intoxicating shade of madness. I'm the one responsible for the gruesome images in my sketchpad Mama stumbled upon that day. And the next. It's like she said when I was seven and I had first discovered art through her burgundy tubes of lipstick—*You'll never be a daughter of the Lord, and you'll never be a daughter of mine.*

My fingers tap against my leg before clutching the robe, a dispersed anxiety thrumming through them. They crave the release as much as I do.

No. I clear my throat, release the material from my death grip. It's just a little paint.

I'm nothing like Adam.

I'm nothing like any of them.

Tugging the robe down and straightening the belt, I wander

through the bedroom. My eyes dart from one corner to the next, trying to pick up any details that may be useful. I'm here for Frankie only, and I refuse to let a single one of the Matthews brothers into my head while I'm here.

If the rest of the place is anything to go off, I can almost guarantee all bedrooms in the ladies' quarters are exactly the same. A second passes before I notice there are no windows. I make my way to the only closet in the room and pull the door open. As large as the oversized bathroom, it's meticulously organized. Expensive-looking black lingerie and silk nighties are lining the left hanging rack, while a row of dresses identical to the one I wore today hangs to my right. Shelving units store six extra pairs of designer heels.

That's it. The only things I will own while I play their little doll.

I creep toward the front door, turn the knob, and crack it open. Peeking through the inch of space, I flick my gaze down the hall, both ways. There's at least one camera to my left, and I can clearly spot two at the right end. With a swallow, I gently close the door and turn around, letting my back fall against the cool wood. Tomorrow, I'll take note of every visible camera in this mansion. Tomorrow, when the sun goes down and the lights go out, I will find out what the Matthews are hiding.

If I can make it until then.

By the time Stella summons me the next morning, Aubrey has already dressed and prepped me.

While she was doing my makeup earlier, I almost flat out asked her if Griff claimed Frankie. I haven't been able to stop wondering since he'd mentioned my sister's flowery scent. But of course Aubrey would never answer a question like that, so instead I settled for, "How does Griff decide who he wants to claim?" She informed me that he never misses out on testing the new hires in the Dark Room, but like she'd said the night before, they usually like what he likes.

That calmed me at the time. His short time in the Dark Room with Frankie likely explained why he recognized her shampoo on me. But my nerves are erratic again when Aubrey sits back against her desk and watches Stella lead me away from the spa area and toward the Matthews' dining room.

Stella's long legs take brisk steps, and I struggle to keep up. She stares straight ahead. "Once you're claimed, your master is to be your only focus."

I nod, and she doesn't wait for a verbal response.

"You'll have primary household duties like the rest of the girls, but your master always takes precedence. You will leave your other duties behind the instant he calls for you. Do you understand?"

Again, I nod.

She stops once we approach the sitting room, then turns to me and exhales. Her eyes brighten when she smiles. "It's a big day for you, Emmy. Are you ready?"

I can only continue to nod because if I say *yes* aloud, I'm afraid my voice will crack through the lie. In some ways, I am ready. Even eager. Every step brings me closer to finding my sister. Every step brings me closer to getting out of here.

I spent last night wide awake in my foreign bed, trying to play out all the scenarios of how this morning might go. Who might be the one to claim me. As much as I hate to admit it, there's no way to ignore the instinct burning deep in my gut that Raife claimed Frankie. Out of all the brothers, he's the one she would have gone for, and on the exterior, she fits his stereotype perfectly.

But what would he have done once he found out Frankie isn't the obedient, demure submissive Stella is? Once he saw her fire, her wings. How far will a Matthews like Raife really go to train their servant? Or furthermore, to punish them?

I gulp down the lump in my throat. There's only one way to find out.

Stella reaches up and gently squeezes my shoulders. "Well, then. Let's go meet your master."

As expected, the dining room is lit like a deep cave. It doesn't matter that it's daytime, just like the girls' rooms there are no windows to let in the sunlight. The entire sight is déjà vu. Each of the Matthews is positioned around the dining table exactly how they were when I met them last night. Felix sits at the left end, Griff at the right. Raife and Adam are side by side at the end opposite me.

Unease settles around me. I didn't expect all of them to be here for this. Does this mean I'm supposed to serve all four, like Aubrey?

A nagging temptation to glance at Adam pulls at my chest. Just one look. One peek at his expression to get a glimpse of his regard for me after the Dark Room. Mindlessly scanning the others, I make out Adam's form in the corner of my eye. But it's not enough. Clasping my hands in front of me, I lift my chin and lock eyes with Raife instead. He's the one I want.

Except it's near impossible to focus on him.

I can sense Adam's heavy gaze on me by the trail of warmth heating my skin. He doesn't say a word. Doesn't shift in his seat or greet me. He doesn't have to. A pulsing energy buzzes off his body, bouncing between us like a circuit stuck on a loop. It vibrates against my bones as if the hard lines of his body are once again pressed against me. His strong hand cradling my jaw. Warm fingers brushing my hair across my neck. Lips softly ghosting over my throat.

"Sleep well?" Raife's question is mocking as he glances between me and Adam.

I clear my throat. "Yes."

He grins. "Fantastic. Stella?"

Delicate fingers intertwine with mine, and Stella leads me toward the Matthews. In the center of the dining table sits a serving tray with a stainless steel dome cover. I look from the tray to Stella, my brows knitted, but she just smiles.

"Eleven minutes," Felix says from my left, glancing down at his watch. "No time for games."

Raife waves a hand. "Nonsense." His lips quirk as he slowly drinks me in from my head to my high heels. "There's always time for games."

"On your knees, slut." The rough command comes from Griff. When I glance at him, his eyes are black, and his lip is curled. I continue to stand, and he runs a finger over his elbow, where I know a cut remains beneath his suit. "You got a hearing problem? *Slut.*"

A rhythmic *tap, tap, tap* pulls my gaze across the table. Adam's leaning back in his seat, the top few buttons of his black shirt undone, legs outstretched. His eyes are honed in on the silver tray between us, his jaw hard, as he continues to methodically tap one finger on the table.

"Knees," Griff barks. "Now."

Lifting my chin, I fall to my knees and flick my eyes to Griff. "Better?"

He quirks an eyebrow. "For now."

"Huh." Raife cocks his head to one side as he stares at me. "Yes, you're right. She does look far better down there. Stella, if you will?"

"Yes, Master." Stella steps around me to reach for the tray's dome cover. She lifts it and sets it aside, revealing a single, thin scarf. A *gold* scarf. "Congratulations, Emmy," Stella says softly as she retrieves the scarf and proceeds to tie it around my neck. "Raife Matthews is officially your new master."

My legs grow heavy, making me thankful I'm not standing. My stomach flutters with a rush of surprise mixed with anxiety. There's something very different about the idea of having Raife as my master versus the moment it becomes a reality. It feels too fast. Too unexpected. Too *easy*. Aubrey may have said he claims almost everyone at some point, but last night in the Dark Room he seemed like he couldn't have cared less about actually claiming me. Not when he'd pawned me off to his brothers for 'relief.'

I drag my gaze back up to Raife's, hoping to mask my suspicion.

A full smile stretches across his sharp face. His dirty-blond hair sits in a perfect, hard shell on his head, his suit crisp, hands folded in front of him. "Well, have you nothing to say, lovely? Are you not as pleased as I am?"

It takes a second to remember my purpose here, to get my act together. Too easy or not, Raife is my key to Frankie, and I'd be a fool not to take advantage of the circumstances. As Raife waits calmly for my response, the *tap, tap, tap* across the table gets louder, faster.

I pull my shoulders back. "I'm more than pleased. I'm eager to serve you." I don't know why I do it, but my eyes shift to Adam like he has a magnetic pull over me. For the first time this morning, he breaks his attention from the now-empty tray and looks straight at me. His finger stops tapping. Something darkens in his eyes as they flick down to the gold scarf around my throat. A muscle in his jaw ticks, his stare narrows, and the next word pours out of me in a whisper like it's meant for one person only. *"Master."*

A chair scraping against the floor drowns out my whisper as Adam abruptly stands.

My breath catches in my throat.

His eyes are midnight blue flames, pure streaks of fire, igniting my skin with a burn that melts my insides. As I squirm under his stare, the feeling dips between my thighs, thrumming with heat. I suck in a gulp of air and press my legs together.

His gaze drops.

My pulse is erratic, but I can't calm myself as I watch him work his jaw from side to side, slowly run a hand across his lips. His intensity fills every inch of the room. He glances up at the quick rise and fall of my chest, then tears his eyes from me as he turns and walks around the table, straight past me and toward the exit.

"Hey," Felix calls, pushing out his chair. "Where are you going? Meeting's in four minutes."

Adam doesn't look back when he growls under his breath, "Not going to make it." He pauses. "Griff, you're coming with me. We're moving my evening appointment up."

He disappears through the corridor, and my chest expands as I'm finally able to breathe. *What the hell was that?*

Griff grunts, shoves his seat back, then follows Adam.

"Goddammit," Felix mutters, shaking his head. He glances at Raife. "Well, we need to leave. Now."

"Yeah." Raife's voice is eerily calm. He's still watching me, a strange, almost pleased, smile on his face. "I'll meet you in the main house."

Felix glances from Raife to me, then sighs. "Fine. Whatever. Just hurry it up." He mumbles something else as he strides out of the room.

"I swear," Raife murmurs, chuckling, "you never cease to

surprise me."

My brows knit. "I didn't do anything."

"It would certainly seem that way, wouldn't it?" He shakes his head. "Stella, you may leave."

"Yes, Master." I don't turn to look when her heels click toward the exit.

"Remove your clothes."

My throat goes dry. "What?"

"You heard me." He rises from his seat and moves the empty tray to the floor, then hops on a chair. "First rule as my secretary: always listen the first time." He reaches over to mess with something on the chandelier. "Ah, here it is."

Hard metal hits the glass table in the same moment that I stand. I'm fumbling with the clasp on the back of my dress when I realize what the object is.

A chain. It's connected to the chandelier at one end. There are two handcuffs at the bottom.

My dress falls to the floor, my knees shaking.

Raife lowers himself from the chair and pushes it back in. He nods toward my bra then glances at his watch, almost bored. "Quick, lovely. I have someplace to be."

My voice is small when I say, "Of course."

I've never been shy about being naked in front of a man. But when he happens to be the same man who fantasized over burning me last night and is now waiting to chain me up, the nerves coil around my bones and squeeze.

I let my bra drop beside the dress, then slide off the thong that was so kindly provided by the Matthews brothers themselves.

"Mmm, lovely indeed," Raife appraises, raking his eyes up and down my naked body. Just as I bend to remove my black high heels, he interrupts the movement with a sharp tsk. "Leave them." He pulls a black tablecloth from a cabinet in the right corner of the room, lays it over the glass tabletop, then pats the material. "Up."

My lips press into a thin line, but I quickly relax them. "Yes . . . Master." I crawl onto the table, my knees sliding along the smooth tablecloth, and wait for the next command.

"Stand and extend your arms to the sides."

I do as instructed. My body stiffens when he clasps the cold, heavy cuffs around each of my wrists, rubbing the skin that's still raw from last night. He tugs at the chain until my arms are stretched above my head, limbs straight as a rod, and my pulse picks up, breaths going shallow.

I close my eyes and focus on my breathing.

"You see . . ." Raife trails a finger up my ankle, his voice soft. "Last night, I couldn't help but notice your aversion to restraints." His cold nose brushes my leg, and he pulls in a long inhale. "I can smell it, you know. Your fear. I have to say"—his fingers inch higher, up my thigh, and my eyes snap open when he strokes my slit—"it's rather addictive." He rubs my entrance with two dry fingers, and I tense in anticipation. But there's no pain when he pushes them inside me. It's a smooth glide, and I know I have his brother to thank for that. He pulls his wet fingers out and slips them into his mouth. "Mmm, yes, just as I'd hoped," he purrs. "I can taste it, too."

He steps away with a reluctant groan and wanders back to the cabinet in the corner. His back is to me as he shuffles through items, then he returns to the table and arranges six candles around my feet. They're tall and white, and they form a perfect, small circle. So small, in fact, that if I were to move my feet an inch or two, I might knock them down. He pulls his lighter from his pocket and takes his time igniting each candle, one by one.

"This tablecloth is made of one of the most flammable fabrics there is. Did you know that?" he asks, his brows rising as though the fact impresses him. "Rayon. It shrinks once it catches fire, and it clings to human skin." When the candles are all lit, he backs away and angles his head, taking in the sight.

The flames tease my ankles, a rush of heat nipping at my skin with every flicker. My throat is tight when I swallow, and a light sweat builds on my forehead. The strain of standing as still as a doll while in four-inch heels is already weighing heavily on my knees and feet.

Raife's eyes dance with admiration. "It's quite dangerous, really. One slip and—well, I advise that you be very, very careful."

He smirks and withdraws a sleek, black phone from his pocket. He holds it out in front of me, angles it. I hear a distinct *click*. "I do wish I could stay and watch, but this will have to do until I get back."

He turns to the exit, and my stomach flips. "Wh-where are you going? You're leaving me here?"

He continues strolling away as he calls over his shoulder, "Second rule as my secretary: don't ever question me." It's not until he's already stepped over the threshold that he pauses and adds, "What's that saying? What doesn't kill you . . ." His words fade off, and I'm left with nothing but his dark chuckle echoing in my ears and a fire dancing at my feet.

chapter nine

"The prince of darkness is a gentleman."
—Shakespeare

Adam

"Aubrey. Meet us out front with the limo," I order, typing up instructions for Felix on my phone while Griff and I pace down the hallway. "Be prepared for a long drive."

"Yes, Master." The redhead gives a curt nod and takes off toward the mansion's lobby.

Few people have proven themselves trustworthy enough to be involved in our dirty work, but Aubrey and Stella are two of them. Stella is ruthlessly loyal as long as it serves Raife, which renders her a liability to me, so I stick to using Aubrey for my own shit. And that's on a limited basis. I prefer to work alone.

My phone sounds. I answer on the first ring.

"You sure you wanna do this?" Felix asks through the line. "I mean, it's daytime in the middle of summer."

I grit my teeth. "I'm not a fucking vampire; the sun won't burn me."

"Asshole, you know what I mean. It's been a long time since you did an actual pickup with Griff, and we both know why."

Doesn't help that you're all worked up, either."

"Don't you have a conference call to make?"

"Yes," he grumbles, "if Raife can get his damn head out of the new hire's ass long enough to show up."

My fingers curl around the phone until the edges dig into my palm. The last thing I need right now is to hear about Emmy fucking Highland's ass. Black hair swinging down her back, blue eyes wide and curious, knees on the white marble and hands clasped neatly in front of her—she was the perfect little hire this morning.

Until she opened those pink lips and let that one, single word spill from her tongue, *Master*. Like it was meant for me. Like she was spelling out my goddamn name.

Burning irritation cuts through me at the thought of Raife's hands on her, and I'm both sickened and fascinated by the fact. It shouldn't send fire scorching through my chest the way it does. The heat is suffocating, making me loosen another shirt button for some fucking air.

Of course, I could have claimed her and owned every move her tongue made from here on out. It would have been so easy. I can't deny it was tempting, even more so when I saw the black scarf Raife originally placed in that tray for her. Like Griff and Felix, he'd wrongly assumed I intended to claim her. In other words, he'd assumed his manipulations had worked on me. Unfortunately for him, there's only one person who controls what I do, and that's me.

Felix's sigh filters through the speaker. "Clearly a subject for another time." My jaw ticks, but I keep my stride steady as Griff and I round a corner. "Anyway, you realize what you're asking me to do is going to start shit, don't you?"

"Since when are you afraid of starting shit?"

Felix lets out a snort. "It'll raise red flags, Adam, and you know it. I had every meticulous step of this operation set up for eight tonight, and you're asking me to move it all up to what, three hours from now? Technicalities aside, how exactly do you think this million-dollar film tycoon will react when we ask him to drop his afternoon plans all for 'Luke McAvoy' to reschedule at the last minute? Especially after everything we've already been pulling on him up till now."

I press my lips into a tight line and stop in my tracks. The tension coiled around my muscles is like a leech digging its teeth into my skin and sucking me bone-dry. All because of a little mouse. And it's pissing me off.

I dip my free hand into my pocket and wrap my fingers around my knife. A knife that got its first taste of Emmy's sweet, crimson blood less than fourteen hours ago. My eyes close as I clench my jaw, stroking the handle with my thumb. Sometimes feeling the weight of the weapon as I walk is enough to calm me, get my pulse under control.

Other times . . .

"Get it done, Felix. I need a damn fix, and moving the appointment up a few hours isn't going to kill anyone." I hear a rough chuckle and glance sideways at Griff. He's shaking his head as he drops the crooked smirk from his face. "Figuratively," I add as an afterthought and resume walking.

There's a pause on the line, the sound of a door closing. "Yup, got it. But hey, I meant what I said earlier about going out. Just take it easy."

Ending the call, I lock my gaze ahead as we approach the lobby's front door. Of course I know what he means, but I'm not about to discuss it like he's a damn shrink. I have only one method of therapy, and we're driving to Pennsylvania to pick it up.

Griff yanks the front window curtain to one side and glances out. He doesn't move, which tells me Aubrey hasn't pulled the car up yet.

I roll my shirt sleeves up to my elbows and slip my hands back in my pockets as I wait, watching the door. Felix wasn't wrong; I can't remember the last time I stepped outside these walls. My pulse spikes with each passing second. It's just a few steps on the pavement till I get to the car, nothing to shit anyone's pants over.

"She's here." Griff pulls the door open and heads out.

Light filters through the doorway, dusting the marble flooring with a golden hue, inches from my shoes.

I fall behind to stare past the threshold. Curl my knuckles. Crack my neck. Then I step outside.

"So," the man sitting across from me folds his hands in his lap, leans back against the leather seat like he owns the limo, "which one of you is Luke McAvoy? I want to know who's been trying to fuck me over behind a screen for the past year."

I cock my head. Drink in his sharp Italian suit, slicked-back hair, snakeskin shoes. He's forty-four, a good fifteen years older than me. And he brought a bodyguard bigger than Griff to accompany him. The man really thinks highly of himself. Hmm. I'll have to see what I can do about that.

"I suggest you answer within the next century, unless you want to find out how thin my patience really is."

Griff, seated to my right, looks at me. He quirks an eyebrow, his black pupils dilating with excitement. He's waiting for my signal. I shake my head.

Not yet.

"Hugo Perez," I mutter casually, adjusting my watch. "The name blends right in, doesn't it?"

The man chuckles dryly. "Yeah? I'm so glad you think so." His lips thinning, he tips his head at me. "Are you Luke? You don't exactly look like a geek who hides behind his computer. But then, you never can tell how small someone's balls are under their suit."

"That *geek* would be my brother, though I'd leave his balls out of this if I were you." Felix must have been feeling particularly Irish when he came up with the latest fictional persona, McAvoy.

Hugo leans forward in his seat. The look he gives me is meant to be intimidating, I assume. "Let's cut the shit. I think you've had enough fun pulling my strings like I'm a puppet over this past year. We both know how this works. You have photos on me; I want them gone. Give me the files now, and you'll walk away relatively unscathed. Or don't, and you won't walk away at all."

I let out a disappointed *tsk*. "You need to work on your threats if you want anyone to take you seriously. I have to say, with a past like yours, I expected more. At least a little originality."

He straightens, his face going rigid. His attention shifts between me and Griff. "What the fuck are you talking about?" Shooting his gaze back to me, he asks, "You think I won't kill over this? Do you really want to test me?"

The silent bodyguard beside him places a hand over the breast pocket of his suit jacket, not so subtly reminding me that he's packing.

"Depends." I tap a finger on the leather seat thoughtfully. "That could be interesting, and we do have a long drive ahead."

The man frowns and looks out the heavily tinted window, finally noticing just how far we've strayed from his precious office building. He flicks his cold gaze from Griff to me, grits his jaw. "I don't care how much testosterone your friend's on, you're sorely mistaken if you doubt what I'm capable of. Now, you will turn this car around and hand over the files, or I will personally slit your neck from ear to ear and smile as I watch you bleed out."

Mmm, I close my eyes and picture it.

Him.

Sitting on my leather seats, just like he is now.

Bleeding out.

My fingers twitch. "Better. Certainly more original." I center my gaze on his. "Except for one key mistake. Threats only work with honesty. The second you light your words with bullshit, they go up in flames."

His face reddens, nostrils flaring. My knife burns a hole through my pocket as I watch the blood rush through his veins.

Not yet.

He lunges. "Just what part of what I said was bullsh—"

Griff has Hugo by the throat in the same instant my knife pierces the bodyguard's jugular. It's a clean kill—aside from the blood spilling over his suit—and leaves him lifeless within seconds. Quicker than I usually prefer, but I only play with my catch if it's on the list. The bodyguard just happened to be in the way.

Hugo turns a shade paler with Griff's grip still locked around his neck. His eyes, however, flash with defiance.

Any ordinary human being would be terrified, perhaps repulsed, in a circumstance such as this one—inhaling the scent of blood, shoulder brushing a dead body, smears of red staining his employee's gaping neck.

Not him, though. We are all cut from the same cloth, after all. To a certain extent anyway. My brothers and I were the cloth; this man, one of the many people who'd held the scissors.

A spark of satisfaction simmers beneath my skin as I soak

in the light spattering of blood coloring his left cheek, his neck. Although it's not his own, the sneak peek of what's to come will have to hold me over until we get to the house.

"To answer your question," I begin, withdrawing a clean cloth from my back pocket and carefully wiping my hand, then the knife's blade, "the exact part of your threat that was bullshit was in pretending you'd personally slit my neck."

His eyes bulge, his voice livid. "You don't fucking kno—"

"Because you're the type to watch someone else do the cutting, aren't you? The type to cash in without getting your hands dirty." I pause mid-cleaning as I give him my undivided attention. "Of course, that's unless you've changed since the last time I saw you."

His brows pull together. "What the hell are you—" Griff loosens his hold as he watches recognition take over the man's face. "But that was—that's not—it's not possible . . ." This right here, those first few seconds our supposed victims begin to piece it all together, this is Griff's favorite part. My brother snarls, sets his jaw. Never taking his eyes off the coward.

Personally, my favorite part comes much later.

"Whether you're going by *Hugo Perez* these days or *Misha* . . . not everyone is fooled."

Finally, I see it. Fear. His face goes sheet-white against the red spattering, a swallow sticks in his throat. His eyes dart to the car door.

The man has no idea what real fear tastes like. Yet.

"Y-you were locked away," he stammers, scooting back in his seat. "Besides, you were just a kid. You don't know what you heard or saw while you were there."

I nod and resume wiping down my knife. "Yeah, I suppose you're right. I could be mistaken."

Griff grunts, then digs his elbow into Hugo's stomach when

the man tries to unbuckle his seatbelt. "Fuck," Hugo groans, doubling over. He doesn't seem to have a high pain tolerance. My lips quirk.

"Maybe I should call Katerina," I suggest. "You know, double-check and everything."

"Katerina—she's been . . ."

"Dead?"

His gaze narrows. "You. You had something to do with what happened the night of her death. Didn't you?" He pauses and eyes the door once more, fidgets with the strap of his seatbelt. "I heard some people started disappearing again."

"Did you now? You've been paying attention." I cock my head to the side. "How many kids in total lost their lives at your hands, do you think? How many innocents filled yours and Katerina's pockets?"

I gently drag the edge of my knife against my palm, teetering on the edge of breaking skin. Beads of sweat are dripping down Hugo's forehead when I look back up.

And, yet, he glares and clenches his fist. "How much do you want?"

I raise an eyebrow.

"I said, how much? That's what this is really about, isn't it? Kidnap the millionaire and use your leverage to get a payday?" He actually sounds hopeful as he glances between me and Griff.

I could almost laugh if his words didn't make my blood boil. "I think you're missing the point, Hugo. Your money is already ours." Felix accesses the accounts of everyone on our list—offshore included—well before we get to this point. It's my job to get the final signatures, but that's child's play once they're in my basement. "What we want is the same thing you want."

He barks a hysterical laugh. "To gouge your fucking eyes out?"

My eyes dance at the coincidence. "We'll get to that. I'm talking about art. That's what you and Katerina attempted to create through *Misha*, wasn't it? That's what you marketed it as, anyway; true and awakened art."

He snorts, though his fear makes it sound like he's choking. "I couldn't give three fucks about her *work*. I didn't even see it half the time, so if you're looking for some kind of payback, you've got the wrong guy. I dealt with the transactions, the money, and that's it. I'm hardly the guilty one here." When I continue silently toying with my knife, testing the pressure of the blade against my skin, he shifts in his seat. "Besides, didn't you hear? I'm the high-profile CEO of a million dollar porn company, not some unclaimed foster kid like you guys. People would notice if I went missing."

I lift one corner of my lips and lean forward, close enough to glide the point of my blade across the bridge of his nose. A familiar jolt of adrenaline courses through me. "Do you ever think about them? The countless kids whose lives you stole?"

Silence stretches between the three of us, the low hum of the vehicle the only sound in the air. A vein in Griff's neck spasms. He's just as impatient as I am.

"Not a single day." Hugo's voice is uneven and breathy, but he manages to smile. My arms flex with the restraint it takes to keep from making him scream. I have a fucking fantastic room for that at home. "They were hardly innocent. The lot of you. Running from the system and wreaking havoc. And by the time Katerina used them for her work, they were practically adults anyway."

My pulse thrums wildly.

Hugo doesn't stop, his voice grating on my ears until they're raw. "You know it, I know it. If she didn't get to them, they would have gone off to become criminals, thieves, even killers." His lips twist, and he eyes me up and down. "So really, we were doing society a favor. I was just smart enough to earn a little—"

The knife, still pressed against the tip of his nose, slides through his skin like butter, only jerking at the cartilage. His piercing scream is delightful, even through the bloody cloth I shove in his mouth as Griff holds his hands down.

"A little early," Griff mutters, giving me a sideways look.

I shrug. So I could stand to work on my restraint.

The fresh flow of blood streams down Hugo's lips, his chin, and my thumping pulse relaxes. When his head lolls forward, I frown. Usually takes more than this before they faint. He was right about one thing—you really can't tell how small someone's balls are beneath their suit.

Raking my eyes along his face, I contemplate exactly what I want to do next with Hugo Perez. Which body part I want to move on to.

The man has always been a coward. Even my teenage self could see that. Those first few times that he had no choice but to enter Katerina's domain, each visit ended the same way—with his head between his legs and puke covering his clothes.

Just like me, one day became two, two became three. Days became weeks. Weeks became years. And just like me, he eventually grew used to it.

The blood. The cries. The screams.

But *visiting* isn't the same as *living* it. Coming and going as you please is different than waking up to it, closing your eyes to it, inhaling it, exhaling it, and soon enough, *becoming* it.

I don't realize I'm squeezing Hugo's hand until I hear a *snap*.

Fuck. I sit back in my seat and close my eyes, feeling the warm thrum of energy vibrate inside me. No, when I work on

Hugo's fingers, he will be wide awake.

I press a button on the center console for the intercom. "Aubrey. Tell Stella to have a bottle of whiskey waiting when we arrive." A satisfied sigh leaves my lips as I sit back, stretch out my legs. "It's going to be a long fucking day."

chapter ten

*"There are maps through your bones and skin,
to the way you've felt and the way you've been."*
—Christopher Poindexter

Emmy

"I pity you like I pity the Devil."

My bones quiver, and the shackles slip against my sweaty wrists. It's not enough to drown out Mama's distant, throaty voice.

"You'll suffer for conjuring his demons, little girl."

I close my eyes, squeeze them hard, and shake my head. *Get out, Mama. You don't belong here.*

"I'll make it end. But only once your soul has been cleansed."

Two hours. The grandfather clock across the room tells me I have been hanging from these chains for two long hours.

"You behave like an animal, and you'll be treated like one."

My knees knock together, a tremble running through them. I'm lightheaded and drenched in sweat, and I haven't seen or heard a thing since Raife's suit-clad back as he walked away. Not until that memory, now twelve years old, found its way back to me. Still echoing in my ears, it won't leave me alone.

"But Mama, I—"

"Don't you dare call me that."

Teeth chattering against the harsh wind, I tried again. "I'm s-sorry, Agnes. I just—"

"Look at it." Mama only ever spoke in whispers and snarls, yet her hushed commands struck me with more intensity than if she had raised her voice.

I shifted my feet, feeling my toes sink deeper into the fresh mud. Then I lowered my gaze to the painting that sat on the ground between us. Streaked with runny lines of red and black, paint blended together as the rain splattered my sketchpad.

"Face your twisted demons like you force me to," she ordered, "because this will be the last time you ever summon them in this house."

"But I'm telling you, Ma—Agnes. I didn't summon any—"

Mama's hand rose so quickly I flinched. She froze mid-air, fingers inches from my cheek, seeming to remember at the same time I did that she never hit me. She never touched me at all. I once overheard her tell Frankie to keep her distance because I could be contagious.

After a tense moment of silence blending with rain patter, Mama lowered her hand to her side. I knew better than to talk back. I did. But this was the most she had spoken to me in seven months, and my heart had filled itself with a silly fluttering sensation that felt a lot like hope.

Hope that maybe she'd listen.

Maybe she'd try to understand that the dark images muddled my brain until it hurt, until I had no choice but to let them out.

That maybe one day she'd look at me like she did Frankie. Not like she loved her—I didn't know if Mama was capable of such an emotion—but even when she was disappointed in my big sister, even when she punished us, Mama looked at her with a spark I couldn't place. A spark that I reminded myself would never flicker for me.

I admit, I didn't make it easy for her. Frankie has always looked just like her, with their blond hair and brown eyes. And from the broken and confusing way my brain works, I was beginning to wonder if Daddy passed down much more than just his looks to me.

"Are you an animal, Emmy May?"

I sniffed and shook my head. "No, Agnes."

"Are you rabid? Are you a stray? Have you not been cared for like a proper child under a roof protected by the Lord?"

"No, Agnes. I've been cared for well."

"Then take a good, hard look at yourself and ask what kind of person would think up such horrors?"

I dropped my head, feeling a sob working its way up my throat. "I don't know, Mama. A bad person?"

She took a step forward and walked around me to the abandoned doghouse. "I'll tell you who," she said calmly. "A child of the devil. A tainted beast. And as such"—I gasped when something cold and hard tightened around my neck—"you will be punished."

Reaching up with shaky fingers, I touched the rusty collar now locked around my throat, then my gaze followed the thick metal to the doghouse where it was secured through a hole in the roof. I felt every drop of blood drain from my face.

"Let us see if your art"—she spat the word—"can save you now."

At the time, those were the most words she'd spoken to me in seven months. After that night, they became the most she'd said since. I suppose it was easier to pretend I didn't exist than it was to exorcise my demons.

Now, as the unfamiliar chains cut into my wrists and the balls of my feet tingle with soreness, I recall that being neglected is a hell of a lot easier on me, too.

A brisk click of heels snaps my head toward the open doorway. A blond secretary blurs past as she proceeds down the hall. "Wait!" My voice is hoarse as it cracks the walls of my dry throat. "P-please. Come back."

The clicks pause, then resume, coming closer this time. The secretary that appears in the doorway is familiar. I squint and realize she'd been setting roses on one of the tables yesterday.

I glance down at her dark red scarf. The color is identical to the handkerchief Griff keeps in his front pocket.

Just perfect.

"Did you call for me?" She tilts her head and furrows her brows, but otherwise shows no reaction at the sight of me chained naked to the chandelier, fire still flickering at my feet. Just another day at the Matthews residence.

I tug at the chains and wince when they rub against the raw skin. "Can you get me down from here?"

Her eyes drop to my gold scarf, then flick back up to my face. She shakes her head. "I'm sorry. Only your master can make that decision." After a pause, she asks, "Would you like a glass of water?"

I bite back a growl. Every inch of my body throbs, whimpering with exhaustion. My head drops to my chest. The thick pressure in my throat screams for me to take her up on her offer, but I won't. I'm helpless enough as it is without someone having to spoon-feed me.

A second passes, then her footsteps fade toward the exit. My gaze slides down, down, to the orange flames that dance with a vibrancy I envy. Melted wax drizzles down the sides of the candles like teardrops.

I lose track of the seconds, minutes, hours. Stop fighting the soreness crippling my muscles, the numbness overtaking my fingers.

The longer I stare into the hypnotizing candlelight, the heavier my eyelids get. My wrists go slack against the handcuffs, my knees buckle, and I think I hear the padded *thump* of a candle falling against the tablecloth, inhale the bitter scent of something burning. But the sea of black curling around my mind is so soothing, I can't bring myself to care.

Voices—hushed and feminine—travel to my eardrums. Something soft brushes my ankle. I stir, shift in place, and a searing pain pierces my wrists. Beyond my wrists, to the tips of my fingers, I feel nothing. Absolutely nothing. The faint sound of metal clinking reminds me I'm chained. A moan seeps past my closed lips.

My eyelashes flutter open, and the dining room blurs into focus.

Aubrey's hair tickles my bare foot, and I cringe at the sting that shoots to my toes. Her grip stiffens around my ankle, keeping it still. She glances up at me and presses a finger to her lips, then resumes wrapping a gauze bandage around my foot. My brows pull together, a sting still throbbing beneath my skin.

The blond secretary from earlier comes into view as she rounds the table. She carefully gathers what's left of the tablecloth and dumps it into a trash bag. No candles are in sight, but a faint singed scent wafts through the air.

Raife sits in the far-right corner of the room, a cell phone pressed to his ear. His lips move as he speaks too low for me to hear, but his eyes linger on the white bandage at my feet. Eventually, he sees me looking at him.

He smiles.

My stomach rolls.

He adjusts his phone, then looks away as he continues speaking. I'm still watching him. My new 'master.' When I boarded the plane to New York, I was certain my employers-to-be wanted sex, and they wanted it on their terms, behind closed doors.

Dress me up, give me a to-do list and roses to set on your tables—it's still sex. Not an easy task, but a simple one.

So why does it feel like they want something else entirely from me?

chapter eleven

> "We stopped looking for monsters under our bed when we realized that they were inside us."
> —Charles Darwin

Adam

A STRING QUARTET. TWO VIOLINS, TWO CELLOS. A SMOOTH AND constant build up before they're competing for the climax.

No, no, that's not right.

A solo. A single cello, slow and haunting. A lazy, rhythmic tap against a drum echoing in the far-off distance.

Yes, that's it.

My solo.

Sometimes it feels like painting. Other times it's poetry. And then there are days like today—it's music, old world and mystic. I have no preference, really. Art is art.

Isn't that right, Katerina?

"How many?" I ask, inhaling his screams and pocketing them in my lungs as I dig the knife a little deeper against his cheekbone then slide it downward. "I'm aware of how many died and had their parts sold. What I want you to tell me"—the slab of skin falls to the ground, my fingers almost as red as his neck. His eyes roll back—"is how many you, personally, sold. How many transactions did you see through?"

I take a step back, angling my head and honing my gaze on his unmarred cheek. It's harder than it looks, making both sides of the face match evenly. But I like to take my time and get it just right.

Katerina took her work seriously in the studio. Fortunately for the victims, she had already killed them by the time she started removing the flesh from their bones. Unfortunately for Hugo, Katerina isn't the only one who can take their work seriously.

Call me a perfectionist.

At least I learned something.

I grip Hugo's neck and squeeze until his eyes roll forward to meet mine. His skin is ghastly from the blood he's already lost, but he likely won't need another adrenaline injection until the next two or three removals.

"I asked you a question," I say calmly. I have to close my eyes to refrain from making the next cut too soon. "How many of their bones did you personally sell for Katerina? Whether it was a hand, forearm, hip, or skull, whether originating from the same body or different ones—what's the total number?"

A wheeze escapes the man in front of me before he manages a faint, "F-fuck you."

My eyes snap open, lips twitch. "Someone is about to be fucked. And it isn't me." I flick my gaze to an electric drill on the stool beside him, and his own gaze follows. It takes him a second to make the connection, but once he does, his mouth falls open and puke hits my shoes.

Really, Hugo?

I set down my knife, opting for the drill. Rotating it slowly in my hand, I inspect it with appreciation. It's not every day I pull this out, but Hugo Perez is one-third of Katerina's infamous underground pseudonym, *Misha*. Only the best for Katerina's business partners.

My index finger presses the trigger. A low *rizzz, rizzz* fills my ears, and it's in perfect harmony with the violin and cello masterpiece suddenly playing so beautifully in my mind.

Huh.

Maybe today is a string quartet kinda day after all.

"Hundreds! Fuck. *Fuck*," Hugo spits out, his chest heaving. "I lost count. I must have run hundreds of transactions for her."

I half-nod, my fingers tempted to wave left and right as I silently direct my own personal orchestra. The *rizzz* continues, and I saunter beside him, pull on the blood-soaked waistband of his pants. I'll have to unchain him for this next part.

"W-wait. Wait! Where's your leniency? Where's my chance? I answered your fucking question, goddammit!"

My movements still. The music halts, and silence rings in my ears. A muscle in my jaw ticks, but of course my voice remains controlled. I taught myself the value of control years ago—it was either that or lose myself completely to the chaos of my mind.

"Were you *lenient*, Hugo, when you listened to Katerina's victims cry in their crates? Or when you knew they were seconds away from death but did nothing?" I tilt my head, rub the bottom of my chin with the drill's handle. "When I was locked up in the studio, listening to them scream, beg to be spared . . . did you *give them a chance?*"

Every muscle in my body tenses. I'm well aware I've lost the emotional capacity I once had. But I remember. I remember exactly what it was like to sit beside them, all of them, as tears streamed down their cheeks and they begged for their lives.

Their reactions only spurred Katerina on. Tears, sweat, choked sobs. To her, that was the only way to create 'true art.'

I don't know if Hugo responds. I don't care, either.

The *rizzz, rizzz* picks up, the smooth, low vibration of a cello resumes, and I finish my fucking solo.

Adjusting the cufflinks on my crisp black shirt, I stroll down the hall toward Felix's office. He called me over half an hour ago, but I decided to reward my hard work with an extra-long shower. With my hair still damp and the fresh scent of aftershave lingering on my skin, I'm feeling particularly fucking good right about now.

My phone buzzes, and I shake my head at Felix's impatience before withdrawing it from my pocket. My steps slow. I narrow my eyes at the screen. What the hell is this? I zoom in on the picture.

Emmy Highland stands on the dining room table. Naked and chained to the chandelier. Her eyes are wide as she stares into the camera, her fingers curled into her palms. With a swallow, I force myself to ignore the bare curves of her body and drop my gaze instead to the candles lit around her feet.

My nostrils flare, my pulse accelerating. After a second, I delete the image, clear the screen, and resume walking. The reaction is illogical anyway. The girl is nothing to me. She signed up for this shit. She can get herself out of it if she can't take it.

Not a minute later, a text comes through.

Raife: Hope your day has been as eventful as mine. She looks so beautiful when she's afraid, doesn't she? She tasted just as good, too.

A growl catches in my throat before I pound on Felix's office door. It swings open, and I barge inside, almost knocking him down. I was having a great goddamn day.

"Fuck. What's up with you?" Felix closes the door behind me and walks back to his desk.

He slips into his leather chair and waits as I pace to the window, grimacing at the rays of light pouring onto the marble floor. I pull the blackout curtains over the glass until the room goes dark.

Better. My muscles loosen with the inky surroundings.

I'm not the only one with an aversion to bright lights, but I spent more time in Katerina's studio than my brothers. I won't pretend to tolerate it for their sake, and they don't expect me to.

I'm about to speak when another text lights up my phone.

Raife: Then again, that was hours ago. You should see what she looks like now.

My grip tightens around the phone. Tossing it on the desk, I watch it slide to the opposite end, near Felix; far enough not to tempt me to respond. I lean forward and rest my palms on the desktop, irritation coiling in my shoulders.

When my phone buzzes again, I don't bother looking. Felix glances toward it, his gaze flicking across the screen, then he groans and rubs his eyes. "You could have Stella send her back, you know. Cut the girl's contract now, before things escalate."

I pull in a long breath, then look up and level my gaze on his. "Since when have I been interested in discussing our hires? Let Raife and Stella deal with them, the way they always do." I pause to work my jaw. "Did you call me in here to talk bullshit or to go over our next play? I want Murphy."

Arnold Murphy is the last remaining chess piece, the final of the three players behind the pseudonym *Misha*, and also the most elusive and cunning. He's been the most difficult to obtain. After a failed attempt to bring him down a few years ago, the four of us agreed to hold off and save Murphy for after Hugo was finished. Who needs a fucking Katerina look-alike when I could finally get Murphy in front of me, face to face, after all this time?

Felix's eyebrows shoot up. After watching my expression, he shrugs. "All right, man. Then let's talk Murphy."

I nod and push off the table, the wheels in my mind already turning. A visual of the bastard tied up, his throat against my knife as he begs for his life, sends a hot rush through me. "We keep it low-key, stay focused on the delivery this time. Do that, and Griff could be bringing him in by the end of the week."

Felix taps a pen against his desk. "You know Raife doesn't want him here until we've completely ruined him. His law firm, his marriage, his fucking reputation. He wants him crushed, and I wouldn't mind seeing the guy watch his perfect life go up in flames before you get to him, either."

My lips curl. "I don't see Raife. Do you? Have you forgotten what happened after the last time we let Raife have his way with this guy? If he wants a say in what goes, he needs to actually be here to discuss this shit." My words bite, but my voice is calm as I turn and head for the door. "Otherwise we do it my way, and that's to cut the fucking theatrics and bring Murphy in."

My phone goes off right as I finish. I tense, turning just enough to see Felix scan the screen. "Speaking of theatrics," he frowns and tips his head toward it, "you might wanna stop by the dining room."

I let out a frustrated breath. He tosses the phone to me, and I slip it into my pocket.

"You're not even going to look?"

"Nah." I turn toward the door. "Some things are better seen in person."

chapter twelve

"I want to be inside your darkest everything."
—Frida Kahlo

Adam

I LINGER IN THE DOORWAY, RESTING A SHOULDER ON THE FRAME. GRIFF'S footfalls approach to my left, but I stay focused on the sight in front of me. Emmy's eyes flutter open. She clumsily straightens, shifting the weight of her body away from the chains and onto her feet. Contrary to the first picture Raife sent me, the chains are now loose enough that her elbows easily bend.

Her legs trembling, she spots Aubrey, who wraps a bandage around her left foot. Then her gaze lands on one of Griff's secretaries as she discards everything on the table's surface. And then she finds Raife. Sitting in the corner of the room, too preoccupied with his phone to fully enjoy the scene he must have handcrafted after I left this morning.

I force my eyes back to Emmy's, fists clenching in my pockets at the effort it takes to avoid looking directly at her naked body. I won't look. I know what would happen if I did—the temptation that would pull at me until I lost all sense of reason. Raife would get what he's been trying to manipulate me into since she arrived.

Still, from the edges of my vision, I see it, however vaguely. Teasing slopes, curves, and dips. A glisten of sweat reflecting off smooth porcelain skin.

Heat erupts inside my veins until it burns. It's been a long time since I've allowed myself such a simple pleasure. My muscles tighten and ripple against the strain of my clothes at just the thought.

One downward glance and I'd see everything. Emmy Highland at her most vulnerable. Ten easy footsteps and we could be skin to skin. Her sweat on my tongue. Hair in my fist. The curve of her delicate neck between my teeth, black strands wrapped around my knuckles.

My jaw grinds from side to side, the cool feel of my knife suddenly between my fingers. The longer I stare, the more it all blends. The dark hair, the pale skin, those fucking eyes.

The heat running through me increases to a searing boil, and for a completely different reason. Hugo's blood still covers the basement floor. The feel of his terror still vibrates through my bones. The kill is fresh on my hands. *Alive* in my mind.

Dark memories and bright white lights take over until they cloud my vision. Choked cries of the past pierce my eardrums and settle inside my chest. I look at the person chained helplessly to my chandelier, and I see *her*.

The woman who destroyed everything.

Kept me locked in a cage, forced me to watch.

As she skinned, gutted, *decorated*.

Snapped a photo and set a price tag on her *artwork*.

Every morning, every night, for 721 days.

An elbow nudges my arm, and I growl. Griff snarls and stalks past me, headed straight for the table. Straight for her. He moves his hand in front of his pants and adjusts himself, his intentions as transparent as the fucking windows in Felix's office.

My strides are long when I realize I'm matching him step for step. My stare locked on one person only. Her head whips to me, then to Griff. Her heavy eyes go wide, and a shiver passes through her limbs. Aubrey and some secretary stumble backward, clearing the way. I reach up, unhook one cuff from her wrist, and her arm falls limply to her side. I unlock the next and catch her damp body before she collapses to the ground, then pull her tightly into me.

"Gentlemen." Raife's amused voice is like a faraway call filtering through the screams still blaring in my mind. "Hands off my merch, please and thank you."

Ignoring him, my shoulder bumps Griff's suit jacket as I exit the dining room with her in my arms and pace through the halls. They both call after me, but I barely register their voices. I don't know what the fuck I'm doing, or what I'm *going* to do—hold the new hire or kill her just to get the screams to stop. My pulse is thumping so violently I feel it fucking *everywhere*—thrashing in my head, my neck, my chest, among other areas it has no business.

I shift her weight so I'm cradling her in both arms, and her head lolls to rest against my shoulder. She's still shivering, but that's the most she seems physically able to do. I keep my eyes straight ahead, strides long, passing door after door in a blur until I'm entering her room in the ladies' quarters.

Standing over her bed, I release her from my grip like my fingers are on fire. It's not gentle, the way her body hits the comforter, and she lets out a soft groan before folding into a ball.

Irritated, I toss a thin throw over her naked body to keep the biting temptation at bay, then I take a step back. And another. Stare straight ahead at the black wall above her pillows, above her head. My skin's hot, my chest pounding the way it does when it's been too long since I made a kill. It makes no sense. My breaths are ragged against the still air.

I should leave.

I *need* to leave.

I know this like I know the sun rises every morning, but my body doesn't move.

I'm about to slip my hands into my pockets to keep me grounded when I remember my knife and drop them back to my sides. Better to keep the weapon away from my grip until I figure out what the hell I'm doing in her room. My knuckles curl until they go white.

Finally, I slide my gaze down. Past the wall, to the top of the pillowcase, to the long strands of hair fanned out behind her. Her eyes are open as she lies on her side, staring straight ahead into the open bathroom across from her, yet she's not really looking. Her irises are blue glass, translucent and distant. Something about the expression makes the rhythm of my pulse normalize a fraction.

I like that she's not really here.

I take a slow step forward, my pants brushing the foot of the bed. Drag my eyes down to her pink lips, then the soft curve of her cheek, her jaw.

She looks different this way. Curled up and absent.

I can't place the tightness that pulls on my shoulders, my throat, at the sight of her like this, but a vague recognition stirs inside me. I've felt it before, even if I haven't allowed my thoughts to wander there in years. I detest the feeling now as much as I did then. Perhaps more.

My brothers and I have a lot in common, one of them being our shared disdain for Katerina. We were all caged. We were all on death row, waiting to become fleshless pieces of art set in a display case. Watching others come and go. But there was one major difference between them and myself.

I was the only *subject* Katerina kept stored inside her studio. My cage placed five feet away from her work table. I was the only person who watched it all—every fucking thing—day after day after day. The only one who spent almost two years with my face lit by rows upon rows of relentless bright lights as she worked, and worked, and worked.

The only one—for the first year.

My second year in the studio, there was another. Another with black hair, pale skin, and those haunting sky-blue eyes. Another who, with one thought, makes my blood boil for entirely different reasons.

But no. I won't think of her. I won't do it now, or tomorrow, or the next day.

She's not like Katerina. They will never be in the same category. She doesn't burn my veins with deep hatred. I can deal with that. Hell, I thrive on it. Hatred's the fuel that keeps me alive. Sofia, though . . . the things she ignites inside my chest are darker than that. Raw. Damaged. Everything I depend on forgetting.

For the sake of keeping my chaos locked inside my mind, packed in tight where it can't escape, I intend to never think of her again.

My gaze slips down to the smooth curve of Emmy's slender neck, her protruding collarbone. The fragile slope of her left shoulder, damp and slumped forward. My fingers squeeze into fists at my sides. I fan them out and roll my tight shoulders back. Before my gaze can travel any lower, I turn on my heel and pace straight out the door. There are many places in this house I should be right now, and none of them are here.

chapter thirteen

"Even the darkest night will end and the sun will rise."
—Victor Hugo, Les Miserables

Adam

(Thirteen years old)

My throat burns like I swallowed a lit match. I wince when I suck in a deep breath, rolling over to lie on my other side, but I don't bother to open my eyes and check the dispenser for water. Eleven months of being locked in here and it still sets my teeth on edge to use the handmade plastic bottle wired to the iron bars like a damn hamster's cage. And anyway, no one's stepped foot in the studio for a day and a half. So there's no one to refill the thing.

It's weird being alone. I want so badly to feel relief in the peace and quiet. To finally get a few solid hours of sleep and forget everything for a little while. But all it does is unsettle me. An unnerving feeling crawls up my spine at the strange absence in the air, and I don't like it at all.

The seconds creep by, each one reminding me I'm still here, and I'm never getting out.

A thunk crashes outside the door, the steady turning of

wheels following. I don't even blink. I know what that sound means.

New arrival.

Poor bastard. I remember being the new kid. Waking up confused and cramped inside a crate. Being lifted onto a trolley and rolled through the narrow, rotten-smelling hall. Dropped off in a room filled with more crates just like mine. More kids just like me.

But that was a different time. A different me. After all the crap I've already gone through trying to survive on the streets, all the messed up things I've witnessed and pulled, I thought for sure I'd seen the worst parts of evil and had outrun them.

Turns out I'd never seen the real thing up close before. And you can't outrun something you can't see.

It'll be a while before the new kid is brought to the studio. For their sake, I hope it's a *long* while.

Moving slowly, I use my forearms to push off the ragged wool blanket draped across the steel flooring. I know from experience how quickly I'll black out if I move too fast after going this long without a meal tray. Once I'm sitting up, I lean back against the cold wall for support as I stare into the empty cage across from me. Two weeks since it'd been set up there, and it's still got no one.

I haven't yet figured out why it's here. Either Katerina decided she's done having only one 'pet', or the thing was set up to taunt me with crap I'll never have.

The new cage is larger than mine, running half the length of the wall instead of one-third. It also has a small built-in toilet and sink, and a plush-ass looking cot with blankets I'm betting can warm one's body even in a freezing room like this one.

I fold my legs into my chest then wrap my arms around my knees, narrowing my eyes. After a second, I force myself to look away, but that only sets my gaze on the display case along the wall to my right.

My shoulders fall forward as I take it all in, the way I do every day. From here, the items behind the glass are passable as art. I never went to school, and I don't know much about the subject, but New York City is full of starving artists camped out on the streets with their hats turned upside down for tips.

Some pieces behind the glass are big, like the skulls. Others are smaller, like the fingers, or long, like the arms. Some are dressed in animal skin, some in feathers. Most are painted—dark and gothic or light and majestic. A few are decorated in the kind of fine jewels rich people lose their shit over. The kind of jewels I would have stolen at the first chance I got if I were still on the outside.

In front of each piece sits a framed card-sized note with a stage name and some bullshit poem. I can't read what they say from this far, and I don't think I want to anyway.

There's a Brazilian thing: *There's no good that lasts forever nor evil that never ends.* I was still a baby when my mom fled from Brazil and illegally immigrated us to America, but I saw it on a bumper sticker a few years ago, and it stuck. Watching Katerina in the studio makes me realize the words are bull. At least the last half.

My lips curl, and a familiar unease stirs in my chest. My eyes dart to the work table not far from my reach. The silver surface is pristine, all shine and gloss. Just like the walls and floors of the place.

I never knew hell would be so spick-and-span.

The door creaks open, and the skin on the back of my neck prickles as Katerina steps inside. Lifting a hand, she flicks the expanse of switches beside the door. The brightest lights I'd ever seen before arriving to this place fill the space. I squint against the harshness. If she only flicks the top two, it means she's just stopping by. But the whole switchboard? That means she's here to work.

A mixture of disgust, turmoil, and apprehension unfolds in my stomach. I get the feeling that if I have to stay in this place much longer, those lights alone will make me go insane.

She takes another step, and the door swings shut behind her. I wait, knowing what's coming.

To my surprise, she isn't alone.

A small girl pokes her head out from behind Katerina's legs. Her little arms are wrapped around the woman's thigh, her eyes scanning the room with a look that reminds me of the apprehension I feel. Katerina pats the girl's hair, and searing hot anger spikes inside my gut.

The hell?

I jump to my feet, grabbing one of the bars for balance when a wave of dizziness rushes straight to my head. Katerina ignores me, ushering the girl to the left—to the empty cage.

My throat tightens, and my breaths grow short, my fingers curling around the iron bar. This can't be right. The girl can't be older than five or six. Katerina never takes them this young.

Once the girl is settled behind the bars, Katerina sets down a large bag I hadn't noticed before. She opens it, then kneels and starts removing items one by one. Old, worn teddy bears, dolls with tangled hair, the kind of packaged kiddy snacks I didn't get to eat even before I wound up here. Last is a large set of oil crayons.

Katerina leans in and gives the girl a hug. I have to rub my eyes to make sure I'm seeing clearly. "You're going to love it here, once you get past the initial adjustment," she says, her voice soft. "Now, Mommy has a lot of work to do and can't miss any more days, okay?"

Mommy? The devil has a fucking kid?

I squint and tilt my head. Of course she does. Replace her tattered white dress with a sleek black one, and the little girl looks just like her. Their straight black hair swings past their waists, and the girl's is straggly like it's never been cut before. Their blue eyes are as close to seeing the sky that I've gotten in eleven long months. Their skin is the same pale shade, like they've never seen the sun.

The girl glances at me, then back at Katerina. She seems unfazed, despite the prison-like bars caging us in, the torn condition of my clothes, my dirty hair, and the odor I know is coming from my cell. Makes me wonder what the hell her life has been like before now for her to be so unaffected.

She nods.

"Thank you." Katerina gives her a peck on the nose then stands and walks to the display case. She opens one of the cabinets at the bottom and withdraws something, then walks back to the girl's cage.

"Baby girl. You still like to color, don't you?"

Again, the girl nods.

"Well, you know Mommy plays with colors, too. And today, we both get to play. Isn't that fun?"

When the girl only continues to nod, unease spreads through my body. Why isn't she saying anything?

"I just prepared this piece last week." Katerina sets down the item in her hand, and my empty stomach lurches until I dry heave.

It's a forearm, nothing but skinless bone.

I've been watching Katerina 'work' for so long I eventually learned to hide my reactions in front of her. Some days, I've even grown numb to it. But seeing her hand someone's body part—a seventeen-year-old who was living and breathing in this studio just last week—to her own kid, that's sick on a new level.

"This boy was very lively," Katerina continues, "but this particular piece of his didn't speak to me like the others. You know, I think you might do a good job telling his story with your pretty new coloring supplies." She spreads the crayons along the cement floor and places the bone between them and the child. "Will you do that for Mommy, Sofia baby?"

Another nod.

"Good girl."

When the child looks back at me with curious eyes, Katerina's gaze follows. The woman smiles, and it makes my skin burn with rage.

I grit my teeth but don't shy away. I stare her down. Katerina moves toward me almost gracefully, her steps soft. When she reaches my cage, she stops and slides a finger down the bars, until her nail traces over my knuckle. I almost snatch my hand away but manage to hold my ground as a growl rumbles up my throat.

Her smile widens, and she angles her head, her eyes roaming along every inch of my face. "This one here, my sweet girl, is our pretty, pretty pet."

The anger in my blood boils until it hurts. My heart races in my chest, my breaths heavy in the still air. I shift my gaze to the small girl, and for the first time, I think I see fear flicker in her eyes. I'm not sure if it's from her mom's words or the livid expression on my face, but I'm glad to see it.

Fear means maybe she isn't entirely unfazed after all. Maybe there's still hope for her.

"In art, some pieces take a little more time to bring out the most vulnerable parts of them," Katerina murmurs, still tracing the angles of my face with her eyes. "But then all the best things take time, don't they? He'll be ready, eventually. The process cannot be rushed."

A muscle in my jaw ticks. I know what Katerina means by that. She wants me to cry, to beg, like the others. She wants to see my fear. In her mind, fear is art, and without it, she has nothing.

What she doesn't understand is that I'm not afraid of death. In this room, I almost look forward to it.

chapter fourteen

*"Watch me. I will go to my own sun.
And if I am burned by its fire, I will fly on scorched wings."*
—Segovia Amil

Emmy

SOMETIMES I BELIEVE I WAS BORN WITH MY SOUL SPLIT STRAIGHT DOWN the middle. Each half of me is a different person. With different feelings, different reactions, different impulses. The worst part about it is the edges dividing me are so frayed I don't think I'll ever be able to sew them back together. Into a person who functions like everyone else. Into a person who makes sense, like everyone else.

Mama would say it's because I belong to the devil.

Frankie would say I am exactly as I'm meant to be.

I'm not so sure either of them would be wrong. And that might be what worries me most.

Long nails brush my shoulder blades as Stella buttons my dress. "Are you certain, Emmy?" Her voice bounces off my bathroom walls.

I nod and lift my hair off my neck so she can adjust my scarf. I keep my eyes on the movements of her hands. The gold material tightens around my throat when she pulls it into a neat knot at one side. Such an elegant collar.

"Yes."

She watches my reflection in the mirror before us. "It would be perfectly all right to take the rest of the day off after a morning as eventful as yours. It is already evening, after all. So long as your master doesn't call on you, it's acceptable, even recommended, to take a break." She glances downward, to the spot below my ankle where I wrapped a fresh bandage around the first-degree burn.

I've been Raife's servant for less than twenty-four hours. If today is anything to go by, I'm going to need to change my approach. I can't expect him to lower his walls if all he sees in me is someone he wants to make suffer. I might never be able to get him to look at me the way he does Stella, but even a small fraction of that could be useful in gaining his trust, getting him to reveal things he wouldn't otherwise.

Finally, I shake my head. I can't allow myself to back out.

I'm well aware that Raife got to me with the stunt he pulled this morning. Seven hours later and I still haven't quite bounced back. A strange hollowness rooted itself in my gut when I was chained to the chandelier, and the feeling is steadily seeping into my nerve endings even now. But the numbness that spread to my fingers this morning has disappeared, which means my body works just fine. I don't need to be present mentally to seduce someone.

"I'm fine," I say faintly. "I'd like to see him."

After a pause, she squeezes my upper arms and her face lights up. She whispers, "Well, he does enjoy surprises."

Raife's voice is quiet, muffled by the wall dividing us. Maybe he's on the phone. What does a guy like Raife do when a secretary interrupts him? Does it please him to see one of us, or does it anger him? I slow my pace behind Stella as she comes to a stop at a door that's been left cracked open. She lifts her hand and knocks softly.

A throat clears. "What is it?" Raife barks. His tone makes the tiny hairs on the back of my neck stand up.

"Master, it's Stella." She looks over her shoulder at me. "I've brought a surprise for you."

A murmur too low for me to understand seeps through the cracked door, then he calls, "Come in."

Stella enters. I wait in the doorway, watching her glide across the dark office and approach Raife. I don't know how she's always so calm and put together, but I can't imagine her being any other way.

Raife sits alone behind a large desk. Blackout curtains to his right block the daylight, leaving his features almost as shadowed as the rest of the room. A small lamp behind him highlights the serious look on his sharp features, an expression that softens only when Stella reaches his side. She bends forward and runs her fingers down his cheek as she whispers something in his ear. She starts to straighten before he grabs her by her ponytail and tugs her back down. I can't hear what he says, but I see him lick—or bite—her neck before he releases her.

When Stella straightens, she readjusts the hem of her dress and turns to me, her pink cheeks and coy smile illuminated by the lamp. She heads my way then nods and winks as she walks past me and down the hallway, the same direction we came.

I keep my eyes on her as her silhouette disappears around a corner, and then on the empty space in her wake. I know I'm up, it's time to make my move, but my neck is suddenly stiff and my heels are glued to the marble.

"Well, don't be shy, love," Raife says quietly. "I hope you didn't stop by just to waste my time."

My head snaps toward him of its own accord. Something about his voice, his words, grates on me.

No, I didn't come here to waste anyone's time. I'm not so sure Frankie *has* time to waste. And there's nothing to be shy about when it's not *me* I need to offer this man, but my body.

My lips curve, though I know my eyes reflect the hollowness still eating away at me. I take one step into his office and close the door. As I take another step, I reach behind my back and begin to leisurely unbutton my dress.

"Shy?" I murmur with another step. "Not at all." By the time I reach Raife, all the buttons are undone. My dress slips to the floor, revealing the black lace bustier I discovered in my closet, paired with a matching G-string and sheer thigh-high stockings. Not my style, but I figured the outfit was in my room for a reason.

Raife leans back in his chair, his eyebrows raised and a smirk pulling on the corners of his mouth.

After rounding the desk, I slip between his legs and sit on his left thigh, then lean in and whisper, "Unless you want me to be." My voice is sultry despite feeling nothing at his nearness. No desire, no racing heart, not even fear.

I run my hand down his silky tie then let my fingers wander lower until I'm massaging his length through his suit pants.

He lets out a half-groan, half-chuckle, and glances over my shoulder. My brows knit as he continues to stare past me, amusement darkening his expression. Just when I turn to see what he's looking at, a yelp escapes my throat as he swiftly pulls me in so I'm straddling him. Unease twists my gut, but I cover it up with a slow half-smile.

I don't know what I was expecting, but it wasn't this. Based on his treatment of me so far, I thought I'd at least have to work a little harder to get this kind of attention from him.

As I lower my lips to his neck and glide the tip of my tongue up to his ear, he moans, and my mind whirls at his reaction. It's the first sign he's given that I might actually be able to pull this off. I might be able to walk out of here tonight with Raife Matthews seeing me as someone to desire. As someone he could potentially loosen up around and maybe even invite into his bedroom—one room in the house I'm willing to bet has no cameras. What better place to hide your secrets?

His breath fans across my ear, cool and minty, as he asks a little too loudly, "Would you be willing to do anything for me then?"

I squeeze my eyes shut, images of this morning flashing through my head. Pulling his earlobe between my teeth, I bring my fingers to his tie and begin to loosen it. "Anything you wan—"

Pain surges through my scalp as my head's yanked back. One hand grips my waist, and then I'm spun around. His hard dick digs into my ass, and my back is against his chest.

My breaths come out fast and short. I try to adjust my eyes to the new view of his office.

The only lamp in the room is now behind me, and it's small enough to leave everything before me a disorienting sea of black and grey. As pieces of furniture take shape, I mentally store each closed drawer away in case I ever find myself in this room alone with time to snoop. It's not until my eyes flick to the right that another, larger, form slowly takes shape as well. I squint while Raife's cold hand runs down the side of my waist then curves around my hip. He dips his fingers beneath the fabric of my G-string, but I'm more focused on the person I now see sitting diagonally from me, in the far right corner.

My heart thumps against my ribcage.

Everything around me goes still as I take him in. The thick dark hair almost falling in his face. His set jaw. Broad shoulders. His hand resting on the chair's armrest. I watch with bated breaths as his fingers steadily go up, down, up, down.

Tap, tap, tap.

A thick swallow passes through my dry throat. I came here prepared for Raife Matthews.

Not his brother.

I squeeze Raife's suit sleeves when two long, thin fingers are shoved painfully inside me. *Fuck.* An ache swells between my legs. Raife's soft, raspy chuckle echoes in my left ear, and the tapping across the room stops. Heavy silence rings in the air for a long, drawn-out moment.

Raife fingers are still inside me, unmoving, when he calls, "I'll make you a deal."

It's clear he's not speaking to me, so I keep my mouth shut and my legs spread. Just how he likes it, I assume.

"A deal." Adam's deep, smooth voice slides past my ears and burns low in my stomach, causing me to clench around Raife's fingers. My heart pounds faster. "I'm listening."

Raife's free hand teases the bottom of my bustier. "I might be willing to meet you in the middle on Murphy." He inches higher, higher, until he's stroking the curve of my left breast. "Perhaps."

When Raife doesn't elaborate and instead cups my breast, then gradually glides his fingers in and out of me, Adam's hand slowly curls into a fist. His gaze finds mine, and he runs his tongue along his bottom lip, then tilts his chin. I pull my own lip between my teeth to keep from squirming as an unexpected tremor flutters between my thighs. Raife pumps faster, but Adam's eyes are locked on mine, holding me captive until all

I see, all I feel, is him. The tension rolls off his body in waves. Electric waves that send a warm jolt through me every time Raife's fingers slide inside me.

Impatience drips from Adam's voice, and somehow it only makes me clench tighter. "The goddamn deal, Raife."

My breaths shorten, and I let my head fall back against the curve of Raife's shoulder if only to free myself from Adam's hold. A cold feeling tries to work its way into my gut—unease, guilt, confusion. It's okay to feel pleasure, I remind myself. It's a *necessity* to get Raife where I need him. It doesn't matter who it's from—which brother, or how, as long as Raife thinks he's the one who turns me on.

There's no way Raife's going to get an orgasm out of me, not after what he did to me this morning—what I can only guess he might have done to Frankie. But I can't help the ripples of pleasure that tease me when his brother is mere feet away, his presence a live wire beneath my skin. His voice, deep and masculine, warming my insides. His eyes piercing mine so intensely it's like he'd go blind if he looked away.

Raife's response slices through my thoughts. "You finish this with my lovely hire, and we'll meet halfway."

My head snaps up, and my pulse spikes. *What?*

Adam doesn't hesitate. "No."

The material of my G-string pinches my skin when Raife's hand disappears, then I'm forced to my feet. I wince when he clasps my wrists together behind my back with one hand and shoves my shoulder blades with the other until my nose almost touches his desk.

"Come again?" Raife asks.

I manage to angle my head in time to see Adam stand and take a few steps toward us. It's not until then that I notice papers in his left hand. "No deal," Adam says. "It's all in or nothing."

His gaze drifts to mine, and a muscle in his jaw ticks. "I don't do anything halfway."

A warm thrill vibrates down my back, making me shiver. I'm the first to look away.

Adam closes the distance between us and tosses the papers onto Raife's desk, just a few feet from my face. I narrow my eyes, but it's too dark to make out the small words.

"Like I said, Felix and I drew out a detailed plan. Put on your big boy pants and read it from top to bottom. *Then* we'll talk."

He turns to leave when Raife firmly says, "Let me prove she wants you, then I'll read the fucking thing."

My entire body stiffens. Apparently so does Adam's because his footfalls halt.

Raife lets out an annoyed sigh and adds, "Top to bottom, three times over, cherry on top, whatever. Take it or leave it, but I'm not reading a word without this deal."

Adam says nothing, though he does turn around. He dips his hands in his pockets and narrows his eyes at Raife before flicking them to me.

"She wasn't wet for me," Raife continues, as though I'm not standing right here, bent half-naked over his desk. I swallow as his words reverberate in my head. I really thought I had him fooled. "She was practically dripping whenever you opened your pretty mouth." He snickers from behind me, and I realize he's not upset. In typical Raife fashion, his tone is darkly amused, even devious.

A flicker passes through Adam's eyes so briefly I would have missed it if he wasn't consuming every fiber of my attention. "Is that so." It comes out like a statement, his gaze burning a hole straight through my skin. Finally, he turns back to Raife, and a breath pours from my lungs. "Sounds like your problem. Not mine."

"Problem?" Raife barks out a laugh. His hold around my wrists loosens as he removes one hand to glance at his watch. "I want to see how right I am about this one." His fingertips dig into my skin, and he presses me hard against the table until my cheek is on the smooth wood. My chest tightens when I realize what he's asking, and my breaths come out in pants. "If you can get her to finish in the next five minutes before my client pulls up out front, I'll read every page of your shitty plan. I'll even discuss it with Felix when I get back. But if you can't . . ." His voice fades, and he inches the papers toward the trash bin with his free hand.

My eyes fall shut. I can't let Adam Matthews bring me to the edge. Not in front of Raife, not when it's Raife I need to somehow convince I want more than the others.

I can't.

When I finally open my eyes, Adam's polished black shoes are moving closer. Every part of my body buzzes to life at the thought of his warm, strong hands on me, and I know I'm screwed if he takes this deal. My only hope is that he'll refuse and walk away. He takes another step, then another, and a swarm of butterflies jumps from my stomach to my throat.

"Five minutes," he murmurs. A simmering heat pulses between my legs at the throaty rasp now coating his low voice. My gaze follows his hands as he pulls them from his pockets, unbuttons his cuff, and pushes his sleeve up. "Deal."

chapter fifteen

"I need someone who sees the fire in my eyes and wants to play with it."
—Unknown

Emmy

My cheek is pressed against the cold surface of the desk, but my insides are on fire. I don't know how I'm going to pull this off, just that I have to. I can't risk Raife turning me away before I get answers, and I have no reason to believe he'll keep me around if he doesn't buy into my desire for him. After inhaling deeply, I wiggle against Raife's hold, trying to stand, but he keeps me in place.

"You're wrong," I finally say, avoiding Adam's gaze. "It's not him I want. It's you."

"Oh, love," Raife says on a breathy laugh. He releases me and steps back, then grins and clasps his hands together like an excited teenager. "Guess we're about to find out, aren't we?"

My arms fall forward, and I grip the edge of the desk, but I don't straighten. God, I don't trust my body not to betray me while Adam is to my left, close enough to feel the heat radiating off him. To see his shirt strain against his broad shoulders when he raises a hand and flicks open the top buttons hinting at his sculpted chest. To swallow down his clean, masculine scent each time I inhale.

I'm screwed.

"Stand up and look at me." Adam's voice is quiet but commanding. The kind of tone you *want* to obey.

I swallow hard, then push off the desk and stand. My gaze is on the floor for a long moment, the thump of my heart ringing in my ears, before I lift my chin and look right at Adam. His blue irises are darker than usual, like an ashy black. It's so dark that if I look close enough, I can almost see my soul reflected in them—secretive. Immoral. *Sinful.*

I suck in a breath, curl my arms around my waist, and turn my cheek. Raife meets my gaze, a wicked tilt to his lips, and my pulse slows a fraction. I don't know why it's so much easier to look at him.

Warm fingers brush the curve of my jaw, and my head is angled back to the man before me. A man who holds every skipping beat of my heart, every uneven breath, in the palm of his hand.

I try to turn my head again, but Adam's grip on my jaw drops to my neck, and I stop. "I want Rai—"

"So you said." His eyes flash, but his tone remains calm. One large hand is curled all the way around my neck, overlapping the scarf. His touch sears my throat, despite the delicate hold he has on me. He leans in, and the stubble of his jaw skims my cheek. "But I have a deal to keep"—he steps into me; I step back—"and the clock is ticking." Another step toward me, another step back.

"You're going to lose," I breathe, just before my shoulders hit the cold, hard wall.

He raises his left arm and presses his palm against the wall, simultaneously caging me in and blocking Raife from my view.

Then he dips his head just enough to look at me fully. Something flickers in his eyes as he traces every inch of my face, and I can't tell if he wants to fuck me or hurt me.

A slow tremor runs through me. Jesus, that should *not* turn me on.

"I should tell you, little mouse," he murmurs. The hand around my neck disappears before he brushes the hair out of my face, and a muscle in his jaw ticks. "I never lose."

Shit.

I snap my knees shut, but not before his hard, warm thigh wedges between my legs, rubbing against my G-string. A spark zips straight to my core at the delicious friction. I bite my bottom lip hard, barely containing the moan rumbling up my throat.

Raife's chuckle sneaks its way to my ears, and I hear the squeak of a chair as he sits.

Without thinking, I bend my elbows and push my palms against Adam's chest, trying to escape before he unravels me. But my arms are forced downward as he moves forward and closes the small gap between us. I gasp when my feet leave the floor and the only thing keeping me up is Adam's strong thigh, my full weight pressing down on him. I squirm, but that only makes me moan as his warmth vibrates against my clit.

When my hips buck against his, every curved dip of his abdomen tenses beneath my palms.

My inhale catches in my throat at the unexpected reaction.

I freeze, my breaths heavy, and take in the shudder that ripples through him as I slowly manage to slide my hands up between our crushed bodies, until my fingers are wrapped around his neck.

Then I angle my chin to look directly at Adam.

His heavy gaze is on mine, his eyelids lowered. His jaw is clenched, chest rising and falling. He doesn't move when I inch my fingers higher and brush them through the thick strands of his hair, messing them up in the process. The tension is stifling, and my chest aches with every rapid thump of my heart. I drag my nails back down, along the back of his neck.

A swallow passes through his throat, and a gust of air pours from my lips.

His eyes flick down, tracking the motion.

His mouth is so close. His skin so warm. I don't even realize I'm leaning in, toward his lips, until his tight grip is on my jaw, my neck thrown back, halting me from getting any closer. My pulse races. With my eyes now forced toward the ceiling, I'm barely able to lower my gaze enough to see him.

He pushes me back an inch until my scalp touches the wall, then drags his grip down my throat, past my scarf, his eyes following every movement. When his hand dips lower, barely skimming the curve of my breasts and lingering just below my belly button, goose bumps erupt from the pit of my stomach to my core.

A faint "Tick tock" sounds behind him.

For a moment, Adam doesn't move.

Turmoil flares behind his eyes. A tendon in his neck bulges. And his gaze drifts back up to mine. It darkens when he catches me staring so intently at him.

Blood rushes through me like a giant wave.

"I don't want you." The broken whisper spills from my lips in one last, useless plea, and it's the same moment I spread my legs further, inviting him in.

His shoulders tighten beneath my grip. I watch as he grinds his jaw back and forth. What I would give to see inside his mind right now, to sense his next move. But for a few painful seconds, he gives me nothing but an icy gaze.

Then his strong hand is beneath my G-string, and an electric heat stirs to life right on my clit.

Oh, god.

My forehead drops to his shoulder as pleasure rolls through me, but his free hand clutches my hair and forces my eyes back to his.

"I said," he rasps, his long fingers sliding all the way inside me, "look at me."

And so I do. With every agonizingly slow pump, every teasing dip, every delicious rub of his thumb on my clit, I look at him. Adam Matthews. My lips part, and I let my pants fill the small gap between our mouths. His eyes go a shade darker, his own breaths shortening as he expertly works his fingers faster, harder.

Fuck.

It feels good. Ripples of pleasure shock me with each slick movement, and I'm already so close. I can taste it in the air between our bodies—my wetness, his heat, our breath.

"Thirty seconds." My broken moans drown out Raife's voice.

I grind against Adam's fingers, chasing it, but the strong grip on my hair slips to my ass, stilling me. I narrow my eyes and growl, and I swear I see his lips twitch. Keeping my hips locked, unmoving, between the wall and his body, he wraps my legs around him so I'm completely opened up, then drives his fingers all the way inside.

I gasp, my jaw falling open, and my skin flushes as hot tingles erupt inside my core. "Oh, god . . ."

He works his hand harder, chasing something I didn't even know was there, and my insides tighten as an orgasm rips through me so violently my entire body shakes. Pleasure surges up my core then ripples between my thighs, leaving me breathless as it goes on and on. I bite down on my lip as the last moan bubbles up my throat, and my legs clench around him.

"Five seconds."

A final spasm spreads from my inner thighs to my toes. My eyes are closed, my muscles mush, as Adam slides me down his hard body.

He keeps me upright with one strong arm, and I watch in a daze as he glances over his shoulder at Raife.

Raife shrugs and reaches for the papers at the end of his desk.

"I'll have it done by the end of the night."

chapter
sixteen

*"Everyone is a moon, and has a dark side
which he never shows to anybody."*
—Mark Twain

Adam

My strides are long, shoulders tense, as I stalk downstairs to the basement. I pass the closed door to my . . . office . . . and continue down the dark hall until I reach the camera room.

The door opens before I reach it. Aubrey's on her game today.

She sits behind the desk, the control panels within reach. Her eyebrows are drawn, her green eyes flicking from the wide display of monitors to mine. "Master." She sounds surprised to see me.

I rarely enter the camera room. But I need a favor, and Aubrey's the only secretary I trust enough to keep it quiet. More accurately, to keep it from Raife.

"I need you to do something for me."

"Of course." Her gaze drops to my pants, where I feel my hard cock straining against the material. She quickly averts her attention, and she actually looks baffled. Certainly not the first time the girl's seen a hard on, but it is the first time she's seen one on me.

She'll get over it. Just like I'll have to.

"How long till Felix relieves you from your shift?"

She glances at the time on one of the monitors. "Twenty minutes."

I nod. "I'll cover for you. Get me all the files we have on Emmy Highland."

She rolls the chair back and stands. "Right away." She starts to walk around me, then pauses, glances back. "Master, if I may . . . Raife's just trying to get to you. It's what he wants."

I let out a breath of dry amusement, my gaze narrowing on the monitors before me when a certain petite girl with long black hair flits across one of the screens. Truthfully, Raife's not my concern right now.

"Get the files, Aubrey."

She's quiet for a moment. Then her heels click toward the exit, and the door locks behind her.

I continue to track Emmy as she enters the ladies' quarters, probably checking out for the night. My feet are rooted to the floor, my entire body stiff and pulsing with an unrested sensation I can't fucking shake.

Her warmth, her wetness, is still on my fingers, tucked inside my pocket where her scent can't get to me. I should have stopped to wash my hands and rid myself of her completely, but my blood was boiling to the point I couldn't see straight on my way here.

My worst case of blue balls yet, and I can't do a goddamn thing about it.

Emmy stops before her door, then glances down both ends of the empty hall before opening it and stepping inside. She makes her way to the bathroom, the one place without a camera, and closes the door behind her.

I let out a frustrated sigh and take a small step toward the monitors.

I remember vividly the last time I fucked a woman, nearly six years ago—just like I recall the terrified look on her pale face. I had one hand locked around her throat with my knuckles going white, and the other holding a knife an inch from her stomach without me even realizing it.

And she was a professional.

By then, I'd already gone through unintentionally scaring the shit out of women when I needed a fix. I quickly learned I needed someone who specifically enjoyed, or at the very least could take it, when I hit that point of blinding release. Every time, I lost all sense of the control I work so hard at maintaining.

I can't even use my own damn hand without losing myself, losing my barely-there sanity, in those final moments of ecstasy. However fleeting, it's enough to give me a sense of what it would be like to lose it all. To threaten unleashing the demons of my mind forever and breaking me down completely. And time isn't on my side. The longer I keep my past locked inside, the more difficult it becomes to contain. I won't risk surrendering my control again.

So I abstain. Like a fucking priest.

With an unhealthy appetite for spilling blood.

The door opens, and I look over my shoulder. Aubrey sets two manila folders on the desk, then glances up at me. "Want me to stay?"

I shake my head, flicking my attention back to the monitor. "I'll text you when I'm done."

"Yes, Master."

She leaves, and soon I relax enough to sit down, pick up the files, and lean back against the seat.

The first file is generic legal bullshit—contracts, payroll information. Not what I'm looking for. I swap it out for the second folder and skim over the few pages of personal info provided.

Emmy May Highland. Born in Presley, Mississippi on October 22, 1997 to parents Agnes and Karl Highland. One sister by the name of Francesca Highland.

I rub my chin and scan the rest of the pages—a picture of the trailer park she calls home, some greasy diner she worked at, a tattooed neighbor she had multiple flings with. Since when do we keep photos of anything other than the hires themselves? I'm about to turn the page when my gaze flies back to the last picture.

Her fling, with a stupid smirk on his face and a beer in his inked hand. The longer I stare at his photo, the more my skin burns. It's irritating as shit, so I tear the paper down the middle and toss it into the trash bin behind me.

A trivial reaction, but fuck it.

I flip to the next page and narrow my eyes. There's a close up of her trailer with a Bible sitting on a stand beside the front porch. Since when is Emmy fucking Highland religious? Angling my head, I trace my thumb along the side of my jaw and notice an old dog house in the backyard with a long, heavy chain sprawled out on the dirt. No dog in sight.

Irritated, I blow out a breath and shake my head.

There has to be more here. Something that ties her to Katerina or Sofia. The resemblance is too coincidental. Or in Raife's words, *uncanny*.

I've noticed it before, every goddamn time I look at her I see it, but today, at the mercy of my hands, there was something too distinct in those sky-blue eyes. Something childlike, a spark of pure vulnerability. It's a look identical to the one I used to see behind bright lights and iron bars every morning and night. A look that haunted me to the brink of insanity every time I shut my eyes for five long years after my escape, before I trained myself to block it out completely.

A look that can't be replicated.

Of course it's impossible. I watched them both die—Katerina at the hands of all four of us the day of our escape. It was a far cry from how we would have done things now. The burning regret of not making her suffer fuels each of us every single day. But we were kids then. Amateurs. No kills to our name.

Except for me.

I had Sofia, and her death was on no one's hands but my own. Despite the promise I made to her.

My grip squeezes the edges of the papers, and my chest tightens in a way I fucking hate. The same way it did when I watched Emmy lying on her bed this morning, limbs weak and eyes glassy.

I drop the file and push off the chair. Something's up, and I'm going to figure out what it is. But right now, the tension coiling inside me is hot enough to implode, and the knife in my pocket is lonely. Just as I pull out my phone to text Aubrey to return, my gaze catches on a page I must have missed sticking out from behind the others.

I pick it up and squint at the image. It's a photo of Emmy taken outside a trailer home that isn't hers. She's wearing skin-tight jeans and a plain black top, holding one hand over her forehead to block the sun. A smile is plastered on her face for the camera, but the sunlight highlights an unnaturally pink tint around her eyes. I tilt the page and notice they're swollen, like she'd been crying.

What the hell is this?

It's standard for our potential hires to send in a photo of

themselves after Stella contacts them, part of the process Raife monitors. But they're usually dressed in something seductive, a genuine glint of excitement in their eyes. They're never fucking crying.

If they were, we wouldn't hire them.

I pick up my phone and dial the last person I want to speak with about this. Well, the second to last.

"Stella Larsson," she purrs.

I look at my watch then dip my free hand into my pocket, keeping my tone neutral despite the turmoil twisting inside my gut. "Who told you to hire Emmy?"

"What do you mea—"

"Did you scout her yourself, like you usually do?"

"Well, no—"

"So how'd she get in contact with us?"

There's a pause. "I . . . don't exactly know."

I grind my teeth. "Explain."

"She called out of the blue a little over a month ago. I went through the interview process as usual, assuming she was someone I had scouted, but when I had her submit her photo I figured there must have been a mistake. She didn't fit the profile at all." Another pause. "So, when I reported the issue to Raife, he instructed me to shred her information, as expected. But then he stopped me and said to hire her anyway."

I lean a shoulder against the wall and cross one ankle over the other. "What gave him this sudden change of heart?"

"He didn't say. He simply looked at her picture and decided—"

"The photo she submitted?"

"Yes, he looked at her picture and decided he wanted to give her a chance. So I booked her flight. But, Mr. Matthews, I'm sure my master would be happy to discuss the case with you personally. Honestly I'm a little uncomfortable answering anything further without—"

"Send Aubrey to the camera room." I hang up and straighten my cuffs.

It's no question why Raife changed his mind after seeing Emmy's photo. I'll bet a single look at Katerina's mini-me filled his mind with all kinds of fantasies on how he could finally quench his thirst for Katerina's rightful revenge. The kind of revenge she deserved and escaped from even in death.

Probably explains all the extra pictures in her file, too. He wouldn't have been able to stop himself from digging up whatever he could on Katerina's doppelganger. And judging from her file, he wound up at the same dead end I'm at now.

Nothing on her ties to Katerina or Sofia. Nothing on how she got our number in the first place. What she's *really* doing here.

Aubrey enters the room, and I stride past her, leaving the files behind.

Raife's manipulations are nothing new. Shit, it's the only reason he's alive. Growing up the way we did taught us to put ourselves first. But where I had a mom to look after me for my first eight years, even if we were homeless, Raife never had anyone. There's no question he would've wound up dead long ago if it weren't for his cleverness, his ability to manipulate. But frankly, it's beginning to bore me.

Emmy Highland, however, just got a helluva lot more interesting.

chapter seventeen

*"Monsters are real, and ghosts are real too.
They live inside us, and sometimes, they win."*
—Stephen King

Adam
(Thirteen years old)

"Mmhmm. Can you tell me more about that?" Katerina's soft voice trickles to my ears. She scribbles something onto a notepad, then leans over the whimpering teenager strapped to her work table. "More specifically, about the feelings that stirred within you when your foster mother struck you?"

I let out a puff of air and shake my head. The girl is a couple years older than me. She has scraggly hair and, based on her answers so far, she was out on the streets for less than a year before winding up here. Really, she had it good. Should've stayed in her foster home—a roof overhead, food in her stomach, a bed to sleep on.

The girl's responses are quiet, a tremble cracking her voice. I know the tone well. She's past fighting, crying, and she's latched onto the only shred of hope she has left—the realization that at least this fucked up interview buys her a little more time.

"You poor girl," Katerina murmurs. "Such beautiful tears you cry. Thank you for trusting me with your story, sweet Jane. I promise to share it in its purest form."

Closing my eyes, I try to block out the bright lights above my head and the thumping in my chest as I lean against the wall. I wish I didn't have to listen to this shit day after day. I cringe with every sob; they ring in my mind as pleas that will never be answered. My fingers dig into the floor below me, my raw skin grating on the rough cement a welcome distraction.

A faint *ting, ting* drags my gaze to the large cage across the room.

The little girl, Sofia, gently taps a colorful bone on the iron bars as she paces slowly from one end of the cage to the other. It's the same bone her mom had her color with oil crayons two months ago.

It's become some kinda routine for her.

The first day she showed up and witnessed her mom skinning a new arrival, she'd sat in a ball, covered her eyes, and rocked back and forth. She still hasn't made a peep. The second day, during an interview, she did the same. And the third. But the fourth day, she'd started this tapping thing with the bone. And she's done it ever since.

I don't get it.

I stare at her for a few moments, letting the *ting, ting* drown out the 'interview' happening beside us. Soon, she stares back. Her eyes are wide, but they're not afraid.

After a while, the only sound in the room is that bone clicking against the iron. There's no more whimpering, no more questions, no more responses. I glance at Katerina.

The interview is over.

Slowly, I turn my head back to Sofia. She's still watching me, but she's set down the bone. And, finally, I understand.

That's why she does it—she's drowning out her mom's voice, the crying, all of it.

She's what, five? And she figured this place out a helluva lot quicker than I did.

The clank of a tray being set on metal draws my attention back to the workspace. The subject's, Jane's, long limbs droop lifelessly over the edge of the narrow table. My breaths quicken as Katerina lifts a scalpel from the tray. My lungs are tight, and I don't realize I'm inching closer until the cold wall is no longer against my back.

No one makes a sound as Katerina makes her first cut.

It's slow. Precise. Drawing the tiniest amount of blood.

She picks another spot, higher up on the arm, and takes her time sliding the blade across skin once more.

It's not until I see it, the deep crimson dripping from the arm to the table, then eventually to the floor, that my lungs open and I can breathe again. I inhale sharply, taking the fresh scent of blood with me, and retreat back to the wall with a snarl.

Over the past 424 days of me being trapped in this cage—forced to listen to one person after the next suffer, then to Katerina's sick murmurs in their ear—I've learned there's only one thing that actually makes it stop. That shuts off the relentless pounding in my head, the guilt, the helplessness, the goddamn lights piercing my eyes.

It might be the needle that initially takes their lives, but the sight of crimson is the only thing that shuts Katerina up and keeps her occupied long enough to leave the others alone. Sometimes it buys us a week or more while she plays with her new project.

In this place, there is nothing more final than the spill of blood on that table.

At least until the room gets wiped clean and a new day

begins, starting the process over again.

But for now, my head has a few blissful seconds to clear. My pulse goes quiet, and I don't have to pretend. For just a moment, I don't have to pretend it doesn't get to me. Because in the silence, as long as drops of crimson flow, nothing can reach me.

chapter eighteen

"Come to me in pieces and exist inside me whole."
—Christopher Poindexter

Emmy

I WIPE A HAND OVER THE FOGGED UP MIRROR AND STARE BLANKLY AT MY reflection. A shiver runs through me as water pools on the tile below my feet. I let the steam soak into my pores and watch as droplets drip from my hair to my waist, sticking for a second before running along the curve of my hips, looping around my thigh.

I close my eyes and slowly chase the water with my fingertips.

Beneath the cold tingles on the surface of my skin, a layer of heat pulses through my veins. I still feel Adam Matthews on me. His strong hand pressed between my thighs, his firm grip on my hair and warm breath on my neck. But it's more than that.

He's everywhere.

Danger sings to me within the depths of his eyes like a long-lost friend. His shadow reaches beyond my skin and summons something deep inside me, something I'm not allowed to feel. Not allowed to *be*.

I grip the edge of the counter as my eyelashes flutter open.

He gets into my head without even trying.

How did you do it, Frankie? Were you strong enough to keep these brothers skirting around the outside of your mind, where they belong? Were you pure enough?

Or did they find your secrets? Did they break you?

Don't worry, silly, Frankie once told me on a quiet laugh. *Only fragile things can be broken.*

Releasing a shaky breath, I hope to God neither of us are made of glass and grab a towel from the door hook. It's still early, and I have secrets to discover. After drying off, I tie the gold scarf around my neck and slip on an ebony silk nighty—the only functional nightwear provided—letting my damp hair hang down my back. Finding no shoes in my closet except four-inch heels, I pad barefoot toward the bedroom door.

Icy nerves claw at my chest, but I reach forward and turn the knob. Then I pause, pushing my shoulders back.

I'm going to get caught. With cameras in every corner, there's no escaping that. For all I know, someone is watching me right now. I swallow back the urge to double-check my room for cameras and step into the hall, forcing my expression to be casual. Innocent.

There are no rules about leaving my room. And I'm the new girl, after all, which is my only hope that whoever catches me will listen to my made-up excuse and let this slide. In the meantime, I'll just have to cover as much ground as possible.

No pressure.

I suppress the shudder trying to work down my spine when I slip by the first camera at the end of the hall. Making a right at the corner, I exit the ladies' quarters.

Instead of a square, the mansion is a really long shoebox. An impeccable, shiny shoebox that keeps its lid secure and snug at all times. The ladies' quarters—holding our bedrooms, dining room, and spa—is on the main floor of two, tucked away at the far right end. Hallways are everywhere, leading from one closed door to the next, until you reach the expanse of the lobby, which I just did.

My nerves squeeze when the clicking of heels echoes to my right. With a thick swallow, I remind myself that I'm an innocent newbie and continue padding across the white marble. There's only one window. It's large, eating up most of the front wall, but heavy curtains cover every corner of the glass.

I don't miss it—the sunlight. The sky. I can't ignore the surge of comfort that soothes me at the bleakness. Even so, I have to wonder why the Matthews work so hard to keep the curtains drawn and the lights dim.

Peeking through the curtain, I stare past the moonlit, manicured lawn and at the wall of shrubbery dividing this building from the front house. It's quiet out, not even a breeze to stir the leaves. Seems odd to have two mansions so close together, especially with one hidden so carefully behind the other.

"Are you waiting for someone?"

I jump at the unfamiliar voice and release the curtain, whirling around. My gaze lands on two blondes in black dresses. I recognize one of them from when I was chained to the chandelier. The other woman I haven't met yet, but both of their scarves are dark red.

Griff certainly keeps busy.

One of them quirks their brow, and I shake my head. "No. I was looking for Aubrey, actually."

"She's tied up at the moment."

I find myself wondering if they're speaking literally or figuratively, but decide not to ask. "Okay. I'll just . . ." I start to step around them, but they both frown, so I stop and point to the bandage on my left foot. "Needed a new bandage. It's not a big deal. I can find one myself."

The girl I'd never seen until now leans down for a closer look. "Is it a cut?"

"A burn."

Her eyes brighten. "Oh, yes." She lifts the hem of her dress and points proudly to a scar on the back of her thigh. "Easy to get carried away, isn't it?" She winks, and I smile and nod because I don't know what else to do. She lets out an easy laugh and gestures behind her. "Go back through the ladies' quarters, to the spa. You'll find some extras stored in the supply cabinets."

"Thanks."

Leaving them in the lobby, I make my way back to the endless halls, but I have no intention of returning to the ladies' quarters until I see what's on the second floor, besides Raife's office. I reach the staircase and lift my foot when a cracked door a few rooms down catches my eye. Chewing on the inside of my cheek, I contemplate. It's possible someone is in that room, which is why the door was left slightly ajar. If that's the case, I could be sent back to my bedroom before I find out what else is upstairs.

Then again, there's a chance no one's there. It's not often a room is left open in this house, and with my luck, all I'll find upstairs are locked doors.

Decision made, I turn and head toward it. When I reach the room and hear only silence, I nudge the door open with my elbow and the pitch-black entrance envelopes me.

A scream catches in my throat when my next footstep swipes through the empty air, and I go tumbling forward. My full weight crashes into something solid. Large hands lock around my waist, and I'm lifted off the ground. Finally I can see again when I'm back in the hallway and released so I'm standing on my own two feet. A burst of air rushes from my lungs, and I look up to see who caught me.

"Lost?" Adam's voice is low, calm, as usual, but his eyes are a full blown midnight storm when I meet his gaze. My attention wanders on its own when I take in the tension coiled in his stiff shoulders, his tousled hair reminding me of when I ran my hands through it.

A tremor rolls between my thighs, and I swallow. Hard.

"Sorry. I was looking for the, um"—I point awkwardly at my foot—"for a bandage."

His gaze flicks down. Then he drags it up my bare legs, past the edge of my skimpy nighty, and lets it drift up my curves before landing on my lips. "In the basement," he says dryly.

The basement? My eyes narrow on the now-closed door behind Adam. Of course. That isn't a room; it's a staircase. I return my attention to his and almost shrink back at his dark expression. "I was trying to find the spa."

A muscle ticks beneath his stubble. "Of course you were."

Warm fingers grip my scarf, and I gasp as I'm tugged forward. I trot behind Adam's long footsteps, my heart thumping against my ribcage as I trip over my own feet, up the stairs and down another hallway.

"Wh—where are you taki—"

He storms inside another room with me at his heels. Stopping once we reach the desk, he pushes a button on the phone but doesn't release my scarf. The heat of his skin sears my neck, and I inhale a sharp breath.

"Yes, Mr. Matthews?" Stella's voice rings through the speaker.

"Bring me a black scarf. Then have Emmy's things moved to my room."

All the air is sucked from my lungs. *What did he just say?*

"But, sir, our guidelines state that all secretaries are to room in the ladies' quar—"

"The guidelines just changed. Now bring me her scarf."

There's a pause, then, "Right away."

The line goes dead, and Adam finally releases me, but he doesn't look at me. He turns away and swipes his palm over his mouth, then yanks the collar around his neck until it opens up. I watch as he takes a breath, the muscles in his back and shoulders tensing, then he slowly exhales and faces me.

He dips his hands in his pockets and sits back against the desk, watching me closely. "From now on, you'll go where I tell you to go. You'll report to me and only me. You'll address me however you want, I don't fucking care, but you do not, under any circumstance, call me Master." Something flashes in his eyes, and my breath shortens with the beat of my heart. "Do you understand?"

My throat goes dry. I wet my lips with my tongue and nod. "I understand."

I wish my voice was strong, but it's just as weak as the rest of me.

If there ever was a time not to be fragile, this is it.

chapter nineteen

"I can resist everything except temptation."
—Oscar Wilde, Lady Windermere's Fan

Emmy

SILENCE SETTLES BETWEEN US. IT'S SO QUIET THE RAPID BEATING OF MY heart thrums in my ears. A heavy current of tension wafts in the air, his gaze unflinching as I reach up and slowly untie the golden scarf. The knot comes undone, and I let the silk slip down my arm to the floor.

He tracks every move I make.

Stella's heels click from behind as she enters the room then appears right in front of me. With a warm smile, she starts to wrap a black scarf around my neck.

Adam pushes off the desk and takes a step toward me. She glances at him, her hands going still.

"I'll take it from here."

"Of course." Without another word, she hands him the scarf, gives us both a small nod, and exits the office.

He studies me for a moment, my heart skipping a beat at the way his eyes trail, lazy and hot, over my face. He takes a step closer, then another. I hold my breath when the heat radiating off his body touches me. He stops, his chest inches from my face, and I feel myself shrink as the full scope of our height difference sinks in. Tonight's the first time I've stood before him without my heels on, and his tall, broad frame threatens to crush all 5' 2" of me with a single move.

My gaze crawls up, up, until I meet his eyes. They're narrowed on me, darkening with every second that ticks by.

Slowly, he brings the scarf to my neck. My skin prickles with awareness as warm fingers and smooth silk graze my throat, leaving a trail of addictive heat everywhere his hands touch. A shiver rolls through me, my eyes threatening to flutter shut. His jaw ticks as he watches my expression. With a rough pull against my skin, he ties the scarf into a knot on my left side.

He doesn't let go.

"I'm going to ask you this once, Emmy Highland." My heart stills as the dangerous hum in his deep voice travels down my body. His stare burns into me, his hold tightening and the material biting into my neck. "Why are you here?"

My eyes go wide, my lips part. He's caught me off guard, and I have no idea how to respond. There's no way I can tell the truth. A spark gleams in his eyes, like he sees everything I'm thinking, and my insides seize.

My scratchy throat rasps the first response that comes to mind. "To serve you."

He tilts his head and takes one final step toward me, his shoes touching my toes. "And *why* are you here to serve me?" His voice is quiet, even patient. Such a contrast to the fiery look in his eyes.

I run my tongue along my bottom lip, my lungs tightening as though his body is stealing my breath. "Because I want to," I whisper. "I want to serve you."

Butterflies whirl inside my stomach as my response fills the quiet office. Right now, with his lips so close I can almost taste them, my words ring with too much honesty.

Adam's gaze darts to my lips, lingering for a beat before he intently scans every inch of my face—searching. Heat floods my skin with each second spent under his scrutiny. I wonder what he thinks he'll find. More than that, I wonder what he already has.

He breaks away, and I almost stumble forward at the sudden absence in the air. His eyes never once leave mine while he leans against the corner of the desk.

I rub my palms against my nighty as I watch him slowly, meticulously, scrub the side of his jaw, his thumb tracing the curve of his lips.

"Leave." The growl makes my toes curl.

"But—"

"Aubrey should be back in the spa now. She'll get you a new"—his gaze flicks to my foot, burning straight through the wound and putting my lie on display—"bandage . . . and show you to my room." A swallow sticks in my throat. "Stay there until you're told otherwise."

When my feet remain frozen against the marble, his brow quirks, and he adds, "Unless you'd rather spend the night with Griff?"

Just like that, my muscles thaw and I'm walking backwards. "Yes, Mast—"

A warning glare and twitch in his jaw stops me short.

"Sir." Spinning around, I release an unsteady breath and wonder how the hell I got myself into this.

chapter twenty

"People don't like it when the flame becomes a wildfire. Fuck them. Burn anyway."
—Erin Van Vuren

Adam

"Hang up the phone."

Raife's eyes brighten when he glances at me. The shithead. He grins and waves me over, cell phone still pressed to his ear and feet kicked up on his desk. I stroll toward him, snatch the phone, end the call, then toss it back.

"Okay, that was a little rude." He lowers his feet to the ground and sits up to slip the phone into his pocket. "That could have been a client."

"It wasn't."

"It could have been."

I sit across from him and relax into the seat, contemplating.

Raife runs our business front. The first dime the four of us ever claimed as a group was from *Misha*, the underground name that now motivates everything we do. It took years, a shitload of trial and error, and hard-as-fuck work for us to become the well-oiled machine we are now. But early on following Katerina's death, Felix worked out how to infiltrate some of her offshore accounts and make her profits ours—under our new names once we'd reinvented ourselves.

Over time, we learned to repeat the process with all the kills on our list. If they made so much as a penny off the shit Katerina, Hugo, and Murphy executed, it's guaranteed to become ours, eventually.

Of course, there's no goddamn way I'm going to live, eat, and sleep off the money that's behind our black souls—hence our front: Matthews House, Inc. Selling cryptocurrency allows us to stay behind the scenes, working online or through Skype, and with three of the branches we developed now topping cryptocurrencies worldwide, it funds our real agenda.

Which is my forte.

Raife is the face of Matthews House, Inc. while I focus on our list, and for the most part, it works—me staying in the shadows. I'm not exactly social.

"They want in," Raife says on a pleased sigh.

"Which account?" I check my watch, then swipe a hand over my mouth, wondering if Emmy is in my room by now.

On my bed.

In my sheets.

"Silver Jack. But I have a feeling that's not what you came by to discuss." I grit my teeth. Raife smirks and folds his hands on the desk. "Hoping I have more *deals* to offer?"

Resting my ankle over my opposite knee, I look him straight in the eye. "She's mine now, Raife."

His eyes flicker with triumph. "Is that righ—"

"Cut the shit. Stella would've informed you by now."

His grin widens in response.

"I came to tell you myself"—I lean forward, ensuring he can read the severity of my expression—"so I could personally see that you understand when I tell you not to fucking touch her."

"Well, now that just doesn't seem fair to the poor girl." His voice drips with amusement. "We both know you won't touch her. You're going to force her to be deprived just because you are?"

Tension pulls my muscles tight, and my fingers rap against the leather armrest. "If I'm not mistaken, I'm the only reason she *isn't* deprived right now."

Raife inches forward so we're level. "Yes, and how was that for you? When she came apart on your hands." Blood rushes to my veins, hot flames dancing beneath my skin as my adrenaline spikes. Raife cocks his head. "Careful with her, little brother, or your precious *control* just might snap."

A muscle in my jaw twitches, and I run my fingers across the bottom of my chin.

Raife is the only one who knows firsthand how close I got to Sofia. The way I childishly convinced myself I was some kind of savior, the promises I made to get her out of there, to give her a chance to grow up and have a normal life. Then how her death almost unraveled me completely.

Before I found an outlet through sex and blood.

Seventeen, eighteen, nineteen—they passed in a blur of ecstasy. And my brothers—before they legally became my brothers—were in as deep as I was when it came to women. For Griff and Felix, that was enough for a while.

Me, I needed more.

I needed red.

But I wasn't the only one who discovered a taste for blood all those years ago.

The differences between Raife and I, however, are immense. I may be unhinged, but I'm constantly working to channel my urges. It never stops, the self-restraint, the need for more.

I make no mistakes.

When Raife gets violent, truly violent, there's nothing controlled about it. It's a wildfire in a gasoline-drenched forest. He cost us one mistake with Murphy already, one that would have ended everything if it weren't for Felix's talents.

I won't risk another slip. Not when I'm so close to ensuring every single person on our list gets what they deserve.

I sit back against the leather, letting out a breath of dry amusement. "You know you can't go back, Raife. None of us can."

Finally, he drops his smile. Black oil eats up his brown eyes. "No, I can't. Just like you can't move forward. You are who you are. *Lucas*." I narrow my gaze at his, but otherwise keep my expression slack. "We all are."

After a second, he opens the drawer to his right and pulls out papers. Then he tosses them into the bin beside him, watching, waiting for my reaction. I know full well it's the document Felix and I drew up this morning. The same document he made a fucking deal to read.

I work my jaw, the only sign of agitation I'll allow myself to reveal.

"Once upon a time," he continues, "you wouldn't have given a shit about my method for madness, so long as I was mad. Remember yourself, Lucas. We were real brothers once, before our empire. Two boys who saw each other for what we were and never had to, never *wanted* to, hide it. You will eventually lose control, and when you do—when you lose every last shred of it until you can't see red from black, right from wrong—I will be here. Ready to back you up, the way you should be doing for me." He leans closer, and my gaze threatens to burn straight through his skin. "Because that's what brothers fucking do."

Carefully redoing the buttons on my collar, I stand. I watch him for a second, taking in the anger simmering behind his words. The mad glint in his eyes that we share.

I lean forward and rest my palms on the desk. "Don't mistake our brotherhood for weakness. I'm the same person I was when we first got out. The difference is that back then, I was a boy who dealt with guilt by giving into every temptation. Shortsighted, unprepared. Uncommitted. I evolved into a man a long time ago." After pushing off the desk, I shove my hands into my pockets and tip my chin back. "I suggest you do the same."

He stands, but I'm already turning away. I don't have time for his shit. We have lives to ruin, and time's a wastin'.

"It's only a matter of time before she gets to you, my friend," he calls as I walk out the door. "And I'll be watching every step of the way."

chapter twenty-one

*"Because, little one, you are not allowed to let go.
The best of us hurt the most."*
—Erin Van Vuren

Adam

(Fourteen years old)

Pink. Blue. Pink. White.

Jesus.

How many pillows does one little kid need?

My ass is sore from sitting in the same position on the cement for so long, one leg bent with my right arm draped over it. But Katerina's got another interview going, and I'd rather watch her tiny clone stack pillows than listen to that woman's voice for another second.

Sofia walks to her cot, picks up her final pillow—pink again—and drags it across the cement, then puts it against the iron bars with the others. I scratch my chin, wondering what the hell she's doing, when she sits on the ground right behind them.

Squinting, I glance from her to the work table next to us then back again. She made a fucking wall. I mean, the thing is small—five pillows can only get so tall—but for a five or six-year-old, it's legit. Blocks the work table from her view perfectly.

She's been here long enough to sense when an interview is coming to a close.

And we all know what comes next.

Blowing out a breath, I rest my head against the wall. It's been months, and the little girl still hasn't said a word to anyone. But I've learned a lot from spending every day and night across from her. She has exactly three dresses, all white, all ragged with small holes, sometimes strings hanging at the bottom. Her bare feet are dirty, like the rest of ours, and her hair is stringy, due for a bath.

At least I assume she gets a bath.

The rest of us get a five-minute hose down once a month—or those of us who last long enough for it, anyway—but Sofia disappears for half a day each month and always comes back clean.

The clanking of metal snaps my head to the right. The burly, bald guy who does our hose downs is here, unchaining the tear-streaked teen from the work table.

"Wh-what . . . y-you're letting me go?" The girl's shaky voice is so hopeful it rips straight through my chest.

She's got no clue.

Katerina runs a hand down the girl's skinny arm. "Oh, darling. Our energies just aren't matching up quite right. It's my duty as your storyteller to ensure we're inspiring each other, understand? I'm having trouble getting that connection from you." She takes a breath and smiles reassuringly. "We have other, more fitting, opportunities for someone as pretty as yourself."

A shriek leaves the girl's mouth, but Baldy clamps a hand over her lips and drags her toward the exit.

Katerina stops him at the door. "Send her to Murphy for redistributing, and bring me another crate. Perhaps a boy?

Someone with enough fire to pull me out of this horrid slump and get our backlogged orders filled."

The door closes, and the room falls still.

My pulse ticks faster, my breath strained, when she turns to Sofia. These aren't feelings I was used to dealing with in the real world—unease, anxiety, helplessness. I've been on my own since I was eight, when my mom disappeared while I was out stealing our next meal, and before that we lived together on the streets. I caught on real quick. Emotions, good and bad, get you nowhere—if you're lucky. Killed, if you're not. Trust no one but yourself, care for no one but yourself.

Simple.

Even in this room, with strangers' screams and bright lights constantly beating against my head—the others in the crates next door aren't so different from me: self-taught to look after themselves. To survive.

We're more adult than any of the 'real' adults here.

Sofia, though, she's not like us. She's too young. Too innocent. Pure enough to be molded.

My knuckles curl as Katerina walks to Sofia's cage. She unlocks it, then sits on her haunches and tilts her head. "Baby, how many times do I have to tell you?" She reaches forward, grabbing each pillow one by one and placing them outside the bars. "This is good for you. Death is a thing of beauty, and it needs to be executed in such a way that does it justice."

Sofia swallows, but it's the only sound she makes.

"You will understand when you're older, working at a table of your own." Katerina points her index finger and taps her daughter's nose playfully, and it makes me sick to my stomach. Like she thinks she's Mom of the Year or something.

She stands and grabs her purse from beside the table then returns to Sofia. My nostrils flare when she pulls out the cuffs for the second time this week, and Sofia's little body stiffens. Katerina wastes no time looping the things around one of the bars and then her daughter's wrists.

My growl comes out quiet. Katerina's head jerks to me.

"What?" I snarl quietly from my spot on the ground, my eyes locked on hers. "Having your own kid in a cage isn't abusive enough for you?"

Katerina's eyes spark with something—interest?—and she turns back to her daughter. She gives her a peck on the cheek. "You'll thank me for this later, baby girl, once you've come into your own."

After a second, she pushes off the ground, locks the cage, and strolls toward me. She stops a foot away and pulls her notepad from the front pocket of her black dress, then flicks glances from me to the pad as she jots something down.

I narrow my eyes. From Mom of the Year to Certified Psychologist.

"This is a real breakthrough, you know," she murmurs. The scratching of a pen against paper nags at my ears. "I've been watching you with her, and I think we're really getting somewhere." Finally, the scrawling stops. She sets her blue eyes on me, and when they soften, it creeps me the hell out. "My pretty pet. I knew I was right about you. There's something genuine here. Vulnerability. Passion."

Gritting my teeth, I break my gaze to stare at the blank wall to my left. She's poison, and so are her words. She doesn't know shit about me. She never will.

The door to the studio creaks open, and I keep my gaze on the wall but follow her movements out of the corner of my eye. A thump hits the ground as a new crate's lowered off the forklift, then Baldy unlocks it.

Same routine every time.

"Hello, there," Katerina says sweetly. "Where's your name card?"

"There isn't one," Baldy grunts. "Been on the streets since he was practically in diapers. No one knows his name. Not even him."

"Is that so?" She's quiet for a moment. "Approximate age?"

"Eh, this one? Fifteen, maybe."

"*This one* is sixteen."

My gaze snaps to the new guy. He's skinny, dirty, like the rest of us. His blond hair looks almost brown, his cheekbones are sunken, his nose pointy. He's still sitting in the crate, peering through the wiry bars, which is weird, because most of them jump out the second it's opened. Weirder still, he looks as casual as I do—leaning back, almost relaxed.

Who the hell is this guy?

"Watch your goddamn—"

"Hush, Mikey." Katerina lowers a hand to the guy, and he takes it, letting her pull him to his feet. She cocks her head. "Not a shy one, are you?"

His eyebrow quirks, and he glances around the room. His gaze lands on the work table. The restraints. The silver tray holding a single needle. "Not so shy yourself."

My lips twitch, but when Katerina chuckles, the unnerving sound wipes my expression clean. "Strap him in," she instructs.

I watch with rapt attention as the guy voluntarily walks to the table, hops on, then lays back and folds his palms behind his head.

This is a first.

When Baldy and Katerina stare at him blankly, he looks up. "Well?"

Katerina's mouth curves, and she snatches up her notepad again. With her gaze and her pen locked on the paper, she mutters, "You heard the boy."

After buckling the restraints without facing a hint of a struggle, Baldy scratches his scalp and turns to leave.

"Hey," Katerina calls, "bring me a chair, won't you?" Her gaze drifts back to the table. "I have a feeling this one might put me through some hoops."

The new guy, staring straight up at the ceiling, grins—fucking *grins*.

I get the feeling a few hoop tricks is the least of what Katerina has to look forward to.

chapter twenty-two

"All the hardest, coldest people you meet were once as soft as water. And that's the tragedy of living."
—Iain Thomas

Emmy

"THIS WILL BE YOUR CLOSET FOR NOW, OKAY?" STELLA ASKS AS SHE hangs the final dress in the smaller of two closets. My stomach tightens at the simple question.

My closet. In *his* room.

I let out a breath and nod.

When I went to find Aubrey in the spa, Stella had been down there too, and she insisted on showing me to Adam's room herself. As it turns out, the brothers' quarters are on the main floor like ours, except they're on the east end.

"Well, then." She slides the closet shut before turning to me, clasping her hands in a way that reminds me of Raife. "I'll leave you to it. If there's anything you need, let me or Aubrey know. All right?"

"Okay."

After she exits, she pokes her head back inside. "And remember, you've had a big day. It's important to get your beauty sleep." She pauses. "That is, if he lets you." Before I have time to respond, she gives a little wave and disappears behind the door.

With my feet stuck to the floor, I gulp as her words echo in my head.

If he lets you.

Adam Matthews, I am officially his.

To serve.

To please.

To be at his mercy.

I bite my lip as I wonder . . . *what will it be like?* Thoughts of earlier today come rushing back—his gaze burning mine, his warm body beneath my palms, strong hand working between my thighs.

Icy guilt stabs me when a heat wave floods my body. I shouldn't feel the way I do. I shouldn't be interested in anything other than finding Frankie. But knowing that isn't enough to make it stop.

I want Adam.

Not just his hand, not just his body; a craving, new and unfamiliar, is gnawing deep within my core for *him*—his shadows and his secrets, the hidden caves inside his mind.

It's twisted, and it's sinful, and it's everything Mama says I am.

My eyes squeeze shut, trying to block out the scolding voice I always hear.

I just need a closer look. A deeper taste. A little touch.

My eyes snap open.

With a shaky exhale and sweaty palms, I walk backwards toward the bed, *Adam's* bed, jumping when the backs of my knees brush its coldness.

I'm supposed to be here for Frankie.

Not for my own dark temptations.

I wipe my palms on my nighty and finally let my gaze absorb my surroundings. The room is slightly bigger than the one I was given, but it's still modest for a mansion. It smells of fresh linens with a hint of his aftershave. A large black rug sprawls across the white tiles, and a single rectangular dresser sits along the wall beside the bathroom.

I flick my gaze from corner to corner, looking for any personal touches, but there are none. A splash of black fabric dangling off the side of the laundry hamper is the only sign someone lives here.

Slowly, I turn and glance at the bed stretched out before me. It's big enough to fit at least six people. The differences between this place and my trailer greet me at every turn, and I don't think I'll ever get used to it. The color scheme, though, I could get used to. Reaching forward, I run my fingers along the cool, smooth material of the comforter. It's cold, just like the rest of the room, and perfectly made, not a wrinkle nor crease in sight.

My eyelids are heavy as exhaustion rolls through me.

Stella was right. I've had a long twenty-four hours, and standing in this silent, dark room, I'm beginning to feel every minute again. I let out a breath and look toward the door. There's no way to tell how long it will be before he arrives.

I wonder what's expected of me. Am I supposed to wait for him before I lie down? Do I draw a bath, undress, light candles? I shake my head. None of those things feel right for a man like Adam.

Not that I've known any men like Adam.

After a moment, I wander to the closets and peek inside the smaller one first, not really looking at the dresses or lingerie before my eyes. I'm stalling, my nerves tight, trying to build the courage to open his. I don't know why it feels so wrong to snoop around his personal space when I didn't think twice about the rest of the house, and yet it's there—an undercurrent of uncertainty, danger, even a twinge of fear.

But it has to be done. None of the other brothers have let me get this close. If there's any chance I might discover something to help me find Frankie, I have to know.

Inhaling sharply, I close my closet and open the one beside it. Rows of pressed, black button-downs and crisp pants line the racks. Three polished pairs of shoes sit on an oversized shelf meant to store at least ten times that many.

Nothing else.

Chewing my lip, I work my way to the dresser and flit through the drawers. A wave of surprise runs through me when I see actual, normal clothes. Not entirely normal—no jeans or T-shirts—but there are immaculately folded undershirts, boxers, and sweatpants. Hesitantly, I trace a finger along one of the pairs of pants, careful not to cause a crease.

Does he actually wear these? I can't picture it at all.

When the bathroom turns out to be as useless as the rest of the space, I remove my contacts then pad across the room, sinking exhaustedly onto the bed. It doesn't feel as strange as I thought it would, being in his bed, although there's nothing to give away that it *is* his bed. The whole room feels distant, clinical. Nothing to offer an ounce of insight into the seductive darkness I sense within him.

I try to stay awake, keeping the light on so I won't fall asleep before he gets here. But soon my eyelids flutter shut, and I drift away.

chapter twenty-three

"Sometimes we reveal ourselves when we are least like ourselves."
—Anais Nin

Adam

My fists tighten, pumping once, twice, at my sides as I pace up the stairs and down the hall. My adrenaline is still going haywire, but it's a vast improvement from last night—when I'd stood outside my bedroom door, knowing who was on the other side. Images of her on my bed, under my covers, turning my blood hot and tempting me to twist the knob.

But I didn't.

I couldn't.

So I called Griff and had him do an impromptu pickup. He wasn't exactly thrilled—the moans in the background made it clear why—but when I told him who was up on the list, it was enough to shift his perspective.

It was a long time coming for Baldy, anyway.

We prepped to pick him up weeks ago, but plans changed when Frederick Fergusson popped up on the grid again. I wasn't surprised to find Frederick became an elementary school bus driver. Not a big stretch from having been Misha's transporter all those years ago, picking up street kids and delivering them to the storage room. They really need to do better background checks.

I reach my door and swing it open, stopping in my tracks when I spot Emmy asleep in my bed, a thin sheet the only thing covering her small frame. I grit my jaw, double-check the time on my watch. Nine o'clock. She's supposed to be in the dining room by now—the only fucking reason I chose precisely this time to enter my room.

Shoving my hands in my pockets, I'm reminded of the dried blood caked under my fingernails. I need my room to myself, and I need a goddamn shower. The sink in the basement only cleans so much.

With a growl, I make my way to the bathroom, lock the door, and ignore the nearly naked woman on the other side of the wall. I take my time washing up and shaving, being intentionally loud enough to wake her. She has plenty of time to get dressed and slip out before I finish.

Once I'm done, I wrap a towel low around my hips and open the door. Emmy is awake, barely, and sitting up on my bed. Her eyelids are heavy from sleep, her hair is a mess from her scalp to her waist, and her little nighty is bunched up at her thighs.

My cock stirs to life on its own, straining against the towel, and the fact only pisses me off more. My shoulders pull tight when she shifts and parts her lips, her sleep-ridden gaze drifting downward.

My eyes turn to slits.

I had a lot of time to think during my therapy session last night.

After more than a decade of being a slave to my demons, I'm damn close to ridding the world of Misha completely. Too close to let trivial temptations like women fuck with my head.

Raife might think Emmy Highland is different—my cock certainly agrees—but in reality, she's just another woman. A woman who pulled our number out of thin air and who I caught sneaking around my house. A woman who apparently has an agenda of her own—which is the only reason I'm risking keeping her this close.

Anything else is just a distraction. A distraction I have no interest in wasting any more of my attention on. Raife can do that on his own.

"Get up."

She starts at my rough voice, but soon she's stumbling from the bed, tripping on the tangled sheet and barely managing to right herself.

I flick my gaze to her closet. Her very *temporary* closet.

She gets the point. After grabbing what she needs for the day, she hugs the items to her chest and slowly glances up at me below long lashes.

There's the little mouse.

"You have five minutes to shower and dress. Then go to the ladies' quarters, where you'll eat breakfast with the other secretaries at exactly eight-thirty every day from here on out. Aubrey has a list of jobs for you. She'll stay at your side from start to finish, and you won't do anything more than a bathroom break without her beside you." I pause, giving her time to absorb my instructions. "Do you understand?"

She licks her lips and nods. "Yes, sir."

Fuck.

"Four minutes."

Her eyes widen, then she rushes past me and closes the bathroom door behind her. Her floral scent hits my nostrils, and my lungs tighten at the feminine smell lingering in the air.

I've never had a woman in my room. Not even when I've

fucked them.

My eyes drift back to the bed's rumpled sheets. The skimpy lingerie hanging in her closet. A bottle of contact solution sits beside a pair of black-rimmed glasses I've never seen before.

I rub a palm over my freshly shaven jaw, frustration burning inside me and pulling my muscles taut.

I gotta get the hell out of here.

chapter twenty-four

*"Some are Born to sweet delight.
Some are Born to Endless Night."*
—William Blake

Emmy

A LOW WHISTLE SOUNDS WHEN I ENTER THE DINING ROOM. AUBREY SITS alone at the table, one leg crossed over the other and her red hair spilling down one shoulder. Her head tilts as she looks me up and down. "Going for a carefree look today, huh?"

"Sorry," I mutter, ignoring the sting at my ankle as my burn flares to life. She pushes a full plate of food toward me once I sit beside her. "Woke up late."

Her lips quirk. "I noticed. The other girls finished their breakfast almost twenty minutes ago."

I push the scrambled eggs around my plate with a fork, Adam's naked, dripping torso still taunting me. His white towel hung low on his hips, letting me glimpse the hard V-shape disappearing beneath it. I knew he was cut, I felt it yesterday when my palms were pressed against his chest, his abs. But that's not the same as seeing it bare, watching the ripple of muscles tense across his body when he spotted me on his bed.

That alone sent a surge of warm satisfaction through me. And when my eyes dropped lower, it only confirmed that at least a part of him wanted me, too.

But then I'd looked back at his eyes. They were as cold as the room encasing us.

He claimed me.

He owns me.

So why doesn't he take me?

"Big night?"

"Hmm?" I take a bite and glance at her, slowly remembering where I am.

She leans back against the seat, still watching me closely. "You've got that look."

"What look?"

"I call it the Matthews Effect."

I pause mid-chew, my eyebrows shooting up. "The what?"

"Happens to all of us." She winks. "You'll understand soon enough. Now hurry up. We've got a job to do."

The Matthews Effect. Finishing my bite with a swallow, I think of Frankie.

Did she feel it, too?

"What's this?"

"This," Aubrey mutters over my shoulder, her eyes skimming the paper in my hands, "is a list of your daily duties."

My brows furrow while I review the checklist. Dishes, sweeping, mopping, assisting with food prep and cleanup.

It's all housework. And it's all in the kitchen.

I blow out a breath and let my hands fall to my sides, still clutching the page. "Wow."

"Problem?"

"Just . . . not exactly what I was expecting."

Aubrey chuckles and starts walking past the ladies' quarters, me following at her side. "Disappointed?"

"No."

Maybe.

She glances sideways at me. "You don't have to do that." When I stare at her blankly, she adds, "Lie. There's no one judging you here."

I chew the inside of my cheek. I don't think I've ever *not* had someone judge me. Every move I make, every word I say. Every piece I paint.

It was the same for Frankie, growing up with Mama, but it was different for her too. She had nothing to hide. No monsters in her head to keep quiet. Mama still scolded and punished her, even more than me once she realized there was no hope for my soul. But that was just for being a normal teenager—sneaking off to parties, hanging with boys. Things I never did. The noise, the trends, the forced small talk and smiles—I never could get used to it.

Instead, I would keep my head down, burying myself in books and school when I wasn't painting. I graduated at the top of my class, secretly envisioning a future I knew I would never have—like going to college, finding a place I might fit in. But Mama wasn't wrong about me. I know how deep my darkness stems, and I know I'll never be free of it, no matter how far I run.

I was Frankie's weird little sister, a loner—identities I still wear on my sleeve. I liked how effectively they kept people away. I was hot enough to get a one night stand when I needed one—when I went long enough without freeing my mind through art that I inevitably caved in on myself. But I was still weird enough that people otherwise left me alone.

Batshit Crazy Betsy was the rare exception. I think her nickname explains why we got along so well.

Frankie, on the other hand, she always fit in. She may have been restless and always searching for something more, but she was also born knowing exactly who she was.

Why would she have thought she needed a place like this?

"I have to say, though," Aubrey murmurs, pulling me from my thoughts. "Your list has to be the most bland I've seen yet. Not to mention the most particular. They don't usually keep us so limited to one area of the house."

That gets my attention. "Really?" My footsteps slow, and I glance at her out of the corner of my eye. "Did he tell you why mine's different?"

"Who, Adam?" She looks at me and snorts. "No, and I didn't ask. If one of the Matthews gives you something to do, you need to trust there's a good reason for it. Always. Every relationship is built on trust, and the relationship between you and your master is going to be the most important relationship you will have for at least the next year of your life. Probably longer."

Following her into a restaurant-sized kitchen, I fidget with the hem of my dress and think her words over. The next year of my life. I can't believe it's only been a little over two days since I signed the contract. So much has happened since then, and I tense just thinking about what else might be coming. When I first arrived, I thought I'd be able to pull this off in less than a week. That I'd be flying back home with Frankie in the seat beside me, safe and sound, by the weekend. At the very least, that I'd be able to reach her somehow by then.

Now, I'm not so sure.

I don't even know where to take my search anymore. She's clearly not here, in the mansion, or I would have seen or heard from her by now. Loud and bursting with energy, she's one of the most outgoing people I know. There's no way I'd be able to miss her.

Unless she left long ago.

Or something happened to her.

When Aubrey leads me through the kitchen and stops behind a long sink, I turn to her, trying to keep my tone neutral. "A year—that's a pretty long time, right? I mean, to commit yourself to something—*someone*—that you know nothing about? What happens when people change their mind? What about those who want to break their contract?"

"What do you mean?" She frowns. "They leave. They'd be giving up their end of year bonus when they do, but whatever. Their call."

"Just like that? It's that easy?"

"Emma, the Matthews are busy men. They have businesses to run and all kinds of things to keep them on their toes. They just so happen to also have very particular tastes and preferences that few outside these walls would understand. So it's Stella's job to find those who *do* understand and who fit their tastes. It would be counterproductive for everyone to keep someone here against their will."

Folding my arms over my chest, I rub my hands on my sleeves. If Frankie left here willingly, why hasn't she contacted me? We've never gone this long without speaking. We promised each other we never would.

Aubrey takes a step toward me, squinting like she's trying to figure me out. "What, did something happen? Are you reconsidering the terms of your contract?"

I shake my head. "No, I'm not reconsidering anything. I just"—I clear my throat, trying to think up an excuse for my behavior—"it's an adjustment, that's all."

She smirks. "Well, sure. I think anyone Adam Matthews claims would agree. I still can't believe he claimed you." Reaching beside the sink, she pulls out a bin filled with dirty dishes. She gestures to the side counter, which is piled with more plates and silverware. "All right, so I'm under clear orders to stay at your side until I'm told otherwise. Guess we'll be double-teaming these."

I glance from the dishes to Aubrey, who's slipping on a pair of gloves. For some reason, I can't picture her doing anything so mundane in this place. "So . . . is this what you do every day?"

Her lips quirk as she shakes her head. "No. Stella and I handle the Matthews' business related needs." Her eyes drift down to the list in my hand. "I'd get started if I were you. You're done for the day only once everything on your checklist is complete, or when your master summons you. Oh, and"—she twists her lips as she takes in the state of my hair and minimal makeup—"I'll let you finish the dishes first, but then we're making a quick detour to the spa. Our masters are known for making unexpected calls. He could come for you at any time."

Warmth flutters through my stomach at the thought, although the hard look in his eyes earlier makes me doubt he'd ever come for me.

I try to ignore the wave of disappointment that pours over me as I turn on the faucet. "So . . . you'll be staying with me all day?"

"*All* day."

I swallow, wondering how the hell I'm supposed to make any progress with her glued to my side.

This is far too convenient.

Something tells me Adam knows more than I realized.

chapter twenty-five

> *"The dark goddess moves within me;*
> *To me she brings the fruit of the hidden."*
> —Segovia Amil

Emmy

DAY AFTER DAY DRIFTS BY IN THE SAME DISAPPOINTING PATTERN. As promised, Aubrey hasn't left me room to breathe, let alone snoop. She's a dedicated servant, just like the rest of them, which surprises me. There's nothing about her that screams *follower*, not the same way I see it with Stella and the others I've met. She's a free spirit with a will of her own, much like my sister, although their similarities end there.

I'm a long way from figuring out the people of the Matthews House.

My duties keep me stuck in the kitchen. The most excitement I had all week was walking in on Griff in the pantry with his pants unzipped and a secretary on her knees, but even that was a letdown. After his behavior in the Dark Room, I expected more from him.

I'm in the same boat I was in when I first arrived a week ago. Each day I'm dismissed, Aubrey walks me to Adam's room. And each day, I intentionally keep our pace slow, soaking in every detail of my surroundings and tracking each camera we pass.

There's no way to sneak upstairs without being recorded, let alone the basement—which is where I've been aching to go. Sometimes I toy with the idea of trying to get away with it anyway.

What's there to lose?

Still, I haven't risked it yet. Each night I go to Adam's room only to find it empty, cold, still. It's lonelier than I thought it'd be. Lonelier than my assigned room in the ladies' quarters. Because now, there are always these kindling sparks of hope, anticipation, and danger building throughout the day that maybe he'll be waiting for me.

That maybe he'll want to see me.

Really see me.

Then I remember who I am, and that no one wants to see the parts of me I try so hard to hide. It's a plain fact, not something I pity.

Frankie loves me, and she's always encouraged me to use art as an outlet. But even she won't look at my paintings. And if she did, she wouldn't see what I do anyway.

Someone like Frankie would never truly see me. She could stare straight at my soul spattered across the canvas. She could tilt it for better lighting. But all she'd ever be is standing at the edge of the cliff, never feeling the dive, let alone the impact of the drop. And if it really came down to it, I don't think she'd want to feel it either.

There's a difference between loving someone as they are whole, and wanting to see all of their pieces. I've understood this for a while now, and I don't fault anyone for it.

I've sought approval from Mama all my life. I've sought

love and companionship from Frankie. I've sought pleasure and a few moments of pure release from art and men.

But I stopped searching for someone to really look at *me* a long time ago.

Although I have to admit: here, in a place where everyone around me is quite possibly as damnable as I am—some even more so—witnessing my own master, the one man whose essence tastes like mine, avoid my presence leaves a bitter sting of rejection in my chest.

Tonight, when we reach Adam's room, Aubrey is on a call so she mouths, "Goodbye," as I slip inside.

It's not until I'm on the other side of his closed door, staring into the vacant room, that the fresh disappointment sinks in, settling right beside the rejection.

I undress, take a long shower, and change into a nighty, just as I do every evening. An hour later as I lie on his bed, with thoughts swarming in my head and keeping me awake, the rejection twists into frustration. It bubbles for a while then seeps into my veins.

He's my *master*.

He claimed *me*.

He won't allow me to serve him, even look at him, yet he keeps me so secluded I can't serve or see anyone else either. Which means I can't get any closer to figuring this place, or these brothers, out.

I can't do another week of this—getting nowhere. I didn't come here to clean kitchens.

Exhaling, I finally close my eyes for the night. Energy hums through my body, somehow riling me up and calming me at the same time. The rational part of my mind remembers what I came here to do. But as the anticipation builds inside me until my stomach tightens, the lines become too blurred to recognize what's what.

    I fall asleep with one thought on my mind.
    Adam Matthews wanted a servant.
    That's what he's going to get.

chapter
twenty-six

"The conversation between your fingers and someone else's skin. This is the most important discussion you can ever have."
—Iain Thomas

Adam

FUCK, I'M EXHAUSTED. I'M ALREADY UNBUTTONING MY SHIRT BEFORE I reach my room.

Among planning my hit on Murphy, prepping our next pickup, and avoiding Emmy Highland, I've been consumed. My blood is on overtime pumping through my veins, and the pressure mounting behind my eyes is barely being held together by a thread.

I'm past due for a kill, and my body sure as shit knows it.

Doesn't help that I've gone over a week with hardly any sleep, thanks to a little mouse occupying my bed. I never did figure out what the hell she was up to when I caught her trying to sneak into the basement last week, but it no longer matters. Aubrey reports that she's been good, no shady shit, so I'm having her moved back to her old room by the end of the day.

I push the door open and stroll across the room, tossing my phone on the dresser and pressing my forefingers and thumb to my temples. Sometimes I think the pressure is thick enough to cut with a knife. I doubt a few hours of sleep will make a difference, but I can't get any shut-eye in the guest room. The pent-up energy coursing through me is threatening to make me do something—or someone—I'll regret if I don't shut it the fuck down.

I resume undoing my shirt when a movement to my left stills me. I glance over to find Emmy standing in the middle of my goddamn room. Her hair is bunched to one side and cascading down her waist. A silk slip hangs on her curves, barely reaching the tops of her smooth, porcelain thighs.

Tension squeezes my muscles to the point it's painful. I grit my jaw, my eyes narrowing on hers because if I let them wander lower, she'll discover firsthand the reason I abstain.

"Did I fail to make your schedule clear?"

She shakes her head and starts to approach me. My expression must make her rethink because she stops and retreats a step.

"Then *why* are you standing in front of me at nine-thirty in the morning? And why the fuck didn't I already know about it?" I snatch up my phone, ready to chew Aubrey out, when five missed texts highlight the screen.

Aubrey: Little situation with your claim, Master.
Aubrey: She won't leave your room.
Aubrey: As in, she is standing in your room.
Aubrey: I really hope you get this.
Aubrey: Testing one, two, three . . .

My fingers squeeze the phone before I set it back down. Then I fix my glare on the mouse instead.

She swallows, juts out her chin, and murmurs, "I'm here to serve you."

Fucking Jesus.

Heat flares under the surface of my skin. Scrubbing a hand

over my face, I turn back to my dresser, fighting to keep my movements controlled as I pull the middle drawer open.

"Believe me, you are serving me by staying in the kitchen. Now leave."

"No."

Slowly, I turn back to her. "What was that?"

She clears her throat, but her fiery expression doesn't waver. "No, *sir*."

My blood runs hot, her words waking my cock without my permission.

She carefully moves forward. "I'm here to serve *you*, and right now"—closing the distance between us, she reaches toward me. When her fingers touch the partially undone buttons of my shirt, brushing bare skin in the process, I tense—"you look like you could use me."

She undoes a button, then her fingers drift lower and she works on the next. I should tell her to get the hell out. Reassign her to one of my brothers. But having her this close, her exhales teasing my skin, her floral scent flooding my nostrils, black hair close enough to fist—it's fucking with my sleep-deprived head.

"Don't test me, mouse," I growl softly. "You know a lot less than you think."

Her fingers tremble against me as she moves down a button, and she lifts her blue eyes to meet my tired ones. "That makes two of us," she whispers.

I flick my gaze between her eyes for a second. When I pull back, her hold tightens on my shirt, and I snatch her small wrists in my grip with a snarl. She shouldn't be this damn close to me right now.

"I get it, okay?" She looks up at me with a soft fire in her eyes. My gaze narrows, registering the quiver in her voice. Both sides of her at once, the mouse and the lion, and I hate both of them for the way they set me off. "You need to rest. That's fine. Just stay still for me so I can help." After a moment, she adds a rushed, "Sir."

Slowly, I release my grip, then shove my hands in my pockets, where they can't touch her.

Her eyes scan my face. "Thank you."

She finishes with the last button and starts loosening my cuffs. The relief in her voice makes my jaw tick. I'm many things, but selfless isn't one of them. She should know better—if she doesn't, she'll learn soon enough.

When she dips her hands beneath the opening of my shirt, pressing her soft palms against my abs, every muscle in my body pulls tight. She slowly slides them up until the shirt slips from my shoulders. It sticks, my hands in my pockets keeping it from dropping fully, and she goes for my belt.

I stop her midway by a fist in her hair. She freezes. I sweep my hand around to her upper throat and force her to look at me.

"Step. Back."

A swallow moves beneath my palm, and I drop my arm. When she backs up, I let the shirt fall to the floor, yank a pair of sweats from the open drawer, and disappear into the bathroom. Fuck. My body feels like a damn furnace. I change swiftly, tucking my knife into a drawer for good measure, and pull open the door.

Emmy's staring at me like she's never seen a man in sweats. Her jaw is dropped, her eyes raking over my torso like she wants to lick me. My cock twitches at the image.

Running my thumb down the side of my cheek, I shake my head and stroll to my bed. She's still staring at me when I pull down the covers and drop on my back, finally shutting my eyes and covering them with a forearm.

After another second of feeling her watching me, I mutter,

"Go." Not that I'll be able to sleep now with my dick hard as stone.

I sense her moving and open my eyes, keeping them partially shielded with my arm. Following her movements as she makes her way toward me, I grit my teeth. Every step she takes fuels the blood coursing through my veins. She tugs at the blanket at the foot of the bed, then gently pulls it up and over me. Discomfort fills my gut. What the hell is this?

When she turns to leave, the bottom of her slip snags on the bed frame, revealing a tight, round ass and tiny G-string.

Shit.

My throat tightens, my skin burns, and the energy pulsing through my veins spikes so fast my vision blurs.

I blink, and she's tugging at the snag.

Another blink, and she's twisting around, her bare, plump ass facing me head on.

Another blink, and my hand is wrapped around her throat, pulling her slowly toward me and onto the bed. I never claimed to be a predator, but right now she's certainly the prey.

chapter
twenty-seven

"Love me like my demons do."
—Akif Kichloo

Adam

Somewhere between the lust drowning my sanity and my black soul clawing to get out, I flipped her onto her stomach. While I hover over her, my grip pins her wrists above her head as I roughly drag my free hand up the back of her soft thigh, then the curve of her ass.

A deep shiver quakes her little body, and I squeeze. I'm unrelenting, filling my palm with as much of her as I can get. My fingertips bite into her skin, but, instead of tensing in fear, she lets out a breathy moan that makes my pulse pound in my ears.

When she grinds her ass against my cock, my entire body constricts, my lungs close in, and fuck, it's been so long—I need to *breathe*.

I need *her*.

Dropping my forehead to her hair, I lift her slip as high as it will go and trail my nose down her spine. I suck in a mix of flowers and clean sweat, then part my lips, pressing them barely against her so my exhales warm her back. She trembles beneath me. I release her wrists as I prowl down her body.

The sweet scent between her legs hits me, and my nostrils flare. I yank the thong off her, and when she tries to turn to look at me, I crush a hand against her back to keep her still. Her breaths come out in pants as she squirms.

Pulling her ass up so she's on her knees—her back dipped and her cheek still pressed against the pillow—I spread her legs and lower my face. My stubble brushes the insides of her thighs, and she groans.

Right now, she *is* my oxygen.

I suck in another lungful of her scent, breathing in her need for me, and my fingers bite into her thighs as the primitive urge to taste her consumes me. I drag my tongue across her slit, from one end to the other, holding her still when she jerks, then I go back for more. Opening my mouth, I suck and pull and lap up her juices, barely registering her mewls beyond the ringing in my ears. It's been so long since I've tasted pussy, and fuck, she tastes so good.

Her fingers find my hair, and she bucks against my face. A snarl rumbles through me as I pull back to bite the inside of her thigh—hard enough to break skin.

"Fuck," she moans, ready to rub against me again when I stop—frozen.

A drip of red leaks from the bite mark on her thigh. Crimson on porcelain, a magnetic contrast that pulls a hypnotic rhythm from my pulse. A dangerous thrumming stirs inside me. I inch closer, blowing lightly on the graze.

A quiver rolls through her, her ass perking up for me, and my cock strains painfully against my sweats.

Black clouds my vision as I lean in, gripping her thigh, and drag my tongue along the small cut.

With her arm still outstretched behind her, she tugs at my

hair, trying to pull me up, but I ignore her, draining each new drop that emerges until the wound swells and turns a seductive pink. I tighten my grasp on her, letting the combination of her tastes blissfully consume me as images of red flood my mind. She pulls again, and a burning frustration tears through me, until my narrowed gaze finally locks on her lust-filled one. She stares at me for a second, panting, her skin glistening with sweat as heat mixes between our bodies.

I grit my jaw, my muscles flexing with need. Her taste is fresh on my tongue, her scent fueling my lungs, both swollen pink spots still in my line of sight. Hunger, greed, turmoil, hatred, and lust splinter down my body, forming a fiery ball of conflicting, violent urges inside me.

Something flits across her eyes.

Something I recognize.

Something dark.

She lifts herself up, the movement taking me with her so I'm sitting back on my calves, with her right across from me. Irritation gnarls in my throat. My eyes turn to slits as I prowl forward, but her slip is on the floor within seconds, and she's climbing on top of me like the bed is scorching lava and I'm her only chance for survival.

Perky breasts brush my chest, her legs wrapping tightly around me as she grinds against my cock through my sweats. She finds my neck and licks, sucks, then pulls my skin between her teeth. A rough groan leaves my mouth. My palms squeeze her ass, and I move her against me, barely containing the agonizing need to pull my fucking pants off and plunge into her until she screams or passes out. She drags her lips to my pecs, then slowly travels down my abs as she licks me, my jaw clenched tight and my breathing ragged.

My cock throbs, aching more the closer she gets to it. I pull her back up by her hair, torment bleeding through my veins at the restraint.

Surprise crosses her features, but it fades as she stops and examines me. Her cheeks are flushed and her lips plump. After a pause, she brings a hand to my right bicep and digs her nails into me. I track her movements as she drags her nails down my arm, tearing the surface as she goes. When she stops, blood seeps from my skin.

She leans forward, her eyes never leaving mine. Softly, she presses her lips to the scratches. My biceps ripple under her touch, and a swallow passes through my throat when she darts the tip of her tongue out to taste.

Motherfucker.

I close my eyes for a second, the pounding in my ears splitting straight through my head and threatening to pulverize any remaining control. She trails a finger over the laceration, the same way I once did to her. My heavy gaze follows her finger as she presses it to her neck, sliding it down to her collarbone and leaving a faint line of red in its wake.

"What the hell are you doing?" I ask coarsely, the flawless image before me burning into my mind—*me* staining her flesh, marking her perfect skin.

She wraps her arms around my neck and inches closer. Her sky-blue eyes hazy and at half-mast. Cocking her head to one side, she parts her lips and lets out a breath, inviting me for a taste.

"Letting you see me," she whispers.

A low grumble moves up my chest. I slide a hand under her hair and palm the back of her neck, telling myself to stop even as my grip pulls her to me. Running my nose along the curve below her ear, I breathe her in. Her naked body goes limp in my arms, but I see the racing pulse in her delicate neck, feel her fingers curl into my hair.

Finally, I taste myself on her, and a slow tremor quakes us both.

A taste turns into a nibble, then a bite. Then I'm sucking on her skin, and her hair is tangled in my fist. My chest hammers, need ripping through me. She claws my neck and mewls when I move off the bed, standing with her naked body coiled around me.

I lift her high enough to pull her nipple between my teeth, my heartbeat drowning out her moans. With one hand still in her hair, I dip the other between us and stroke her wet clit. She jerks and tugs my pants down slightly, rubbing her hot pussy against my cock, and my lungs constrict. I stiffen, a surge of adrenaline seizing my muscles as I faintly recognize that I'm spiraling. She squirms and tugs at my sweats again, then pulls my ear in her mouth and sucks.

My blood pumps so hard it's blinding, specks of black appearing and dissipating.

Fucking shit.

I throw her on the bed and whirl around, fixing my sweats. Running both hands through my hair, I squeeze and pull at the strands as I pace across room.

What the fuck am I doing?

Bracing one palm on the wall, I drop my head and close my eyes, forcing the blistering heat inside me to die down so I can breathe *oxygen* again and regain a little fucking control.

I haven't lost it in six years, and even then it wasn't like this—spiraling before I even got my damn release.

The bed creaks, and my back stiffens. "Don't."

She waits in silence for a long moment while I steady my breaths, my pulse. My cock doesn't seem to get the message, no thanks to Emmy's scent still clouding the air, her touch lingering on my skin. When I speak next, my fingers dig into the wall as though it could restrain me from pouncing on her again.

"What do you need?" I bite out.

"Wh-what do I need?" Her voice is out of breath and confused, and it only frustrates me more.

"What's it going to take to get you to follow some goddamn instructions?"

"What?" She sounds stunned at first. But when she opens her mouth again, fire coats her words. "What's it going to take? I want *you*. I—"

"More money? A different master? A plane ticket home?" I pummel straight through her answer as if she wasn't speaking, because the one thing she named isn't a fucking option. "Name your price, mouse."

The bed creaks again, and this time I hear material shifting before she's approaching from behind. She pauses. I can picture her body tightening in anger without having to look at her.

Pushing off the wall, I turn to face her.

She's put her slip back on, her hair a mess and her skin still flushed. Her eyes are fuming, but her chin is held high.

Because deep down, she's not a damn mouse.

"If that's the way we're doing this," she finally says, "fine. I want different duties. No more being stuck in the kitchen or other housekeeping jobs. I want to do something of value. And without a babysitter glued to my hip."

My gaze narrows, suspicion spiking inside me. "Something of value."

She nods. "Things that actually matter for your businesses. Like what Stella and Aubrey do."

Taking a slow step toward her, I mutter, "And what do you know about my businesses?"

She pulls her shoulders back. "The kitchen wasn't exactly

eye-opening."

My lips twitch despite the irritation still coiled around me. "No, I don't suppose it was. And you realize what you're asking?"

Her eyes flicker with uncertainty, but she wipes it clear. "Yes."

I rub my chin, genuinely considering her terms.

With a request like that, she's clearly still up to something.

I could pawn her off to one of my brothers and avoid having to deal with her altogether. But then I see images of their hands on her naked body, and the urge to slice off their dicks consumes me. Not great for our relationship. The most obvious solution is what Felix already suggested—cut her contract and get her far outside these walls. Eliminate the risk for good.

Obvious choice, yes, but after today, that's not an option for me either. I'm not so sure I'm done with her yet—and I sure as fuck don't want anyone else having her.

"I'll think it over." A buzz vibrates on the dresser. I glance toward the sound then back to her, thanking whoever the fuck it is for interrupting. "For now, you can manage one more day in the kitchen."

I don't wait for her to respond before I'm walking to the dresser, revealing none of the tension still gripping me as I press the phone to my ear.

"Go ahead," I tell Felix.

The door clicks, and my shoulders relax a fraction. Funny how being fucked isn't nearly as pleasing as I remember.

chapter
twenty-eight

> *"She wore her scars as her best attire.*
> *A stunning dress made of hellfire."*
> —Daniel Saint

Emmy

My heart races when I leave Adam's room. I keep my eyes forward and my steps brisk as I walk through the halls, desperate to find a spot where I can be alone. One of Raife's secretaries passes, and I manage a small nod but otherwise forge ahead until I'm near the spa and locking the bathroom door behind me.

I let my weight fall against the wall, close my eyes, and I just breathe. My skin tingles everywhere, deliciously sore from the pressure of his strong hands running all over me. I can already feel the bruises forming.

I've had rough sex, gentle sex, some unconventional and everything in between. I've never considered myself someone who leaned one way or the other, because it was never the *act* I was after—it was the release. Those blissful moments of pure, blind ignorance an orgasm provides, shutting the world down around me.

But this . . .

With a swallow, I reach for my inner thigh and stroke the raw bite mark. His starving tongue, the tremors rolling through him, the unapologetically depraved look in his eyes—this was so much more.

He was so much more.

Instead of ignorance, I tasted what it might be like to finally be me. I didn't give a show this time. I had no plan, no calculations. No scolding voice inside my head.

For a little while, I was free.

Adam—he was unhinged. Shameless. Everything wrong and everything right. And he held the key to my cage in his palm.

I jump at a knock on the door.

"Emma? You alive in there?"

It's almost normal now, hearing Aubrey address me as Emma. "Just a sec."

Adam's heat still warms my skin, my sore muscles reminding me of only him. I close my eyes again, letting the sensations sink in for one final moment.

I hope it lasts.

Pulling the door open, I step into the hall and face Aubrey.

Her eyebrows lift as she scans everything from my wild hair to the torn hem of my nighty to the faint marks on my thighs. Stepping closer, she places her hands on my cheeks and stares into my eyes for a few long moments. Soon, she goes from squinting with concern to giving me a satisfied grin.

"What are you doing?" I ask, my cheeks still squished between her palms.

"Just working out if that look in your eyes is you losing yourself or finding yourself."

My brows knit. "And?"

She drops her hands and steps back with a knowing glint in her eye. Then she spins on her heel and heads toward the spa's exit. "And I think we need to clean you up because the kitchen isn't going to service itself." Just as I start to follow, confused, she looks over her shoulder and winks. *"Emmy."*

Is this what you felt, Frankie?

Did you let yourself go to this place? To one of *them*?

Her question from our last conversation comes as a whisper in my ear: *If you had the chance to get away, and I mean really get away—forget Mama, forget it all. Would you take it? If there was a place you could finally just be you. All of you. Would you do it, Emmy?*

My chest twists as I place a tray of bread rolls in the oven, then start preparing the rest of them.

Frankie might be good and whole, but everyone is flawed. And in our case, we had a mama who never failed to remind us of it. A mama who saw Frankie's strengths and treated them like things to be cleansed of. I watched it suffocate Frankie, Mama's constant punishments and attempts at purifying us.

Sometimes I wondered if I was suffocating her, too. She was all I had growing up, and she knew it. It hurt each time she left, but I never blamed her for needing to get away.

I could have said no that day. I could have lied so she would've stayed home. She may not have believed me, but I could have at least tried.

Now—as a cold, absent sensation slowly replaces Adam's lingering hold on me—I wonder if it was really such a bad thing for her to come here. What if she found whatever she was seeking, and then she really did leave, safe and sound, of her own accord?

The Matthews are not good men. I don't need more evidence

to know that. But none of the secretaries are here against their will. In fact, they seem to enjoy serving the brothers.

After pushing the next tray in the oven, I glance at the clock. Aubrey stepped into the hall for a phone call three minutes ago. Turning around, I wipe the back of a hand over my damp forehead.

Even as I try to understand Frankie's absence, the nagging in my gut doesn't relent. It's a sharp, stabbing feeling, and I know I can't just assume she's okay. I need to see it with my own two eyes.

There *has* to be something more I can do. Something more immediate than my current plan's turned out to be.

Slipping my shoes from my feet to my hands, I tiptoe toward the door Aubrey took. I press my ear against the cool wood, and listen for her as I work out my next move. The spa is the closest part of the house, and Aubrey's desk might have something helpful. It's a slim chance, but it's also the only thing I might get away with in this slight window of time. After overhearing Aubrey's voice behind the wall, I'm about to rush toward the other exit when heels click toward me.

Shit.

Aubrey opens the door just as I slip back behind the oven.

My heart races, my eyes focused on the bread rolls baking, as if looking at her will give me away.

"Hey. You okay?"

"Yeah," I breathe.

"What's up with the shoes?"

"Huh?" I glance down at the shoes still in my hand, and my grip tightens. "Oh, they were hurting my feet." Setting them on the floor, I kick the heels out of the way and clear my throat. "I rarely wore heels before I came here."

She's typing something into her phone when she approaches

me. "You'll get the hang of it soon."

"I was wondering," I mutter, turning on the sink and washing my hands. I wait until Aubrey glances up from the screen to continue. "What is it the Matthews do, exactly?"

She returns her attention to the phone as she answers, "Cryptocurrency."

I frown. I don't have much experience with the internet, but that sounds pretty clean. "So, why all the cameras?" I bite back all the other things I could add—why are there two mansions? Why the lack of windows and constantly closed shades? Why the secretiveness?

Aubrey looks up from the screen again. She shrugs, like the answer is obvious. "They have enemies." After a second, she adds, "And maybe a few trust issues."

"Just a few?" Adam's deep voice pulls my attention to the open doorway, and my skin prickles with awareness.

He's leaning so casually against the doorframe that I might doubt this morning ever happened if it wasn't for the evidence marking my body. He takes a step forward, his eyes finding mine, and my pulse immediately responds.

"I've thought your request over." He pauses, his gaze sweeping the room before returning to mine. "No deal."

What? "You said—"

"I said I would consider your request. And I did. I don't like it." Aubrey slowly backs away, but Adam's shoulders stiffen when she almost fades from view. His eyes go dark, and he growls, "Stay."

I can't deny a feeling of satisfaction at seeing that maybe he isn't so unaffected after all. A tiny smile lifts my lips, and his jaw ticks.

When Aubrey rushes back to stand beside me, his muscles relax slightly. "As I was saying, no deal. It takes work to get to where Aubrey and Stella are. It's not something you can have just by asking. I will, however, make some adjustments."

I perk up at that, my spine straightening. "Okay . . ."

"You'll be moving back to the ladies' quarters. Tonight."

I bite down on my lip, trying to hide my disappointment.

"And instead of housework, you'll begin catering to Aubrey, assisting with any duties she wants help with."

"Really?"

His eyes narrow. "You'll be sitting some things out, but for the most part, she's still at your side constantly. Understand?"

I nod, barely refraining from letting a grin stretch across my face. Still not ideal for investigating, but far better than being stuck in the kitchen. "Yes, sir."

•

chapter
twenty-nine

"The scariest monsters are the ones that lurk within our souls."
—Edgar Allan Poe

Emmy

It's strange seeing the four of them lounging in leather seats, gathered in Raife's office for a meeting. It just looks so . . . normal . . . from out here in the hall. Aubrey leads the way, although I'm the one carrying a tray in one hand with their drinks. When I told her I was a waitress before this, she shoved the tray into my hands and said she always spills. If I knew that's all it was going to take to be allowed into these morning meetings, I would have told her three days ago when I first started assisting her.

Serious tones fill the air as the brothers talk amongst themselves, only quieting slightly when we enter. Aubrey makes her way across the room and gestures for me to get started.

Griff is closest to the door, so I give him his drink first—plain coffee, which surprises me considering what the others are having. When he grabs the mug, his fingers cover mine and hold. I lift my gaze to his, a shiver sliding down my spine when I meet his beady black eyes. His lips thin before twisting up.

I'm about to pull my hand away when his grip tightens. What the hell?

"Is there something else you need?" I mutter, trying to avoid gaining any more unwanted attention.

"I'll tell you what I need—" He stops suddenly, glancing behind me and gritting his jaw.

After an eternity, he grumbles and takes the drink, releasing me in the process.

Relief rolls through me, and I chance a peek over my left shoulder, the direction Griff had been looking. Adam sits back against his seat, legs spread, slowly running his thumb beneath his bottom lip. He's looking at Felix, but his attention on me is like an invisible grip warming my skin. Something flutters in my stomach. I notice the bags under his eyes, despite his freshly shaven jaw and otherwise sharp appearance.

Moving to Felix, I lower the tray and hand him a whiskey.

"There's been no movement," Felix is saying, looking between Adam and Raife. "Other than covering up the kid's shit, he's staying quiet."

I frown before remembering I'm not supposed to be listening. Not that I'll stop, but I don't have to give myself away either.

I move on to Raife, who sits at his desk with his hands clasped behind his head.

Raife's chuckle sends goose bumps down my arms. "Yeah, well, preparing to run for state senate will do that to a man." His eyes follow me as he speaks, but I pretend not to notice.

A deep grumble sounds from Adam's direction. "He won't get that far."

"I don't know," Raife murmurs. "I certainly like the idea of waiting till he does. More people to see it all blow up in his fucking face."

Griff grunts from behind me. "I second that."

"We've been over this. I'm not wasting my breath on it again while we could be discussing today's . . ." Adam's gaze finds me, and he grinds his jaw, ". . . appointment."

My curiosity spikes more with every word they say. What the hell are they talking about?

"Everything's prepped on my end," Felix says, checking his watch then nodding at Griff. "His wife rescheduled her dental appointment, so you might want to wait an extra hour before doing your pickup."

Finally, I reach Adam. For the first time, he looks straight at me. His eyelids lower, and I swear he's burning me from that look alone. When he reaches for his glass, his finger grazes my thumb and warmth zips through me as my senses come alive.

I've barely seen him over the past week. Not for lack of trying, but he always seems to be locked inside one room or another. My cravings for his voice, his touch, the sinful fire in his eyes—it eats away at me stronger than anything I've felt before.

My bite mark pulses as his gaze travels down to my thigh. His fingers tense around the drink just before he snatches it from my hands.

I jerk when Aubrey leans over me to exchange a file under her arm with the one beside Adam, and Raife barks out a laugh. When I narrow my eyes toward him, he's not looking at me. He's looking at Adam, much in the same way he did the very first night I arrived here. Like the pair of them are sharing a private joke—one that Raife alone finds amusing.

I swallow and back up a step, wishing I knew what those looks really meant. Turning to find Aubrey, I spot her leaning over Felix's shoulder. She's stroking his tie and whispering in his ear. Felix's lips turn up, then he's pulling her mouth to his and licking her face off. Awkwardness seizes me as I just stand there, not knowing if I should wait outside or stare, so I choose the latter.

She pulls up for air and walks toward the exit like she'd been simply stopping in for a quick hello.

I glance back at Adam, desperate for one more look, one more anything as long as it's from him—but his stare is fixed on the blank wall opposite him.

A crazed spark flits across his tired eyes.

My brows pull down, but Aubrey grabs my hand and tugs me from the room before I can figure out what's going on with him.

"Knock, knock," Aubrey bellows through Felix's closed door. I pull back to look at her. This is the most casual I've seen her act with any of the Matthews.

"Yeah, come on in."

She looks at me, and her lips curve up like we're in on the same secret. But she hasn't told me why we need to make a stop in Felix's office, so I don't get it. I follow after her anyway, more curious than I let on because I've never seen the inside of his domain.

She strolls toward him with me trailing behind, then rests her ass on his desk and places one hand on her hip. She tilts her head to reveal a mark I hadn't noticed on her neck. A hickey? "Really? Are we in high school?"

My eyes widen. I didn't think we were allowed to speak to the Matthews like that. Not that it isn't a perfectly normal way to speak—anywhere else.

He smirks, his eyes locked on hers as though it's just the two of them in the room. "You said nothing permanent this time. It just came to me." He shrugs. "You know, heat of the moment and all that."

She rolls her eyes. "Raife doesn't like it."

Felix wipes a palm across his mouth and adjusts his bowtie. "Yeah well, Raife's not the one who discovered you and invited you here. So it could be said that, on principle alone, I win." He grins.

A smile lifts her lips, and she mutters something in agreement, but I've stopped paying attention. Three huge monitors sit on Felix's desk. Two of the screens are black, but the third and largest one is lit up with small squares.

Each square reflects a camera's view of different rooms of the house.

My stomach tightens at my discovery. So Felix is the one monitoring the cameras. Right now at least. It's not much, but it's the first thing I've stumbled across that could be useful somehow.

Lip-smacking hits my ears, and Aubrey waves for me to leave as she mounts Felix's lap. "You're on break," she murmurs through his mouth. "You're welcome."

My lips quirk. "Thanks."

I quickly exit, closing the door behind me, and chew on my lip. This is the first time she's let me go on break without her. I glance at the camera at the end of the hall, a rush of adrenaline pouring through me as ideas formulate in my mind. The person on watch is a little preoccupied at the moment.

Before I miss my chance, I travel down the stairs and turn left, stopping only once I reach the basement door. It's cracked open again. I'm either remarkably lucky or terribly unlucky. Nerves wrack me as I flick my gaze down the empty hall and slip inside. A pitch-black cloud swallows me, just like before, but this time I'm prepared for the staircase. Finding a rail to my left, I carefully make my way down.

The stairs lead me to a wide, dimly lit hallway with cameras at both ends and several doors lining each side. Deadly silence fills my ears, and I breathe it in. It's not easy to get a quiet like this, the kind that's still and thin, fragile like it could break at any moment.

I slide my shoes off and carry them in my left hand, then slowly pad through the basement. There are four rooms I can see, but the hallway curves at the end, hinting at more. Each door is open, lights off, nothing but shadow over clinical tiled floors. After passing the third room, I glance over my shoulder and slink into the fourth.

A cold wave of disappointment floods me as I look around. There's nothing here. Literally. Other than a column running from the ceiling to the floor, it's a vast expanse of nothingness.

Irritation gnaws at me. I risked getting caught over this?

I take in the room once more. Something doesn't feel right. Why have a basement filled with empty rooms? And why would Adam be down here? After creeping further inside and still finding nothing, I exit and duck into one of the other rooms. This one is exactly the same, except there's a metal table just a few feet from the column.

Slowly, I approach the table, intense curiosity pulling each footstep forward. A rectangular tray sits tilted in the center. My throat tightens as my eyes trace the sharp instruments laid out side by side. Reaching forward, I let my fingers graze the scissors from top to bottom, then I drift to the scalpel. My heart thumps a little too loudly, almost echoing against the hollow walls of my chest. I pick up the instrument, cock my head to one side, and lightly skim the thin blade along the inside of my index finger.

Strange thoughts seep into my head as I wonder how deep

it cuts. If the red liquid it spills pours out in a rush, or if it trickles down, like in my paintings.

With a jerk, I drop the instrument and step back when a *thunk* sounds from down the hall. Heavy footfalls hit my ears, blending with the echo of the scalpel hitting the metal tray. Darting from the room, I race down the hall and up the steps, my pulse on overdrive, my breathing hard. Once I'm alone in the hall, with the basement door cracked beside me, I pause and rest against the wall.

As my breathing slows, my ears fill with Aubrey's voice . . .

They have enemies.

And maybe a few trust issues.

chapter thirty

> *"See, the darkness is leaking from the cracks.*
> *I cannot contain it.*
> *I cannot contain my life."*
> —Sylvia Plath, Three Women

Adam

I pace into the basement and find Griff already in room three, where my tray lies prepped and waiting. He's got our latest hit unconscious and halfway chained to the column as he works on the guy's ankles.

I inhale the moment, letting it seep into my bloodstream as I wait for the calm to kick in.

This is it.

What I fucking needed.

My jaw ticks as uninvited images continue to devour me—Emmy's naked body wrapped around me, her nails piercing my skin, my blood on her neck. I'm standing in front of my next kill, yet she's still all I fucking see. A growl catches in my throat as I stare straight ahead—trying to will her taste, her body, her subtle hints of madness from my mind.

Andrew isn't supposed to be here right now. I'm already

pissed at having to move him up an entire damn month. After over a decade, I'm finally down to the last four people on my list. With the exception of Murphy, who we've been after for years, I need to preserve and savor them as long as I can. Because fuck if I know what I'm going to do once my list runs dry.

Raife and Griff have other plans—other lists. Enough to keep them at this for at least another decade, thanks to being dealt some shitty hands before winding up with Misha. It's a fucking wonder the two of them never met before the studio. They're both from the shadiest streets of New York, both survived things I never had to go through. They won't call it rape, won't talk about it, but that's what it was. Griff's abuse was from his own father before he got fed up and took to the streets; Raife never had a father, but their pasts before Misha are similar in ways only they can understand. So they have their own lists. It's something we've discussed at length over the past year, along with some tempting offers they've made for me to join them.

But it doesn't work that way. If the hit doesn't have a stake in sucking my soul dry, then I gain nothing by taking their life. A random kill is useless to me.

With my hands in my pockets, I glance at the pathetic excuse before me—his balding head drooping, his scrawny frame limp. A coward who could hardly look at us when he slipped our food trays through the bars, day after day after day. Watching kids come and go, sustaining our caged lives until Katerina or Murphy decided our fates. This one, was perhaps the weakest of them all.

When Griff finishes, I tilt my chin toward him. "You staying?"

"Nah." His lips curl. "Piece of shit's not worth my time."

I nod, and he paces from the room.

He's right. It's a shame I had to move this one up at all. My mind thinks I'm permanently blue-balled; my bones are screaming for any fucking fix I can get, and it's a shit combination. I narrow my eyes on him, irritation coiling around my shoulders.

When Emmy walked into our meeting this morning—her long hair swaying like it remembered me, her blue eyes wide and begging me to bring out the rest of her dirty secrets—it took everything I had not to drag her back to my bed.

Fuck.

Stepping forward, I smack Andrew's cheek a few times to wake him. He stirs, struggling to open his eyes. That won't be an issue in a moment.

I dig my knife from my pocket and toss it beside the tray. Squinting, I step toward the table.

The hell?

The scalpel is lying halfway on the tray, half off. I'm meticulous with my equipment, and my brothers know it. They wouldn't have touched my shit. It's rare that I use the instruments as it is; they're mostly here for nostalgic purposes, and the scalpel was one of Katerina's favorite tools.

Running the backs of my fingers down my jaw, I can't help but recall a certain mouse trying to sneak in here.

"Wha—what . . ." I glance at Andrew as he comes to. "What's going on?"

Finally.

I move toward him, stopping inches from his face and tilting my head as I watch the fear take over. His eyes go wide, his body shaking before I even introduce myself. Funny how quickly they realize something's wrong with this picture when they're the ones strapped down.

"Hello, Andrew." I slip my hands into my pockets, closing my eyes for a second as I will the calm to wash over me. Usually, the adrenaline comes first when I enter the room and see them waiting. Lately, however, adrenaline is all I fucking feel, boiling inside me and threatening to split me open. I need to jump straight to the goddamn calm. "My name is Adam, but you might remember me better as Lucas Costa."

Confusion wrinkles his forehead. I'd usually give them a minute for the recognition to sink in, but at the moment I couldn't give a fuck. With my veins on fire and the pressure in my head steadily increasing, I'm a bomb seconds away from imploding. He'll put the pieces together soon enough. Whether it's before or after the cutting begins is up to him.

I'm about to go for my knife when I stop. Glance back at the tray. Pick up the scalpel.

It's cold, showing no signs Emmy's warmth touched it. But I know she was here. Bringing the instrument to my nose, my chest hammers as I slowly inhale. I try to picture her petite body in my kill room, wearing her little black dress with the silver blade in her delicate palm. Fuck me if the image isn't flawless.

After taking a deliberate step toward Andrew, he whimpers as I lift the instrument, deciding where to start.

All it needs is a little *red* . . .

After a scalding shower, I dress and send a quick text to Aubrey. My fingers feel stiff as I type, my back tense and straining against my shirt.

Moving Andrew up was a fucking waste.

As soon as she responds with their location, I make my way through the halls and to the spa, trying to pretend my insides aren't burning up. I find them with one of Raife's secretaries—Carrie? Carol? Aubrey stands in front of the girl, putting stuff on her face, while Emmy is behind her with a hairbrush.

Working my jaw, I lean back against the wall. Then I just watch her.

Raife's secretary's giggles grate on my eardrums as she drones on and on. Aubrey is attentive, if a little annoyed. Emmy, on the other hand, isn't here. Her hands go through the motions, but her eyes are absent. Lost. I've seen that look before, when she was curled in a ball in her room.

At that time, I liked it. Now that I've seen, *felt*, her wildfire, it only aggravates me.

Because now I know she's hiding.

"You're needed downstairs," I say to Aubrey.

All three of them jump, but I only really came here for one.

Surprise, mouse.

"Yes, Master." Aubrey helps the blonde up and gestures to the door. "I'll go now."

After Emmy sets the brush down, she stares at me. She's back, and her eyes are locked on mine, but something's still off.

I think of my kill room, and my eyes narrow. "Enjoying your newfound freedom?"

Some of the fire returns as her lips tilt up. "Is that what we're calling it? Sir."

I quirk an eyebrow. "When you have the luxury of going on little adventures, yes."

She swallows. Her chest rises and falls beneath her tight, little dress, and it drags my eyes downward.

I push off the wall, and she runs her tongue across her lip. Apparently that's all it takes for my cock to stand at attention these days. Fucking great.

Gritting my teeth, I warn, "Be careful where you step, little mouse. There are some holes too deep to dig your way out of."

chapter thirty-one

> *"She's a strong cup of black coffee in a world that is drunk on the cheap wine of shallow love."*
> —JM Storm

Emmy

GOD, I NEED MY PAINTBRUSH. I FEEL IT BURNING.

The craving.

The *need*.

It itches in my fingers, and it burns in my chest. I close my eyes and think of the colors I would use. Dark shades, blue and black, blending with white to create a brilliant chaos. Then I'd dip my fingers in cherry red and drag them down the center.

It looks just like him.

My master who won't have me.

When that doesn't help, I focus on forming a plan to return to the basement. Then I remember the scalpel, the way my heart thumped when I held it and the morbid colors that ran through my mind.

I don't understand my reaction. But I'm not so eager to go back.

With every moment that passes, my worries for Frankie

intensify. I watch everything the Matthews do, yet I still don't feel any closer to finding her. If I don't find a clue that makes sense soon, I might have to resort to Aubrey. She's just as loyal as the others here, maybe more so, but there's also something rebellious about her. I have to hope it's enough for me to trust her.

But so much could go wrong.

It's against the rules to even discuss previous hires. And if she rats me out and they discover I was never supposed to be here, I could be sent home on the next available flight. Then there's the possibility the Matthews are somehow behind Frankie's disappearance—and asking Aubrey about it would be my downfall.

"Ouch!"

I cringe as the naked secretary before me shrieks, squeezing the sides of the massage table beneath her.

"Sorry. Still new to this."

Not exactly reassuring, but Aubrey only showed me how to wax yesterday. Who knew it'd be so easy to get lost in thought while hunched over a woman's private parts?

There are things I can't assist Aubrey with, and ever since Adam caught me snooping—again—two days ago, she won't let me go on breaks without her. This morning she's in the basement, so she sent me up here to work in the spa.

So far, I've seen all the brothers but Felix pass through there. Raife, though, spends most of his time in the front mansion. When I asked Aubrey about that yesterday, she said any business meetings and Skype calls take place there, so he spends more time in that house than this one.

The secretary scowls at me while she dresses. Maybe I should care, but I don't. I just want to be left alone so I can finally search the space. The second she leaves, I'm at the front desk. *Aubrey's* desk. With a quick glance to my right and left, I pull open each drawer one by one, my fingers trembling against the handles. Snooping is a lot more nerve wracking when it's Aubrey or Adam's personal space.

Frustration builds under my skin as all I find are useless supplies. When I open the last drawer, my eyes narrow. There's a journal. Pulling the drawer back further, I keep the book tucked inside as I flip it open. My shoulders fall forward, and a quiet grumble escapes me when I see what notes fill the pages. Waxes, facials, other appointments. It's just a goddamn log book. Flicking through the pages faster and faster, my heart rate picks up with every second that passes.

I almost miss it when the name jumps out at me. My stomach leaps to my ribcage, and my fingers still.

Francesca. Full body wax and sugar scrub exfoliant.

I grip the book, pulling it out of the drawer and searching for any other details. There are no last names. No dates either. Based on the number of pages I went through before finding this one, it had to have been at least two months ago, maybe three.

I trace a fingernail over the letters of her name.

Was this you, Frankie? My eyes fall shut as I hold the book to my chest. *God, where are you?*

"Forgot my scarf."

"Shit." My whole body jerks at the voice, and the log slips from my fingers before crashing to the floor.

When I look up, the secretary from earlier is standing right in front of me. She glances from me to the book on the floor, and her brows furrow. "What are you doing?"

Clearing my throat, I bend to pick it up. "What do you think?" I flip to the most recent page, where her first name *Anabelle* is written, and grab a pen from desktop. Checking her name off, I keep my tone casual. "I'm filling in the log, of course."

She crosses her arms over her chest and looks me up and down, but I pretend not to notice as I tuck the journal back into the drawer. I don't relax until her footsteps fade toward the waxing rooms.

When she returns a second later, she stops and watches me as she ties the blue scarf around her neck.

I rest my hip against the desk and arch a brow. "Is there something else you need?"

"You headed to lunch?" She places her hands on her waist and glances at the clock behind me. "It's five past."

"Oh, um . . ." I wipe my palms on my dress and push off the desk. "I'll be there soon. I should probably get Aubrey first."

She shrugs. "Okay."

Relief blows through me. We walk out together, then break off in opposite directions as I head down the hall toward the basement. Leaning against the wall beside the door, I wait for Aubrey to come out and think back to my sister.

Sugar scrub exfoliant. That doesn't sound so bad, right?

After a few minutes pass without seeing a soul, I slide to my butt and sit on the ground.

More time passes and another blond secretary comes clicking down the hall toward me.

She frowns and looks at me funny, stopping at my feet. "You okay?"

I nod. When she doesn't move, I add, "Waiting for Aubrey."

"Oh, you'll be waiting for a while. She was sent out on an errand."

I let out a groan. "Thanks."

I'm about to pull myself up when the door opens. A shadow looms over me, and I slide my gaze upward.

A flock of tiny birds take flight in my stomach as I stare up at Adam's hard eyes, unshaven jaw, and the vein popping in his neck. He was buttoning his shirt cuffs, but stopped midway.

With my chin angled to see him, I place my palms flat on

the floor to push myself up, but his expression distracts me. I blink when his dark eyes cloud over. It's the strangest thing, like he's looking straight through me. Sitting here with his large form shadowing me, I've never felt so much like the mouse he always calls me.

I suck in a breath as he stares at me, his brows crashed together and his entire body tight like he's brimming with restraint. After a moment, he squints, scrubs a hand down his face, and stalks past me.

The air whooshes from my lungs while I watch him leave me.

Again.

chapter thirty-two

> "Damaged people are dangerous.
> They know they can survive."
> —Josephine Hart, Damage

Adam

I TURN ON THE BATHROOM FAUCET AND SPLASH COLD WATER ON MY face. After shutting it off, I grip the edge of the marble counter and stare past my haggard reflection.

All I see is her. Sitting on the floor with her sky-blue eyes blinking up at me. She looked exactly like her. So small, with her knees bent and her long black hair blanketing her little body.

I shake my head and rub my eyes. Fucking Emmy. Even in her absence she's climbing under my skin and lighting a match. She's stolen my sleep, consumed my thoughts with images of her, deprived me of the calm my kills are meant to bring, and now she's got me seeing things I didn't ever want to see again.

But fuck, I swear I saw Sofia flicker through those eyes.

(Fourteen years old)

"Let's jump back to more recent times," Katerina says. "Tell me about the alley on 5th Street. Specifically, I'd like to hear more of the sexual violations. I don't imagine it's easy, sacrificing a piece of yourself for security."

The scrawny teen tilts his chin and twists his lips, like he's thinking seriously about her question. I shake my head. After thirty minutes of this, I'm surprised Katerina's let him go on this long.

He mutters, "No, I don't imagine it is. And how does that make you feel? Knowing the price you pay for sacrificing your sanity?"

She exhales slowly, her patience wearing thin.

My lips twitch. At least he's entertaining.

"I'm going to give you one more opportunity," she begins calmly, "to open up for me. I'll make it easy for you. Why don't you pick a topic or incident, and we'll build on it from there?"

He chuckles. "How thoughtful."

A *clink* across the room pulls my eyes to Sofia. She's still handcuffed to the cage. She's pulled her knees up to hide behind them, but I can tell she's peeking between.

Watching.

Listening.

I wonder how many of their words she actually understands. But then, I guess it's not about the words. I feel it, the way everything around us soaks into my bones. The tone of their voices. The stillness in the air. The scratching of a pen on paper. And that's just the interview.

"Don't be afraid," the kid strapped to the table says. I glance at him. "I'm here to listen. Was it your childhood that made you this way? Do you have mommy issues, or did Daddy sneak into your bed?"

I expect Katerina to be angry, but she only smiles and slips her notepad into her pocket. She stands, stepping closer to the boy, and leans in. Stroking his dirty-blond hair, she murmurs, "So young and ignorant. Not everyone needs a traumatic childhood to access their true impulses. Some of us are in tune enough with our inner selves to light our own path. While others need to be guided." She inches closer and presses a kiss to his bony cheek. "They need to be abandoned." Another kiss on his other cheek. "Used." A kiss on his nose. "Raped." His chin. "Beaten and starved." Lastly, his forehead. "And left to die."

For the first time since his arrival, the new kid doesn't have a comeback. When she backs away, his lips are thinned and he's glaring at the ceiling.

She pats his leg. "There, there. Everything happens for a reason."

She walks to the door, pulls it open, and disappears for a minute. When she comes back, Baldy is with her. She nods toward the table. "I need more time to observe this one. Lock him in with my pet."

My ears perk up, and I straighten against the wall. She's never sent another kid to my cage before.

Baldy unstraps the guy, drags him toward me, unlocks the cage, and tosses him in. He lands on his stomach, too weak to catch himself. I know the feeling. As Baldy locks us back up, Katerina walks over and angles her head, watching him struggle to stand.

With a sigh, she turns to Baldy. "Take me to the storage room. I'll handpick a crate myself."

Baldy leads the way, but Katerina stops beside Sofia's cage. She kneels. "I'm sorry it's been such a slow day. Mommy just needs a little inspiration." She reaches a finger through the bars to tap her daughter's nose. Sofia closes her eyes, like she's absorbing the touch. "I love you, baby."

Katerina and Baldy leave together. My tense muscles relax when all but one of the lights go out, and the door closes behind them.

I watch as my new cellmate shifts his attention to Sofia. For a second, he just watches her. Then he turns to me. His brows furrow as he lowers his gaze to my spot on the ground, against the wall.

"Shit. How long have you been stuck in this place?"

I shrug, not wanting to tell him it's been over a year and a half. I don't know why the question feels so personal. Instead, I ask, "You really don't know your name?"

He smirks again, and I narrow my eyes. I've never seen any of the kids here do anything but cry, beg, or stare blankly. I'm an exception, but I've never smirked. It's weird. Kinda refreshing, too.

"No. Who needs one, anyway?" He swipes a hand through his dirty hair, then glances back at Sofia, cuffed to the cage and hiding behind her knees and hair. He tilts his head in her direction. "Already grooming an apprentice, huh? Bet she'll make her mommy proud someday."

I shake my head and push off the ground to stand. I don't know why that sends a surge of anger through me. Doesn't he see that she's just a kid? A *real* kid? Until she arrived, I'd never really been around someone so little. Never seen such a small kid up close, how innocent their eyes are.

"She's a kid," I growl. "She's still good."

He barks out a chuckle, and Sofia's whole body jumps. "Kids aren't good. They're dumb, which makes them *appear* good. And besides," he glances back at her, and she trembles under his glare, "she's her mother's daughter. There's no fighting what's in her blood."

chapter thirty-three

"Who's to say that dreams and nightmares aren't as real as the here and now?"
—John Lennon

Emmy

AFTER ADAM DISAPPEARS AROUND THE CORNER AND MY BREATH catches up to me, my eyes drift to the basement door left hanging open in his wake. I finally stand and straighten my dress. He stalked off in such a hurry he didn't check to make sure it closed behind him. His hard expression is still stuck at the forefront of my mind, bags beneath his eyes and a vein popping in his neck.

He's slipping, and I ache to know why. I may not have signed up for Adam Matthews, but I'm here now. I'm here to serve him.

I want him to use me.

I want him to show me everything.

My heart skips when I take a step closer to the basement, torn between dreading going back down there and feeling compelled to. I tell myself it's just my search for Frankie that pulls me in that direction, but I know better. And that's what scares me.

The clicking of heels down the hall makes my decision for me. I slip inside, close the door behind me, and take a breath. Removing my shoes, I grip them in my sweaty hand and slowly make my way down the pitch-black staircase and to the hall. I'm almost to the same room as before when a large form blocks my path. I halt before we crash.

Lifting my eyes, I take a slow step back as my gaze meets Griff's.

He inches closer, making me slink further back with each step he takes. I bump into the cold concrete wall, and I swallow. *Shit.* I played his game once. I don't think I have it in me to do it again.

"There are cameras everywhere, Emmy," he breathes against my neck. "Someone is always watching." My breaths quicken when he slips a hand beneath my dress. "Something tells me your master wouldn't like finding you here."

I try to push him away, but he doesn't budge. "Something tells me he wouldn't like you touching me, either," I manage.

He grunts and steps closer until his huge body crushes mine. My shoes slip from my grip, landing with a *thump* on the floor. His fingers pull on the string of my thong, and his wet mouth skims my ear. "I find that hard to believe. You think I don't notice the way he avoids you? Not only would he let me fuck you, he'd sit back and watch. He doesn't have the balls to touch you himself."

When I bring my knee to his groin, he catches it, blocking the movement with his arm. A slap stings my cheek and whips my head to the side. "*Slut.* It's my job to acquire people and get them where I want them," he warns, his voice ragged. "I'd try to get comfortable if I were you."

The burn of his slap trickles through my cheek and down my neck. In the back of my mind, a little voice tells me to keep my mouth shut. I can't risk getting thrown out. Or worse. But sometimes, I can't stop the words that bubble up my throat.

With my head still cocked to the side and my eyes narrowed on the wall, I whisper, "All this for a quick fuck? Are all your women sick of you?"

His sweaty palm clutches my neck, and my back drags along the wall as he lifts me off the ground. "You think this is about a quick fuck?" he spits. He leans in and slides his tongue up my cheek, where I still feel a sting. "This is so much more."

I try to swallow, but it gets stuck in my throat when his grip tightens. My lungs squeeze, latching onto any thin streams of air they can. Suddenly he releases me. Just as I catch my fall and inhale, he grabs me again, then flips me so my back is against his chest. With one arm locked around my ribcage and the other around my hips, carrying me like I'm a doll, he marches us up the stairs.

I kick and struggle against his hold. "Get off me! Let me go—"

He clamps a hand around my mouth. "Shut the fuck up. Raife is waiting."

A shiver crawls up my spine. *Raife?*

He takes us through the halls until recognition hits me. Adam's room is just a few doors down. Which means Griff's and Raife's must be close, too. When we reach a room I'm unfamiliar with, he unlocks it, releases me, and shoves me inside.

I stumble forward before looking up and taking in my surroundings. My eyes widen.

The bedroom is identical to Adam's—except for the four naked blondes sprawled on the bed, each of them toying with golden scarves between their fingers. They're watching me, two of them wearing seductive smiles, the other two with curiosity—as though I'm the unusual piece in this picture.

Raife sits at the foot of the bed, his hands clasped on his lap and a smirk on his face. "Hello, lovely," he purrs. "I've missed you."

I tense when Griff moves behind me. His fingers brush my dress, and he pops each button open, one by one, snapping the thread and letting the buttons fall to the floor.

"What is this?" I ask, my voice shaky.

"This," Raife murmurs, "is called show and tell."

When I frown, his chuckle fills the room.

"Not for you, of course." He eyes something to my left.

I follow his gaze to find a small, silver video recorder on his dresser, the little red light on it blinking. My brows crunch together. "Why are you—"

"Ah-ah," he tsks, "that's a reveal for later."

My dress slips from my shoulders, and I shudder as it drops to my feet, leaving me in a black scarf, sheer black bra, and matching G-string.

"Come." Raife pats the bed. "Sit."

My throat closes as I flick my eyes from him to the women. It's not them who intimidate me so much as Raife's expression. I've seen him so rarely since Adam claimed me that I almost forgot how dangerous the devious glint in his eyes is.

My palms dampen, and I keep my feet rooted to the floor. "I'm under orders to only follow my master's instructions."

Something dark flits across his brown eyes. When he grins, the combination is pure madness. "In that case . . ." He unclasps his fingers and signals the women forward with a wave of his hand. "You don't have to do a thing."

The first woman to slink from the bed is the one who offered a glass of water when Raife was my master. Her hair is pulled back in a loose bun, and her brown eyes are locked on mine. When she takes a step toward me, stroking the extra scarf in her hands, the next girl follows. I know this one, too. Her hair long and billowing down her back, she's the one who perked up at seeing my burn mark before proudly displaying her own. She smiles and winks as she walks forward, like she thinks she gets me. The other two I've seen only in passing, and they follow in a straight line, all four of their movements feline.

The woman with the bun reaches me first. She tilts her head, her eyes sliding down my body, then lifts her arms and gently pushes my hair off my shoulders. As she leans in and blows on my neck, the other three surround me.

Delicate fingers trail down my back, my stomach, then silk is teasingly curling around my waist. Nerves jump to my throat as sensations from the last time Raife had me restrained resurface. Cold unease spreads through my veins, mixed with a feeling I can't shake, that I'm doing something wrong. I'm not supposed to be touched by them, by Raife, by Griff—I'm Adam's.

I stumble forward when they urge me toward the bed, their bodies blocking every side of me.

"Shh, it's okay," one of them whispers.

"You need to trust them," another says from behind.

Hands nudge my hips, my back, but I can't see anything but blond hair and tanned skin, and my heart is pounding, and I just want Adam.

When I continue to hesitate, my feet dragging, Raife says, "Would you like Griff to assist you?"

Gritting my teeth, I finally relax against their shoves and allow them to usher me the rest of the way. Raife pats the bed again, now with triumph in his eyes.

I dart a glance at the blanket with a swallow, then look back at him. This isn't like the other times, when I had to play along. I'm not his anymore. I don't want to play.

"I'm not yours," I whisper, my voice intentionally submissive in hopes of countering the disobedient words. I don't know how far I can push before he'll snap. "I shouldn't be here."

He drops his smile, his eyelids lowering. "I think we both know how true that is." My breath hitches, and a cool tremor runs straight to my toes. "But as long as you're in this house, you belong to me. Get. On. The. Bed."

I can't stop my fingers from trembling as I oblige, questions gripping me.

He knows I'm not meant to be here? What else does he know?

The other women join me one by one, forcing me further into the mattress then pushing me onto my back. They branch out, stopping to sit at different corners of the bed. Smooth silk wraps around my wrists and ankles, each of them tying their extra scarves around me, spreading my arms and legs, then looping the material through the bed frame to keep me in place.

My chest rises rapidly with the thumping of my heart as I find Raife's calculated gaze. It's strange, the way he almost reminds me of Adam. They're both powerful, effortlessly seductive, and driven by darkness.

The core difference is: when I look into Adam's eyes and he bares his soul, I see everything. I can touch his madness and his passion. I can taste his dark colors on my tongue then swallow them down to burn in secret with my own. But Raife, when I look into his eyes, I see nothing beyond the glints of mania. He's so convoluted by the darkness waging inside him that any soul of his is buried past the point of no return.

Raife lets out a long sigh as he takes in my expression. "Don't tell me you're a virgin when it comes to women," he mutters, frowning with feigned disappointment.

I narrow my eyes despite my racing pulse. Something tells me he already knows I've only been with men. Not that it matters. I suspect that has little to do with the real reason he brought me here.

"Well, I think you'll enjoy it. Or at least my brother will. This is one of Griff's favorite pastimes."

Griff's lips pull back in a partial smile, partial snarl. He stalks toward us, the bed creaking and leaning to one side when his bulky frame plops down. His beady black eyes drift along my body. "I usually do a lot more than watch."

Raife glances at Griff, one corner of his lips lifting, and my stomach tightens. "All in due time, brother."

All four of the women around me lean in at once. Hair tickles my neck, my stomach, my thighs. I tense in anticipation, wondering what Raife really has planned for me. He's all about performance, and I have a feeling this is just Act One. Hands, fingers, lips—I don't know who's touching me where. Someone licks the curve of my neck, while another slips her hand beneath my panties.

Betrayal slithers around my chest and squeezes.

I watch through streams of golden hair as Griff traces every movement, every woman's hand on my skin. His eyes darken with each second, and soon they're bottomless pits sucking in the view.

My body stiffens when Raife stands. He vanishes from sight as the bubbly blonde with a burn appears inches from my face. A soft smile lifts her pink lips, and she runs her fingers down my cheek.

"It's okay," she coos. "We're just here to relax you."

I jump as something cold skims my left palm. Lifting my chin, I turn my head, trying to see past all the hair and bodies. When my gaze lands on the instrument above my hand, my throat goes dry.

A scalpel.

I glance at Raife, who watches me as he takes it away and

carefully lines silver instruments side by side on a nightstand right beside the bed.

Scalpel. Scissors. Saw. Clamp. Forceps. Other things I don't know the names of. Lastly, a knife.

My breath comes out ragged, fear spiking my voice. "Wh-what are you d-doing?"

He leans toward me, pushing someone else's hair from my face as he does. "Don't you remember?" His lips touch my ear, and I tremble. "Show and tell. Now smile. You're on camera."

He moves back slightly and locks his gaze on mine. Deadly anticipation stirs in his eyes, something that tells me he's just getting started.

I don't think I'm ready for Act Two.

chapter thirty-four

*"She who walks the floors of Hell
finds the key to the gates of her own Heaven,
buried there like a seed."*
—Segovia Amil

Emmy

I squeeze my eyes shut when Raife disappears, seizing up as the groping continues. Hands paw at every part of me, tugging my hair, pulling at my bra, teeth skimming skin and tongues tracing curves. I yank my sweaty wrists against the ties, breathing in, out. I can't stand the helplessness, not knowing what's to come.

Keeping my eyes closed, I think of the scalpel, how close it is to my grasp. I remember the touch of the tiny blade teasing my finger and long for the silence that swept over me when I held it in the basement.

I want Adam.

I want *me*. Not this girl restrained to the bed with anxiety clutching her lungs.

Deep voices travel to my ears, and I vaguely listen to Raife when he asks, "What are you waiting for, brother?"

A low grunt rumbles through Griff's throat.

"I've brought her to you on a silver platter. Your very own Katerina. Don't you remember when she cut into you while you still breathed? Don't you remember what she did to you?"

I suck in a breath, my heart pounding faster in my chest while his words blare in my ears. Cold chills grip my mind, and I squeeze my eyes tighter.

The bed creaks, and I picture Griff standing. A light sweat breaks out along my body.

I can't do this.

I can't do this.

"Don't be shy," Raife murmurs to his brother. "There's no one to stop you this time."

One by one, the hands touching me fade as the girls move away.

"Leave," Raife barks.

A succession of *Yes, Masters* echoes through the room, then the door opens and closes. A shadow looms over me through closed eyes. My heart pounds against my ribcage, my hands curling into fists.

I cringe at the sound of a zipper sliding down then clothes falling to the floor. I know it's Griff without looking. The bed tilts as he crawls toward me, then thick thighs are locked around my waist.

"Look at me, little bitch."

With a quivering breath, I open my eyes, immediately wishing I could close them again.

Red splotches climb up his throat and color his cheeks. His beady eyes are endless black holes, the way I've seen them once before. Only this time, Adam isn't here to save me.

He's naked, fisting his cock as he stares at me, and bile rises in my chest. White marks pull my gaze to his stomach, where scars upon scars line his torso.

"I'm going to fuck you, Katerina," he rasps, "and it will hurt so much worse than the way you fucked me."

Katerina.

Katerina.

Katerina.

Why do they keep saying that name? My head hurts, and I just want them to stop. Stop talking, stop looking at me, touching me—just *stop*.

A shiver makes my teeth chatter as Griff reaches for the scalpel. I shake my head, try to back away, but the ties around my ankles keep me in place. Adam's warning resurfaces in my head. *Be careful where you step, little mouse. There are some holes too deep to dig your way out of.*

"Wh-where's Adam?" I stammer, wishing he wasn't so right. "I want to see him."

Raife's cold voice makes the hairs on the back of my neck stand on end. "Are you really so loyal to someone who can't stand you?"

I swallow hard at his words, wishing they didn't hit so close to home. I know it's not true—not when Adam looks at me, touches me, the way he does. But no one has been able to stand me for long, not even my sister. I can't stop his words from digging into my chest.

Walking on his knees, Griff slowly approaches my face. He continues to fist his cock with his left hand, and when he tries slapping my lips with it, I snap my head to the side. He releases his length to clutch my jaw, keeping me still. A growl finds its way to my throat, but it gets stuck when he sits on my chest and forces my jaw wide open. I watch with wide eyes as he brings his right hand behind him, then a sharp blade presses lightly into my stomach. He rubs himself against my chest as he devours my expression.

It cuts skin, and pain slices through me, my stomach burning against the blade. The same moment a scream leaves my mouth, he jams his cock down my throat.

chapter
thirty-five

*"Knowing your own darkness is the best method for
dealing with the darkness of other people."*
—Carl Jung

Adam

"Bullshit." Pulling out my phone, I check for missed texts, but there's nothing.

Felix shrugs. "I called Aubrey. She said you're the one who sent her out."

Glaring at the screen in my hand, I flick open the text thread between me and Aubrey.

What the fuck?

Me: I need you to make a supply run. Stella has a list for you. I'll deal with Emmy. We're not to be disturbed under any circumstances.

I squeeze the phone as I pace around Felix's desk. "Pull up the cameras. Emmy's room first." He clicks his mouse, then her bedroom fills the screen.

Her *empty* bedroom.

"Do a quick run of the rest of the house."

A minute later, Felix glances at me. He shakes his head, then blows out a breath because we both know which are the only rooms without cameras. I'm already charging out of his office when I hear his seat roll back and his footfalls as he chases after me.

My gaze is locked straight ahead, but the only thing I see is my grip crushing Raife's neck, his eyes bulging out of his fucking head.

"Chill out, man," Felix says, jogging behind me. "You need to cool the fuck off, *then* strangle him. Otherwise you're gonna kill him."

My eyes narrow as I think his words over. Killing Raife sounds remarkably appealing.

My phone vibrates in my death grip. Blinded by rage, I almost don't bother to check it, but then it goes off again.

Raife: She's a trooper, this one. And hey, at least someone's finally fucking her. Amirite?

A two-second video clip below his text plays automatically, on a constant loop, and my perception goes red.

It's Griff.

Shoving his dick in Emmy's wide open mouth.

Over. And over. And over.

"Well, shit." Felix's grumble over my shoulder is underwater, my ears drowning under the frantic beat of my heart.

We reach Raife's room, and I shove the door open, storming inside with enough fire in my veins to burn the fucking room down.

"Oh, look who finally came to join—"

Raife's words die on his tongue as I grab him by the throat and yank him off the foot of the bed. Even with his neck turning red, the asshole smirks.

A rough grunt pulls my attention back to the bed. All my blood rushes to my head, spotting my vision. Griff sits over

Emmy's face, thrusting even now, with his grip forcing her jaw open. Her little body writhes against the mattress, her long hair tangled around her torso, but the fuckers have her tied down.

Slamming Raife's face into the dresser, I stalk across the room and onto the bed, curl one arm around Griff's neck, and press the tip of my knife to his gut with the other. He freezes—which is lucky for him because if he so much as breathes too hard, he's losing blood tonight.

Emmy's panting fills the air, and I feel her stare on my skin. But I don't allow myself to look at her. I'm barely seeing clearly as it is.

"You have four seconds to untie her."

"Fuck yo—"

I dig my knife into his stomach, and he snarls. Griff is no stranger to pain. He was Katerina's only subject who wasn't given the luxury of death before she began her work. But I know his scars like I know my own, and I just intentionally tore one of his open.

"Three seconds."

He growls, his arms flexing like he's bracing to fight me, so I tear another scar open, pulling a grimace from him. He may be bigger, but I'm both faster and more resourceful. After a minute, he shifts, moving off her, and my lungs expand as I release him, finally able to take a damn breath.

I keep my glare fixed on him until both her wrists and ankles come loose, then I flick my eyes to Raife when he strolls toward me. His suit shirt is partially untucked, and a red mark highlights his forehead from when he hit the edge of the dresser.

His steps are slow and carefree, making my blood boil beneath my skin. I grip my knife and envision slashing his fucking throat. Griff might have been the one on top of her, but he was the puppet. This was strategic. Meticulously planned to make

Griff go off like the ticking time bomb he is. It's the reason Raife is so easily able to pull his strings—Raife sees Griff's weakness ignite before his eyes and soaks those flames in gasoline. I see mine and crush the flame between the tips of my fingers before it has the chance to take me down with it.

At least I did.

Before *her*.

A soft, feminine groan sounds beside me as Emmy pulls herself up, close enough the tips of her hair brush my fingers, and it takes all my goddamn willpower to keep from looking, touching, breathing her in.

When Raife reaches me, I lunge.

My forearm crushes his neck against the wall, my chest heaving as we stare each other down. The knife burns my palm, begging to be put to use. Raife sure as shit deserves it. In all the years we've known each other, all the bullshit we've been through, it's never come down to this. I never thought it would.

But he crossed a motherfucking line today.

He doesn't fight me. Of course not, this is what the asshole wanted. His brown eyes brim with life as he darts them between me and my knife. "That's it, brother," he croaks. "Don't hold back."

"So this is it?" My voice drips of the red hot ire burning inside me. "Your big fucking plan?"

He grunts against the pressure of my arm, then his lips curve. "We both know it's already working. Don't pretend you don't think about it, hurting her. Just wait till," he chokes, then tries again, "just wait till you see her now. She's even more of a doppelganger when she's marked in red."

A snarl works its way up my throat, my fingers coiling around my knife. I've had enough of his manipulations for one night.

"Adam . . ." My body stills at her soft voice rasping my name behind me. When she does it again, my shoulders constrict. "Please, Adam. Don't listen to him."

My chin jerks halfway toward her on its own, like she has some power over me I don't fucking recall granting. Raife's low chuckle pisses me off, so I drop my arm from his neck to elbow him deep in the gut. He curls forward, clutching his stomach and choking through coughs. I finally turn around to face her.

She's still on the bed, but she's scooted toward me. She sits on her knees, her ass on her heels, blue eyes wide and set on me with her arms wrapped around her stomach. Her hair is spilling over both shoulders, hiding her upper body in a wild mess of thick, black strands, and fuck my chest for lurching at the sight of her.

I grit my teeth. My pulse thrashes against my throat at the restraint it takes to keep from hauling her against me. But if I do, if I give in to the temptation—it will all be over. Once I turn it on, letting myself go, I don't know if I'll be able to turn it off again.

When she unbinds her arms from around her stomach to crawl toward me, slivers of crimson flash through her curtain of hair.

My jaw ticks, then I'm right in front her, wrapping her hair around my fist to reveal her body. She gasps and jerks back, and my gaze narrows on her bare stomach. My lungs compress.

One, two, three slashes, ranging from the size of my thumb to my middle finger.

Crimson rivulets dance from her waist past her belly button, some smeared across her hip bone.

Her pale skin blurs to a cloudy black and back again as my adrenaline pumps too fast to see straight. Temptation flares to life inside me, my muscles clenching with the compulsion to touch, to taste, to bite. I want it all. But something else stirs deeper, too. Something I'm far more accustomed to than temptation.

I thought I'd felt rage before. Now an inferno eats me alive.

With my shoulders heaving, I turn to Raife.

Still with his back against the wall, a grin stretches across his face. "There you are," he whispers.

The edge of my knife is pressed against his neck before he can blink.

He made his choice. Now I'm making mine.

Before I can act, soft fingers run down my cheek, cup my jaw. My glare still leveled on Raife, a low growl rumbles through me as I try to process the warmth on my face. Raife's eyes dance with amusement, and the inferno beneath my skin tries to crawl its way out.

"Adam . . ." The sound of my name rolling off her tongue slides past my eardrums, heavy like syrup. "He doesn't have to win."

When the fingers on my jaw tug downward, I snarl, reluctantly tearing my gaze from Raife to find that Emmy has slithered between us.

Her chin is angled up, her large eyes round and desperate. "Adam." She lifts to the tips of her toes, forcing herself in my line of vision, and caresses my stubble. I close my eyes to ease the tension coursing through me, but that only makes her soft skin feel ten times heavier on my own.

Her palms slip to my neck, curling around me, then she's climbing onto me like she did once before. She winces through the movement, but doesn't stop. My breaths are hard, my jaw twitching as she wraps her legs around me and latches on.

Her lips reach my ear, and she whispers, "Master. Take me away with you."

For a minute, I don't move. The rage radiating inside me is

suffocating. But when her voice rings in my ears long after she quiets, her disobedience echoing all around me—*Master. Master. Master*—my hand eases away from Raife's neck.

He smirks the same moment I slice the knife across his cheek, from his ear to his lips. In a matter of seconds his face twists from pain to anger to betrayal. Then eventually, satisfaction.

Son of a bitch.

I wipe the look off his face by slamming his head back against the wall, and he groans.

Emmy's arms squeeze my neck tighter, her short breaths on my skin and her thighs clenching around my hips, warmth rubbing my cock. My muscles contract painfully. I grit my teeth as I shut my knife and slip it back into my pocket, then wrap my arms around her. I have to force her higher to stop the friction before I lose my fucking mind, I'm wound so tight.

I pin Raife with a final glare. "This isn't finished."

His lips twitch, fresh blood from his cut dripping toward them, and he rubs the back of his head. "I'll be waiting."

After swiping the recorder off his dresser on my way out, I grip Emmy tight and pace toward my room.

Every fiber of my being burns with the weight of these past weeks, and every bit of it revolves around the mouse latched onto me. My body is so tight with tension I'm fucking shaking against hers.

As we're swallowed into the depths of black halls, it all hits me at once like a train on full speed crashing into a brick wall.

I may be her master, but she owns me, too.

And if I don't make it stop, it's going to fuck us both.

chapter thirty-six

> *"You are terrifying and strange and beautiful.*
> *Something not everyone knows how to love."*
> —Warsan Shire

Emmy

My body slumps against Adam as he holds me. I mold into his hard form like he's the canvas and I'm the paint. Resting my face in the curve of his warm neck, I can't keep my eyes from fluttering shut.

Everything aches. Both sides of my jaw throb as they swell, and my stomach is raw. Adam shifts my weight in his arms to shove open his door. He strides into the room, lowers me on the bed, and drapes a blanket over me. My eyes drift open when he stalks to the dresser, tossing the recorder on it. He grabs his phone from his pocket, punching keys.

I watch him closely through heavy eyes. The way he clenches his jaw, his thumb darting across the screen. A vein in his forehead looks like it might burst.

He won't look at me.

After a second, he slides the phone across the dresser and works the buttons of his shirt. His movements are stiff, like he's refraining from tearing the material apart.

"Adam," I say faintly, exhaustion draining me.

He tenses, the muscles in his shoulders constricting.

"I just . . . I wanted to thank—"

The door opens, dragging my gaze to Aubrey. When I look back, Adam's already in the bathroom, the lock clicking behind him. My chest deflates as I stare at the closed door.

When Aubrey removes the blanket and starts slipping off my shoes and scarf a few moments later, she's nonchalant to the point I wonder how often she deals with stuff like this. I wince when she cleans and dresses the open wounds. But I'm glad she works in silence. My body sinks into the mattress, and my eyelids lower.

Soon, she covers my naked body again, and I find someplace between restlessness and sleep.

I drift in and out for a while, my mind wavering from clarity to fuzzy clouds, then back again. Somewhere along the line I faintly register movement in the air as Adam paces from one spot to another. I don't know how much time has passed before I feel, then see, him watching me, but sleep tugs at my consciousness and pulls me back under its spell.

When a crash whips me from my subconscious, my eyes flutter open to find a room cloaked in darkness. It's not long before I spot Adam's broad, shadowed form sitting on the ground—his back against the wall, elbows resting on his knees and hands gripping his hair.

The video recorder is in shambles on the floor beside him.

After a moment, I realize he's shaking. It's not a small, illusive shake. In fact, I don't think 'shake' does it justice at all. Waves of intensity radiate off him, tension rolling through his muscles like thunder roaring beneath his skin. I swallow as I watch him in utter silence, not daring to make a move.

Not because I'm scared.

Because I'm captivated.

A violent war wages inside his head, and it shows with every twitch, every clench, every ripple overtaking him. He doesn't just blend in with the darkness surrounding us. He sucks it dry with every inhale then feeds it with each exhale.

It's madness begging to be released. It's pain so forbidden you can't cry. It's an explosion of everything I am when I reach my darkest days.

And I've never seen it look so beautiful.

Peeling the covers off my naked body, I slip from the bed and drift toward him like an invisible rope is tied around my chest. His energy is the grip tugging me closer. I carefully guide his hands to his sides and crawl into his lap. He doesn't look at me, but his knuckles curl and his breathing picks up. For a long moment, I just stare into his shadowy eyes in admiration.

I reach up, bringing my hands to both sides of his face, and lazily trail my nails from his temples to the bottom of his chin. A tremor slides over him, vibrating against me. When I cup his cheeks with my palms, he finally looks at me.

"Does it hurt?" I whisper.

He narrows his eyes, a swallow passing through his throat.

"When you lock yourself away like that, does it hurt?" I drag my fingers to his thick strands of hair. "Can you tell me . . . can you tell me what it's like when you let it out? Is it everything I imagine?"

His gaze flicks between my eyes, and I wonder how much of me he sees. Here I am, completely naked, yet I feel so deep in layers I can hardly breathe.

"I want you to show me. I'm not afraid."

A low rumble escapes his throat as he allows his gaze to wander lower, his lips twisting as though he's in physical pain. "You should be. I would tell you to run"—his strong hand clutches my throat, and I gasp as somersaults go off in my stomach—"but I'd only catch you. And then I'd crush you."

"So crush me," I breathe, my chest pounding to a new beat. "I don't want to be whole anymore. I want you to see my pieces."

It's in the moment his pupils expand so wide they're completely black that I know.

There's no going back.

chapter thirty-seven

> *"Love me like the moon intended.*
> *All the way through the darkness."*
> —A.J. Lawless

Emmy

With Adam's hand still locked around my neck, he drags his thumb along the bottom of my jaw, lifting my chin until my head falls back and I'm staring at the ceiling.

My pulse thumps against his grasp.

He slides his palms down my body, his movements agonizingly slow, but there's nothing teasing about the way he does it. His grip is firm, burning into my skin and branding every curve. From my collarbone to my breasts, to my waist then my hips, he leaves a trail of goose bumps everywhere he touches.

I shudder when he presses his face to my exposed neck. He breathes me in and tastes me with his tongue, a rough groan rumbling through him. He wraps his strong arms around my back, then pulls me in so tightly I have to suck in a breath. We're flush against each other—breasts to chest, stomach to abs—as he pulls my skin between his teeth. My eyes fall shut because, fuck, I never knew it could feel so good to have someone clutch me like I'm their life support.

A gruff sound vibrates against my neck before he prowls forward, and my back hits the soft rug. I try to lift my head to watch, but his grasp finds my hair, keeping my scalp on the floor. His hand is everywhere, avoiding only the bandages as he travels roughly down my body—squeezing, digging, bruising—and I swear he's trying to crawl under my skin.

Breathing heavy, I lift my hips, instinctively seeking friction. Giving a low growl, he clamps my pussy with his large hand and shoves me back to the floor. A deep-rooted moan escapes my lips, the raw strength of him making me quiver. He quiets me by sucking on my bottom lip and biting down, hard.

It's the closest we've come to a kiss, the tang of blood hitting my tongue, and I return the favor by scraping my nails down his shoulder blades. He grunts and takes it, his muscles flexing under my hands, and, *god*, it feels so good not to hold back.

His raw, carnal energy is the match to my flames. In this moment, I don't care if I'm swallowed up and left as ash scattered in the wind.

At least then I'd get to fly.

His forehead dips, and he inhales my hair, then his fingers are snaking up my ass, spreading my cheeks apart before roaming back down and stretching my slit. He expertly traces both areas with his fingers, like he's memorizing the feel of me.

My skin is set ablaze as I bite down on his neck. A rough sound climbs up his throat. He plunges two fingers deep inside me, bending and flexing, and my jaw drops.

"Oh, god . . ."

When his thumb presses on my other entrance, I gasp. He doesn't enter, only teases as his forefingers pump ruthlessly between my thighs, and tingles erupt straight to my core at the combination. Just when I throw my head back and close my eyes, his hand disappears.

I protest through a breathless groan, but he's already hauling me to my feet.

I only catch his gaze for a second as he moves behind me, but one second is all I need to see it. His expression is clouded over, his hair wild and falling over his forehead, his muscles rippling—but it's the look in his eyes that makes my heart stutter.

It's smooth dark syrup dipped in madness, then rolled into a blanket of obsession and pain.

It's *savage*.

My toes curl as I soak it in. I've never stared directly into eyes quite like his. And, yet, my chest aches like he's calling straight to me.

I'm spun around and bent over the bed, his hand pressing down on my back. My pulse races when my cheek touches the cool sheets. A glint of silver on the nightstand catches my eye. I swallow, realizing his knife is less than an arm's reach from us, already open.

Without warning, he shoves his cock deep inside me. A strangled groan rumbles from his throat at the same moment an intoxicating mix of pleasure and pain shoots through my body. He pulls me up so my knees are on the bed, his chest heaving and his breaths blending with mine. Bracing the inside of my thigh with one hand and clutching my breast with the other, he has every curve of mine flush against him while he slams into me, again and again, stretching me to my limit.

My mouth falls open as I take it, my thighs clenching from the addictive sensations rolling over me. It's primal, the way he fucks me. Like he's trying to fuck a lifetime of demons free.

I'll take it all. Everything he gives me.

I bring my hands up and behind me to clutch his shoulders, and he somehow pumps faster. Our skin is slick with sweat, my damp hair tangled between us. He drags his hand from my thigh to my clit, his fingers working as hard as his cock, and I can't stop the mewls from pouring out.

I release one of his shoulders to tease his bicep and forearm, getting high on the delicious ripples of muscles flexing as he rubs my clit.

"Fuck," I moan, dropping my forehead as pleasure rakes over me.

A deep rumble vibrates from his chest to my back. His thrusts become violent as he loses control, then his hand disappears from my breast and curls around my neck, squeezing. I stiffen, but his fingers only continue to sink into my throat.

"Adam," I pant, gripping his arm.

He fucks me harder, the hand between my thighs grasping as firm as the one on my neck. *Shit*, he feels so good, even as his growls become so animalistic they're unrecognizable. I breathe through tight lungs, inhaling the darkest parts of him.

So this is his freedom. I wonder what it tastes like.

My gaze slides back to the open knife beside us. The smooth silver that yields so much power. I want to feel it—the power. I want it for myself. My heart pounds against my ribcage as he pushes me closer to the edge.

"Adam," I half-breathe, half-moan, a faint thread of reason trying to break through, warning me against the sinful creature I am. But a stronger voice latches on too; one that lurks so deep I'm not sure I've ever really met her. And she urges me not to resist it—the burning longing that swells inside me whenever I taste Adam's darkness.

I don't want to resist. I don't want to be good or bad or spared or cursed.

I just want to explore whatever's inside me.

I want the freedom to *be*.

When he squeezes so hard a choked cough escapes, I stretch my arm as far as I can and reach for the knife. My fingertips graze the handle, then a thrill courses through me when it's finally in my grasp.

For a second I stare at it, soaking in the way his rough thrusts blend so perfectly with the power in my palm.

I gasp when he snarls and frees my neck, suddenly pulling out of me. He spins me so I'm facing him, his gaze darting to the knife, and I swallow.

His eyes are crazed with lust and darkness, his breathing heavy, and a vein pops in his forehead. Possessive or possessed, I don't know the difference right now.

The longer he watches me, the more his breathing calms. His expression clears slightly, and his brows crash together when he glimpses my neck. I still feel the invisible weight of his hand clutching me, and I know it's red—or worse.

His jaw ticks, his lips thinning, and he closes his eyes for a minute.

When he opens them again, his gaze flicks back to the knife in my hand. Shadows flit across his expression. "What are you doing?"

I clench it tighter, absorbing the strange feel of the weapon. For so many years I've painted the colors it draws from our skin. I've closed my eyes and been flooded with them—reds and blacks, mangled bodies and broken bones. But I've never stood and held in my own two hands the tool that spills the blood. Not like this.

I'm teetering on the edge of unfamiliar territory, and somehow I sense the rush is greater than the fall.

Cartwheels go off in my stomach as Adam watches me brush the tip of the weapon from my hip bone past my bandaged wounds and up to my ribs, like it's a feather.

His nostrils flare, his grip finding my waist. I almost groan when a heavenly zing surges up my body. The tormented way he's looking at me, the dangerous weapon in my control, the freedom of just *being*—the combination is toxic, and I'm drunk on it.

"What are you waiting for?" I coax softly, moving the knife's point in slow circles around my belly button. "Fuck me, Master."

A deep grumble fills his chest. I grow warm at the raw beast inside him. The beast that calls to me and soothes the bleakest parts of my soul.

I place my free hand over the ridges of his abs, then slowly slide up his hard chest until my fingers curl around his neck. Moving the knife to my lips, I dart my tongue out and drag it from the handle to the tip.

A long tremor rolls through him, and it's the sexiest thing I've ever seen.

When I lower my mouth back to the base of the knife, he dips his head so our noses almost touch. Waves of heat fill the gap between us, and the room goes so still all I hear is our breathing and my throbbing pulse. I gently bring the tip of my tongue to the smooth, flat surface of the blade. My breath hitches when he does the same on the opposite side. His eyes are locked on mine as we run our mouths from one end to the other, finding the same rhythm. When we reach the top, our tongues brush for a mouthwatering second before he drags his along my jaw and down the side of my neck, tugging my head back by my hair. My eyes flutter shut, and a long moan bubbles from my core.

Strong hands grip my ass and squeeze. With his lips attached to my neck, he pulls me up and paces across the room, my legs wrapped around his waist as he lowers me onto the dresser. He glides his palms against my thighs and spreads me wide open. After curling one hand around my fist so we're holding the knife together, he fucks me deep and slow.

Jesus.

Tangling my free hand in his hair, I clutch him as I meet him thrust for lazy thrust. Goose bumps prickle along my body, his breath skating over my throat. Quivers run through his muscles like he's never felt anything so satisfying, and I finally understand.

I finally get why it's the *act* of sex people seek, not just the blissful ending. Why people drag it out instead of claiming their release right away.

This. This is everything.

Bodies melting together as you set each other on fire. Peeling back your mask and baring your soul. Surrendering yourself to another while owning every part of them.

His teeth skim my jaw, crossing over to the other side of my neck. His hand grips my shoulder as he goes deeper, drawing a shiver down my spine as he fills me.

God, it feels so good.

I dig my nails into his back with my free hand, and he groans as he releases the knife, leaving it in my grasp, to lift me off the dresser. My legs curl around his hips before he strides across the room and shoves my back against the wall.

Bracing the wall with one hand, he drives into me faster, harder, pulling mewls from my throat with every thrust. Panting, I wrap both arms around him, clawing and gasping as I grind, clench, and quiver.

"Oh, fuck." My eyes flutter shut. Pleasure pulses through my core and squeezes. "Adam . . ."

A growl rumbles through him as he bites my collarbone and grips me harder. He fucks me with everything he has. My jaw drops, spasms spreading like wildfire along my limbs. Rough grunts vibrate against me as he loses himself, his whole body trembling like my own, and it unravels me. My muscles seize from the pure intensity rocking through me. *Shit.* Wave after wave hits, and he clamps my face between his fingers and thumb, forcing my eyes open so we're staring straight into each other as we come apart.

The look in his eyes steals the breath from my lungs. His eyelids are lowered, his face twisted—almost pained—as a deep shudder tears through him. My chest heaves when I finally start to come down, and warm liquid spills over my fingers from behind his back.

What the hell?

With my bones heavy and spent, I slide my hands up and over his shoulders so I can see them. My eyes widen as red cloaks them, the knife still in my grasp.

Oh my god.

"Adam . . ."

He just stares at me, clutching my waist like he might never let me go as the darkness simmers. Something unfamiliar, warmer, seeps into the deep blue of his irises.

"I'm so sorry," I whisper, dropping the knife and bringing my shaky, blood-stained fingers to his cheeks. "I-I don't know how—I didn't realize—"

He leans in and sucks my bottom lip between his teeth, teasing me with his tongue. Even as confusion clouds my eyes, delicious sparks explode inside my chest. My entire body is still shaking with need for him. When he releases my lip, my shoulders slump, and I inch closer, silently begging for more. Instead, his arms squeeze around me, as though being flush together isn't close enough, and he drops his damp forehead to mine. Heavy breaths pour over me as his eyes fall shut, and for a moment, he just holds me.

I can't quiet the thumping of my heart, and I don't want to. My head spins with bliss. I want it to last forever.

Just as I start to sink into him, his hands curl around my legs, and he lowers them, sliding me down his body until I'm on my feet. Coldness scatters along my skin at his absence, and an unpleasant shiver chases my spine.

I'm not ready.

His eyes darken while they roam over my body—skin flushed, coated in his sweat and blood. His Adam's apple bobs up and down. I step forward, but he turns away and swipes a hand down his face.

My gaze rakes over his shoulders and back, across the blood marring his muscles, and I gasp. The coat of red hides the depth and width of the cut, but I can see enough to tell it's not superficial like my wounds. He'll need stitches.

Dragging his fingers through his hair, he stalks toward the bathroom.

I follow after him, my hands shaking. "Adam—"

He stops at the door, tensing, but he still won't look at me. "From now on," he rasps, "you're mine. In every sense of the word. You're not to leave my side. Tell me you understand."

My heart stutters, and I whisper, "I understand."

chapter thirty-eight

*"It's rather easy to shine in the light,
but to glow in the dark—that's mastery!"*
—Rick Beneteau

Adam

(Fourteen years old)

"No, but really," the sixteen-year-old with no name says, a devious grin on his face, "what would you do to her?"

I shake my head and lean back against the wall, closing my eyes.

"Come on." He nudges my elbow. "Don't tell me you haven't fantasized about hurting the bitch. Killing her. Burying her alive."

My lips twitch, because he has no idea.

Before I came here, I'd seen four deaths. Two at gunpoint, one a fist fight gone wrong, and the other a heroin overdose—all people like me on the streets. I thought those were gruesome at the time. Normal, but gruesome.

After a year and a half in this cage, I've learned a lot. About death, murder, art. About people: no matter what their differences were outside these walls, once they're strapped to that table, they're not so different after all. I've learned about reality—the lies we tell when we're trying to convince ourselves any reality exists at all. Fuck that. There's only what we think we see, and even that fantasy doesn't last.

Mostly, though, I've learned about myself.

No one ever tells you how far you can fall inside your own head.

Opening my eyes, I turn to face No Name beside me. He's still dirty as fuck, and his eyes and cheekbones are sunken in. I'm probably worse off, but at least up until last month, when I was alone in here, I could pretend I wasn't.

"I've thought about it," I mutter, my gaze flicking to the empty table on our right, then to the little girl across from us coloring on a skull. "I think about it every day."

No Name smirks, something dark dancing in his eyes. He's a crazy fucker, but then so am I. His crazy is just a little louder. I think he's lucky for that. Probably feels a helluva lot better than the crushing weight of keeping everything in your head.

"You wanna know what I do to her when I close my eyes?" He leans in even though it's just the three of us here. "I tie her up. Naked. Then I pour gasoline on her body and toss in a match. Burn, bitch, burn."

I watch as Sofia glances at him. She continues coloring, but I know she's listening.

I've been talking to her more, trying to get her to talk back. It never works. Sometimes, though, when I say stupid shit to see if she knows how to laugh, her lips quirk. I like it. It reminds me of when I was her age and I used to laugh with my mom. It didn't happen much, but maybe there's goodness in that. This way, I'm able to remember every single time.

No Name shifts beside me. "Well, I thought burning was a good one," he continues. "Heard from some of the other crate kids that that's option three."

I arch a brow. "Option three?"

"Yeah, you know. Option one: become an art display. If that doesn't work out, then Murphy pulls you for option two: sex trading. But then there are the kids who are too fugly for option two and they won't sell for enough to be worth the trouble. That leaves option three: burn the body." He clicks his tongue. "You know. Evidence and all that."

I grit my teeth, but continue watching Sofia. Sometimes seeing there's a little kid here helps remind me to chill the fuck out, because little kids aren't supposed to listen to shit like this. They're not supposed to be here at all.

"Really? That's it?" No Name shakes his head. "Man, I really thought you'd be more into this, now that I see what you sit through every day."

"What are you drawing?" I nod toward Sofia, ignoring him.

She jumps, then looks from me to the other kid. After a second, she continues coloring like I didn't say a word.

"Why you talk to the devil's clone, I still don't get," he grunts.

"She reminds me of something."

"Yeah? What?"

I shrug, not really sure myself. It's more of a concept, really. An idea of what could be. What should be. Something he and I lost our chance at ever having a long time ago. Sometimes I think she's lost it too. That Katerina has already sucked her dry. But then her lips quirk when I do something stupid, and I know she hasn't.

"Wanna show me?" I ask, trying again.

This time she pauses. She puts her crayon down. Then she holds up the skull, turning it so I can see the front.

My jaw spasms.

"Holy shit," the kid beside me mumbles through a chuckle. "That's fucking twisted."

It's red. All of it, from top to bottom.

Except she's caked on so much of the crayon that it actually looks like a bloodbath.

I swallow, No Name's question about Katerina echoing in my mind. Yeah, I think about what I wanna do to her.

"You're pretty good," I mutter, a bitter taste on my tongue. "Looks just like the real thing."

She beams as she turns the skull back around, her smile wider than I've ever seen it. Well, she should be proud. It's impressive for a fucking five-year-old to capture blood so well.

I'm just about to rest my head against the wall when a small voice pulls my gaze across the room again. I squint, realizing she's singing as she goes back to coloring. She's not actually using words, but still, I've never heard her hum before.

Until now, I'd never heard her make a sound.

I don't recognize the tune, but it's slow and soft. Kinda creepy, actually.

"Creepy shit right there," No Name echoes my thoughts.

The corner of my mouth tips up as I lean back and close my eyes, listening. We're all screwed in the end, but there's something about knowing I played a part in getting the girl without a voice to sing.

Even if she is covered in red.

chapter
thirty-nine

"I desire very little, but the things I do consume me."
—Beau Taplin

Adam

I TAKE MY TIME SHAVING, STROKE AFTER SLOW STROKE, KNOWING EMMY waits for me just outside the door.

My jaw ticks beneath the razor as last night replays in my head. Over and over, I watch her mouth fall open as I fuck her, hear my name on her tongue when she comes. Feel the burning slice in my back as she loses herself, then her soft, stained fingers sliding down my face.

Shit.

Tossing the razor beside the sink, I lean forward and splash cold water on my face. My wound aches at the strain, still raw with the stitches Aubrey gave me several hours ago. I keep my eyes shut for a minute. Everything inside me starves for Emmy, urging me to peel back whatever other dark secrets she's hiding behind those innocent eyes.

In all the years prior to abstaining, I'd never had a woman able to pull me out of it—out of the blinding depths that take over those final moments I relinquish my control. Yet Emmy did. Then she went and outdid me. Seeing her soul stripped of pretense as she held my knife, as my blood decorated her skin—it was fucking spellbinding.

I don't know how, or when, she got under my skin, but she's liquid in my veins. I feel her with every beat of my pulse. There is no avoiding her. For better or for worse, she's shackled to me now.

I step into the bedroom and pace to my closet, grabbing a black button-down and slipping it on. Turning as I work the buttons, I spot Emmy leaning against my dresser. She's raking me over, licking her lower lip like she wants to do that climbing thing she does.

My cock is weak. He immediately stands at attention.

I grit my teeth as the sutures below my shoulder graze my shirt. The sting makes me think of Emmy's euphoric expression when she stabbed me, which makes me want to fuck her again, which is irritating because I have shit to do and can't spend all day between her legs.

Fuck. That image doesn't help.

A quiet growl rumbles through me. "Keep looking at me like that and I'll need new stitches before my meeting."

She bites her lip but drops her gaze. Intrigue and guilt. Interesting pair. She thinks she did something wrong last night. And, yet, she liked it.

She works so hard to hide herself. Makes me curious who made her think she had to in the first place.

Once I'm fully dressed, I walk to the dresser and grab my phone, opening a text from Felix. "Let's go," I mutter without looking up.

"But I'm not presentable. I have to stop by the spa."

I arch a brow, then bring my gaze to hers. "You're not what?"

She shifts her feet, gesturing from her face to her heels.

"Presentable. For you." When I say nothing, she adds, "Hair, makeup, nails..."

I look her up and down. She's in her uniform—tight black dress and heels. Little fucked up since that's the same thing Katerina wore in the studio, but everyone has issues, and we stopped trying to make sense of ours a long-ass time ago. Her hair is down, black and long. Her lips are soft and pouty. Light freckles I hadn't noticed before dust her cheekbones and the bridge of her nose. Her blue eyes are bright and centered on me, right where they should be. She looks fucking perfect to me.

I rub my palm down my jaw, my eyes flicking back to those lips. I had my first taste last night, but it wasn't enough. I wanted to shove her mouth open with my tongue. I wanted to take that part of her too.

But I don't kiss. It's one line I won't cross, not even with her. Kissing is intimate, and I don't do intimate.

Tearing my gaze from her mouth, I turn and head for the door. "You're fine," I mutter, staring straight ahead as we exit. "No more visits to the spa, understand?"

There's a pause, my words echoing in the hall as she trails behind me.

"I understand," she says softly.

Something about her tone makes my shoulders stiffen. It's warm and affectionate, two things that don't belong anywhere near me. I'm made of ice, a place where warm things go to die.

Clenching my fist, I stop just outside Raife's office door. When I finally look at her, I know my expression is as cold as my soul would be if I had one. But the second I find her wide eyes already locked on me, her chin tilted and her lower lip between her teeth, unspoken words I didn't anticipate burn painfully inside my mind.

Instead what comes out is, "You're here because I'm your

master." *I can't function without you.* "Your duty is to serve me." *I'm chained to every move you make.* "That's all this fucking is." *You're all there fucking is.*

Her gaze drifts to my clenched fist, and when she drags it back up to meet mine, she gives a slow nod. "Yes, Master."

Heat coils around me, pulling my muscles taut as her voice lingers in my ears. Working my jaw, I push the door open. "You and following damn instructions."

Her lips quirk before she passes me and makes her way toward my usual chair, diagonal from Raife's empty desk. Still standing in the doorway, my eyes flick from Griff to Felix. "Where is he?"

Felix brings his glass of whiskey to his lips. "In the front house. We got another offer for a buyout. He's shutting it down."

Griff grunts as his gaze trails Emmy, pausing on every curve, and my eyes narrow. "You don't get to look at her," I grumble, tracing my fingers over the knife inside my pocket. I feel Emmy watching me, but my focus is on Griff.

He shifts his attention to me and scowls. "Since when do you make my decisions?"

"Since you broke the rules and lost the right to make your own."

He snarls but keeps quiet.

Just as I move toward Emmy, the door opens behind us. Raife strolls inside and heads to his desk, slowing halfway when he notices Emmy leaning against my chair. I grit my jaw. In light of professionalism, I'd planned on waiting until after the meeting to finish what he started yesterday. But one wrong move and that flimsy plan goes to shit.

Typical Raife, he opens his mouth before he even circles his desk. "Well, isn't this sweet." He smirks as he glances between us, and I instinctively move closer to her. "I gotta say, I'm impressed you're still keeping it together, brother. Must be a pussy made of magic." He winks at her, then runs the back of his fingers down the fresh cut I left on his cheek. "Gonna have to test it for mysel—"

I'm behind him before he finishes his sentence. I pull his hands behind his back and use my leg to shove him against the desk, keeping him rooted to the spot. After whipping my knife open, I hold it with my free hand less than an inch from the vein in his neck.

Griff stands, braced to fight. Felix stays in his seat and downs the rest of his whiskey.

Raife's deep chuckle makes the knife brush skin. "Finally," he groans. "Yes, old friend. Throw away the key and come out to play."

A dry smile tips my lips. I tighten my grip on him. "Not today, brother. This revenge isn't mine."

The room falls silent, and Felix shifts in his chair as he watches me transfer my focus to Emmy. Confusion etches into her forehead, her eyes locked on mine in silent question.

Moving the knife from Raife's neck, I extend it to her. "A cut for a cut."

Raife wasn't the one who tore into her stomach, but he may as well have been. And with all the shit he's pulled on her since her arrival, I know she's burning to make him pay.

A swallow passes through her throat as she stares between the knife and Raife. I can almost feel the anger, burning like fire, under his skin.

His eyes turn to slits. He digs his shoulder into me, but I hold him in place. "You're gonna fucking regret this, Adam," he seethes. "No fucking way would I let Katerina cut into you."

I shove him against the desk, hard enough to pull a groan from him. "She is *not* Katerina," I bite out. "She had nothing to do with any of that shit."

He barks out a laugh and shakes his head, his chest heaving. "You so sure about that?"

My gaze narrows when I glance at Felix, but he just shrugs. Griff's lip curls as he watches Emmy. When I look at her, her eyes are wide and she's shaking her head. "I have no idea who Katerina is, Adam. I swear."

Uncertainty grips my veins, despite the fact I know that's Raife's intention. Emmy isn't lying. Anyone could see that just from her expression. Still, the resemblance is too striking to keep any of us from questioning it. Not to mention her age. She would have been exactly Sofia's age at the time we were there.

I watched Sofia die with Katerina. I've seen Emmy's file, her family, her home.

Gritting my teeth, I slide the knife across the desk. Emmy's gaze drops, and a shaky exhale pours from her mouth. She takes a slow step forward.

Raife's fucked with her enough.

chapter forty

*"Her soul was too deep to explore
by those who always swam in the shallow end."*
—A.J. Lawless

Emmy

I WRAP MY FINGERS AROUND THE KNIFE'S WARM HANDLE AND LET THE full weight of the weapon settle in my palm. It's heavy and powerful. It feels like Adam.

Warmth trickles into my bones as I look back at him.

His muscles strain against his shirt as he forces Raife to straighten, and his eyes run so deep I'm sure he holds my soul in them. If I stare too long, I could drown in his depths.

Until Adam, no one had ever offered me something like this. The right to own myself and all that affects me. He's granting me his trust, and with that, I can't help but trust myself.

When Raife's glare pulls my attention to him, a shiver crawls up my spine. Still, I inch closer, until my hip brushes the desk.

"I don't know who Katerina is," I say again, this time to him.

"So you've said." He stares daggers at me as I untuck his

shirt, and I'm actually grateful.

I'm so used to his theatrics—from the Dark Room to the chandelier, leaving me to burn then setting me up for Griff. Anger dances in my lungs and climbs up my throat. I almost swallow it back down, but then I remember I don't have to.

I don't have to pretend.

Leaning forward, I unbutton the lower half of his shirt then slide my gaze back to Adam. Hesitation burns in my gut as I watch him, letting the knife's tip hover below Raife's ribcage. I don't know what I expect—for him to change his mind now that he sees me going through with it? To reject the side of me that finds pleasure in being able to make Raife pay? Whatever I'm waiting for, Adam doesn't give it to me. He patiently observes, his eyes tracking my every move.

Finally, I make my first cut. It's shallow like mine, but still enough to feel the tear beneath my fingers. As the blade slides across Raife's skin, his muscles tense, but he doesn't make a sound. I don't want to see his expression, so I stare at his stomach. It's pretty, really, if you focus on the colors and the way they spill. His red is the same shade as Adam's, a slightly deeper hue of crimson than mine, and it runs down his body like it's trying to escape.

Moving an inch lower, I start on the next. My breaths come out soft and weightless, and I'm drifting with each gentle movement. If the knife were my paintbrush and his body the canvas, I'd blend some black with the crimson to make it murky like his soul. Then I'd add a splatter of cherry around the edges to top off the madness that it sprouts. I think he'd like it, stripped down but maintaining the flare he loves so much.

The third and final cut takes a little longer since it's the largest. Letting one end curve up more than the other, I tilt my head and smile. It looks just like one of his smirks.

After a moment, when the rest of the room comes back into view and I look at the stained weapon in my hand, I feel the blood drain from my face. With a long exhale, I take several wobbly steps back.

"Well, that was . . ." Felix pauses, clears his throat. "Unexpected."

My gaze finds Raife's, and goose bumps race down my arms. I've never seen his eyes run so dark.

"And now, *brother*," Raife spits, his eyes latched on mine. "Still so certain there's no Katerina in her blood?"

I have no idea what he's referring to, but the insinuation is clear. I close my eyes, wishing I could take it back. I didn't know it would feel like painting. That it'd be able to carry me away. And now they all know it, too.

Back home, I worked in solitude when I put my brush to the canvas. Art is a private piece of me. Now, I may as well have displayed all my canvases for the Matthews to inspect. When my eyes dart back to Raife's torso, torn and red, I swallow hard.

No, I'm far worse than a girl who paints madness on a canvas.

Today, I painted with blood.

It takes a minute to find the courage to look at Adam. If he didn't see enough to reject me before, he will now. They always do.

When I meet his gaze, a warm tremor ghosts through my body. His eyes are hooded, his posture constricted and intense. Yet there's something gentle, familiar, behind the depths of his eyes and in the set of his mouth. I think I could get high on that look alone.

He releases Raife but doesn't take his eyes off me. With each slow step he takes toward me, I'm left a little more breathless. When he reaches me and leans down, his arm curling around my waist, I shiver. His lips touch my ear, and his warm breath skates over my throat. "You look stunning when you're not hiding."

My eyelids flutter shut, and I whisper, "I don't want to hide. Not from you."

"So don't." When he nips below my jaw, my toes curl. "Show me everything."

chapter forty-one

*"Crawl inside this body,
find me where I am most ruined—
love me there."*
—Rune Lazuli

Emmy

THE TOES OF ADAM'S SHOES CONNECT WITH MY OWN AS HE WALKS INTO me, guiding me backwards with each step he takes toward the office's exit.

"Hello?" Felix calls. "Meeting, anyone?"

Raife's bitter voice follows, but I can't make out his words over the hypnotic beat of my heart. Before we reach the threshold Adam slips his hands under my dress and grips the backs of my thighs. He drags me up his body until my legs lock around his hips. His tongue finds my neck, his grip holds me close, and a sigh pours out of me as he walks us into the adjacent room.

My head lolls to the side as his lips move toward my ear. When I scan the room, spotting an empty desk and leather sofa, I murmur, "Whose office is this?"

"Mine now," he rasps, kicking the door shut behind him.

He crushes me against the wall, supporting me with one

hand and undoing his pants with the other. A warm flutter in the pit of my stomach dips between my thighs as he works his zipper, my breath shortening in anticipation. I wrap my fingers around his neck, and he shifts me enough to yank my panties down my legs.

He pulls back to look at me, his eyes darting between mine for a long moment. I lick my lips, and his gaze drops. His pulse races against my palm, *thump, thump, thump.* Then he slams his cock into me with one hard movement, and a rough rumble tears through his chest as he fills me.

My head slumps back against the wall, my eyes falling shut. *So full.*

"Fuck, Emmy," he groans, his forehead dropping to mine. For a second, he stays like that, our heavy breathing permeating the air as we absorb each other.

Slowly, he pulls out then glides back in. A long shudder passes through him. He does it again and again, smooth and methodical, and I can't stop a shiver from wracking my body.

God, yes.

I grip his hair and roll against him.

Lightly cradling my jaw with his fingers, he angles my head so I'm looking at him. His shoulders are tense with restraint, a thousand flames burning in his eyes and melting my sanity.

"How did it feel?" he croaks, deepening his strokes. He leans down, his eyes closing as his nose brushes my cheek. "How did it feel when you cut into him?"

My chest squeezes as I watch Adam. The barely contained gentleness of his touch on my face. The agony coating his voice. As though every bone in his body depends on my answer. "It felt—" A moan spills from my lips, the sensation still lingering in my mind as he continues to fuck me slowly. "It felt like . . . like art."

A tremor rolls through him. He lets out an uneven breath as his lips brush my ear, his smooth jaw stroking my cheek. After a second, his pumps become a little faster, harder, and his voice turns gruff. "Are you an artist, Emmy?"

I close my eyes, sinking into him. "I don't know what I am," I breathe. "I just . . . am."

He stares at me so intensely it peels back the layers of my soul, one by one. When I feel naked and cold, I try to turn my cheek, but he holds my chin in place. My heart skips a beat. I have no choice but to bare myself.

Releasing my jaw, he slides out and holds me as he crosses the room. He lowers me on the sofa so I'm sitting, then drops to his knees and yanks my ass to the edge.

"What are you—"

I gasp, my pulse skyrocketing as he wraps his lips around my clit and sucks. I squirm with every pull and lick, then jerk when he fills me with his tongue. A shock of pleasure makes me clench, and I drop my gaze to his head between my thighs. I clutch his hair and grind against him, watching him let me relentlessly fuck his face, and holy hell, I take it back—*this* is the sexiest thing I've ever seen.

With a growl that vibrates straight to my core, he digs his fingers into my hips and pulls me flush against his mouth, like he's feasting on his last meal and isn't willing to miss a single drop.

"*Shit*. Adam." I squeeze my eyes shut. Crackling sparks explode inside me, one after the next, making me jolt against his mouth. "I-I'm coming."

Waves of pleasure slam into me hard, and my eyes roll back into my head before I finally come down. Sighing breathlessly as the gentle aftershocks roll in, I sink into the sofa like melted butter.

With a long moan, I force my eyes open and look at him. He's still between my thighs, but his eyes are locked on my face, soaking in my expression. He wipes his mouth with the back of his hand, then brings it to my stomach. His lips graze my belly button so softly I can almost pretend it's a kiss.

I stroke the back of his neck, captivated by the shivers rolling through him with every brush of my fingers. When he pulls back and tugs my dress over my hips, I frown. "Wait. What about you?"

He stands, his eyes darkening in a way that makes somersaults flip in my stomach. Bending down and caging me in with his palms against the sofa, he leans into my neck. His teeth nip at my scarf, pulling it down, and he flicks the tender area beneath with his tongue. His lips brush the spot so delicately I shudder.

God, can he see what he's doing to me?

As though reading my thoughts, he lifts his chin, scanning my expression while skimming my lips with his. I part my mouth, breathing out and watching him close his eyes as he breathes me in.

"Don't worry," he murmurs, his deep voice husky. "I'll get mine."

Before I can respond, the door swings open and Adam is pulling me up beside him. Griff's enormous frame blocks the doorway as he narrows his eyes, darting between me and Adam, then the sofa behind us. He scowls, his gaze lingering on me. Adam's warm hand curls around my waist, and he leads me forward, watching Griff with every step. His hold on me is effortlessly possessive and delicious as ice cream on a summer day.

I swear I see him wink before he says, "Thanks for your hospitality. Brother."

chapter forty-two

"Let your plans be dark and impenetrable as night, and when you move, fall like a thunderbolt."
—Sun Tzu

Adam

With my grip locked around Emmy's waist, I head down the hall and back to Raife's office. I'm fucking hard as shit, but my cock is going to have to get over it. I step inside to find Raife absent and Felix collecting the papers on the coffee table.

I narrow my eyes. "Short meeting."

Felix flicks his gaze up to me, shakes his head, and shoves the files under his arm. "It's done, man."

"What's done?"

"Murphy." He walks up to me and adjusts his bowtie. "Raife is setting up his pickup for later today as we speak."

I grit my teeth, clutching Emmy tighter against me. "What the hell are you talking about?"

"They already sent a file straight to Murphy. It has all we've got on Misha. His involvement controlling everything from Katerina's crimes to the sex trading, burning the extra bodies—even their romantic affair. Anything we were able to dig up."

My jaw ticks. That's nothing new. In fact, it's exactly what we sent Murphy when we first tried to get to him several years ago. At the time, he proved with ease that none of it was strong enough to connect him directly to the crimes. Not that we expected it to. We don't need 'hard evidence.'

We lived it.

We were set to move forward—until we weren't. It wasn't until Felix discovered a particular photograph buried deep in Murphy's private files three years ago that Raife lost it, and Murphy slipped from our grasp.

The photograph was of a sixteen-year-old boy, naked, with dirty-blond hair, sunken-in eyes, and hollow cheeks. Written in permanent marker at the bottom: *No name. Due for redistribution.*

Raife stalked Murphy, barged into his house in the middle of dinner, and stabbed him in the stomach from behind. Of course, if Raife had followed protocol and planned for a proper pickup, he would have known there was a guest in their restroom at the time, who happened to be an off-duty cop. A dirty cop in Murphy's pocket, but a cop nonetheless. Raife barely escaped without getting shot.

The only fortunate thing to come out of the experience was that Murphy didn't link Raife's current identity to *No Name* from fifteen years ago.

Murphy had no idea how personal that night really was.

It was easy to assume his attacker was one of his many disgruntled, cheated clients, and Murphy's fear of damaging his delicate reputation overrode any impulse to seek justice. He already had us—anonymously—threatening to leak Misha, and a stabbing in the midst of all that would hurt more than help. He thought offering us a shit-ton of money was enough to make everything disappear and reset life to normal.

And it was.

It had to be.

For a little while.

It was dumb luck that Raife didn't get caught. Murphy did investigate us harder than shit after that incident, however, and he came too fucking close to connecting all the dots and figuring out our identities. If it wasn't for Felix's talents, he would have too. He would have reburied us before we made it out of our own graves.

Releasing Emmy, I refill Felix's shot glass with a bottle on the table and down the whiskey. "What aren't you telling me, Felix?"

Emmy tracks my movements, her brows furrowed as she shifts her gaze from Felix to me.

Felix scrubs a hand over his face. "You, ah, wanna send her downstairs to Aubrey for a few?"

I squeeze the glass in my hand. "She stays."

He blows out a breath but answers me. "They didn't send the file anonymously this time."

The hand at my side curls into a fist. *Fucking idiots.* "Of course they didn't."

"We've been going over this at some of the meetings, but lately you walk out or spend them doing kil"—he glances at Emmy, clears his throat—"in the basement."

"Bullshit. You fucking know this plan is shit, and you knew I'd shut it down if I found out about it. This was purposefully outlined in my absence."

He rubs the back of his neck. "Look, man. When you walked out this morning I was gonna wait till you got back before moving forward, but we all know you've been distracted lately. And Raife had other ideas. Your little show didn't help." He waves a hand between me and Emmy, and a breath of dry amusement leaves my lips.

Convenient. Raife the puppeteer. If Emmy doesn't break me

down enough to lose any sense of boundaries, at least she distracts me. Either way, she works to his advantage.

"The files we sent him are encrypted, all right? He's the only one who will be able to figure out who we are based on the clues I've left him. As far as the duplicates we're releasing—"

"What fucking duplicates?"

"The ones I set up to automatically release to all major news platforms tomorrow morning, once we've got Murphy in our hands. Those are anonymous. There's no way to trace them back to any of us."

"So that's the plan? Get Murphy here by the end of the day, then take Misha public?"

"Fuck yeah. Raife still wants to see his reaction while he watches everything fall apart."

Shutting my eyes, I press my fingers to the bridge of my nose.

"What's the problem?" Felix steps closer. "You get Murphy, Raife gets his publicity stunt. Everyone wins."

"Yeah," I mutter, shaking my head. "I've been trying to convince him to bring Murphy in for weeks, and he suddenly decides he agrees? For no fucking reason?"

He shrugs. "Maybe he's sick of waiting, like the rest of us, and figured he'd compromise so you both get what you want."

"We're talking about Raife, brother." Setting down the glass, I shove my hands in my pockets. "Nothing is ever that straightforward."

Emmy shifts beside me. "Adam . . ."

Felix glances away, his face twisted in thought. "Maybe. But this shit seems sound enough to me."

Still fixed on Felix, I grumble, "Raife. Fucking polar opposite of *sound*. How exactly does he expect to pull off a quiet pickup with a man like Murphy? An operation like this takes extensive planning, more than usual, unless you want his disappearance to lead back to us."

He shrugs. "We fucking know that, man. I've still got everything tapped, so we can watch and listen to every move Murphy makes. And besides, this plan might be new, but it's not far from my original idea."

"I believe your *original* idea was more in line with mine. Pick him up quietly, pull any loose ends out of him, peel his fucking skin, and close this shit down."

Emmy flinches from beside me, and my gaze finds hers. She's staring straight at me, her eyes wide. *Fuck.* I rub my chin. Since I'm chained to her anyway, I figure she'll be discovering more than she'd bargained for soon enough. But, yeah, maybe this is too much information for her to soak in at one time.

Looking back at Felix, I work my jaw. "It's your fucking shit show. Lemme know when he's ready for me. If we get that far."

Delicate fingers brush my arm. "Adam."

My gaze snaps to hers.

"What's going on?" she asks, her lips turned down.

I take a slow step toward her. Slipping my fingers below her chin, I lift her head and rake my eyes along her face. Light freckles. Velvety lips. The gentle strokes of her voice, like a softly played instrument. So easy to presume she's innocent. Her eyes, however, are on fire. There's nothing quiet about them. Even after flinching at the mention of peeling someone's skin, she's determined to know more. Perhaps now more than ever.

I don't know what I was thinking.

She doesn't resemble Katerina at all.

I stroke the pad of my thumb along her plump bottom lip. "You'll know soon enough."

She watches me curiously as I turn toward the exit, but that's all she's going to get right now. Some things can't be explained.

chapter forty-three

*"The darkness that surrounds us cannot hurt us.
It is the darkness in your own heart you should fear."*
—Silvertris

Adam
(Fourteen years old)

SOFIA'S GENTLE HUMMING FILLS MY CAGE. AFTER SEVERAL MONTHS, I actually look forward to hearing it, and I drift asleep to the sound.

"Hey." No Name nudges my bare foot with his. "You up?"

Opening my eyes, I shift against the wall, my ass numb from sitting in the same position for too long. "Yeah."

"What do you think that song is?"

I shrug. "Maybe it's a nursery rhyme."

He huffs a half-chuckle. "Even I know that's no nursery rhyme."

Sofia flicks her gaze to us. When she spots me looking at her, she smiles. She's been doing that more lately, when her mom isn't here. One corner of my lips lifts, and her grin widens before she goes back to coloring the fibula she's been working on all day.

"What are you gonna do tomorrow?" I ask No Name.

He smirks, tapping one of the bars with a wrist bone Sofia gave him yesterday. It was an accident, really. Katerina was about to do her millionth interview on him, so she pulled him out of the cage. When she got annoyed at him for lifting up her dress before they even made it to the worktable, she threw him back in with me, and he shouted after her, "Hey, throw me a bone."

Sofia took it literally.

And here we are.

Tap, tap, tap.

No Name scratches his chin with his finger, like he's thinking hard about his answer. "Pluck Katerina's hair out one by one and set her on fire. Then I'm going to the storage room next door to check out what chicks she's been hiding. I'm gonna fuck them while we watch her turn to ash."

I arch a brow and shake my head. We started this stupid game a few weeks ago. I don't know why. Maybe it helps to pretend we're not in a cage. Truthfully, though, I go out of my way *not* to imagine it—getting out.

Releasing a breath, I rest my head against the wall and scan the studio. Steel walls. Metal table. 'Art' display.

The inside of these walls are all I've seen, day and night, for almost two years, and I feel nothing like I did the day I walked in here. I *think* nothing like I did. She fucking broke me, and honestly, I'm scared shitless of what I'd do if I got out of here alive.

"Your turn," he mutters.

I twist to see him. He's watching me closely, something disturbed flicking in his eyes as he waits for me to take my turn. The thing is, my answers always have the same pattern. And I don't even have to think about it because it's all I picture.

"I'll start with her ears. Cut slowly from top to bottom, sawing the blade against her skin till they come right off. Then I'll wish her luck with her interviews now that she can't hear worth a damn, and I'll take my time carving out her eyes. Hard to admire art without the view. Then I'll stand back and watch the blood stream in waves down her pale skin till she bleeds out."

The room is quiet for a moment, nothing but Sofia's soft humming in the air.

"Shit." No Name grins from ear to ear. "You never disappoint. I'm going to have to break us outta here just to see you run loose."

My lips quirk, but it's humorless. I don't want to know what I'd be like out there. It's something my cellmate talks about a lot, getting out of here. He's always planning something.

After a second, I glance across the room. "Hey, Sofia."

She falls quiet, her crayon going still against the fibula when she looks at me.

"What do you think? Would you ever want to get out of here?"

She just stares at me, like she doesn't understand the question.

"If you could live in a normal house. If you could go outside, play. Would you want to?"

A swallow moves down her throat, and she nods.

"Yeah?" I glance at No Name but he's looking at me like I'm crazy, so I turn back to her. "Would you . . . would you talk?"

Her eyes dart to the bone in her hand, and she fidgets with it for a long minute. When she lifts her head again, she nods slowly.

No shit. Blowing out a breath, I sit up straighter. I angle my head and squint as she sets down the half-painted fibula and folds her knees up, wrapping her arms around them.

She really can get out of here, can't she? I bet she's even young enough to still make a life after this shit.

"You're kidding, right?" No Name chides. He leans in and mutters, "I'm smart enough not to free Katerina's spawn, not even if my life depended on it."

Ignoring him, I tip my chin toward Sofia. "Hey. It's okay. Maybe we'll, uh . . . maybe we'll figure something out."

Her eyes lock on mine, and something I've never seen sparks in them. Something that looks a helluva lot like hope.

The door slams open, and she jumps.

All the lights flick on at once, making each of us squint in unison.

"This one here," Katerina says from the open doorway, gesturing toward the cage where No Name and I sit. Someone stands in the hall, but I can't see anything except their shoes. "I've been trying very hard with this one. He reminds me of Pet in some ways, so I held out, thinking there was hope. I'm afraid months under heavy evaluation have only proven he's not like Pet at all, below the surface. There's just something missing." She looks at the kid beside me, frowning, and my eyes narrow. "Heart. That's it. He's missing heart, and I cannot connect. I'm afraid it's time to call a spade a spade and redistribute."

No Name stands, a smirk on his face. He fucking winks at me.

I shake my head, my lips tipping up. The sly son of a bitch. Guess that's one way to get out. "You know where you'll be redistributed, right?"

His eyes darken, but as quickly as the shadow shows up, it clears. "No way I'll let it get that far. Just need one foot out the door, man. One foot out the door."

I turn back to Katerina just as she reaches forward, toward the man hidden from view. Her gaze drops while she smooths out his tie, extending the material enough for me to see bronze. I squint, unease uncurling in my stomach. It's strange as hell watching her touch anyone so intimately—especially when he touches her back, stroking her arm with the backs of his fingers.

Finally, the mystery person steps into view. I've never seen him before, but I know right away who he is. I hear his name from at least one of the adults around here on a daily basis.

Murphy.

He's tall and fills his tan suit. I have no clue what kind of suit it is, but I've stolen from enough rich people to know it's fancy as shit. His hair is gelled to one side, his shoes shined, and he stands like he runs a hell of a lot more than this underground operation. I'll bet everything he touches turns to gold.

"Holy shit," No Name mutters, taking in Murphy's wealth, just like me. "Him. I wanna be him when I get outta here."

chapter
forty-four

*"Behind the most beautiful eyes,
lay secrets deeper and darker than the mysterious sea."*
—YLD

Emmy

CHEWING MY CHEEK, I WALK ALONGSIDE ADAM. HIS STEPS ARE BRISK, and I'd be falling behind if it weren't for his hand on my waist, guiding my pace.

I can't stop thinking about his conversation with Felix. Encrypted files. Tapping someone's lines. *Peeling his fucking skin.* A shiver runs through me every time Adam's deep voice repeats that softly in my mind, and I wish it was cold instead of warm.

I've been letting my guard down. Thinking maybe my sister really did leave on her own accord and just needs some time alone. It's not such a far stretch now that I'm here. Now that I've seen the women are willing. Now that I've experienced the strange and magnetic appeal of this world. Or as Aubrey called it: *The Matthews Effect.*

But the fact is: I still know next to nothing about these brothers.

About Adam.

I look sideways at him, openly staring. He doesn't glance at me as he continues walking down the hall, but his fingers dig into my waist, like he feels me watching him. His warmth sinks through my dress and melts my skin. Facing forward again, I don't think before I'm placing my palm over his hand and entwining my fingers in his. He stiffens but doesn't move away.

When he opens the door to the basement and leads me down the stairs, my stomach tightens into a million knots. He's never let me in this part of the house. I dart my eyes toward him, but it's too dark to get a read.

He takes us to the second room. Lingering in the doorway, I release his hand and let him pass me. He flicks his gaze in my direction, but he doesn't say anything or make me enter. Instead he moves toward an empty metal table near the column. His face is hard, but his posture is relaxed. Comfortable enough to suggest he's down here often.

My feet are glued to the threshold.

Butterflies swirl in my stomach and my palms are clammy, which only confuses me more. I wish I knew if these reactions were from excitement or fear. It shouldn't be the first one. Not when I know Frankie was here. What would she have done if she stumbled upon that tray? If she'd seen half the things I have?

Adam reaches under the table and pulls open a hidden compartment beneath. After removing a silver tray, he sets it on the table's surface and closes the compartment.

Something twists inside my gut every time my eyes shift to him. I've shown him things no one else has seen. Offered him the darkest parts of me. It feels unnatural hiding anything from him now.

I fold my arms over my chest, glancing away. "Adam . . ."

He looks over his shoulder and cocks a brow.

When I stay quiet, he turns back to the tray and adjusts the items lined on top. I can only see his side profile, and his back blocks most of the tray, but I don't have to step closer to know what's displayed in front of him.

"Is there something you want to say?" A corner of his lips twitches, but he stays focused on the task at hand—whatever that is exactly.

I close my eyes, willing the words on my mind to escape. Despite everything I've seen, it feels hurtful and bitter to ask him what I need to. I don't know what it would do to him. If it would break some unspoken trust between us.

But then I think of Frankie, and I have to. Every second spent with Adam pulls me deeper into the addictive vortex between us, and Frankie slips further away.

A rattling sound snaps my eyes open. Adam is withdrawing a thick chain from the compartment below the table. A chain not unlike the one Raife used to tie me to the chandelier.

He drags it toward the column, his movements strong, full of purpose, and I clear my throat, finding my voice.

"Adam. Would you ever—have you ever—" I swallow. *Why is this so hard?* Opening my mouth again, I push the words off my tongue. "Have you or your brothers ever seriously hurt any of the secretaries?"

He halts, bent forward with the chain in his grip. He tilts his chin toward me, but not enough to meet my gaze.

"I mean, to the point lines are being crossed? To an extreme?" I know what Raife and Griff have done to me, the horrible way it's made me feel, but I haven't seen any of the other women here treated the same. At least not to the point they disliked what they were doing. Could the same be said for everyone, though?

The chain drops with a *thunk*, then Adam is stalking toward me. He stops when he's so close I have to lift my chin to see him.

His narrowed gaze darts across my face, and my heart falters.

He cocks his head to one side, his eyes dropping to my scarf, and my bruises feel electric under his scrutiny. When he inches closer and dips his chin, my pulse picks up as our lips almost brush. I inhale his masculine scent like a shameless addict.

"You tell me, Emmy. Was I *extreme* enough for you last night?"

This. This is my problem. I can't think straight when I'm with him. He makes me never want to think straight again.

When I lick my lips, his gaze follows my tongue. "That's not what I meant."

I start to look away, but he grips my chin with his finger and thumb.

"Then explain, Emmy," he growls quietly. "What *did* you mean?" He flicks his eyes between mine, searching, then grits his jaw when I don't answer. "We have no use for people who don't want to be here." He drags his thumb along my lower lip, something flickering in his eyes, and he rasps, "If you're having second thoughts—"

"No. I want to be here. With you." My words hang between us. It scares me how true they are. "It's not me. I just . . ." My voice trails off, and his eyes burn with frustration.

"You just what?" he grits out. "What are you keeping from me?"

My eyes widen. "I'm not keeping any—"

"Bullshit." His hand dips below my jaw, his body tensing and his breath skating over my lips.

A warm shiver rolls through me. "What do you want from me?"

"What do I want?" His nose skims my cheek, then his smooth, deep voice reaches my ear. "Loaded question for a mouse." My skin warms when he pulls my earlobe into his mouth and sucks, and Jesus, I wonder what I wouldn't give him.

"For now, however," he murmurs, pulling back slightly, "I want to know what you've been hiding."

"I told you. It's not me—"

"Who is it?"

"What? It's—it's—"

"Who. Is. It?"

"My sister," I burst, and my eyes fall shut.

Shit.

A long pause stretches between us, and I don't open my eyes again until I hear his low voice. "Your sister?"

I nod, my neck stiff. My confession either saved Frankie. Or destroyed her.

He drops his hand from my face. "Francesca Highland."

My lungs squeeze. "You know her."

"No." He shakes his head and steps back, running his palm down the side of his jaw. "Her name is in your file." I frown, but he doesn't wait for me to respond. "What about her?"

"So . . . you don't remember her?"

He arches a brow and pulls his phone from his pocket when it buzzes, glancing down. "Why would I?"

Blowing out a breath, I shift a few steps to the right and lean back against the wall. My secret's out. It's all or nothing now. "She came here about nine months ago. She was one of your hires."

His eyes narrow when he looks back at me.

"She went by Frankie."

"Tall? Blonde? Tanned?"

"Yes!" I'm nodding my head up and down like a bobblehead until his lips slowly tip up. Pausing, I glare at him. "Funny."

Slipping the phone back in his pocket, he shrugs. "If it isn't

Aubrey or Stella, I don't deal with them. And if I don't deal with them, I have no reason to learn their names."

Silence spreads between us as unspoken words fill the gaps. He didn't 'deal with them.'

Until me.

My stomach flips, but then I remember something Aubrey mentioned when I first arrived. "Except for one. There was another girl you claimed before me, wasn't there?"

"If you can call it that." His expression hardens, and he works his jaw. "Chalk it up to Raife and his reminiscing for another life. I only claimed her to shut him up, but I never spoke to her, let alone knew her name. She requested a new master by the end of the week, thank fuck." Running his thumb below his lip, he takes a step toward me. "What does your sister have to do with anything?"

I take a deep breath, then lift my chin and look at him head on. "I think she might be missing."

He cocks a brow. "And you suspect we had something to do with it."

"I don't know. I think it's . . . possible?" Darting my gaze to the metal tray, I pull my bottom lip between my teeth. "All I know for sure is that she came here, and I stopped hearing from her soon after."

Adam narrows his eyes. "So she was Raife's."

"What?" My brows knit. "Why do you say that?"

"He's the only one who doesn't allow outside contact. Distracts them from their—"

"Devotion to him." I roll my eyes. "Of course it does."

I think his lips twitch, but it's so slight I can't be sure. He flicks his gaze to the table then back to me, as if contemplating. After a second, he nods at the exit. "Let's go." He moves toward me, then his warm hand finds my lower back and he's steering me toward the hall.

I try to ignore the tingles that erupt at his touch. "What are we doing?"

"Going to find your sister. She's distracting you from your devotion to me."

chapter forty-five

*"You are my blue crayon,
the one I never have enough of,
the one I use to color my sky."*
—A.R. Asher

Adam

"Yeah, get me whatever we have on Francesca Highland."

"Right away, Master."

Ending the call with Aubrey, I open the door to my office and step aside for Emmy. It isn't until she's walking past the threshold, her shoulder brushing my chest, that I realize what the fuck I'm doing—holding a door open for a woman for the first time in my life—and I snap the hell out of it.

She lingers in front of my desk, running a hand over one of the two leather seats. Making my way to the opposite side, I watch her as I loosen my cufflinks and roll up my sleeves.

So this is the real reason she's here. Or was. I glance at her black scarf, and satisfaction rolls through me. Not her only reason now.

My eyes narrow on her as I think it over. "We didn't reach out to you."

She shakes her head even though it wasn't a question.

"How'd you get our number to begin with? It's not something we hand out freely." I lower myself into my chair, leaning back and stretching my legs out.

She chews on her cheek as she sits across from me. "My sister."

"Not so loyal, is she?"

"No. It wasn't like that." She sighs and glances away just as the desk phone rings.

I hit the speaker button. "Go ahead."

"Master, we don't have any record of a Francesca Highland."

I rub the bottom of my chin, flick my gaze to Emmy. "You sure about that?"

"Positive. You're welcome to check for yourself, but . . ." her words peter out, and my jaw ticks.

The records are kept in the front house. I would have to walk across a wide, sunlit lawn to get there, which isn't exactly at the top of my to-do list.

"Thank you, Aubrey." Hanging up, I lean back against the seat and tilt my chin. Emmy's forehead is creased in confusion, her head shaking. Aubrey is efficient. If she wasn't, I wouldn't rely on her. "Well, mouse. It seems you've made a life-altering mistake."

"It's not a mistake." Her voice is assertive, but her eyes flicker with doubt. "I saw her name on a log in the spa."

I rest my hands on the armrests and wait for her to explain.

"Well, not exactly. It was just a first name, and I guess it's a pretty common one. But still, it can't be a mistake. I heard her. My sister was on the phone with Stella the day she left."

"What exactly do you think you heard?"

She lets out a sigh and sinks deeper into the chair. "I was just getting back from, um . . . visiting a neighbor"—she darts her eyes away, and my hand clenches into a fist as a certain photograph of a guy with tattoos appears in my mind—"when I saw Frankie through the trailer's window. She was transferring a number from her palm to the bottom of her dresser. I walked around to the back and started to come inside, but then I overheard her through the cracked door. It was weird. She was hushed and secretive—nothing like usual."

When Emmy pauses to run her tongue along her lower lip, I grit my teeth. This conversation would be far less distracting if she would just keep still.

"She said she'd be ready to start right away, that she was honored to have received an invitation. She mentioned a contract, too, and something about confidentiality. Then she took off that same night. I waited to hear from her, and when a few months passed without a word, I called the number under her dresser. Stella answered." She shrugs. "You know the rest."

Tipping my seat back, I mull her words over. "So that's why you were crying in your photo."

"Oh. No." She picks at her fingernails, something I've never seen her do till now. "You saw that? I, um . . . my mama and I aren't exactly close. I'd been trying to talk to her about finding Frankie, making sure she's okay. It didn't go so well, that's all."

Her mother. I trace Emmy's movements, the way she rubs her neck, then tugs the bottom of her dress and swallows. I want to know why the woman makes her so uncomfortable. I want to know what Emmy's mother did to make her react this way at the smallest mention of her.

My collar tightens around my neck, itchy as fuck, as I realize I want to know everything. Who she was before she came to me. Who she wants to be now.

I won't push it. When she gives me those parts of herself, it will be on her own. Eventually, she'll tell me.

Eventually, she'll give me everything.

Reaching up, I loosen the top few buttons of my shirt, but that doesn't provide the relief I need. I'm hot everywhere, and why the fuck is my desk so wide? She's like a full room away from me. Biting back a growl, I let my gaze drift to the curves of her body. The parts of her I can see, touch. The only parts that should occupy my mind.

Her smooth skin begs to be touched, making my fingers curl around the chair's armrest. The angles of her face are round, soft, and I'm disappointed that her spattering of freckles is barely noticeable from here. When I find her eyes again, they're shiny. I squint, something uncomfortable burning hotter in my chest with each moment I watch her. I don't know when the hell my focus shifted back to her face, but fuck if it hurts to look away.

Irritation grips my veins. Murphy is going to be here in less than twenty-four hours, and more than likely not alone. I don't have time for this shit. And since Emmy fucking ruptured my ability to function solo, neither does she.

Tearing my gaze from her, I scrub my palm down my jaw and watch my cock-blocking desk instead. "Why are you crying?"

She shifts in her seat. "I'm not crying."

"Your eyes are . . . doing that glassy thing." Fuck, that was smooth.

She huffs out a snort and rubs her stomach, where her bandages are. "It's called being upset. I'm worried." When she sniffs, I slowly bring my eyes back to hers. "I just don't get it. I was so sure she was here. I mean, she had to have been. Right?"

I twist my lips, needing the fire in her eyes to come back so my chest can feel normal again.

Goddammit.

Hitting speaker, I dial Aubrey's extension.

"Yes, Master?"

"You still in the front house?"

"Yup."

"Try searching for a Frankie instead."

There's a pause, then, "No Frankie either. But . . . wait, I remember Frankie." Emmy sits up straight. "She was here this year, wasn't she? Came in with her personal belongings even though we told her not to?"

I shrug, even though she can't see it. Why the hell people expect me to know this shit is beyond me.

"Yes," Emmy pipes up, her head bobbing up and down. "That's her."

I narrow my gaze at the phone. "Why didn't she finish her contract?"

"I'm not sure exactly. Stella handled Frankie's departure on her own. I do know she was scouted while modeling in New York, and I believe that had something to do with her leaving so suddenly. Some agency had reached out to her with another opportunity."

I cock an eyebrow at Emmy, and her shoulders slump forward. "A modeling opportunity?" she whispers, like she's talking to herself.

"Thank you, Aubrey."

"Of course, Master."

The line goes dead, and I watch Emmy's brows furrow. "Well?" I mutter. "Sound like something your sister would have done?"

"I—yes. I guess it does, but . . ." She shakes her head, folds her arms over her stomach. "I just thought . . . I thought she would have written to me. But maybe it really is that simple. I mean, why wouldn't she take an opportunity like that? And who knows?" She pulls her lip between her teeth and glances at her feet. "Maybe not writing for a little while was what she needed.

A break from m—from everything. I wouldn't blame her."

I tilt my head, thinking the situation over. Truthfully, it fucking stinks. And it has Raife's scent all over it.

We might be fucked up, but our Matthews House business is legit as far as legalities go. We worked with the best lawyers to ensure it was, back when we first started this shit with the secretaries. That was six years ago—after my last sexual *incident*, among some other shady encounters my brothers were involved in. Griff being accused of rape, twice, almost burned our plans to ash before we even started.

Ground rules are simple, really: blondes only—to keep shit like this from happening—only women who get off on what we have to offer, they come to *us*, and a standard year-long contract is the sweet spot. That's typically as long as they can take before they want out, and it keeps them from expecting any further commitments from us. As far as contracts go, nothing explicit is stated aside from their secretarial duties, but our hires know what they're getting into from the start. If the contract didn't make it clear, the Dark Room certainly does. They sign up willingly and with all the right secretarial paperwork. They're compensated beyond fairly and can leave at any time. We don't hide or wipe out employee records.

Unless there's a reason to.

chapter forty-six

"Embrace the glorious mess that you are."
—Elizabeth Gilbert

Adam

"REALLY. I'M NOT HUNGRY." EMMY'S STOMACH GROWLS AS SHE STARES past the doorway at the dining table, the scent of eggs and bacon wafting into the hall.

Grabbing my phone, I pull up my text thread with Aubrey. "Your stomach disagrees." My fingers dart across the keypad, but when Emmy still doesn't move, I shift my eyes to her. I didn't plan on doing a kill in front of her; however, I haven't exactly worked out how to leave her behind either. Regardless of Raife's motives, Murphy is finally coming, and I'm going to end him. "The next twenty-four hours are going to be . . . eventful. You don't eat now, you might miss your chance. And your appetite."

She frowns but eyes the table again, her feet slowly moving toward it this time. "All right."

As she makes her way to the table, I stay in the hall and wrap up my text to Aubrey.

Me: Look into the agency Emmy's sister went to work with. I want to know who they are and how they were able

to contact her while she was here. Also, confirm that she did arrive and when.

Aubrey: Yes, Master.

Slipping my phone into my pocket, I glance up to see Griff walking my way.

He stops right in front of me. "Big day ahead."

I clench my teeth when he flicks his gaze to Emmy. "I thought we talked about the new rule, brother. You don't get to look at her."

His eyes flash, and he doesn't answer. But he does look away from her.

"You guys should be proud," I murmur, taking a step toward him until we're almost nose to nose. "Going behind my back twice in two days."

Griff's lips twist up. "Someone needed to move forward, whether it was you or Raife, and you know it. Raife just happens to be the one getting the ball rolling. Who am I to deny him?"

"Considerate."

He narrows his gaze. "I didn't come find you to rehash."

"So spit it the fuck out already."

"There've been some changes this morning. One of your kills is going to be here sooner than expected."

A snarl works through my throat, and I grab Griff's collar, pushing him back against the wall. "You have no business fucking with my plans. There's a reason I've been slowing them down."

"Yeah?" He shoves my hand off him and pushes off the wall. "You guys may have saved my life, but when you start treating a chick better than your brothers, you need to look at your fucking priorities."

We stare at each other for a minute, him looking as aggravated as I feel, and for the first time in a long while, I remember it.

The day I met Griff.

(Fourteen years old)

Fists slam down on the table, the teen's body straining against the straps as he fights. Katerina walks a slow circle around him, trailing a fingernail along his body as she does.

"So many scars," she whispers. "Poor Griffin. You've suffered so much."

He huffs through her coaxes, still not saying a word. He's refused to speak since she began this interview almost an hour ago.

"You can fight. You can kick and growl like an animal," she murmurs. "But you will eventually have to speak." She flicks her gaze around the room. "Do you see this small space? It feels cramped with the two cages and my artwork, doesn't it? But this, this is a lot more than just a room. There's history in these steel walls. You see, bomb shelters have many uses, many models, and this one in particular has a way of holding everything inside its walls. There's not so much as a crack beneath the door to let its essence out, and such closeness allows my art to speak to me long after my subjects are gone." She pulls back and inhales sharply. "Can't you smell them?"

I close my eyes for a split second and swallow. Not because of what she's saying, but because I can.

I can smell them.

Sofia jumps when the steel door swings open. Baldy's fingers grip No Name's arm as he shoves him toward my cage. The kid is naked, glaring and using his hands to cup his shit. I knew he was taken for pictures; I should have guessed they would have been nude.

Baldy is about to unlock my cage when Katerina strolls over and eyes No Name up and down.

She shakes her head. "I'll never understand the use of children as sexual objects. Completely twisted." She unlocks the cage herself and steps aside for Baldy to shove him in before locking it back up. "If Murphy hasn't transferred him by the end of the week, move him back to the storage room."

"It's still full." He pushes No Name's clothes through the bars then nods toward the kid on the table, Griffin. "We've got his spot open but there's already a new arrival scheduled to fill his crate."

"Figure it out." She gazes at Griffin, the wheels in her mind spinning. "I have an idea for this one. It will take a few days, though, then another week of prepping him for sales. I can't have distractions."

Baldy quirks a brow, then he nods and exits the room.

When Katerina heads back to taunt Griffin some more, I turn my attention to the buck-naked kid before me.

"Shit." I shake my head. "Didn't really think this one through, huh?" It's a sick attempt at making his smirks come back, but now that he's leaving, I realize it's going to suck without them.

His glare shifts to me, but after a second, his lips tilt up. "You underestimate me," he says under his breath.

My brows crash together. I match his quiet tone when I ask, "What'd you do?"

He nods toward the door Baldy just walked out of. "Remember his keys?"

I squint, scanning his body for something I missed. Even if he did manage to swipe them, where in the hell would he have stored them? "Yeah . . ."

He licks his lips, rubbing his stomach. "Best breakfast I've had all year."

"You are a crazy son of a bitch."

He smirks. "Fuck right I am. The crazy son of a bitch who's getting us out of here." He pulls his dirty jeans over his hips, then slumps down on the cold floor beside me. "You meant what you said about all the shit you wanna do to them, right? To these fuckers in charge?"

I rest my head back against the wall and picture it, letting two years of fucked up desires flood me. The way it eats through my skin and burrows beneath my bones grips me more like a compulsion than a desire.

After a second, I nod. "I don't think I have a choice." *And I don't think I want one either.*

"Good." He spits on the floor then wipes the back of his hand across his mouth, his eyes going black. "You and me. We're in this together, right?"

I slide my eyes to him. The only kid I've met who might be more fucked up than me. The rattling chains pull my attention back to the teen strapped to the table. Griffin's eyes are just as black as No Name's while he continues to struggle.

Hmm, so maybe not the only one.

"Yeah," I mutter. "Together, man."

chapter forty-seven

*"She didn't need to be saved.
She needed to be found and appreciated, for exactly who she was."*
—J. Iron Word

Emmy

AFTER SWALLOWING THE LAST BITE, MY FORK CLATTERS AGAINST THE plate when I see Adam shove Griff against the wall. He's clenching Griff's collar so tight his knuckles are white.

Pushing out my chair, I collect my dishes and set them aside then rush toward them. Griff is already turning his back and walking away by the time I reach Adam.

"Hey," I say softly, running my fingers down Adam's arm. He's staring at Griff's back, his fists clenched and a vein bulging in his neck. "Hey, what's wrong? What'd he do?"

He's still watching Griff when his phone dings. He pulls it out of his pocket and swipes the screen, his movements tight. After a second, he grits his jaw and slips it back into his pocket.

Finally, he turns to me. His gaze drifts along my face, eventually landing on my eyes. "Frankie's sudden modeling gig popped up four weeks ago."

My brows knit. "Okay?"

"How long have you been here?"

I glance down, thinking it over. When I look back at him, I'm more confused than ever. "Four weeks."

His hand finds my waist, gripping tightly, then he's guiding me down the hall.

"Where are we going?"

"To find Raife and figure out what the fuck he's up to."

When we reach Raife's office, it's empty, but Adam bulldozes straight to his desk, opening drawers and flicking through files. I make my way around the desk and move the computer mouse until the screen whirs to life. But of course it's locked. A garbled noise of frustration escapes my throat.

Adam glances at me, his lips tipping up at one corner. My stomach flips at the warmth igniting behind his eyes.

When he looks back down at the opened drawer before him, his gaze narrows. He whips out a file, tossing it on the desk and flipping it open. My eyes widen as I see photograph after photograph filling the folder.

Mama on her knees in prayer. Priest Henry scattering holy water around the trailer to cleanse the space.

My stomach twists at the third picture. I reach toward it, picking it up and staring into the flames. Mama found the canvases I hid under Frankie's bed. Some of them anyway. She's standing over them in the yard, watching them burn to ash. Right beside them is another box. My pillowcase, clothes, the pictures Frankie and I took together and hid away—none of it is recognizable now.

I close my eyes, willing the tears forming along my lashes not to spill. I don't know why it hurts. I should know better than to expect anything else by now.

When I open my eyes, Adam is watching me closely. I want to turn away, but the look in his gaze holds me captive.

He gives the slightest shake of his head, his voice low and commanding. "You don't get to hide anymore. Not from me."

After a second, my shoulders relax, and I let out a shaky breath. Relief floods me at not having to try. I don't want to anymore. I nod, and he withdraws another photo from the pile.

I frown, squinting as I look it up and down. It's a man I've never seen before, but I know who he is. He has dark hair, and a small blond-haired baby, bundled in a pink blanket, is in his arms.

"Your father?" Adam asks quietly.

I don't speak for a moment. I only heard Mama mention Daddy once, and that was to Frankie. She said he couldn't confront giving himself fully to the Lord. That he made his choice and would suffer eternally for it, but she and Frankie didn't have to do the same.

That's the thing about Mama, though. Whenever something threatens her beliefs, or her journey to Heaven, she forbids it—or them—from being spoken of under our roof. She is happy to pretend we never existed at all.

"If you can call him that," I finally whisper. Setting the photo down, I flip to the back of the file and see copies of my birth certificate and social security card. Behind that is a copy of Frankie's and Mama's, too. "What is all this? Why does Raife have it? Why has he been watching my family?"

Adam runs the backs of his fingers down his jaw, his expression thoughtful. He pulls out his phone and starts on a text. "He thinks he knows something about you, and he's determined to work it out."

I chew my lip, curling my arms below my chest. I've heard enough of Katerina now to know what he's referring to. "Well, he's wrong, you know. He's searching for a connection that doesn't exist, and it's only going to drive him more crazy when he realizes it."

I'm trying not to let the thought affect me, but I can't ignore the bundle of nerves tightening in my chest. Not only for myself, but for my sister who's innocent in all this. I've seen Raife's crazy side. And something tells me that's only a glimpse of it. I don't know how much more of him I'll be able to take.

A shadow flits across Adam's eyes when he takes in my expression. A second passes, his gaze running along my face, then he rakes a hand through his hair and shoves the file back in Raife's drawer.

His grip is around my waist before I know what's happening, and he's lifting me off the ground so my ass is on the desk. I suck in a breath as he steps between my legs, his body warming mine through our clothes. He slides his hands beneath my dress and cradles my bare thighs, his thumbs stroking small circles over my skin.

"Is Raife your master?" he asks, leaning down so his lips almost graze mine.

"No," I breathe, my fingers finding his biceps and pulling him closer.

He pulls my bottom lip between his teeth and sucks before releasing it. A shiver ghosts through my body, settling low in my stomach. "Who have you given permission to get under your skin and make you *feel*?"

My eyes flutter shut. "You."

A soft growl rumbles through his chest, and his grip digs into my skin. "Have you given Raife the right to own any part of you?"

With a thick swallow, I shake my head. "No."

His touch disappears from my left thigh, and his fingers tilt my chin up. He brushes his nose against mine so gently I'm sure I'm melting into a puddle right in front of him. Then he slips his hand around my hair and tugs. Hard.

I open my eyes to find him staring down at me, his blue irises burning as deep as the delicious fire he's dipped my soul in.

"Every emotion you summon or swallow back, every reaction you allow him to pull from you—it's yours. He owns nothing. He controls nothing. You are yours to give, and yours alone."

I choke back a wave of emotion that climbs up my throat. Do I really hold so much power? Images from my life flit through my mind—the neglect, anger, desperation, pain—and I'm not so sure. But when his thumb tenderly grazes my lower lip, and he's looking at me like those are the truest words he's ever known, I wonder if maybe he's right. Maybe I do hold more power than I thought.

My body slumps against his, and a single tear slides down my cheek.

He inches closer, runs his tongue from the bottom of the tear to my lashes, and a shudder rolls over me. "Not everyone knows what to do when they come across a snowflake in the desert," he murmurs. "You get to decide"—leaning into my neck, he breathes me in—"who gets to share you. And who doesn't."

"You, Adam." I press my lips to his jaw, wrap my fingers in his hair. "You do. You already have every part of me."

He leans in and bites down on my neck, making my thighs clench around his body. When he sucks, it's like he's trying to take a piece of me with him.

"I know," he rasps.

When a knock taps on the door, I jump. He pulls back to glance over my shoulder, but he keeps me tight in his grip.

"Did you want me to wait?" Aubrey's voice filters to my ears, and I wiggle against him so I can look at her.

She winks when she sees me, then returns her attention to Adam.

He holds my gaze for a second, like he's deciding on an answer, before shaking his head. "No. We don't have time to wait."

He steps out from between my legs and pulls me off the desk. As I straighten my dress, I dart my eyes from him to Aubrey. "For what?"

Adam tips his chin toward her. "Aubrey's taking you to my room. You're going to stay there for a minute while I find my brother and shut this shit down for good." I follow after him as he heads toward the exit, and he looks at me once more. "Stay together. And don't leave my room. Got it?"

Aubrey and I nod our heads in unison.

Just as he leaves, I call, "Adam."

He stops, looking over his shoulder.

"Why do you put up with him? Raife?"

He cocks a brow. "Because I owe him my life."

chapter
forty-eight

> *"Lips red as blood, hair black as night,*
> *bring me your heart,*
> *my dear, dear Snow White."*
> —Queen Ravenna

Adam

(Fourteen years old)

ONE AFTER THE NEXT, STRANGLED CRIES ESCAPING THROUGH GRITTED teeth rattle my eardrums. Hatred tears through my bones the longer I watch, but I can't look away.

I've never seen it done like this.

Thin streams of blood slip across Griffin's broad torso. He flexes under the scalpel as Katerina cuts, swirling her hand and making shallow designs like he's her fucking sketchpad. My eyes are glued to every tick of the blade, my veins strumming with bursts of energy I don't understand. The scent of fresh blood and sweat thickens the air, his pulse straining against his neck and his skin flushed, and this—this is how I would do it.

Griffin, he doesn't deserve it, and every cut only makes hatred seep deeper into my chest. But to do this, to dig into the flesh of those orchestrating this whole shitfest, to watch them suffer through each stroke of the blade and remember every single person who died at their hands . . . I inhale the stench and swallow it down, letting the sensation fill me. Jesus, I've never felt anything so satisfying.

"You're doing well, Griffin," Katerina coos. "I knew you'd show me everything through your eyes if I connected to your past. I do wish you'd discuss the boys who gave you these scars, but this is emotion enough." She smiles, her voice sounding distant. "I believe your pieces might just be the most honest of them all by the time I'm done with you."

She glances over her shoulder at me, the scalpel still rotating in her hands. "What do you think, Pet? Surely yours will be more beautiful?" I narrow my eyes, but she's already turning back to the other kid. "Yes," she hums to herself. "My sweet, sweet pet."

Katerina halts when the door is shoved open.

No Name taps my side just as Baldy walks in. "Here," he whispers, extending his palm and dropping something cold and metallic in my hands. "Slip them into your waistband."

I glance down to see two small silver keys, grimy with dirt . . . and shit.

"Quick."

Tucking them into the waistband of my pants, I drop my hands and lean back against the wall.

Katerina's hushed voice hits my ears, and I stiffen. "And you're just discovering that they're missing now?"

He shrugs and scratches his head. "I haven't needed to use them for the two days you've had this one in here. But now we've got that new arrival I mentioned"—he points a thumb toward the open door, where a crate sits. The kid inside is hunched over but alert, flicking his gaze over his surroundings—"and I can't get into the storage room."

"I'll let you in, and we'll discuss this further." Her tone is impatient as she leads the way toward the exit, and they disappear into the hall.

I waste no time reaching my skinny arm around the bars and sticking the first key into the lock. When that one doesn't work, I try the next. The cage door swings open, and I let out the biggest fucking breath of my life.

"No fucking shit," No Name mutters, a grin stretching across his face.

The first genuine smile in almost two years lifts my lips. I might have pursued this escape for Sofia, but now that the taste of freedom is on my tongue . . . I may as well embrace it.

I nod toward Sofia's cage. "Go. We have probably less than a minute."

He darts to Sofia's cage, unlocks it, and she steps aside to let him pass. When she looks at me, I wink. She hugs her teddy bear to her chest, smiling.

Sofia knows the plan. As best as she can anyway. I explained it last night in terms I think a five-year-old would get, and I may have left out the details about what would happen to her mom. She also knows the whole plan could crash and burn before we even get started, and to pretend she knew nothing about it if we're caught.

No Name pulls open the lid to her toilet. He wets a piece of toilet paper and places it over the overflow pipe, then unscrews the float. After putting the lid back on, he works on the sink, clogging the drains. When Katerina's heels start clicking toward us, he grabs the handcuffs beside Sofia's cage and scurries back into ours, closing the door behind him. Neither cage is locked, but we just have to hope she doesn't notice yet.

Katerina returns to the kid at the worktable, apologizing or some bullshit, and I stare at Sofia's toilet. Water is already trickling down the sides, but it's not anywhere near enough to cause the kind of damage we want.

I look at No Name, and he nods. "I know, man," he whispers from beside me. "It's cool. I told you I've done this before. I just need to get back in there and blast the sink faucets. I mean, it won't be quick, but I'm gonna check out the pipes too. I can make do with Katerina's bloodstained tools if I have to. A bunker like this, especially underground, will hold water like a fucking sinking submarine."

I'm not so sure, but I've never tried to flood a place either. And anyway, it's the best we've got.

"All right," I mutter. "I'm up."

Shaking out my hands, I take a breath and stand. *Shit.* A rush of nausea grips my forehead, and I steady myself on the bars. Our water's been out all day. Oh, the fucking irony.

"Katerina," I call, my dry throat burning like sandpaper.

Her hand freezes above Griffin's bloodied ribs. She looks back at me, her eyebrows shooting up. "My pet. To what do I owe this honor?"

I force my expression to look desperate, my lips turned down. "I need to talk to you. Please. This"—I gesture to Griffin, the blood dripping to the floor—"I can't take it. It's too much. I'm gonna fucking be sick." That part might be true, but I have my deteriorating physical state to thank for that.

Her head tilts, and she sets down the instrument. Griffin's body relaxes against the table, his chest going up and down with rapid breaths as Katerina steps away. Her eyes soften with each step she takes toward me.

"Is that right, my sweet boy?" She reaches the cage, and I move slightly to the left for what I'm about to do. "Is it painful for you to watch? Seeing someone suffer before they're put to sleep?"

I nod slowly, keeping my body relaxed. When she inches closer, I swing the door open and lunge. She gasps as No Name and I double-team her, shoving her inside and locking the cuffs around her wrist. My chest hammers straight to my ears. No Name locks the cage door while I reach between the bars, forcing her to the floor by securing the cuffs around the water dispenser, just a foot above the ground.

Her forehead connects with one of the bars, and she winces before staring up at me. "My pet." She sounds genuinely hurt, and my face twists with disgust. "You tricked me."

Holy shit. Yes, we fucking did.

Turning for Sofia's cage, I don't respond. We don't have time to waste on Katerina. No Name gets to work on the sink while I lower to my haunches in front of Sofia. I've never been this close to her, and she looks even smaller from here.

"Hey," I mutter, trying to smile even though my adrenaline is through the roof. "You still sure about this?"

She nods, her sky-blue eyes twinkling up at me.

When a familiar humming fills the room, all three of us look back at our old cage. Katerina is sitting cross-legged on the floor, watching us, and fucking singing. Except she's *actually* singing, lyrics and all. She's too quiet for me to make out all the words, but I catch something about children coming with her, into some kind of garden. A cold shiver shoots down my spine, and I break my gaze away before her level of psycho sucks me in any more than it already has.

After a second, I pull myself up, grabbing ahold of the bar this time for support. Glancing at No Name, I wipe my sweaty forehead with the back of my arm. "I gotta get those crate kids out, man."

He arches a brow, flicks his gaze to the hall. "You still sure about that? We might not have enough time."

I shake my head. "Stay with Sofia. I don't want her seeing that room."

When No Name's eyes dart to Sofia, he barely contains his loathing. It pisses me off, but I don't have a choice. I have to leave him with her. There's no way I'm walking her into a room overflowing with street kids stuffed in crates, especially when I don't know how they'll react once I break them out.

"Fine," he grumbles, "but you won't have time to come back and get her after all that. I'll bring her out with me. I'll make sure she's safe."

I cock a brow. *Yeah, no fucking way.* "Nah. I got her." Shifting back to Sofia, I soften my voice. "I'll come back for you."

She hugs her teddy bear tighter.

"Go, Lucas," No Name says, angling his head toward the exit. "Unless you want this to take all night. I still have to get to those pipes."

No Name turns away, and I head to Griffin. Shit, he's tore up. But the wounds are mostly superficial. Might be fatigued, but he should be able to stand. I grab a white cloth from beside the table and wrap it around his torso, then unstrap his wrists and ankles.

When he looks up as I pull him forward, our gazes lock. For a second, I'm taken aback by the black holes staring into me. I saw him before she strapped him down. It was obvious even then he'd been through hell already. But the look etched into his face now? It's like Katerina carved his heart out and left him to bleed.

I don't know how you come back from something like that.

Maybe you don't.

Maybe none of us will.

He grimaces as he slides off the table, but he walks pretty good as long as he leans on me. Just as I step foot into the hall, a small voice stops me solid.

"Promise?" it squeaks.

I look over my shoulder. Sofia is standing in the cage's open doorway, peering up at me.

When I don't respond, she hugs her stuffed animal. "Promise you'll come back for me?"

Something turns hollow in my chest, and I don't know what it is, but it hurts and soothes all at once. I can't believe she spoke, for me.

Finally, I nod. "Promise."

I start to turn, but Griffin stays rooted to the ground. Frustrated, I tug him again, and when he still won't budge, I look beside me to find him glaring at Sofia hard enough to burn a hole through her head.

A growl sounds from low in my throat, and my knuckles turn white around his arm. "You coming or staying?"

After a second, he rips his gaze away, wincing when I drag him down to the storage room. It's the only door in this short hall, other than the exit at the top of the built-in ladder behind us. I unlock it, and we enter a room of rotten stench and dark corners.

Crates line the walls side by side, piled on top of each other in stacks. Arms as skinny as toothpicks immediately reach out, grabbing for us, and parched voices climb over each other to be heard.

"Help—"

"Get out while you can—"

"Don't leave me here—"

The hair on the back of my neck stands on end, and I try to ignore the voices since my head is already pounding without every shrill cry.

"Here." I set Griffin on the ground so he can rest, but he

grunts and struggles back to his feet. He gestures to our left, where a single bolt cutter and a fire extinguisher lean against the wall.

I grab the bolt cutter and make my way toward the first crate. It's holding the new kid that was just brought in.

"What the fuck do you think—" Baldy's gruff yell is cut off when the fire extinguisher connects with the back of his head. He falls in a lump to the floor, right in the middle of the doorway. Griffin lowers the extinguisher, grimacing as he wraps an arm around the bloodied cloth on his stomach.

"Shit," I pant, my pulse ringing in my ears and competing with the shouts around us. "Thanks, man."

"Guess I owed you, right?" he huffs, leaning against the wall and sliding to the ground.

"Guess so. Hang on."

Returning to the crate in front of me, a fresh sweat breaks out on my skin as I cut the padlock.

The new arrival comes stumbling out, his eyes darting from me to Griffin. He's breathing hard, but his pupils are dilated with excitement.

What the hell?

"Thanks. I'll stay and help you." He nudges his chin toward Griffin. "Or I can get that guy out of here before he passes out. Your call."

My brows pull together.

"I'm Lex," he adds, like that somehow matters. "So what's it gonna be?"

The kid could be making a break for it, but he'd rather risk getting caught. Fucking weird.

I glance at the wall, my thoughts swinging back to Sofia. I need to get her the hell out of here. I want to tell him to get her instead. But I don't know him worth shit, and I hate that I can't take the risk.

"Get him," I finally mutter, pointing to Griffin. Then I pick up the bolt cutter and move toward the next crate. "Heads up, there might be alarms."

"You kidding? I know alarms better than I know my way around the streets."

"Also, you'll probably run into someone along the way." I glance back once more, my tone serious. "Kill them if you need to."

The new kid's lips quirk. "After this? Shit, with pleasure. I'll light their fucking souls on fire."

My head tilts. I like this one.

He takes Griffin, and I continue busting crates open, one by one. Exhaustion cripples me more and more by the second. Most of the kids say nothing, pummeling straight through the room as quick as their weak legs can take them. Some of them pat me on the back or shout thank yous. Many are crying.

When I get to the final row and my eyes start to blur, the bolt cutter slips from my sweaty grip. I wince as I bend to grab it, and black spots dot my vision.

Fuck.

I rest a hand on the wall, waiting for the spots to clear like they usually do, but they only get worse. Keeping my palms on the wall, I force my legs to move blindly toward the studio.

I have to get to Sofia.

I *have* to.

I take another step before I'm plunged headfirst into darkness, and I'm falling down an endless tunnel.

"Hey." Something smacks my cheek. "Hey, man. Get up. Right the fuck now."

Another smack, and I'm being dragged to my feet. My eyes drift open as I'm lugged forward, one arm draped over someone's neck. It takes a minute for my vision to focus, but soon I'm able to make out No Name. He grunts as he pulls my dead weight. With a groan, I manage to work my leg muscles and push myself forward with his help.

I look around, realizing I'm still in the storage room. Lifting my hands, I turn them from back to front. They're wet, along with the back of my pants and shirt. "Shit. Shit, shit, shit." It's shallow, but water covers every inch of the floor.

"Yeah, say that another ten times and you're getting there. You fucking passed out. You'll never believe how lucky I got, though. There's a damn garden above us. Already busted the main pipes by the time I found the hose, then got the hell out of here right after closing the studio. I thought you and the girl were long gone. Took me forever to realize you weren't one of the kids outside." He lifts his left hand, fresh blood smeared across his palm and fingers. "Had to go through some shit to get back down here. You owe me, man."

My brows crash together. "Sofia . . . You closed the studio?"

"Of course. I thought you had her. 'Nah, I got her.' Remember that?"

The adrenaline comes rushing back full speed, and I'm tearing free from his grasp. Sofia can't swim. I know because I asked last night, and she shook her little head. I storm past the empty crates, water sloshing at my feet, and get to the studio's closed door, then shove. "Give me the fucking key."

"I don't have the fucking studio key," he growls. "As far as I know, only Katerina had that one."

My throat tightens, my lungs constricting as I glance up at

the shoebox-sized, rectangular window at the top of the door. "Give me a lift."

"Are you crazy? We don't fucking have time for—"

"Giving me a fucking lift!"

He stares at me. I know my face is red, my eyes bulging like I might kill him with my bare hands if he doesn't, but I think I really might.

"Fine," he grits.

He crosses his fingers together and flips his hands so they're palm up. Stepping onto his palms, I use the door for balance and peek into the slit of a window.

The room is halfway flooded. Katerina floats at the bottom, cuffed to the bars with her eyes wide and black hair floating in streams around her head. I shift my gaze to the right and swallow when only the bars of Sofia's cage are visible from here.

Just a few feet in front of me, though, a pink teddy bear drifts along the surface.

Oil crayons hover above the floor.

And the tips of long black hair poke out from between the bars. Floating, just like her mother's.

chapter forty-nine

"Don't play with the Devil, he always cheats."
—Anonymous

Adam

I BARGE INTO FELIX'S OFFICE. WHEN HE SEES MY EXPRESSION, HE HANGS up the phone.

"Let me guess," he sighs, rubbing the balls of his palms against his eyes. "You're looking for Raife."

"Do you know where he is?"

"He's in the basement, but he cut the cameras down there a while ago." He loops his pointer finger around his ear and whistles the universal *coo-coo* tune. "He's officially lost it, man. Wanna pop in?"

My gaze narrows. "Not yet." Raife's trying to get me downstairs, but that's not how this is supposed to work. I go where I want to go. "I need your help."

"Anything, brother."

"Can you access Raife's computer from here?"

Felix scoffs. "Can I access—" He waves a hand through the air and sits up in his seat, then his fingers are flying across the keyboard. "Look, the dude's off his rocker. So whatever this is,

I'm in. What do you need to know?"

My shoulders loosen slightly, and I lean forward to see the screen, resting my palms on his desk. I might usually work solo, but it's good knowing I still have a brother on my side. Especially this one.

Felix was always the sanest of our group, even before we met him. When Felix—or 'Lex' at the time—was nine, he lost his family in a car accident gruesome enough to rival the basement after a kill. He barely survived himself. After getting hooked on OxyContin by the age of ten and being tossed around in the foster system, he started to prefer the streets. It was easier to get his oxy there anyway since his doctor cut him off. When the four of us broke out of the studio, Felix stuck to us like a wolf who finally found his pack. And when he met Aubrey in rehab years later, she became a part of our pack too.

I nod toward the computer, grumbling, "Raife's been obsessing over this Emmy/Katerina thing. I need to know what else he has on her. Anything to clue me in on what's going on inside his head and what he's up to."

He's quiet for a minute, flicking through shit like it's as easy as one, two, three. "Got something. Looks like he accessed it this morning, after our meeting. It's related to Kentucky."

I straighten and fold my arms over my chest, squinting at the screen as he opens another file.

Kentucky.

We went back there once since the night of our escape, and that was weeks after everything went down. I tried to return sooner for closure regarding Sofia, but my brothers—or, back then, new friends—insisted on waiting till things cooled off, so we didn't get arrested for murder. At the time, I fucking lost it on them. Even made an anonymous 911 call later that night despite knowing she was dead. At least they could get her body out of that tainted shithole.

Years later I realized it was good they stopped me. I would only have gotten us all locked up. Or worse.

When we finally did return, it was nothing but a big, green piece of land covered in trees. There were a few cottage-type properties on it, but not a single thing to reveal Misha or an underground shelter.

We eventually learned Murphy owned the land. Still does. And that a lot of money can cover up a lot of shit. Add a lawyer and politician to the mix, and the guy is virtually bulletproof.

"Here we go."

It's a video. Felix hits play, and we watch as a news reporter films in front of a hospital. The footage is raw and unedited, her hair blowing in her face and the sound intermittent.

"Mere hours ago the young girl was transferred to this very hospital in delicate but stable condition. She was discovered in an underground bunker on Wiley Road thanks to an anonymous call made to the police station at four-fifteen this morning."

My fingers dig into my shirt sleeves as her words reverberate in my ears. "What the fuck is this?"

Felix's mouth is hanging open, his eyes stuck on the screen.

"It appears that the child had been submerged in water from her chin down for an extensive period of time, reaching safety by using iron bars to climb above the water's surface. The exact time frame is not yet determined. While her injuries primarily seem to be bruises, likely caused from gripping tightly to the bars for such an extended period, she has experienced severe mental trauma and is not speaking at this time. At present, we are unable to identify the child. Authorities are actively working to identify her and trace any living relatives."

The screen goes black, and Felix starts clicking away again, but I'm fucking frozen from the inside out.

There's no way this is legit. I researched Misha, Sofia, everything about that place. We all did. And what we wound up with was the mother of all cover-ups. There was nothing to trace back to Murphy or any of the others there. Anything in the underground communities and black market had been wiped clean. And as far as Katerina and Sofia, it was like they never existed. Neither of them had records, not even a birth certificate to their names.

"Shit, this is impressive," Felix mutters, scrolling through something coded on his screen. "The asshole undermined me and hired an outside hacker to dig this up." He lets out a low whistle. "Gotta admit, I'm seeing a little green with envy here. This shit was buried deep, bro. As in, the footage was never released. Actually, it was shut down mid-report." There's a pause as he sits back, rubs his chin. "Huh. So if Raife just received this clip this morning . . . after you let Emmy cut him up . . ."

My lungs are so constricted I can't take a goddamn breath as I storm from Felix's office.

"Well, fuck *me*," he murmurs, jogging down the stairs behind me. "I swear though, dude, if this becomes a habit, I'm not going to chase after you next time."

My lungs are on fire, my pulse thrashing so hard I'm seeing black stars by the time I reach my room. I swing the door open, stopping in my tracks as I notice Emmy's absence. My gaze finds Aubrey tied to the bed, duct tape covering her mouth.

"What the fuck," Felix growls, pacing past me.

The fuck is right.

Felix strokes her hair then places his fingers on the edge of the tape. "This is going to hurt, baby." She nods, and he rips with one quick movement.

"Fuck!" she shrieks.

I grip the doorframe, one foot already out the door. "Where's Em—"

"He took her," she pants as Felix leans down and frees her wrists. "Fucking Griff took her."

chapter fifty

*"Do not feel lonely,
the entire universe is inside you."*
—Rumi

Emmy

GRIFF'S FINGERS DIG INTO MY ARMS, THE TOES OF MY HEELS DRAGGING on the floor as he hauls me down the dark basement hallway. My breathing is thick, my hair sticking to my damp forehead. I wriggle against him but can't get him to budge with my arms tied behind my back, and muffled whimpers are all that get through the tape over my mouth.

He takes me to the third room. The lights are off, leaving it pitch black, but I know someone is here.

Soft weeping bounces off my ears when I'm shoved forward and into some kind of metal crate. My nose hits one of the bars as I fall face-first, and I choke on a curse before straightening so I'm sitting up.

My eyes are wide as I look around, my heart slamming against my ribcage.

What the hell is going on?

"Emmy." It's a whisper, or maybe a cry. There's a sniff, then another broken, "Emmy."

I glance toward the familiar voice, to my right. After a moment, another crate takes shape. Slender fingers are curled around the bars. Behind them, a feminine face surrounded by long strands of hair stares at me. I lean closer, my heart rate picking up as the shapes of her eyes come into focus, her small nose, her high cheekbones.

Frankie.

I slam my shoulder against the bars, trying to get to her, and a shooting pain races through my arm. When I try calling her name, all that comes out is a stifled shriek, and Jesus, frustration boils in my blood until my eyes burn with unshed tears.

"Shh," she hushes me through quiet sobs. "He'll hear you." My brows knit, and she adds, "My master."

My eyes dart around the room again. A shape forms around the column, big enough to be a person but also too clunky. I continue looking but don't see anything, or anyone, else.

"I'm so sorry, Emmy," Frankie whispers, pulling my gaze back to her. "I had no idea you'd try to find me. I just needed—I just needed to . . . I don't know what I needed. But I never meant to lead you here. I'm so sorry."

I focus on my breathing—in and out, in, out. God, I want to yell. At Frankie. At Adam. At fucking Raife. But mostly at myself.

Why didn't I try harder to find her? Why did I let this place suck me in so deep?

I squeeze my eyes shut when harsh, bright lights fill the room, and they water when I open them again. I can't tell if it's from the harshness or if my tears have finally spilled.

I scoot backward as the form I'd spotted against the column earlier is suddenly directly in my line of vision, clear as day. It is a person. Except chains are wrapped around his chest and ankles, keeping him upright, and his head is hanging low. He's unconscious.

"You know . . ." Raife's voice slides past my eardrums, and a tremble runs through me as I try to spot him. "I wasn't so sure at first. I mean, I knew it was too coincidental. Enough for me to lock Frankie away in the front house when you made my fucking day by inquiring about employment."

Oh my god. She was here the whole time? Locked up?

I turn to Frankie, and my eyes well up. She shakes her head and whispers, "It's okay. It's okay."

"If you saw your sister here, safe and sound, what was to keep you from leaving? Nothing. And I needed time to observe you. What started out as pure fascination quickly evolved when I realized it couldn't all be a coincidence. But fuck, your mom knew how to cover her tracks. And this one"—he turns to Frankie, his lips tilting up. "She is talented at keeping secrets. You guys really had me going there."

My brows pucker, and I glance at Frankie again. Tears slide down her cheeks.

"Katerina wiped her existence off the map, then did a home birth with you—brilliant. Just brilliant. As far as the world was concerned, you didn't even exist, did you, Sofia?"

I shrink back as the lights somehow grow even brighter above our heads. My breath turns shallow and my dress feels itchy.

Sofia. Katerina. Sofia. Katerina.

"I apologize." Raife steps into view, his shiny shoes and suit-clad legs level with my eyes. "Are the lights making you uncomfortable? I thought you'd feel right at home."

Anger spikes in my chest, and I lunge toward him. He chuckles when I crash into the bars.

You have the wrong fucking person, psycho! I want to scream.

"I know." He kneels so our eyes are level. His head cocks, and disgust twists his face as he stares at me. "You're confused. But I researched this subject thoroughly for you—repressed childhood memories and all that psychobabble." He flicks his gaze to Frankie, and she swallows. "You had quite the traumatic childhood even after going to live with your aunt, it seems. I'd say I'm sorry but . . ." He stands, letting his incomplete sentence hang.

"Stella. Now, if you will." He winks when he glances back at me. "One final thing to set the mood, and this should do the trick."

A soft, feminine voice drifts through the air, so quiet I think my mind is playing tricks on me. It gets louder, and I shift in my spot, looking around the room. The voice is everywhere. In the corners, on the walls. In my crate and in my ears.

I know this song. Somehow, I know it.

Come little children . . .

I squeeze my eyes shut. Why does it hurt?

I'll take thee away.

No, no, no.

I try to bring my palms to my ears, I try to make it stop, but my wrists are stuck behind my back.

The song only gets louder, and soon it's seeping into my bones and filling my lungs. My knees fold up, my hair curtaining my face to block out the patches of light my eyelids can't close off. I need to stay out of the brightness. It's where bad things happen.

Blue eyes, black hair. She's looking down at me.

I shake my head. It's not real.

But it is. Her eyes are so *real*. Her touch when she flicks my nose with her finger, her quiet laugh when I smile. It vibrates on my skin, and I know it's real.

The images, the voices, they won't stop. They flood my brain until it hurts.

She tells me she loves me.

I'm her *baby girl*.

I want to say something to her; I want to speak. But then I remember I can't. I can't. Because I know what happens when people speak to her for too long.

There's so much crimson.

Smooth bones in my hand.

Just paint, I tell myself. Paint it red.

It looks just like the real thing, he said.

You did good, he said.

I promise I'll come back for you.

chapter fifty-one

*"Come back to me . . .
even as a ghost, even as a shadow,
a raven at my door, a scar upon my body—
for it is in my trembling, shrinking heart, I hold the things we thought
we lost."*

—Segovia Amil

Adam

Soft music filters through the basement hallway. I pace forward, fists clenching at the old, familiar tune. When I enter Room Three, lights blind my eyes.

"Fucking shit."

I stop in the threshold, holding my forearm over my brows. My muscles tighten, a low thrum stirring in my ears and blending with a song from my past. Unless the sun is down, I've hardly set foot outside over the past decade, never mind a fully lit room.

I can't stand the way it fucks with my head.

"Come, Lucas. Step into our blast from the past."

"Turn those fucking lights off," I growl, a mild sweat working beneath my skin.

A second later, the room dims, and I drop my arm.

What the hell is this?

A body is chained to the column, the head hanging low, but it's the crates in front of it I can't figure out. I step closer, squinting at the blond-haired girl I faintly recognize, her cheeks wet, her trembling fingers curled around the crate's bars. When my gaze flicks to the crate beside hers, my chest hammers so hard it's about to tear through my fucking skin.

Emmy sits curled in a ball. Her arms are tied behind her back, and her head is bent toward her knees. She rocks back and forth, her soft humming in sync with the song.

A snarl rips through me as I lunge forward and yank on the door, but an all-too-familiar padlock keeps it from budging. My grip tightens around the door, and her faint floral scent hits my nostrils. The smell makes me freeze. I watch her slow movements, forward and back, her long hair blanketing most of her body, and for a second I can't breathe. Her humming seeps into my ears and sits heavily in my chest. I grit my jaw, try to turn away, but my neck is too stiff.

It can't be her.

It's not her.

I *killed* her.

"Ask her sister." Raife's words are low and taunting.

I'm playing right into his slimy hands, but I glance at the crate beside her anyway. The blonde widens her eyes as she stares from me to Raife.

"Go on," Raife tells her. "Tell him who your *sister* really is."

"Raife. Shut your fucking mouth." The room goes quiet, nothing but Emmy's humming and the song playing on a loop. "Frankie. Explain."

She shakes her head. "I don't know—I don't know everything—"

"Start with what you do know. Don't cut any corners."

A lump passes through her throat. She flicks her eyes to Emmy then back to me. Her gaze slides down to my clenched fist around the crate.

"Okay," she whispers. "Okay."

I nod, my jaw ticking harder with every second she's not talking.

"I was ten when Emmy showed up. I don't know, I didn't understand it. She didn't have a name, but the men who brought her to us said she was Mama's niece."

"What men?"

Her eyes water. "I told you, I don't know. I swear. They were dressed nice, real professionals. They helped her get some papers, and the next thing I knew she was a part of our family. Mama wouldn't talk to me about it, and Emmy wouldn't talk at all, but my neighbor Betsy told me Mama had a sister once. I never knew about her. She said Mama's sister was adopted, and that she was something evil. No one spoke of her."

An irritated grumble rises up my throat. "What happened to Emmy?"

"Well . . ." She swallows, glances down at the floor. "Mama said . . . she said Emmy needed to be cleansed of her past, and of her own Mama. After the priest came, she told Emmy stories all about her life now, telling her this is the only life she's ever had. She tried to get Emmy to repeat her new name back to her, to tell her she understood that I'm her sister and she's her mama, but Emmy—she wouldn't say a word."

My gaze slides back to the crate in front of me, and my stomach twists. *She wouldn't say a word.*

"So"—Frankie closes her eyes and takes a deep breath—"so Mama locked her in the doghouse and repeated over and over again who the Lord is, who Mama is, who I am, who *she* is— Emmy May Highland from Presley, Mississippi—until Emmy finally echoed it back at her."

"How long was that?" My voice is low, fury gripping my lungs. When Frankie doesn't answer, I snap, "HOW LONG?"

"F-forty-two d-days," she whimpers through sobs. Her body shakes, and she wraps her arms around her chest. "It took forty-two days for her to believe it. I-I snuck out to lie with her every night. I begged her to just say it. Say what Mama wanted. I d-didn't know what to do. But I swore. I swore from then on I would always be there for her. I would be her sister. I would be the best sister she ever had."

My eyes shut as the fire in my lungs reaches my throat.

"I love her. I really do love her like my sister," Frankie whispers. Her words only irritate the flames. "I even tried to love her art. I knew it was important. She had to get it out. But sometimes . . . sometimes I could hardly look at it, and I worried she saw right through me. Eventually the guilt—it just ate at me more and more every day. I had to get away. From Mama, from everything. I always had to get away." She pauses, thank fuck, then looks around the room and mutters, "A-and now look what I've done."

I slip my fingers through Emmy's crate, stroking the soft strands of her hair and rubbing them between the rough pads of my fingers. She won't stop rocking. Singing. Shaking.

Sofia.

Emmy.

Whoever she is.

Somewhere along the way, she weaved herself so deeply into my veins I can't fucking inhale without her breathing life into me. When she first arrived, I wanted to get under her skin. I wanted to see if I could break her without even touching her.

But, fuck.

I had no idea I'd already broken her.

chapter fifty-two

> "There cannot be a passion much greater than this—
> it wells up in me, makes my heart ache . . .
> until my eyes brim with water, until my lashes grow dark."
> —Segovia Amil

Adam

"And so," Raife's voice gnaws at my eardrums, "the spawn of the bitch *becomes* the bitc—"

I don't know I'm moving until my fist connects with his ribcage. He keels over, sucking in a breath, then he locks his arm around my back. Wrapping my hand around his neck, I throttle him and shove him backward when Griff's form appears and a punch lands on my right side. Pain shoots through me, but I don't loosen my hold.

Griff goes for my neck, but Raife sputters, "No. Let him," and Griff halts mid-swing.

I narrow my eyes, relaxing my grip. What the fuck is he really up to with all this shit?

Raife's lips quirk, and he darts a sideways glance toward the column beside us. "You didn't even try to see who it is."

Gritting my teeth, I flick my gaze toward the unconscious

man. I take in his sharp suit, the gelled hair parted to one side.

Murphy.

A satisfied exhale blows past my lips. Releasing Raife, I stalk toward the man and lift his chin. Energy zips through my fingers at the mere touch. Fuck, it's electrifying, having him this close to me after all these goddamn years. The man who was always a mystery. The ghost hiding behind his wealth and conducting everything Katerina did from a safe distance.

He thinks himself a god, the egomaniac, which is what the name Misha initially represented. He might have played one for a little while, but his body is as frail as any of ours, and his soul is blacker than the deepest pits of Hell. He deserves to rot in all the ways Katerina escaped.

For a moment, I allow myself to close my eyes and inhale his scent.

"That's right," Raife purrs, his voice growing closer. "You can finish him *right now.*"

My eyes snap open. When I pull back, distancing myself from Murphy, a painful sting reminds me I'm going against my instincts.

"What happened to your elaborate plan?" I flick my gaze around the space, taking in the lack of screens. "Felix hasn't released anything to the media yet. And not so long ago you risked everything to kill Murphy yourself." Stepping aside, I gesture toward the limp body. "Now's *your* fucking chance."

We both want our revenge; the chance we missed with Katerina. Why isn't he taking his?

Raife glances at the crates then back at me. "Plans change. This morning has been . . . illuminating for me. As you know, I'm not always a selfish man, Lucas. I've brought you a gift. Two, really. The chance to end Misha *and* Katerina's bloodline—personally." He steps toward me, his chin dipped. "So you see, I'm choosing our brotherhood over my own desires. Will you do the same?"

I stare at Murphy, compelled. My fingers twitch with the impulse to grab my knife. Murphy is mine. But so is Emmy. And the weird stabbing sensation in my chest when I see her in that crate is fucking painful.

"Give me the key."

"Key? What key?"

"The fucking key, Raife. Give it to me before I cut your damn throat."

A smirk lifts his lips. "There is no key. Don't you remember how efficient I am at hiding them?"

I prowl toward him, braced to knock him on his ass, when my fucking phone dings. I'm tempted to ignore it, but Felix wouldn't text unless it was urgent. With a frustrated breath, I click open the message.

Felix: Watching the cameras and something's not right. Two shady SUVs are coming straight for us. Fast.

With my grip tightening around the phone, I slowly bring my gaze back to Raife's. "You didn't cover your tracks?"

He doesn't answer. Instead, he tips his chin toward Griff. Griff bumps my shoulder and walks around us.

"Brother." Raife clasps his hands in front of him. "It's time for this thing between us to come to a head. You and I have had our differences long enough, and frankly, I fucking miss the old you who wasn't so"—his face twists—"uptight. The one I set loose when we first got out. But the fact is: we're down to the last few people on this list of ours. We all need to move on, one way or another."

I shift when something drips behind me. Frankie's sobs get louder, and rage boils beneath my skin, making my muscles spasm. Griff is holding a container, encircling both crates in one thin stream of gasoline and, in the process, drenching the air with its stench.

"We don't have much time," Raife continues, rocking back on his heels. "Murphy's people will be here any moment, ready to lock us up or kill us. And you, Lucas, have a pressing choice to make. You can save Sofia and her cousin. Or, you can choose our brotherhood and finally taste the revenge on Murphy we've been craving for years."

Griff's mouth twists up as he moves to Murphy and encircles the column in a matching thin stream of gasoline.

"But we don't have time for both." Raife glances from the crates to Murphy, and he rubs his palms together. "So, what will it be? The rotten girlfriend, or the man responsible for endless suffering?"

I work my jaw, watching the man I've called my brother since I was a kid with new eyes. This is low, even for him. "I make my own calls."

His eyes flash. He whips something out of his pocket and shrugs. "Tell that to your precious Sofia."

With a single flick, the lit match is on the floor and a low ring lights up around the cages. One more flick, and the ring around Murphy does the same.

"Oh, shit." The female voice snaps my attention to the doorway, where Aubrey stands with her jaw dropped.

"Get the hell out of here," I growl, my knife already in my grip. "Now."

She stares between my knife and the crates then nods before rushing back upstairs.

Emmy's humming grows louder, her rocking faster. I lift my foot to step toward her, and the flames spread when Griff pours another short stream of gasoline. I freeze, my vision clouding with fury.

"My bad," Raife murmurs. "Forgot to mention that every step you take in that particular direction earns the girls another dose of gasoline, closer to their crates."

When Griff tips the container to add more, I charge.

He stumbles back at the impact, the open container dropping from his grasp and sliding across the room until it crashes against the wall. The spilled petrol branches out and connects with the ring around Murphy. Flames shoot in a thick line from Murphy to the container before erupting in tall bursts along the left wall.

I knock Griff to the floor and slam his head against it, trying to knock him out instead of having to use my knife. He curses and grabs my neck, squeezing hard before rolling us over so I'm on my back. A sharp spasm works up my spine. He tightens his stranglehold, and my lungs close up. When I'm on the brink of passing out, I use all my strength to drag my knife across his stomach.

"*Fuck.*" He releases me to clutch the wound. Blood seeps through his shirt and onto his hand. "Just let the bitch burn, you pussy!"

His eyes widen, and before he can make a move, I jump to my feet, yanking him up and lugging him closer to the column. The fire is climbing, but the excess chains dangling from the knot behind Murphy are long enough to reach safely. I shove Griff onto the floor so he's sitting upright then secure them around his torso and arms, less than a foot from the flames.

"Fuck you," he spits, grimacing as the metal digs into his wound.

"Pretty sure you're the one getting fucked."

I wipe the sweat from my forehead and glance at Raife when my phone dings again. He's clenching his teeth while he watches Griff, but he makes no move to interfere.

He's too stubborn. And too naïve if he still thinks I'll play to his tune.

Checking my phone, my gaze shoots across the smoke-fogged screen as quickly as possible.

Felix: Get the hell out. Murphy's men are in the front house. Ten of them. All packing.

I spot Murphy from the corner of my eye, looking beautifully helpless. After years of orchestrating everything Katerina did, then getting away with it and living like the god he thinks he is, he deserves to fucking die the most painful death. He's practically moving my legs for me when I shift toward him. Then Emmy's form flashes in my mind, bound and shaking within a low ring of fire, and a stronger force urges me to go the opposite direction.

Shit.

Revenge is all my soul knows. It's the only thing I've lived and breathed for almost as long as I can remember. With a painful swallow, I tear my feet away from him. It kills me, two different instincts seizing my bones. I pull at my hair, trudging toward Emmy because she fucking owns me.

A chuckle rips through it all, and my movements slow when my gaze lands on Raife's.

Shaking my head, I'm tempted to change course and smash his face in. But he's a distraction, and if I let him win, I won't get Emmy out in time. Instead, I position my knife, aim, and throw.

Raife's hands shoot up to block his face. "Fucking *fuck*!" He slowly lowers his arms, peeking to his left where the knife landed in the wall, two inches from his ear. "Well, shit." Panting through coughs, he wipes his sweat-drenched forehead with the back of his hand, then slinks along the wall till he's standing in the doorway.

I reach Emmy in the same moment Raife glances at the

crates, the fire, then fucking smirks. "Tick tock." And the asshole is gone.

My fists clench, a snarl working up my throat.

"The flames!" Frankie's shriek tears through the basement. She coughs, pointing to the wall across the room. "They're coming closer!"

Flames eat up the left side of the room, inching toward us, and smoke clouds the air. I move forward when a low choking sound snaps my attention to Murphy. His head is still slumped forward, his eyes closed, but his brows are puckered and broken moans escape as he slowly comes to.

Well, shit.

"Hurry, get Emmy," Frankie cries. "Please, hurry."

Emmy. My head pounds as sweat drips down my hairline. I flick my gaze across the room, searching for something to open the crates. After a second, I bolt toward the exit and enter Room Two, where my table is. Yanking out the bottom compartment, I shove the drill aside and grab two nut wrenches, then race back into Room Three.

"Get me the fuck out of here, asshole! Stupid damn—" A coughing fit takes over Griff's snarl, and I don't bother to look at him as I pace straight to Emmy.

Thank fuck the giant flames by the wall haven't yet reached the low ones circling the crates. My shirt clings to my damp shoulders and back, and my lungs burn with each inhale. I try to focus on the tool in my grip instead of the blurred images of the past bleeding into my mind. Stepping over the orange blaze, I place both wrenches on either side of the padlock's ring and shove them in opposite directions. The lock snaps open, and I pull Emmy into my arms.

I hold her close, feeling her melt against me, and carefully peel the tape from her mouth. It comes off easier than it should from the sweat dampening her skin. *Shit.* My pulse skips a beat as I breathe her in. Every bone in my body throbs, and I know it's not just from exhaustion.

My forehead touches hers.

Griff's coughs jerk my head up, and my own lungs start to close as the smoke becomes almost unbearable. With my gaze fixed on Emmy curled in my grip, I stand and move toward the exit.

I'm getting you out this time. I'm fucking getting you out.

"Wait! Don't leave me!" Frankie is staring at me, her cheeks red and wet, her eyes round.

I growl, everything inside me burning to get Emmy the hell out of here before it's too late. Risking it once was enough. I start to leave again because I'm not in the business of saving goddamn lives when Emmy's moan makes me stop. Her hair covers her face, her limbs weak, and fuck, she'll never forgive me if I leave her sister.

Stalking toward the exit, I lower her against the hallway wall, my hold on her lingering longer than it should. I lean forward, brushing the hair out of her face and cupping her cheek. Sweat and tears wet my palm.

I press my lips to her ear. "I'll come back for you."

Her eyes remain closed, and she doesn't respond. Swiping my thumb across her jaw, I tear myself away, my pulse hammering as I dart back into the room. I bust Frankie's crate open and pull her out, then lift her over the flames and release her.

"Fuck you, Lucas Costas!" Griff's choked bellow pierces my ears, and my spine stiffens. "I'll fucking kill you and your little whore!"

My shoulders constrict. "Frankie, stay with Emmy." She nods and rushes toward her sister.

When I turn around, it's not for Griff. The asshole paved his own path. Instead, I lift my shirt collar high enough to cover my nose, partially blocking the smoke from hitting my lungs, and pace toward the coward sagging against the column. The lucky shit passed out again. Fumes and flames lick at my skin and seep past my nostrils, the blistering heat pure ecstasy as I imagine what it will do to Murphy.

He isn't going to miss his own show.

I strike him across the cheek, then grab him by his shirt and shove his spine against the pillar. Finally, he groans and his eyes slowly open. He squints, then immediately joins Griff's coughing fit. When his brows shoot to the ceiling and the panic takes over, I step back. "Welcome to hell, motherfucker."

After pulling my knife from the wall, I exit the room without looking back and shut the door just as muffled cries of pain spill through the cracks. Frankie sobs harder, but she's wrapped her arms around Emmy and managed to lift her sister off the ground. She takes a step forward, toward the exit, and yeah, no fucking chance.

I pry Emmy's body out of Frankie's grip and haul her into my arms. I try not to think as I lead them around the corner and toward the garage exit. When gunshots ring from upstairs, I tense. Fucked up or not, I just lost one brother. And the bumps racing down my arms at the shots fired make me wonder if I've lost a second.

And Murphy. It still wasn't the death he deserved. My muscles are close to crippled with the anger that seeps into my veins at that. For the second time, a leader of Misha got off too fucking easy.

Kicking the back door open, we enter the underground garage. One, two, three cars are already pulling out, blondes behind each wheel and filling the back seats. My adrenaline kicks up as I watch them go and realize I don't have my keys since I never leave the damn house.

A black Mercedes comes to a screeching halt in front of us. The driver's window rolls down, and Aubrey jerks her head toward the vehicle. "Get in."

Felix grins from the passenger seat. "Yeah, man. Right about now would be great."

Frankie is already opening the door and sliding across the seat to the other side. Ice cold air from the A/C blasts on my damp skin when I slip in after her, hugging Emmy to my chest and closing the door. My back sticks to the leather as the wheels tear against the pavement, and I use my knife to free Emmy's hands from the rope.

I'm still on edge, every part of my body on high alert. My arms are stiff around Emmy, and I look down. Her eyes are closed, her long lashes casting a shadow above her cheekbones. Her breathing is even and peaceful, no sign of the shit she barely escaped from. With a tightness in my throat I'm fucking sure I've never felt, I sweep the loose strands of hair from her face.

My pulse slows as I watch her. The pace of my breathing falling into sync with hers.

I press her into me and dip my head, letting my lips graze her forehead. Letting her scent, her softness, her breaths fill me. She's delicate in my grip, so much like the mouse she tries to portray.

But she's never been a mouse. Maybe she was never a lion either.

With the number of times she's been burned and risen from the ashes, I'm starting to think she's an entity all on its own. I'm a mere mortal next to her. And fuck if I'm not her willing prey.

chapter fifty-three

> *"Life is going to break your heart.*
> *Remember to say thank you."*
> —Maya Luna

Emmy

My weight sinks into something hard, a chest rising and falling against my cheek. My eyes are so heavy I want to keep them closed forever. But soft bumps vibrate beneath our bodies, rocking me, and I force my eyes open to take in my surroundings. My hazy gaze takes a second to focus on the blacked-out window across from me. The backs of leather seats to my left.

I'm in a car.

Blond hair moves into my line of vision, and Frankie's glossy brown eyes meet mine. "Emmy," she whispers, a fresh tear spilling over her lashes. "It's okay now. We're going home."

She scoots closer and curls an arm around my waist. I want to respond. I feel like I should. But I'm disconnected from my body, the images in my brain so fragmented and overcrowded that exhaustion whirs through me at just the thought of trying.

Pieces still flood me in waves. Some connected to voices. Others drowned out by bold colors. None stringing together in the clear path I need.

After shifting my gaze up, my heart squeezes when I find Adam staring down at me. His deep blue eyes are intense but tired as they scan my face. His thick hair is tousled in all directions, his body tense beneath mine. Behind those distressed yet piercing eyes is a soul that speaks to parts of me I don't quite understand, but I certainly *feel*.

I see a man.

I see a boy.

I hear sweet words and feel the way a smile once played on my lips for him as he sat behind bars and gave me things no one ever had.

Friendship. Hope. Trust.

But then the betrayal sinks in. He didn't just earn my trust. He ripped it straight from my five-year-old chest.

My eyes flutter shut as I fall back against him, the weight of a thousand bricks pressing on my heart. As I drift away, I wonder what's going through his head when he looks at me.

I wonder if he sees them.

The bruises he left on my soul.

I shift my head against the pillow, the mattress dipping as movement stirs beside me. A sigh pours from my lips while I stretch my arms. I feel like I've been sleeping for days. My brows knit as my sister's face materializes in front of me again. Except this time, it's comforting. This time, I reach for her hand, and a soft smile lifts her lips. My body relaxes when she strokes my hair with her free hand, and I think my eyes are wet.

"Frankie," I whisper, my throat dry. "I'm so sorry. Everything that happened, it was all because of me. Because of who I am. None of this would have happened to you if I didn't show up at your door that day—"

"Shhh." Her smile spreads, but her eyes are wistful. "You don't ever need to apologize to me. I should never have let Mama treat you the way she did." She swallows, her gaze darting between my eyes. "There are so many things I wish I could go back and do differently. So many things I wish happened differently or didn't happen at all. But not one of them involves you becoming my sister. I'll happily sneak you paint and canvases for the rest of our lives." I choke out a laugh, and her eyes water. "No, fuck that. No more sneaking around. I'll cover Mama's trailer walls with blank canvases and fill the floors with buckets of red paint for you."

A sob strangles my chuckle, and she smiles, wiping a tear from my cheek with her thumb.

"Frankie?"

"Yeah?"

"Where the hell are we?"

She snickers, her shoulders shaking softly. "Well, we're back in Mississippi. Remember that inn? Buffalo Creek?"

My nose scrunches, and she laughs.

"Yeah, it's crappy, but it's quiet too. I think we all needed a little time to ourselves anyway. Two days was just right."

"Two days?"

She shrugs. "A day of straight driving, then a day here—"

My eyes widen, and I start to sit up, but she pulls me back down. "Adam—"

"Adam's here." She tips her chin toward the bedroom door. "He's barely left your side since we arrived, except to pace through the living room. And let me tell you, the man looks like he's about to punch something. I tried talking to him, but . . . he's not much of a talker, is he?" I swallow back a laugh, and I hate that my body vibrates with the deep-rooted need to see him. I don't want to want him after what he did to me. "He's kinda scary, actually. But, like, in a highly fuckable way." She grins.

After a few seconds of silence, though, reality creeps back in and our faces go somber again.

"So," I whisper, "what are you gonna do now?"

"Me?" She rolls onto her back, staring up at the ceiling. "I can't believe I'm saying this, but I think I found a new appreciation for home. I'll probably stay for a little while, make Mama suffer before I head back to New York."

"You're leaving again?" As I say the words I've said so many times before, they sound different to my ears. There's nothing hollow in my chest. No desperation. No fear of being alone.

It's just a question. A question whose answer no longer has the power to hurt me.

I glance away, letting the unfamiliar sensation soak in. My time at the Matthews House was many things. I'd never truly been on my own before, and the broken pieces of my soul ache to be mended. Still, all I can feel is stronger.

"Yeah, I think so." Frankie's lips tip up. "I made some great friends before signing up with the Matthews, and I think I can really get far there. But maybe I'll let Mama take me to church a few times first—after having Priest Henry cleanse her of her demons." She winks, and we both chuckle. When she turns back to me, she whispers, "What about you?"

I let out a long sigh. "I'm not going home." My brows furrow. "I don't think I really have a home. But I think . . . maybe that's okay. Maybe home isn't a place anyway."

I hold a hand over my chest and take a breath, absorbing the strange feeling of my broken pieces trying to sew themselves back together.

"Yeah." Frankie's hand squeezes mine, and she nods. "It's so much more."

chapter fifty-four

> *"There is true life somewhere inside this body,
> claw your way through until you find me."*
> —Maya Luna

Emmy

IT'S THE STRANGEST THING, LOOKING AT YOUR REFLECTION AND SEEING someone you don't recognize. My hair is wet from my shower, and a shiver runs down my bare body despite the warm steam clouding the bathroom. I lean over the sink, pressing a hand to the glass. I can't stop staring.

I've thought before that my soul was split in half.

Now I finally know why.

I wish I could talk to her. Sofia. I would tell her she's right. Life isn't a fairytaie, and for some of us, nightmares are real. If we're really unlucky, they make a home inside us, wrapping their claws around our souls.

But then I would tell her she's stronger than she knows. And sometimes, that's enough.

My fingers curl against the mirror, and tears prick my eyes.

It has to be enough.

I jerk when Frankie's voice hits my ears. "Mind if I hop in

the shower before you take me home?"

Wiping a tear before it falls, I grab a towel and curl it around my body, then open the door. I force a smile. "Yup. I might have used all the hot water, though."

Frankie pulls her towel back, steps around me, and snaps it against my ass.

"Ouch!"

She grins and closes the door before shouting, "Now we're even."

I shake my head and walk to the little black dress draped over the bed. Aubrey washed it for me this morning, but it's still going to be weird putting it on now that I'm back in the real world. I drop the towel and slip it on, getting it over with. First thing I'm going to do when I drop Frankie off is borrow some of her clothes. If Mama hadn't burned my belongings, I'd pack a bag of my own. Not that I know where I'm headed, but I kind of like that.

There's something freeing about being able to create my own future. One that doesn't chain me to my past. I've spent enough time confined, I think. It's time to see what happens when I fly.

A soft knock raps against the door, and my chest tightens.

I still haven't seen or spoken to him yet. Adam. I don't know how to when the ache in my heart is still so tender. That night he left me may have happened fifteen years ago, but to my mind, it may as well have been yesterday.

"Hey, Emmy?" Felix's voice filters through the closed door.

I clear my throat and walk toward him, turning the handle. He's still in his suit—suspenders, bowtie, and all. "Hey."

He glances down, rubs his neck. "I'm heading out with Aubrey for a minute to grab us some food. Any requests?"

A form shifts behind him, and my heart lurches when I spot

Adam. He's standing not even ten feet away, leaning a shoulder against the wall with one hand in his pocket. His chin is dipped, but a muscle twitches in his jaw and his eyes are honed in on me.

I swallow, still watching him when I answer Felix. "Whatever you guys want is fine. Thank you."

He nods and walks toward the exit, where Aubrey is already waiting for him. "Be right back," he calls as he leaves.

Then we're alone.

Adam pushes off the wall and steps toward me. For a second I'm frozen. Every bone in my body is determined to stay where he can reach me, where he can touch, hold, taste me. But my heart knows better.

I move to slam the door shut, but he stops it with his shoe.

With my hand still on the knob, I look away. "Adam, don't."

"You've been avoiding me." His words are strong, smooth, but when I face him there's desperation in his eyes.

The look only hurts me more.

I let go of the knob and distance myself from him, turning my back and folding my arms across my stomach.

God, it's so fresh.

Every word from his lips.

I promise I'll come back for you.

Every minute behind those bars.

Baby girl. You still like to color, don't you?

And every second that followed after he left me to die.

I'll let you in on a little secret Lucas didn't tell you. Promises are made to be broken. People like you and your mom? You deserve to die.

I snap back to reality when Adam steps closer, his warmth on my back. Rough fingers trail up my bare arms, and a shudder runs through me.

"I trusted you," I whisper.

His hands freeze.

I step forward, out of reach. "I waited for so long." A sob works up my throat, but I force it down. "Even when the door closed. Even when I climbed as high as I could and water still reached my mouth. I waited. I still thought . . . I thought maybe . . ."

The air is so still it feels frozen. Images, sensations, emotions—I've opened the floodgates, and now I'm drowning in them.

I hear him swallow, and I whirl around.

He's looking anywhere but at me, his fingers working his collar like it's too tight to breathe.

A rush of anger surges through me. My eyes narrow, and I move forward.

"Do you have any idea what it's like? To watch your mother drown right in front of you?" When my toes brush his shoes, I lift my chin and grit my teeth. This would be so much easier if he'd just back away. Why won't he back away? "To be so scared you can't breathe? Can't cry? Can't call for the one person who was supposed to—who was supposed to—" My words choke on a sob, and I hate it.

I step around him, my arm brushing his shirt, and he catches my wrist, keeping me in place.

He holds my gaze with his, the coldness in his voice not matching his eyes. "I wanted to be there—"

"You abandoned me!" Tears stream down my cheeks. I tug my hand, but he only grips it tighter. "You left me with *Raife*. Was that part of your plan from the start?" My words hang between us, and I know I'm being ridiculous, but they spill out on their own. I can't stop the conflicting mix of emotions gripping me. "Did you tell him to lock the door after he took the key too?"

A low growl works up his throat, and he walks me backward until my spine hits the wall. I suck in a breath.

"What key?" he grits.

The door to the bathroom opens, but neither of us break our gazes. I narrow my eyes. "The key he took from my mom. The one he used to lock the deadbolt."

Something flickers in his eyes, and a vein pops in his neck. He places his palms on the wall on either side of me, then he leans down, his lips grazing mine. "I came back for you, Emmy."

My heart skips in my chest, and butterflies jump from my stomach to my throat.

"I came back," he rasps, his shoulders rippling with tension. "I never meant to abandon you. I was a fucking idiot. I thought I could do it. I thought I could get everyone out of there." His eyelids lower, and he dips his head so he's somehow closer. His breath skates across my skin. "I fucking failed you."

His nose brushes mine, and I run my tongue over my lower lip. His gaze drops, his lips parting, and just when I think he might kiss me, he pushes off the wall.

All the air releases from my lungs at once. My chest is pounding, and I can feel the disappointment all the way to my toes.

He turns away, runs a hand through his hair, and clasps the back of his neck.

I can't tear my eyes from him. The banging in my chest makes it harder to breathe with each second I stare.

He came back.

He came back for me.

chapter
fifty-five

*"Madness, as you know, is like gravity.
All it takes is a little push."*
—The Joker

Adam

I SCRUB A HAND DOWN MY FACE, FLICKING MY GAZE TO THE CLOCK ON the wall again in between pacing. It's been two hours. Their trailer is seven minutes away. How long does it take to say a fucking goodbye?

"Hey," Felix calls from the mini kitchen to my right. "Deep breaths, man. In and out."

I snarl, and he chuckles, shaking his head.

I'm tempted to look out the window again, but the sunlight rips right through my head every time I do. We already had to hang a spare blanket over the glass. It's sunny as shit in August, and the curtains here might as well be non-existent.

Jesus, I don't get the painful sensations running rampant inside me. Two days of her resting, then she leaves right after she finally talks to me. The adrenaline racing through me is ready to burst. I keep going for my knife, thinking the feel of the blade in my hands will calm me, but it doesn't. My chest burns, and my lungs are too tight to pull in enough air. I try to focus on somehow getting to my last two kills for some goddamn relief, but all I can think about is *her*.

I've even tried distracting myself with other things. Felix and I have talked in length over these past couple days. For a while, we monitored the house through the camera access he has on his laptop. Watched the police raid the place, trying and failing to get info off the software Felix fried and from the desks Aubrey cleaned out before she organized getting the secretaries to our extra vehicles.

Call it bittersweet. All I feel is bitter.

Nothing is foolproof. There's still shit to lead back to us and what we've been up to. And then there's Raife. Felix and I went through the backlogged recordings; Raife, with Stella's help, walked away from the bullet he took in his side. He's somewhere, his heart beating and his Emmy/Katerina obsession most likely thriving. But we've escaped death, prison, and worse before. Recreated ourselves and found sources of income behind screens. We can do it again, and better this time. As far as Emmy is concerned, if Raife comes looking for trouble, he'll find it in the form of my knife in his throat.

None of that is behind the tension in my muscles and craving in my bones.

The last words Emmy spoke to me were filled with loathing, and before that, she didn't speak to me at all. I watched her sleep, seeking something to fix me, but all that built was a weird ache in my chest. That shit was worse. I need her to look at me with something other than pain and venom. I need to feel her grip me back when I hold her. I need her exhales to saturate my lungs.

My body can't seem to function without her, so it's basic fucking survival I'm concerned about.

"Dude, we're missing it," Felix mutters, pulling my thoughts back to the room. He grabs the remote from the counter and turns up the volume. "Showtime."

I step closer, my eyes narrowing on the screen. Felix wasn't kidding the other day when he said the files were set to automatically release to all major platforms.

". . . that the investigation into the murder of attorney and soon-to-be Kentucky state senator elective, Arnold Murphy, is still ongoing. However, officials have since acquired further evidence of the atrocious acts committed by members of *Misha*, an underground criminal group Murphy allegedly operated and oversaw. Fifteen years ago, Misha reigned in the black market, with records showing millions of dollars gained through sex trades and . . ." the brunette reporter folds her hands over the desk, a swallow passing through her throat as the first image appears in the upper right corner of the screen, "selling the disembodied bones of kidnapped minors."

It's bright when I spot it. Colorful and lively. It can't be more than four inches long on the screen, but in person, it's closer to nine.

I remember this skull. The way Katerina carefully glued the peacock feathers on all sides but the face. The white paint that lingered on her fingers long after she smeared the color across each cheekbone. I also remember the forearm that belongs to the same subject, a bone Katerina once handed her daughter just before asking if she still liked to color.

My lungs constrict more with each second I stare at it, making every inhale feel like a goddamn chore.

I wasn't expecting this. Actual photographs as real as my memories, maybe more so. I refuse to look away. I'm a part of it, Misha and that very skull. They're embedded into my soul, stitched with the blood I've witnessed and drawn.

When the image changes to spotlight a small white notecard sitting in front of the skull, Felix pauses the TV and cranes his neck toward the screen.

"Fly for me," he reads aloud. "I'm not a bird. I'm not a swan or a dove above your head. Perhaps my wings are made of dirt from the earth below your feet. Perhaps my soul, the very air you breathe. My heart is fire; don't get too close, for you will fall to ash deep in the shadows. Don't go too far, for you will thirst for me like you would a cascading waterfall in the desert. I'm not a bird, for I am you, and you are me. I'm not a swan, for I am everything, you see? I'm not a dove. I'm only human with dreams of being set free. Won't you fly for me?"

Silence expands in the room when Felix finishes. His eyes are stuck to the TV, his body as still as the news reporter on pause. "Hell," he whispers. "Katerina makes us look normal." He shifts his gaze to me then winks. "Well, me at least."

I pull at my collar and squint at the walls, certain they're inching closer. Was this room always so damn small?

Felix hits *play*, and as the news reporter resumes speaking, I glance at Emmy's bedroom. It's so empty. A strange rhythm erupts in my chest, each beat lingering like an echo. Digging my knuckles into the area, I try to rub the irritating sensation away.

So fucking *empty*.

". . . and a string of those allegedly in connection with Misha at one time or another have reportedly begun disappearing over the past several years, including Hugo Perez, the well-known CEO of Shaggy Entertainment Industries who was officially reported as missing on July 22nd of this year. While there are currently no leads on the person or persons behind the disappearances, viewers are being encouraged to speak now if they have any information on—"

"Cut it off."

Felix looks over his shoulder, his brow shooting up.

I press my fingers and thumb to my temples, attempting to quiet the throbbing in my head.

A second later, the screen goes black. It doesn't relieve any of the tension from my body, but it does shut that reporter the hell up. I blow out a breath. What the hell is taking Emmy so long? I flick my gaze back to the clock, then the shaded window, my shirt feeling too tight across my shoulders.

Felix walks back to the kitchen, watching me as he passes. He doesn't say anything as he places our leftovers in the fridge. After a minute, I pace into Emmy's room, stopping midway and wrapping my fingers around the doorframe.

Fuck this.

"Dude, wait—"

I barely hear Felix when I barge past the exit. Within seconds, I'm in the shoddy lobby and blurring past two young receptionists. The news is on, that reporter's grating voice filling the space, and one of the guys behind the desk is clapping his hands.

"Serves the bitches right, though. Doesn't it?"

"Yeah, man. Sick shit right there."

"Call the person behind the disappearances a hero and move on with your damn life, reporter lady!"

Sunlight beams in my eyes as I push the front doors open, and I groan. My head pounds like a hammer is swinging inside my scalp. *A fucking hero.* Those kids don't know what in the hell they're talking about. Draping an arm over my forehead, I take a step forward, no clue where I'm headed, just that I fucking need her. The rays of light creep past my arm and beat on my skin and eyelids. My throat tightens a little more with each step I take.

When the light closes in on me, cutting off my breath, I curse and bend forward, placing my palms on my thighs and trying to suck in some goddamn air.

What the fuck?

I start to turn around, but specks of black dot my vision. Where the hell is Emmy?

chapter fifty-six

> *"This is my confession.*
> *As dark as I am, I will always find enough light to*
> *adore you to pieces with all of my pieces."*
> —Johnny Nguyen

Emmy

I REST MY HEAD AGAINST THE SEAT. MY EYES ARE SET ON THE FAMILIAR houses flicking by, yet all I see are peacock feathers, bright and blue, bones and paint, white and smooth. After saying my goodbyes to Frankie, I stopped by Batshit Betsy's trailer to say hi, and the news was on. But the images featured felt off to me. My child self saw many things, but not one memory is as clear as that skull I just saw on screen.

I've always painted pictures of them, skulls and other . . . parts. I paint them just as I recall. There are no peacock feathers. No perfectly proportioned streaks decorating their cheekbones. There is white, and there is red, and there are black bursts of agony hiding behind the oily remnants of flesh that were stripped from them.

Watching that reporter, the images, I just wanted it to stop. I was ready to tear the cord straight from the wall if I had to.

Batshit Betsy wouldn't have it. "Hate me if you wanna, but you can't ignore these things forever."

She wasn't done at that either. She went on and on about Mama and Katerina, even when I covered my ears with my hands.

"Never know what you're gonna get with a closed adoption, you know. The family just wasn't ever the same after Katerina, 'specially Agnes. Two of my cats went missing when they were kids, and I swear to this day it was that woman who did somethin' to 'em. Shame, really, to see a brilliant mind weighed down by so much evil. Her poetry was dark, I s'pose, but it was music to my soul. Matter o' fact, she won contests 'round here for years."

Ugh. I jab the window button until fresh air whips at my face, and I close my eyes.

I don't want to know Katerina. I don't want to remember that the only mother who ever told me she loved me was such a horrifying person.

I do, however, have hopes of getting to know Sofia better.

One day.

"Hey, you all right?"

Dazed, I turn to face Aubrey, who has one hand on the steering wheel and the other hanging out the window.

"We can drive around a little if you want. I'm sure the boys will survive without us a bit longer."

The boys.

Adam.

Oh god. Did he have to watch that, too? Is he still watching it now, those images flashing in his eyes, that reporter's voice drilling into his ears?

I chew on my lip and shake my head. "No. I have to see him." I have to hold him. I need him to hold *me*. I haven't been able to shake the ache for him since I walked away with bitter words on my tongue. And now . . . god, now, it hurts so much worse.

"Wait—" Aubrey slows the vehicle, focused on something outside her window. "Is that . . . Is that Adam? He's *outside?*"

I lean forward to see past her, squinting through the sun. Adam is bent forward, one hand on his thigh and the other rubbing the back of his neck.

I'm unbuckled and out of the car before it comes to a full stop. "Adam!"

My eyes burn at the sight of him. I've never seen him like this, and I don't think I can take it. I race across the street and slide my fingers into his damp hair.

His eyes are wild when they lock on me, unhinged and desperate. My heart stutters at the look alone. I take his hand, and I'm about to pull him toward the inn when I spot the rays of sun seeping past the glass windows, reflecting on the floor.

Darting a glance back at the car's blacked-out windows, I jerk my head across the street. "Come on." He doesn't move at first, his posture tense, muscles straining against his shirt. I step close enough to press my body against his and curl my arm around his torso. My voice is stronger than I feel. "Come with me, Adam."

When he steps forward, I breathe a sigh of relief and guide him toward the car.

I need him to be okay.

I need *him*.

Aubrey slips out of the vehicle, leaving the keys in the ignition, just as I get him settled into the backseat. I pull the door shut and climb onto his lap so I'm straddling him, then cup his face in my hands.

"It's okay," I breathe, leaning forward and softly pressing my lips to his forehead, his cheek—careful to avoid his lips. We haven't kissed, and even though I want to so badly it hurts, I won't make him cross that boundary. "Everything is going to be okay."

His gaze trails along my face as if he's making a mental map of every curve, every freckle. "Emmy," he croaks, his voice rough like he hasn't spoken in days.

"I'm here," I whisper. *For you, I'll always be here.*

When his large palm covers my hand and squeezes, I inch closer.

The longer I stare, the more I get lost in him. His expression is so pained, his muscles tensing against me and his skin burning hot. "You left me," he rasps, his grip finding my waist and pulling me in tight. "I don't know why I can't—I can't fucking breathe—"

"Shh . . ." I tilt his chin up and run my tongue across the thumping pulse in his neck. A swallow moves down his throat. Bringing my lips to his ear, I tangle my hands in his hair. "I couldn't leave you if I tried. Don't you know that? You're a part of me now. You've always been a part of me."

A tremble vibrates from his body to mine, like a tangible current in our souls. It's the most divine thing I've ever felt. Without thinking, I lean back, lift my hand, and drag my fingernails down my upper arm the way I once did to him. Specks of crimson illuminate my skin, seeping from my wound as if pulled toward him.

He lets out a broken groan as he stares, mesmerized.

"Do you see it?" I whisper, running a finger over my cut and tracing it down his warm neck. He wears me like I was made for him. "Do you see yourself in me?"

His eyes squeeze shut, his fingers slipping to my hips and digging into me like he can't get me close enough. When his breathing gets hard, rough, he grinds me against him. A warm flutter zips between my thighs. He's just trying to close the gap, but I want more. Doesn't he know I want everything?

And in return, I'll give him all of me.

I grab the bottom of my dress, sliding it a few inches up until it's over my hips, then I wiggle and slip my panties off. His eyes snap open. He grits his jaw, his gaze trailing down my bare skin and leaving a shiver wherever it lands. But he doesn't make a move to touch me. His body is stiff, and I wonder if he even can right now. Slowly, I reach between us and work his zipper.

We watch each other for a long minute, all the things I want to say to him racing through my head. I don't know how to be sentimental. Not aloud anyway. Maybe that's my biggest secret of all. Sometimes the feelings in my heart feel too large and delicate to release into the world. Sometimes it's easier to say everything and nothing all at once.

Can I keep you? I silently ask from below my lashes, with nothing more than a heavy swallow.

Leaning closer, I blow on his skin and drag my nose against his stubble. I slide my palm to his chest. A solid *thump, thump, thump* races beneath my hand.

Will you let me into that place so deep your darkest secrets hide with ease?

The air thickens between us. Soon it's a sweltering stream of sunshine coating our bodies. When I pull back and his gaze flicks between mine, there's something I've never seen before. It's exposed and vulnerable. It makes my chest pang in a way I've never felt. My lips part to breathe it in, and I swear I get high on Adam Matthews.

A shaky breath pours from his mouth, like he hears every word I can't speak. Lifting his hips, he tugs his pants down. He tilts his head, skims his lips over my open wound. Then he presses his mouth to it so gently a tender ache swells inside my heart.

He's inviting me in during his most exposed moment. Warmth seeps into my soul. For a moment, I'm lighter than someone so capable of darkness should be allowed.

I curl my hands around his neck. Then I lower myself onto him. My eyes flutter shut as he fills every inch of me. An agonized groan tears through him, and he angles his head to look at me. His hands find my ass and squeeze, but instead of keeping them there, he brings them higher, higher, until he's cupping my face. He never breaks his gaze as I grind delicious circles, and my heart skips at the intimacy of it.

I've never been held like this during sex. I never expected something so small to be like an anchor keeping me bound to him.

After a second, I quicken my pace, and he drags one hand down to grip the nape of my neck; the other finds my waist. A long tremor ripples through his body, and hell, everything about him feels so *good*. Mewls spill from my lips, one after the next, as the sensations build and build with every roll of my hips.

When I find his eyes, they're hooded and consumed with raw hunger.

God, lust is scorching hot on him.

Throwing my head back, I grip his shoulders and ride him hard. Greedier than I've ever been. A rough noise rips through his chest, and he raises his hips, thrusting deep enough to make me gasp.

Soon, his hands drift to my hair, and he pulls my face to his. My rhythm slows, each movement more satisfying than the last. His eyes are intense as he holds me so close our parted lips brush. My breath fills his mouth, and he inhales each exhale like he needs them to survive.

And I think he might.

I think we both might.

It's gradual the way ecstasy grips me this time, rolling through me in long, full waves. My nails dig into his shoulders, and moans fill the car as I ride him faster, chasing every drop of it.

He pulls my lower lip into his mouth, his hands guiding my ass and grinding my clit against him just right.

"*Shit*. Adam."

"Fuck." He slams into me, curling his arms around my shoulders and pumping so deep shockwaves clench my core, one after the other.

I scream out at the same time a ragged groan tears through him, his muscles trembling beneath my touch. My eyes fall shut as tingles spread to my core and disperse down my thighs. I collapse against him.

"Holy fuck," I breathe against his damp neck, every muscle in my body spent and satisfied.

His chest pounds against my own, his breathing heavy. His hand grips my hair, and he tilts my head back so I'm looking at him. We stare at each other, his brows puckered and his eyes tortured, and I don't understand.

It takes a long minute for my heart rate to slow. "Adam." I swallow, my gaze bouncing between his eyes and his lips. "Why are you looking at me like tha—"

He crushes his lips against mine, his tongue plunging into my mouth and tangling with my own. Devouring me, he steals my breath with every stroke. Tingles sizzle down my skin, my hands shooting to his hair and grabbing, tugging, twisting.

His kiss is carnal, desperate, and filled with all the torment I saw in his eyes. Tilting my head, I take everything he gives me, and I give him more.

When he finally tears his mouth from mine, it's to trace open, hungry kisses along my jaw and down my neck. "I think—" His rough voice vibrates against my throat, his arms curling around my waist and gripping me like nothing else exists. "I think I—*fuck*, I love you, Emmy."

My heart thunders in my chest, and a thousand somersaults flip in my stomach. His words sink into my bones, filling my veins with heat as I rewind them in my head over and over.

Leaning back, I cradle his jaw in my hands. His eyes pierce through me, layers of vulnerability hiding behind the torment, and his chest goes still like he can't breathe without my response.

"Yeah," I finally whisper, my words broken with emotion. "I fucking love you, too."

He swallows, his eyes darkening while my words hang in the air, and I curl into his chest. He holds me like that for a long time. So long that my eyes, prickling with tears, flutter shut.

Pressure builds and vibrates under my skin. It's strong enough that I'm sure it's not meant for just one person to contain.

He grips me tighter, and I nuzzle my nose against his neck.

We have everything we need to survive.

epilogue

> *"Everyone wishes to ascend.*
> *But it is through the descent that you see the truth up close."*
> —Maya Luna

Emmy

I squeeze my fingers around Adam's, so tight they ache. He doesn't stop me.

Maybe he knows I need this small, tangible thing right now. Maybe he needs it too.

Dirt and dried leaves crunch beneath our feet, protesting each step. Even the land urges us to leave. Miles of trees surround us, long and thin and casting shadows in all directions as though trying to frighten us away. The clouds are grey and murky above our heads, the sun nowhere in sight; at least it's one piece of nature that's accommodating us. Soft drops of water fall to the ground and decorate our skin. It should be beautiful.

If we were anywhere else, it would be.

It's been four months since the news on Misha was released. I haven't been tracking the stories, yet versions of our past follow us everywhere.

For a while, we received unsolicited articles at the inn where we were staying. We knew Raife was forwarding them to us because the signed *Sofia* in his handwriting at the bottom gave him away. When he realized Adam and Felix were able to figure out his and Stella's location no matter how many times they moved, I think he got cold feet because he sent a postcard. From the North Pole. With a picture of cold feet. There was a note, too, but it was a single line, and it wasn't meant for me. Not directly, anyway. *Fate always finds those who run from it. For now, goodbye my old brother and friend.*

We haven't heard from him since. But even without Raife, Misha is everywhere. Civilians still talk about it, spreading rumors with hushed whispers and disapproving eyes. Like it's something they read in a celebrity gossip magazine.

I heard the woman drowned her daughter so they could die together, like some final poetic act.

I'll tell you something, people these days are too trusting. It's exactly why I never go anywhere without my 9mm.

It's a conspiracy. There are entire societies, secret dungeons in every city, waiting to take our kids even now. We'll never be safe again.

Can you believe they're calling him the Ghost of Misha? Naming and praising the person responsible for all those disappearances like he's some sort of hero?

A murderer is what he is. Just as guilty as the rest of them. For all we know, he was one of them.

Then there are the posters, flowers, peacock feathers, and other offerings adorning tree trunks and abandoned buildings all throughout the states. Some of them pray their gift is enough to keep their loved ones safe. Others give thanks to the Ghost of Misha for protecting them and their children. Then there are those that anonymously praise Misha for their 'brilliant' and 'transcending' art. I get sick to my stomach every time I spot the latter. I'm just grateful Adam doesn't have to see them.

There are days he goes out, like today, when the sun is hiding and I'm at his side. But every day is a journey for the both of us, a slow and intimate dance. I'm reveling in each intoxicating step we take together.

I angle my head to stare at the man walking beside me. His footfalls are long, his jaw set, and his intense gaze focused straight ahead. His shirt sleeves are folded up, revealing the tendons bulging in his forearms. His hair is damp, wild, and falling into his eyes.

The Ghost of Misha.

He shows me that side of him every minute of every day, whether intentionally or not. It lives in the shadows beneath his eyes. In the electricity that zings through me when his fingers brush mine. The way he curls his large hands around my smaller ones when I hold his knife. Each act breathes life into the darkest and brightest pieces of me.

My feet halt, and I suck in a breath when we reach a worn picket fence.

It's a garden.

Come to my garden.

A pang strikes my chest.

I know this spot as intimately as I know her song. But it's not easy sorting out the scattered images in my mind.

I flick my gaze all around, resting a hand on the fence's splintered wood to keep my wobbly legs from giving out. I can feel it, the way the sunrays warmed my skin when I sat right there, within reach of where I stand now. I'd be alone for hours at a time, sometimes longer, while Katerina disappeared beneath the garden. Once, when she returned for me, she sat in a bed of roses, and she held me. Her blue eyes sparkled, reflecting the kind of love I would later ache for from Mama. Then, Katerina sang. I sank into her, and she stroked the side of my face, leaving smooth, red stains on my cheek, in my hair. I saw it out of the corner of my eye, the lifeless body maybe five feet behind her, but I was too busy soaking up any attention I could get to try to care, or try to understand.

How sick it is that a garden hiding years of torment feels more like home than Mama's house ever did. It looks different than I remember, though. An old friend, childhood ghost story, and total stranger all rolled into one.

There are no more colorful flowers dancing in the wind. No butterflies to sparkle in the sunlight as they watch me come and go. Now, weeds overtake the stone pathway I used to follow when she led me to the cottage for bath time. Thick vines climb up the cottage walls at the garden's center. Full bushes bleed into one another. And forgotten waste, pieces of wood and broken pipes, are piled up.

The place is as dead and as alive as my mother is.

"You can change your mind." Adam shoves his hands into his pockets, staring down at me through squinted eyes. Raindrops slide down his olive skin, from his jaw to his neck, and disappear beneath his undone collar. "All you have to do," he says lowly, "is walk away."

My breaths shorten, and I stumble back a step.

For a fleeting moment, I see him so clearly. *Too* clearly. The boy I once knew. He's right here, inches from my face, and god, I can't do this. I can't take the unexpected guilt washing over me.

"So can you," I whisper, a swallow sticking in my throat as I break my gaze from his. "You can walk away."

He's been a part of me for so long, before I even knew that he was. It's excruciating to think of what being here—seeing *me* here—is doing to him. I'm the daughter of the woman who took his life without lifting a finger. Her clone. Her apprentice before I knew what an apprentice was.

I'm not wallowing. These are facts.

Something the man in front of me must be more aware of in this moment than ever before.

A bird whistles from the distant trees. Raindrops pitter patter on the leaves. And a twig snaps as he takes a step toward me.

I gasp when his thumb slips into the belt loop of my jeans, and he tugs me forward so I crash against his chest. Fingers graze the bottom of my jaw, and my head is lifted so I meet his eyes.

"Where you go," he murmurs, his voice rough, "I go." His nose skims mine, and my eyes shut. "Do you understand?"

I nod, water pooling behind my lashes as I find his gaze. I don't know when I became this huge crybaby, but it's annoying as hell. "Yes."

"Good. All you have to do," he repeats, "is walk away." He tips his chin, scanning my face. "Is that what you want?"

"No." An uneven sigh escapes me. I shake my head. "I can't. I have to do this. I *want* to. Don't you?"

A muscle in his jaw ticks, and he gives a barely perceptible nod. "Let's go."

He waits for me to take the first step, then his hand lands on my waist, and he follows where I lead. The garden pulls my feet forward, luring me to the one place it knows we need. The one place we once belonged.

Soon, silver shines through fallen leaves and unkempt brush. I look at Adam, and he's already moving over the hidden door built into the dirt. He pulls out the keys, *our* keys, and narrows his eyes on the padlock.

The property was put up for sale at a ridiculously low price. With Murphy's murder, and speculation about his involvement in Misha still circulating, it got no hits.

That is, until us.

Well, technically until Emmy and Lucas Miller, thanks to Felix.

But these keys are to the cottages, not a bunker that was never disclosed. Adam tosses them to me and checks his other pocket, withdrawing a shim he made out of a can when we parked the car. He fixes it to the padlock, expertly pulling the tabs from side to side, and the lock pops open.

A loud creak bellows through the tree-ridden acreage when Adam yanks the door open.

From up here, it's nothing more than a black hole. A shiver runs through me, and the combination of fear and excitement is strangely stimulating. I crane my neck, then inch closer and let the provocative draw of darkness pull me down the rusty ladder.

A thump sounds from beside me when Adam's feet hit the ground. Light pours from the opening above our heads, and gentle raindrops drizzle onto the ground. Together, we silently consume the place that molded us so long ago.

"It's so small," I whisper, taking in the short, narrow hall and two steel doors just a few feet apart. When I was a little girl, I could have sworn an army of guards could fit in here. But now, Adam's form is so much larger than it used to be. He makes the walls look like they were built for hobbits.

He swallows, his fist curling once, twice, before he strolls toward the first door.

The studio.

It's cracked open. An inch of space inviting us in like the room was waiting for our return. His knuckles brush the door, and it swings open the rest of the way.

This time, he takes the first step.

I hold my breath, then follow.

The first place I look is to my left, foolishly expecting to see shelves of 'art' encased in glass. Of course, there's nothing but a steel wall and empty space. I tell myself I'm relieved, but a dark corner in the back of my mind—the part that craves familiarity and a glimpse of the madness in my blood—is wilting in disappointment.

When I glance to the right, my heart stops.

I don't know when I slunk deeper into the cramped room, but my fingers are wrapped around the cool iron bars, and an ache I can't place throbs where my heart should be. They're so thin in my grip now, the poles, my middle finger and thumb overlapping.

The cage door is just a footstep away.

Wide open.

Calling to me.

Missing me.

My throat burns. If I were brave enough to venture inside, I'd be able to touch the rusted child-sized sink along the far wall. The mini toilet I once had no idea would spur the plan that led to our eventual freedom.

But that's not right. Not completely.

I close my eyes, ashamed to admit the feelings of comfort rolling through me. If the outside is freedom, why is it that, years later, standing on the inside, I finally feel my wings? They're not white and weightless, but black and exhilarating. Like they were made just for me.

A soft *thud* across from me pulls my attention to the only other cage in the room. My grip on the bars tightens when I find Adam. He's inside his cage. Sitting on the floor. His back against the wall, one knee bent with his elbow resting on it.

My heart lurches at the overwhelming sense of recognition.

"Adam," I whisper, my voice cracking. There were so many

times as a little girl I wished I could crawl into his cage so he could comfort me.

He gazes up at me, something dark flickering in his eyes as he runs a thumb along his jaw, and I don't understand how he could look so perfect in this place.

Electricity jolts from the tips of my fingers as I push off the bars. With my attention locked on him, I slip off my shoes and press my bare heels to the cold floor, the way they always were before. The way they're meant to be now. Then I take slow, purposeful steps toward the other half of my bleak yet remarkably full soul.

My mind and spirit were broken in this place once. It's possible that it will break me again. Maybe once, or maybe a thousand times over. But this time, I will be reborn.

Leaving my cage behind, I slip into his with an ethereal sensation lightening my steps. He straightens his spine, angles his chin, and scans me up and down in a way that makes me wonder if I look as different as I feel. I lower to my knees, crawling the last few feet toward him. He wraps warm arms around my waist when I curl into him, pressing my back against his chest.

Taking in my empty cage from this angle, I breathe slowly. So this is what it's like, looking through his eyes.

"Adam?"

His hands tease the hem of my T-shirt, the rough pads of his fingers ghosting over my bare midriff. "Mmm?"

A shudder rolls over me, and my head falls back against his shoulder. "Are you feeling as delirious as I am right now?"

A soft laugh shakes his body against mine. Hummingbirds do flips in my stomach. "I'll tell you a secret, my lioness." His lips graze my ear, warm breath fanning across my neck. "We're all a little delirious."

I jerk my head toward the ceiling, where somewhere above

ground, normal people roam. "Even them?"

"Especially them." He nips my neck, and I think I dissolve into a puddle in his lap.

If this is what delirium tastes like, I want to strip down and bathe in it. My eyes flicker toward the bars that once held me in, and something tightens in my chest. I yearn to touch them. Stare at them. Paint them.

The steel walls that once trapped me are now the embodiment of power.

We own the keys. We own the land.

In the same way we own our bodies, our hearts, our souls.

Down here, with him, I don't have to drown out the rest of the world. I can finally let go, in the truest sense of the words.

This place is no longer my cage. It's my domain.

Whether we decide to dress it in red paint or dance in its ashes, we pull the strings now.

"Welcome home, baby," I whisper.

His strong grip pulls me closer, and his entire body relaxes against me. He rests his chin on my hair. "Welcome home."

The End

Katerina's Song:
Erutan—*Come Little Children*

acknowledgments

One of my beta readers said to me, "Sometimes I read something so ridiculously twisted that I have to wonder how the author even thought of it in the first place." Firstly, thank you? I think? And secondly, I guess I should credit Melanie Martinez for her song "Dollhouse," because one look at that music video and I knew I wanted to write a dark romance. Combine that with my addiction to poetry and the TV series Dexter, and you get my first dark romance and my 'ridiculously twisted' book baby, *Dancing in the Dark*.

Writing this was challenging in all the ways I hope to experience as a writer, primarily in mentally bringing me to places I wouldn't ordinarily go. It was hard, and there were times I thought I wouldn't finish. I lost count of the number of emails I sent my writing besties during the first portion of this book, begging them to tell me why I ever thought I could write a dark romance—because I sure as hell didn't have an answer. Luckily they had more faith in me than I did (love you, Danielle and Samantha!) because I soon became so engrossed in Emmy and Adam's story that I couldn't be bothered to come up for air.

If you're reading this, I can't tell you how much I appreciate you taking a chance on my books. I wouldn't be able to write without readers like you, and I owe you the biggest thanks of all.

To my husband and children, thank you for your endless support and inspiration, and for putting up with my scattered writer's brain.

To my proofreaders, Juli Burgett, Nicole Campbell, and Mamta, thank you for your sharp eye! To all those who beta read my manuscript in its roughest forms and helped make it shine— Shalini, Toni, Brittany B., Brittany M. (guess Brittany's are just awesome like that), Jacqueline, Erin, Brooke, Ivy, Jordan, and everyone else. You were each so wonderful to work with, and I couldn't value your time or your feedback more.

To my girls, my besties, my soul sisters, Samantha Armstrong & Danielle Lori. Love you guys.

To my incredible editor Sarah Collingwood, who has also become a close friend, thank you for your brilliance and devoted support!

To my wonderful cover designer, Amy Queau, and interior formatter, Stacey Blake, thank you for giving my book the perfect finishing touches it needed to be complete.

Final note to readers: Please take a second to leave an honest review/rating on Amazon and Goodreads!

I'll see you on the next one. :)

Love,
Tawni xx

coming next from
T.L. MARTIN

New Adult Contemporary Romance
BLUE SKIES

All Blue Everest wants is the wide open sky above her head and the soft earth beneath her feet. And maybe to spread a little love where she can. When she gets the opportunity to live with a father she's never met and to enroll in public school for the first time, she brings her optimistic and free-spirited nature with her.

But it's not long before she meets her polar opposite, Joshua Hunt, whose hard edges resist every smile she sends his way . . .

Hunt's never met a girl who smiles so easily. It can't be normal. Combine that with the flowers in her hair, constant daydreaming, and a knack for sticking her nose where it doesn't belong—and he wants nothing to do with Blue Everest. He's got enough going on without her distractions, and everything, everyone, he cares about is depending on him to stay focused.

Blue's ready to go wherever the wind takes her, and Hunt's determined to steer his own ship. But sometimes the wind changes course, pulling two people into a rough and devastating storm that can crush the strongest of hearts. And sometimes, it takes more than you ever thought you were capable of to get back to blue skies.

CONTENT WARNING: contains sex, profanity, and sensitive subject matter, including suicide.

connect with me

Sign up for my newsletter to receive occasional updates about new releases.:
officialtlmartin.com/subscribe-new-release-updates

Follow me on Instagram to see bookish posts, along with pics of my cute kids. ;)
www.instagram.com/t.l.martin

Like my author page on Facebook,
www.facebook.com/tlmartinauthor

Follow me on Amazon,
and catch me on Twitter.:
twitter.com/tlmartinauthor

www.officialtlmartin.com

officialtlmartin@gmail.com

Printed in Poland
by Amazon Fulfillment
Poland Sp. z o.o., Wrocław